D0408659

ME AND MY DADDY LISTEN TO BOB MARLEY

NOVELLAS & STORIES

ME AND MY DADDY LISTEN TO BOB MARLEY

ANN PANCAKE

COUNTERPOINT
BERKELEY

Stories were first published in the following magazines:
"In Such Light"—*The Harvard Review*
"Mouseskull"—*The Georgia Review*
"Arsonists"—*The Georgia Review*
"Dog Song"—*Shenandoah*
"Coop"—*Quarterly West*
"Said"—*Chautauqua*
"Rockhounds"—*Agni*
"Sab"—*Chattahoochee Review*
"Me and My Daddy Listen to Bob Marley"—*Water~Stone Review*

Library of Congress Cataloging-in-Publication Data

Pancake, Ann.
[Short stories. Selections]
Me and my daddy listen to Bob Marley : novellas and stories / Ann Pancake.
pages ; cm
ISBN 978-1-61902-464-9 (hardcover)
I. Pancake, Ann. In such light. II. Title.

PS3616.A36A6 2015
813'.6--dc23

2014034176

Cover design by Briar Levit
Interior Design by Megan Jones Design

Counterpoint Press
2560 Ninth Street, Suite 318
Berkeley, CA 94710
www.counterpointpress.com

Printed in the United States of America
Distributed by Publishers Group West

10 9 8 7 6 5 4 3 2 1

In memory of Philip E. Sullivan, 1927-2014

"And gladly would he teach, and gladly learn."

—Geoffrey Chaucer

CONTENTS

IN SUCH LIGHT 1

MOUSESKULL 71

ARSONISTS 97

DOG SONG 117

COOP 145

THE FOLLOWING 155

SAID 173

SUGAR'S UP 179

ROCKHOUNDS 235

SAB 255

ME AND MY DADDY LISTEN TO BOB MARLEY 265

IN SUCH LIGHT

ONE POPCORN GIRL fringe benefit was a pass for two to any showing at the Alexander Henry Theater. Janie usually took her mentally disabled uncle. During the movie, the two of them would get drunk on Southern Comfort she'd smuggle in in a pimento jar and mix with a Sprite they'd buy at concessions. Janie's favorite spot was the first few rows, where she felt swallowed by the screen, but Uncle Bobby insisted they sit in the back row on the aisle for the quickest exit in case of fire. In scary movies, he shrieked with laughter, whooping and wheezing at unexpected and inappropriate moments in the movie so he could later say, "I wasn't scared of that movie! I just laughed at it! I just laughed at it, Janie!" Janie would scoot down a little lower, pull her knees up against the back of the seat in front of her, and feel thankful for how few people she knew in Remington and for the way the on-duty popcorn girls wouldn't be in to pick up trash until after the credits were done.

The one day in May when the Alexander Henry had done all its summer hiring, Janie had stood in line with seventy other people, many in their Sunday clothes, her seeing the country in those clothes. She glanced down and wondered what the others saw in hers. The job seekers huddled out of the rain under the short eaves of the storefronts north of the theater marquee, gaunt men with white shirts bunched at their waists, younger men in pool-blue leisure suits and tennis shoes. Women wearing double-knit slacks in tropical colors and faux silk shirts, others humped into dresses, their legs battened down in thick brown hose. Eventually the thumb-shaped theater manager strolled out, squinted up and down the string of jobless, and shouted, "If you didn't bring something to write with, you might as well go home!"

The people who needed the money the least ended up getting the jobs, and Janie knew even then she had gotten hers because she had the college-girl wherewithal to bring a pen and because the manager recognized her grandparents' last name. Plus her looks, such as they were, not that she'd ever thought them much, but throughout the summer, Gus would now and again pronounce, "Nobody wants to come to the movies and see an ugly popcorn girl."

She was staying with her grandparents that summer and only working part-time as a kind of convalescence after "running herself down," as her grandmother would say, during her first year of college. She wasn't sure what her grandparents thought had run her down—it had all climaxed a few months earlier in a mysterious infection that had her sleeping sixteen hours a day and made her gums bleed—but she had to believe they thought it was overworking, which it was partly, instead of overdrinking, which it was mostly. She was sixteen years younger than Uncle Bobby, which made him thirty-four that summer, but his mental age was about thirteen and a half. Hers, when she was drunk, she calculated at fifteen.

This was 1983, and in West Virginia, you could still legally drink at eighteen. By the time she'd been in Remington two weeks, she hadn't made any friends, but she and Uncle Bobby had found their places. After supper, while her grandparents watched the *MacNeil/*

Lehrer Report, she and Uncle Bobby slipped off in her blue Chevette to Ramella's on Fourth Avenue and drank White Russians. She and Uncle Bobby went to Gino's Pub and drank pitchers of urine-colored Miller. She and Uncle Bobby hung out in the basement garage across the street drinking Bud, while Nathan, Uncle Bobby's neighbor, smoked pot and worked on his bike.

Often when she'd gotten home from a popcorn girl shift and she and Uncle Bobby were sitting on the front porch, Uncle Bobby would say, "Tell me again about the cat shit," then snicker into his hand.

Janie would pretend she didn't know what he was talking about. "What do you mean?" she'd say. Or, "What was that word you used?" She knew he found the cat shit story thrilling because her grandmother allowed no cussing in the house, and certainly never an utterance as vulgar as "shit."

"Ah, Janie. C'mon! C'mon now! Tell me!"

When she knew he couldn't wait a second longer, she'd give in. "Gus tells us, 'Scoop the cigarettes out the ashtrays with that thing you clean cat shit with.'"

At that, her uncle would erupt into howling brays that sounded like an elephant. Janie wasn't sure why he laughed so hard, but no one else laughed at anything she said, and she'd take what she could get. When he'd finally come down enough from that fit to put together a few words, he'd say, "Remember that time I took you all to *Black Beauty* and Ben lost his mittens?"

Ben was her brother, a year younger than she was. Uncle Bobby had asked her this at least once on each of her twice-a-year visits to her grandparents' over the thirteen years since the incident had happened. "Yeah," Janie would say.

Then Uncle Bobby would laugh beyond elephant, beyond cat shit. He'd pound his thighs with his fists, and his face would bloom red, his eyes squint shut with his effort to hold back from outright screams. Her grandmother did not permit screams.

She hadn't grown up in this city, but her grandparents and her mother had, and Janie could remember not just the *Black Beauty* incident, which occurred when she was five, but seeing *Mary Poppins* in the Alexander Henry when she was no more than three. Remington, West Virginia, at eighty thousand people, was the biggest city in the state at the time and the only city she'd ever known. She remembered being driven through Remington to visit some aging relative or another—back then, there'd been legions—and her awe and disbelief at how far they could drive and not stop seeing houses. Almost every time her family came to Remington, she and Ben were taken to a movie at the Alexander Henry, and the Alexander Henry was the grandest and most elegant place Janie had ever entered. In McCloud County, where she grew up, grandeur was found only in nature, and the palatial and luxurious not at all.

The theater itself, where you actually watched the movie, was the largest room she'd seen in her life, triple the size of the high school gym back home, and that didn't even count the balconies and mezzanines, the lobbies and the catacomb of bathrooms. You padded down the lush carpet enveloped in a dazzle world of scarlets and golds, as though pipe organs had been sacrificed, trumpets unwound, then resculpted into resplendent spirals and scrolls. These framed the stage, feathered the walls, where Midas-touched vines twined columns, and figures of berobed women and bearded men gazed and glared among petrified fruits and urns. Over the box seats mounted on the walls, golden swag upon swag of voluptuous satin soared clear to the towering ceiling, and from the boxes themselves spilled fabric like knights' horses' finery, emblazoned with flags and ensigns and shields, the box seats all the more impressive for never having people in them. If Janie stared long enough without blinking before the lights went down, she saw faces in the ceiling.

Many times the Alexander Henry outglamoured whatever was on the screen, and occasionally Janie watched the walls instead of the movie. There was even a full curtain that drew back to let the show begin, a curtain in heavy folds the dried-blood color worn by kings in the Old Testament, and its velvet stateliness extended to dense drapes along the walls through which you swam, your hand in Grandmother's or Uncle Bobby's, to reach a narrow passageway lit by little half-moons if you had to go to the bathroom in the middle of the show. "The show," her grandparents still called the movies, and her uncle did, too, and it had been a real theater at first, for vaudeville and plays and concerts. Her grandparents and Uncle Bobby remembered those days.

The Alexander Henry was not even the same species as the rinky-dink theater in Janie's own hometown, population two thousand, with its dull linoleum lobby under bald fluorescent lights. The seats soot-colored, walls as well, the theater's single adornment an obnoxious illuminated clock advertising a car dealership. And the way you knew everyone there even if you pretended you didn't, and how you weren't allowed to take your Coke to your seat, had to drink it standing in the back, but your shoes stuck to the floor anyway. When Janie was little and she got mad, which she often did, and threatened to run away, which everyone ignored, it was to Remington she knew she would go. Remington, West Virginia, Janie saw as real life. The life real people lived and the one she'd reach after she suffered and struggled through the one she'd accidentally been plunked in as a baby. The Alexander Henry was the highest echelon of that real life, the one not many attained, but one she just might if she worked hard enough.

When she was still a kid, at least, that's how Janie saw it.

SOME AFTERNOONS, WHEN both she and Uncle Bobby were off work, they hung out in his room and listened to his 1960s record collection. Paul Simon, Joni Mitchell, the Beatles, Joan Baez, Bob Dylan—Uncle Bobby had them all, while Janie, of course, had just missed them, her born not only in the wrong place, but in the wrong time as well. She lay on the blue pile carpet with a Pink Panther for a pillow so her ears were nearer the speakers, the music rushing into the empty parts of her, never quite topping them off. Beyond the windows, humidity coated the house like liquid glass, the air-conditioning a seal against it. Uncle Bobby's room, built onto the back of her grandparents' small bungalow after years of money put away, felt like a hideout then. Afternoon time, hovering time, wait for the true time, which was what might happen at night. And coiled in the hideout, the music transfiguring her, only Uncle Bobby present, and the anticipation of drinking that night, for whole minutes Janie could kick clear of herself and be who she wished she was.

Uncle Bobby lounged in his blue recliner, nodding to the beat, his little Yorkie terrier mix, Tina, of the wise face and the bad breath, curled in his lap. Uncle Bobby had actually seen Joan Baez in concert, had seen Paul Simon, at the Remington Civic Center always by himself, and such history, along with Uncle Bobby's being more city than her, gave Uncle Bobby areas of superiority over Janie despite his other handicaps. Now Uncle Bobby was telling of his and Janie's recent exploits as though Janie hadn't been present and they'd already rushed into legend.

"And remember, I came out of the state store, and I tripped, and I fell down! But I held that bottle up! It didn't hit the ground! I didn't break it, did I, Janie? Did I?"

"Nuh-uh," Janie said.

She turned onto her stomach, the carpet showroom clean. Uncle Bobby worked in the bigger of Remington's two hospitals, and before he'd been promoted to laundry, he'd spent a decade as janitor. During that period, he'd collected the pennies caught up in his broom, and when Janie was seven, she'd spent a whole morning counting all of them for him. Occasionally now he found in the dirty laundry abandoned stuffed animals, and after a two-week lost-and-found probation period, he washed them, carried them home, and displayed them in his room. Most were bland teddy bears, or dogs and monkeys with fur so fake it made your fingers squeak. The Pink Panther was Janie's favorite because of the softness of his fabric skin, like flannel or beaten-down towels. It was the E.T. Uncle Bobby adored. That had been the big movie the summer before, and Uncle Bobby was first smitten, then obsessed. He'd bought her an E.T. cake for her eighteenth birthday the September before, and by some divine intervention—divine intervention was not rare in the life of Uncle Bobby—an E.T. doll showed up in the laundry in the winter. It now sat like a big-eyed god on top of an oversized jewelry box Uncle Bobby had gotten from the house of a dead "maiden aunt," as he called her, the jewelry box in turn on top of his well-dusted chest of drawers. This E.T. was not to be handled.

"—and then there was a knock on the door!" He was onto the night her grandparents had gone out of town and they'd made strawberry daiquiris. Nathan and his girlfriend Melissa had stopped by for that one. "And here it was the church people with the church directories!" Uncle Bobby collapsed into elephantine peals, Tina vaulting from his lap, Uncle Bobby convulsing, bent at his waist. "I couldn't believe it! I couldn't believe it! Could you, Janie? Could you?" He exploded again, then abruptly swallowed the last laugh and commanded in a grave baritone: "E. T. Phone home."

"Where'd you go yesterday afternoon, Uncle Bobby?" She hadn't expected to say it even though she'd been speculating since it happened.

"Huh?" He sobered immediately. Like her, he'd been caught off guard. "What do you mean, Janie?"

"Yesterday afternoon. After you took your shower. After work. Where'd you go?" Janie raised up on her elbows to watch his face.

"Oh." He paused. Closed his mouth with a loud smack. "To visit a friend of mine."

"Who?"

"Just a friend of mine. You don't know 'em." The face armored up. The tone a challenge. "Anything wrong with that?" Then she saw him whisper the same words afterwards, as he sometimes did, as though the spoken words left a shadow in his mouth that made him have to say again.

Often Janie visualized the uneven operations of the uncle brain, which, according to family lore, had been damaged by dehydration when Uncle Bobby fell deathly ill as an infant. Some parts had melted in the heat, Janie saw them tarnished and clotted together like clock guts after a fire—the part that did numbers, the part that managed cause and effect, the part that gauged how funny things really were—while other parts in that dark, crowded space still gleamed and whirred, unscathed—the part that could sustain a conversation, the part sensitive to her grandmother's tireless social skill drills, the part that remembered things. The memory had overgrown in compensation, and Uncle Bobby could recite his grandmothers' phone numbers and addresses clear back to the 1950s, even though one grandmother had moved several times and both had been dead for almost a decade. He knew the ages and birthdays of most people on Kentworth Drive, and he recalled trivial incidents from ages ago with the most unlikely details in brilliant relief. As he was doing now, Uncle Bobby retelling, as Janie put away Joni and plunked down Janis, a favorite story twenty-five years past of how his sister and her friends had put a water sprinkler on the porch of a mean neighbor lady, knocked, and ran. It was a story Janie had heard at least twenty times before. Because this was another characteristic of the uncle brain: certain clock innards had melted into granite-hard configurations—Uncle Bobby was "set in his ways," her grandmother would say, he "had his routines"—and for this reason and others, most people found dealing with Uncle Bobby someplace between irritating and maddening.

"I think she deserved it. I do, Janie. I think she got what she deserved. Don't you, Janie? Don't you?" And there was another reason, the imprisonment in the tag question, his snaring of others in tedious conversations by demanding a response to everything he said by adding "Huh, Janie? Huh? Huh, Janie? Huh?" until you said, "Yeah," back. The tag questions were an offshoot of Uncle Bobby's know-it-all-ness, a quality Janie found fascinating given his IQ, Uncle Bobby's treasure trove of authority gleaned mostly from the black-and-white movies he watched on cable TV. "How do you know?" Janie would ask. "Saw it on one of these old movies," he'd say.

And now he was onto a lady at work who'd been rude to him, another fixation of the Bobby brain, the infinite slights, the corresponding self-righteous indignation. Different family members had different Uncle Bobby survival techniques, and most family members used a combination of several: avoidance, stoicism, humor and teasing, almost always at his expense, and when none of those worked, the occasional no-longer-suppressible outburst. But Uncle Bobby, for some reason, had never bothered Janie much.

Janie knew it didn't bother people at all when they were little. You noticed it then, the difference, but it didn't get on your nerves. It was when your own brain grew to where it passed Uncle Bobby's that the trouble started. First the struggle for control—who was boss of whom? who child? who adult?—and then, it never entirely resolved, the impatience with him, the frustration, the exhaustion. She'd seen it in each of her older cousins when they became teenagers, she'd seen it in her brother Ben. She'd even felt it a little herself when she was thirteen or fourteen. But this summer, she felt it hardly at all. Part of the spell of the summer, Janie recognized it even then, was the way she and Uncle Bobby almost matched.

". . . . and he said they broke up."

"Huh?" Janie said.

"I was talking to Nathan last evening while you were at work, and he said him and Melissa broke up again. But they got back together the next day."

"Oh," Janie said.

DURING HER FIRST few weeks in Remington, she'd gone out with two boys, one with an eleven o'clock curfew who kissed with his teeth, the other the kind of well-behaved smart boy who reminded her too much of her secret self. She and Uncle Bobby spent more hours in the garage across the street with Nathan and his bikes.

Nathan had two motorcycles, the one he worked on and the one he rode. The one he worked on, a 1972 Harley-Davidson, he loved with a nearly feral ferocity and hated even harder. Sometimes he'd stroke his hand across its cam cover, its forks and fender, explaining to Uncle Bobby and Janie its extraordinariness while Janie nodded gravely and said, "Wow. Huh." The way she did with McCloud County boys when they talked about football, cars, and deer hunting; the way she had more recently with WVU frat boys as they talked about football, keggers, and "brothers." Other times Nathan cussed the bike with a fury like a fuse had burned up from his stomach and detonated a bomb in his mouth, and once Janie had seen spit, not fly from his mouth, but bubble up at its corners, she'd seen it foam. While she and Uncle Bobby sat at a safe distance in their lawn chairs near the garage door in silent, but sincere, sympathy.

A full-sized stereo sat up on a shelf—there was another one, Janie would learn, in Nathan's bedroom, yet another one in the living room—tuned to WAMO, the Tri-State's classic rock, and Nathan always had in his dorm-sized refrigerator a case of Budweiser, which he'd share with them even when he wasn't talking. Now and again he'd share his pot, too, skinny roaches in little stamped-tin ashtrays he'd lifted from Johnny's, his favorite biker bar, the dirty ashtray, its slender string of smoke, a tantalizing aberration among the tools Nathan'd neatly rowed across the floor. The garage was unlike any working garage Janie'd ever seen, its sterility, its orderliness, the smell of clean concrete, not even an oil stain on the floor, and she'd wonder was it Nathan or his mother who kept it so. "Wacky weed," Uncle Bobby would snigger. "Left-handed cigarettes," then snuffle-squeal with laughter. Janie with one ear pricked always for Nathan's mother to come down from the living room, but his mother never came. Often Nathan paid little attention to them, but it was enough to know he wanted them there. Plus, the never knowing what he might do next. It was hard not to watch.

Once, when she and Uncle Bobby were sitting by themselves in the dark on her grandparents' front porch, Janie said, as offhandedly as she could muster, "What do you think about Nathan?"

"Nathan?" Uncle Bobby paused. "Oh, Nathan's a good friend of mine." He paused again. Janie heard his rockers stop. Then start. "I've known Nathan since he was born. I've known Nathan since he was born, Janie."

There were photos at her grandparents' house of her and Nathan and some other neighbor children playing together as little kids, but he was way bigger than she was in those photos, and she could barely remember Nathan before this summer she'd moved in. He was four years older than Janie, but now he was exactly her height, Uncle Bobby a full head taller than they were. But when he wanted to, how big Nathan could make himself. A fuse for that, too. Janie never hung around guys that much older than she was, and normally, she'd have been too shy, but with Uncle Bobby along, and the Budweiser, the pot, after half an hour, she felt as cool as anybody else. Besides, Nathan had a girlfriend, Melissa, who was a year older than he was. They'd already been together three years, and Melissa wanted to get married, but Nathan wasn't ready. "I'm just not ready to settle down," he'd tell her and Uncle Bobby, head hung, his voice glistening with pain. "Why can't she understand that?" Janie and Uncle Bobby nodding, growing a little, glowing, in their role as Nathan's confidantes.

He worked from seven to three as a bank teller, and if Janie didn't have an afternoon shift herself, at 3:20 she'd hear his '76 Scout slamming down Kentworth Drive. She'd slip to the window of the front bedroom to watch Nathan park and walk to his house in long heavy strides as though invisible boots weighted his feet. Him leaning forward from his shoulders, his head tucked down, his brow, too, the posture at all odds with the three-piece suit. A half-hour later he'd emerge from the garage on the riding bike in black leather. Then what that Yamaha would do. To the quiet street, the respectable yards, the middle-class 1920s brick homes with their mostly elderly residents, hardworking, churchgoing, now honorably retired. In one instant of ignition, that motorcycle slashed the whole scene to shreds.

Nathan's moodiness was mesmerizing. One second throwing his tools and beating the concrete floor with his fists until Janie'd look for blood (she never saw it). The next smiling at Janie from under droop-lidded eyes and asking if she liked the way he'd shaved his beard and let his moustache stay, as if what she thought mattered. Fifteen minutes later, an anguished confession that he and Melissa were again "having some problems," she just "didn't understand him," his deep voice making what could have been a whine come out a moan. He'd even ask them for advice, which neither she nor Uncle Bobby, sober or high, had any idea how to give.

One night the heat stayed so heavy it drove her and Uncle Bobby off the porch and down to the steps between their yard and the street in hopes of a little air moving. She'd gotten home from the theater an hour before. Now, as she and Uncle Bobby perched in the streetlight, she listened half-eared to her uncle, listened with the other ear and a half for the sound of Nathan's bike turning off Norway Avenue and onto Kentworth Drive. But what she heard instead was Nathan's front door open.

She lifted her head. Nathan floated, silent and gray, across his dim lawn and the street. He stopped a little off to the side of them, just out of the streetlight's beam. He was dressed in a polo shirt and a pair of shorts. He usually favored black T-shirts, and Janie could remember him in shorts just once. The legs looked strange naked. His feet bare, too. Janie felt braver, and sadder.

"Well, Bobby," he said. "It's for sure."

"Uhh-hmmm," Uncle Bobby nodded, knowingly.

"It's over."

"Yep," agreed Uncle Bobby, the conversation camouflage, decades of practice of acting like he knew exactly what you were talking about whether he had an inkling or not.

"This time . . ." Nathan halted. He swallowed. "This time. It's for good."

"Umm-hmm," said Uncle Bobby.

Then Nathan looked directly at Janie. He had his head tilted to one side, almost limp. The pale legs. The bare feet, one heel scuffing gently at the grass.

"What do you think, Janie? Three years, and just like that. It's all gone." He halted again. Janie peeked at his face to see if she could catch in his eye what she thought she'd heard. Then she looked away. "All because she just can't wait on me a little while. That's all I asked."

"I'm sorry," Janie finally said. "I'm real sorry."

Nathan drew a deep breath.

"Well. Good night, you all."

"G'night," said Uncle Bobby.

"Good night," said Janie.

Once he'd gotten far enough away that she figured he wouldn't turn back, Janie watched him. He flowed up the steps and vanished into the house, and a week later, Janie was riding the motorcycle behind Nathan.

BY THAT SUMMER, they'd docked the Alexander Henry's glory by cutting the opulent theater of Janie's childhood into a big central box with two smaller, rectangular theaters at its sides. They'd bought an adjacent shoe store and converted it to hold a fourth screen. The popcorn, she discovered, arrived from someplace else in big plastic bags they stored on a landing over one of several sets of basement steps. Ronnie, the gentle year-round usher, scuttled up railings in his slick dress shoes and threw down the bags to waiting popcorn girls, and the "butter" they poured out of plastic jugs that listed coconut oil and yellow number something as ingredients one and two. When kids twelve, ten, eight came in for R-rated movies, Gus would march them to the pay phone—"Oh, that's just awful! That's awful, Janie!" Uncle Bobby said when she told him this—and sell the ticket after he got whatever passed for parental permission over the phone. Some of the candy was left over from the 1960s—the Chuckles wouldn't give under your thumb no matter how hard you pressed—and Gus marked them down to a "special price," then ordered the popcorn girls to "really push 'em."

"Ooooo. I wouldn't eat those." Uncle Bobby screwed up his face. "Would you, Janie? Would you?"

"And this one lady who's worked there twenty years. She says there's ghosts in the bathrooms." Janie stopped and looked at Uncle Bobby. His face got serious, then worried, just a little. "She says somebody died of a heart attack down there in one of the stalls, and people have been seeing the ghost ever since."

"Oh." Uncle Bobby was stroking Tina's back, and now the strokes went a little faster, a little harder. Janie saw Tina brace. "I don't believe that. I don't believe that, do you, Janie? Do you?"

Janie thought.

"If I saw a ghost down there," he said, "I'd just laugh at it! I'd laugh at it, Janie!" Tina slipped behind the couch. "Do you believe that, Janie?"

"Nah," Janie said. "It's just what they say."

Most of the new hires at the Alexander Henry were girls from the in-town college, and if they hadn't known each other before becoming popcorn girls, they had friends who had. They were all sorority girls, at least in type. Not the snobby and mean variety, but the variety who knew how to make themselves look cute even in red popcorn girl smocks and health department regulations about loose hair, who knew the right girl giggle or quip for every circumstance, who stayed cheerful and pleasant always, as though they'd never recovered from their high school cheerleader careers. They treated Janie the way they'd treat a person they were visiting in a children's hospital or a nursing home: with kindness, then forgetfulness, never with inclusion.

The other three were long-timers, year-rounders. Besides Ronnie, there was Tommie Sue, a long, pointy woman with high, hard hair who held between her fingers always a phantom cigarette. She had worked at the Alexander Henry for twenty years, longer than anybody else, longer even than Gus, and she reminded him of this regularly without ever speaking to it or of it. Both she and Betty drove into Remington from someplace out in the country, but not the same place, and Betty was snowman-shaped, with a constant sad smile and a tiny silver cross riding her large breasts. Intelligent, competent, organized, Betty had put in fourteen years and usually sold tickets, something the popcorn girls weren't trusted to do. Tommie Sue was vinyl and wire. Betty, cottonball and artificial flowers. And although neither of them was more like Janie than the sorority girls were, they were far more familiar. They could have come straight out of McCloud County. They were the ones she'd been around all her life.

It was Tommie Sue who told about the people who had died. When all the movies were at least an hour deep, when the counters had been wiped, the cups restocked, the ashtrays cat shit-cleaned under Gus's military eye, Tommie Sue would lean against the back of the concession stand between the pop dispenser and Betty, crack her back, cross her arms, and start. The sorority girls tended to cluster at the other end of the counter, where they murmured among themselves, what party, what boy, what bar. While Janie shuffled around the middle, not sure what to do with her hands.

"You were here, Betty, weren't you, when that big chunk of plaster came down off there and on that guy's head?" She gestured with her first two fingers squeezed together to the rococo molding that ran between the high ceiling and the wall. Betty nodded. "Must have hit him just right. Knocked him dead on the carpet." Tommie Sue rolled her eyes back in her head a little to remember. The gold-flecked mirror behind her reflected her dark, undyed hair, defiant, the few white strands as fine as cobweb and invisible in the atmospheric lobby light.

From across the room, poised to prop the theater doors the moment the *Return of the Jedi* credit music rolled, Gus glared at Tommie Sue. Tommie Sue, at least eight inches taller, gazed evenly back. "Worst one was the manager before Gus. Blew his brains out in the office upstairs while he was counting receipts. If that wasn't a mess."

"You all get ready for this exit!" Gus yelled. The sorority cluster bustled into place. Janie stood at attention over the candy. After a long minute, Tommie Sue reached under the counter, picked up a big stack of the booklets that had come with that year's James Bond, *Octopussy*, and strode out into the lobby. She flagged them in front of the departing movie watchers.

"Pussy programs! Get your pussy programs!" she sang.

THE FIRST WEEK, Nathan asked Janie to ride with him almost every day. She'd only been on a motorcycle a few times before, and soon she understood. The absence of metal, you closer to dying, and how that shouted all the life in you out to your edge. The way you soared into vaults of odors and the tastes that they carried, then left them as rapidly behind, all the layers of real a car kept you from, and the heat of the muffler against the inside of your calves and what happened to your skin if they touched.

They'd cross the 18th Street Bridge and ribbon down some of the straightest roads Janie'd ever seen, along the Ohio River on the Ohio side, her looking back across at West Virginia. She loved that on the bike, she didn't have to talk, didn't even have to look at or be looked at by him. Them just hurtling forward, her straddling his hips, the bulk of his jacket against her cheek, the smell of his clean neck, his back to her always. Her riding not just the bike, but his back.

He took her places that she'd been only dimly aware of before, places her grandmother never passed on their childhood excursions to Sunday school, to the Remington art museum, to the Alexander Henry. With Nathan, she traveled under horizons of coal power plants, heaving up out of their own steam and effluvium like daymare mirages, menacing unoccupied castles, the cooling towers monstrous squat beakers, some mutation out of a chemistry set. The oil refineries with their perverse metal trees, overtall, spindly, their flares rippling, biblical, each crown a sterile altar. They ripped past hulks of plants even more mysterious, seeping noxious stenches that gummed the roof of your mouth, many of the buildings painted a color that matched their stink, putrescent chartreuses, vomitous creams.

When they didn't ride along the river, Nathan favored an east side outskirt of abandoned or almost warehouses and factories, the streets there usually empty, and always of cops. The structures formed a three-story sheet metal ravine, their echo spectacular, the motorcycle a contained and rainless thunderstorm ricocheting between walls. The deserted hulks seeped not just eeriness, but somehow anger, even surprise, but Janie and Nathan were shielded from all that by the speed of the bike. Them rocketing past enigmatic geometries, cylinders and chutes, cupolas and cones, past towering red letters threatening head injury and limb loss, past windows, if not shattered, so spider-infested Janie could make out webs at fifty miles per hour. These were places that used to make things, not chemicals, electricity, gasoline, but things you could actually touch, and now the vegetation rising, the weeds shrouding, pressing, fecund, wanton, "plants" and "plants" Janie'd think in her alcohol haze, noticing for the first time how the word had been stolen, but ultimately the first plants had won.

The last evening of that week, they pulled over at a spot Nathan knew along the river. They hid the bike in the brush and pushed down the bank through kudzu and briar. The stillness after the bike shocked Janie's ears, the *chung* of insect slowly returning, and Nathan, halfway down, remembered to hold back the blackberry vines. At the bottom, they reached a decaying dock over river water the color of dirty tires. Nathan sat cross-legged on the punky boards, pulled out his Baggie and papers, and rolled a joint with ostentatious expertise using a fold in his jeans on the inside of his thigh. He sucked in and held, then passed the joint to Janie, who imitated him, like she'd been imitating pot smokers since she was fifteen. And instantly—reflex, too soon for the drug to have reached blood—her tight places loosened. The pot shortened the distance between Nathan and her, why she smoked, why she drank. It was not, she told herself, escape, but its opposite. To connect her, to make her more there.

Nathan passed the joint again. The opaque river water under them, its slow, invisible poisons. The coal barges silently sliding. And then he was taking off his clothes. The leather jacket, the black T-shirt, his engineer boots, his Levi's. He stopped at his briefs. They had not had sex yet, and Janie'd never seen him strip down, although the truth was, even after they did begin having sex, she'd never see him completely naked in light. He slipped over the dock edge and into the river before either of them said anything.

Janie stared, his body vanishing under the charcoal-colored water, surfacing, him whipping his bangs out of his eyes with a violent shake of his head. Janie watched, the pot continuing to dissolve the hard holding in her, burning away at her self-doubt. Nathan broke surface again, gulped, and dove, the white briefs soaked translucent, the skin of his buttocks visible through them. And as she watched him, Janie understood she wanted to undress, too, and a part of her was surprised and a little scandalized. But then she was untying her shoes, rolling off her socks. She hesitated, glanced up and down the river, then unbuttoned her blouse. She was standing on the dock in her jeans and her bra, her shirt wadded against her stomach, her hunched a bit forward, when Nathan came up and turned towards her again.

He treaded water, a little too far away for her to clearly see his face. He called, "You better not get in here. It's nasty. I always shower soon as I get home."

Then he was pulling his sleek, filth-rimed body back up on the boards. Janie's fingers already stumbling to rebutton the blouse. She wondered if the tugboat captains had seen. And at first, along with that embarrassment, a sting that Nathan hadn't wanted her in the water with him. But right after that she told herself he'd warned her not to come in because he cared.

After two weeks of motorcycle rides and one week of sex, she guessed they were a couple, but she didn't know how to find out for sure. Uncle Bobby seemed to think they were a couple, too. "Nathan came over and asked me, he asked me, 'Bobby, do you think I should ask her out?' But I didn't tell you." He nodded to himself, solemn. "Because I know how to keep a secret. I know how to keep a secret, Janie. Did you know that?"

She knew that. The story of Nathan's consulting Uncle Bobby became an immediate favorite in Uncle Bobby's anecdote repertoire, and after he'd told it three or four times, Janie realized he interpreted it as Nathan asking his permission for her, much like a suitor asking a father for his daughter's hand in "one of these old movies."

Now she lived listening always for the comings and goings of the Yamaha, of the Scout. Her life a hover of anticipation of the next journey through those mysterious backways, not country, not city. Her grandfather muttered his displeasure, but mostly kept it to himself, while her grandmother, who carried indestructible, if unfounded, faith in Janie, found the romance charming. When Janie and Nathan thundered through the metal canyon, Janie couldn't help but think of her grandparents. A few of the factories still operated, at least parts of them did, and in shot-spattered signs, Janie, even stoned, recognized some names from her grandfather's tales.

Her grandfather's narratives were more résumés than stories. Recitations of his jobs since age thirteen, when he delivered on his bicycle empty bottles from a drugstore to a bootlegging apartment on Third Avenue. The bootlegging was the first step in his bootstrap chronology, through the glass factory, Owens Illinois, the nickel plant (how Janie'd always pictured this as a child, a flower blooming nickels), the job teaching welding, all arduous rungs in his hand-over-hand pull to the American Dream. Which he did attain, in his late forties: a real-estate appraisal business he finally established after Janie's own mother had left home. And she thought of her grandfather, too, as she and Nathan stormed past the rows of neat and grime-inlaid little houses behind their chain-link fences and their FOR SALE signs, her grandfather at the supper table lamenting all the lost homes, large and small, shabby and stately, in this city where he'd lived and worked all his life. The city that had rewarded that hand-over-hand climb, now on the verge of losing its station as largest in the state as people and money drained out. She could hear the hurt in his voice and the humiliation, too, in both of her grandparents, while Janie could not understand. The contrast, still, with McCloud County. McCloud County, now that was humiliation.

Gradually she learned that Nathan's parents, a university professor and a high school teacher, were mortified that Nathan had dropped out of community college. He confided in her that they'd bribed him to go back, but he couldn't be bought. Janie suspected that they'd pulled strings to land him the bank teller's job, where, she also gradually understood, Nathan didn't want Janie to see him. Nathan behind the bank counter was very hard for her to visualize, and the softness of Nathan's hands always surprised her, especially given all the work he did on the Harley. The hands of boys in McCloud County, even if it was basketballs they handled more than tools, had all been harder than Nathan's.

Once, she and Nathan were saying good night after parking the Yamaha in the basement. Janie's back against the cinder block wall, Nathan's face tucked under her jaw and into her shoulder, their hands entwined where they hung at their sides. Lulled by the tenderness of the moment, and pot, and arousal, Janie, who almost never spoke without thinking the words first, heard herself whisper, "A banker's hands."

Nathan jerked the hands away. He stepped back. His shoulders cocked, the compact body engorged, and Janie, even startled, marveled at how he could amplify himself at will. And right then, more than any other moment in her life except with her mother, Janie thought she was going to be hit. Then she wasn't.

That was the first time the temper was directed at her. But seconds after he flared, he folded. He slumped against a tool bench, his arms crossed, shaking his head, and Janie saw how badly he hurt. She felt guilty for having been mean, even if she hadn't intended that.

His eruptions cast his sweet parts into brighter relief. The way he always checked to be sure she was dressed safely for the bike. The soft way he held her hand in the movies and didn't go farther. His acceptance of Uncle Bobby. Probably because like she had, Nathan had been around Uncle Bobby his whole life, he took Uncle Bobby's peculiarities for granted and usually handled Uncle Bobby like her family did. Not with kindness, exactly—it was impossible to be always kind to him—but with stoicism on good days, suppressed irritation on others, and mild teasing regularly to vent some of the pressure. Uncle Bobby didn't confuse or scare Nathan, didn't make him uncomfortable like he did most non-family members, who either avoided Uncle Bobby or overtried. Janie knew there was not another person in Remington who could hang out with her and Uncle Bobby without her feeling embarrassed. She and Uncle Bobby and Nathan together felt irresistibly familiar.

One long drawn-out twilight she and Nathan were sitting with their backs against the flood wall, the gravel and ground rubble under them, the grass right beyond their knees almost as high as their faces. Two motorboats gashed the river. The bleared sun stifled itself behind the lowish Ohio hills. The joint was moving between her and Nathan when he murmured, "You know, if we're ever going to be close, you have to talk to me more."

Janie's head knocked softly back into the cement. Her body flushed a strange and pleasant warmth that dissipated into confusion. No one, lover or friend, had ever said anything like that to her before. But now she saw that she hadn't even realized she and Nathan rarely talked, and also she saw the stark truth of what he said. She didn't know what to say back.

THOSE EVENINGS WHEN she didn't work or ride with Nathan or when they rode very late, she and Uncle Bobby would return around 9:30 from Ramella's or Gino's or a six-pack shared in the Chevette at the riverfront park and head straight to the pantry, where they'd gulp a gob of peanut butter. Uncle Bobby had taught her this technique for eluding alcohol detection, and Janie had to admit it was more effective, not to mention more imaginative, than her own strategy of chewing Freshen-Up gum. After, they'd pause in the doorway of the TV room to greet her grandparents, their empty ice cream bowls beside them. When she and Uncle Bobby escaped to the front porch, where their breath was less likely to be noticed, Janie always felt herself darken and narrow with shame, which she never felt in front of her parents, whom she believed deserved whatever they got.

As she passed through the dining room and living room of the small house, straitjacketed in the concentration of the moderately drunk person trying to appear sober, objects came into focus that were ordinarily blurred. The house brimmed with precious things, worked-hard-for things, each one cherished by her grandmother. Ceramic Swiss children in petrified lederhosen. China plates with pastoral scenes. A chiming wooden mantel clock, blown Blenko glass, an elegant rolltop desk, needlepoints by her grandmother, roosters and flowers gilt-framed and hung. On the footrest before her grandfather's chair lay the day's newspaper divided into sections, the white pages to be thrown away, the sales circulars and coupons—Big Bear, Foodland—carefully sorted out.

Outside, the heat was finally receding though the humidity was not. Uncle Bobby dropped into his webbed rocker lawn chair and worked it energetically. Janie stretched full-length on the porch swing, reached one hand over her head for the chain, and began her own languid rock. Out of habit, part of her ear pricked for Nathan even though she knew he'd stayed in tonight because his parents were having his older sister and her husband for dinner.

The front door cracked. "Can you all please turn out the lights and lock the door before you go to bed?" her grandmother called. "And sleep tight."

Shame geysered through Janie again, as deep and shuddery as grief. And then, it was grief. Because her grandparents were among the very few people in the world who loved her, she knew this, and they were the only ones who saw her not as she was, but as she could be, yet she could not stop being as she was.

To douse her guilt, she started to talk. Tonight, Uncle Bobby would listen to her first. As she usually did, she spoke to the ceiling her plans for after college. At some point during her freshman year, her ambitions had leapfrogged Remington, and now real life, if she could reach it, lay in an unidentified place out of state. Most of her post-college plans hinged on her becoming famous because leaving West Virginia seemed so outlandish, fame was for Janie the only imaginable route out. The problem was, famous for what? She couldn't do anything well but read.

She told Uncle Bobby she was going to write books, and she told him what would happen after that. "Mmm-hmm. Mmmm-hmm," Uncle Bobby agreed in tune to the thud of his rockers, and she knew he was nodding despite it being too dark to see, "Uh-huh, Janie. Uh-huh," brightly, Uncle Bobby taking for granted that of course Janie would do such a thing. She left out the part about how "running herself down" had affected more than her health. How if she didn't pull up her grades next semester she'd be on academic probation. She didn't mention how she'd taken a creative writing course the semester before, how the teacher had written throughout the margins of her story in green ink the single word "unclear" and finished with a sentence about lack of dramatic tension—Janie wasn't sure what that was—and a tepid note of encouragement that brought alive to Janie for the first time the saying to "damn with faint praise." She'd dropped the class because, she'd told herself, it gave her more hours at her grocery store deli job. Janie not only left all that out, but by the time she'd finished talking about her plans to the confident accompaniment of Uncle Bobby's "uh-hmms," she'd forgotten all of it, too. Talking to Uncle Bobby made her brilliant and brave and even obliterated her greatest fear: even if she managed to get through college at all, she'd likely end up back in McCloud County as a junior high English teacher.

"Why don't you write a story about the time I took you and Ben to *Black Beauty* and Ben lost his mittens?" Uncle Bobby asked when she finally finished. "Why don't you write a story about that, Janie?"

"Well," Janie said. "Maybe one of these days I will."

Then it was Uncle Bobby's turn. Tonight he was in his righteous argumentative mode, operating from the know-it-all part of his brain. The people he'd quarrel with were always absent, sometimes actual individuals who'd told him something he didn't want to do or believe, sometimes straw antagonists—their nonexistence didn't dampen his passion—who represented abstract somethings he considered offensive or ridiculous. Now he was recalling the time he took the Greyhound to McCloud County to visit Janie's family, but the bus driver had forgotten to stop in their town because, Uncle Bobby claimed, he was distracted by a woman with "dimensions"—dementia, Janie translated—who wouldn't stop talking about her false teeth. Uncle Bobby had ridden another hour to Winchester, Virginia, before the driver caught the oversight. Strumming her thumb along the links of the swing chain, the tang of rust sharp against the night scents of the junipers around the porch, Janie returned the Uncle Bobby favor, confirming, regardless of what he said, "Mmm-hmmm. Mmm-hmm."

He fulminated on to the rhythm of his rockers, the indignity of having been forgotten on the bus, the stupidity and insensitivity of the driver and the false teeth lady, while Janie, the swing jangling end-to-end under her hand, imagined Nathan in his single bed, his room barren—she'd seen that room now—as though he'd stripped out everything from childhood and not known what to put back. "What I should of done, Janie, was tell him off. Next time, I'm just gonna tell him. Would you? Would you tell him, Janie?" The alcohol lowered her gently tonight. She remembered an incident as a preschooler when she'd brought Uncle Bobby a book and asked him to read to her. Her confusion when he couldn't. That was one of several early times she'd noticed something different about him—his turtle phobia, for instance, or the way he said *animules* for animals and *legotards* for leotards—but he was the youngest of her mother's four siblings, and Janie attributed his inability to read, along with other young things he did and young ways he was treated with his being the family baby.

Now Janie could tell from his volume and tone that he was winding down. Like he did for her, she joined him for the landing—"Yep, I hear ya. I hear ya"—while Uncle Bobby petered out, "And so forth and so on. And what have you," Janie agreeing, "Mmm-hmm. Mmm-hmmm," until he went silent except for his rockers on the floor, and Janie giving a final commiseration, "It's awful, Uncle Bobby. It's just awful." And then, both of them finished, Janie nearly sober, she asked, "Where'd you go this afternoon after work?"

Almost every other day now, he'd been leaving the house without asking her to come along. This didn't hurt her feelings, but it made her intensely curious because under normal circumstances Uncle Bobby wanted her with him whenever possible. The last two times she'd asked him where he'd gone, instead of saying, "Oh, to see a friend of mine," he'd said, "Oh, just down to the Coin Castle."

The Coin Castle was a video arcade across from the Convenient Mart about a half-mile from her grandparents' house. This answer made her suspicious because Uncle Bobby was terrible at games in general and video games especially. The answer also worried her. She knew that although most of the neighbors loved and looked after Uncle Bobby, who'd passed their papers for years and who raised record levels for the annual American Cancer drive, there had been incidents, always involving teenagers and kids, like the ones who hung out at the Coin Castle. Uncle Bobby giving boys money, no one ever uncovering for what. Uncle Bobby buying beer at the Convenient Mart for underage kids. An episode several years ago when a couple of teenagers had talked Uncle Bobby into buying them an old jeep. After that, her grandfather, a staunch believer that a man should have at least a little control over the money he earned, had to take away Uncle Bobby's checkbook.

And then there had been an event vaguely sexual, so vaguely sexual that Janie wasn't sure if she'd overheard her parents talking about it or just made it up. Because eavesdropping was how she'd learned all the stories of the taking advantage of Uncle Bobby. They had never been told to her directly. She had overheard them shared among adults, and when she did overhear the stories, she immediately regretted hearing them: a teenage boy again, again, the boy with the upper hand. A fragile place under her heart drew in on itself and pinched, that snarl of emotions, including hurt and helplessness, also defensiveness and shame, those last two the most confusing and complicated of all. It was like her family's privacy and their territory were being trespassed upon. Only family should know Uncle Bobby's vulnerabilities, and if Uncle Bobby was to be teased or told what to do or manipulated, he was theirs to tease and tell and manipulate.

"E.T.! Phone home!" Uncle Bobby tried to change the subject.

"What do you want to go to Coin Castle for?" she asked.

Uncle Bobby snicker-chuckled his you've-caught-me-in-something-but-I'm-trying-to-act-like-it's-nothing laugh. "To see a friend of mine." He snicker-chuckled again. "Anything wrong with that, Janie? Anything wrong with that?"

AFTER EACH SHOWING, the popcorn girls had to drag garbage bags into the theaters and pick up under the seats. Spilled pop running from theater top to bottom, dirty Pampers in *Snow White*. The occasional greasy grocery bag from homemade popcorn snuck in. Halfway through the summer, *Psycho II* came to one of the side theaters, and the sorority girls decided to get scared. "I'm not going in there this time, I just won't do it!" A squeal. "I'm petrified!" "My God, I had to go in there Saturday night after the last show, and, I swear, something moved, I'm not making this up, something moved behind the curtain along the wall." Once when Janie herself was picking up, she pushed behind that curtain and ran into Kimberly. Kimberly shrieked so loud even Betty came running, then all the sorority girls collapsed into the nearest seats in hysterical laughter until Gus busted in and yelled at them.

Everybody said they felt the hauntiness in the *Psycho* theater, but everyone acted like it was a joke, so Janie did, too. Inside her, though, it didn't seem funny at all. Just stepping into the dim, empty theater, she'd feel the prickle left over from the screen, the pretend horror having somehow leaked off the film and infected the walls and the seats. But far worse than the *Psycho* theater, Janie knew although no one else appeared to, were the bathrooms.

Out in the lobby, Tommie Sue continued to tell. The attempted murder on the sidewalk under the marquee, a jealous husband waiting for his cheating wife to show up with her date. The more recent seizure in the bathroom, a lady's legs thrust rigid out a stall door, her heels tom-tomming the tiles.

"And then that guy who had a stroke during *Porky's*, that was just last year, right, Betty? And it happened during a matinee, that's what the coroner said, and here nobody noticed him until after the last show on a Saturday night. I don't know who was supposed to be picking up that day."

Betty shook her head. She didn't either.

"But there as we were closing down, that usher—I can't recall his name, I think he was from over in Chesapeake—he tried to shake the guy awake. And a mouse jumped out of his mouth."

Betty shivered and cupped her cross.

"We never saw that usher again."

As always, Janie would be standing between Tommie Sue, on the end of the counter nearest ticket sales, and the sorority girls, huddled at the other end past the pop machine. During the stories, Betty would swivel around on her ticket-seller stool and listen without smiling—these were the only times Betty did not smile—and that Betty, practical, even-tempered, cheerful, Christian, never questioned a syllable Tommie Sue spoke and affirmed many with nods made it all triply terrifying.

"And that's not all," Tommie Sue said, her big, round, darkish glasses amplifying bigger, rounder, darker her cloudy black eyes. Just then Gus barreled around the corner to catch them idle. Tommie Sue didn't blink. "That ain't even counting what all's happened in the old parts." She said her *ain'ts* with an elegance.

Gus clapped his hands on his hips, the bloated keychain quivering on his belt like a grenade, and glowered at Tommie Sue. He had to lift his chin to do it. Tommie Sue stared back, a nonchalant blankness. "Somebody get down there and check those restrooms!" Gus blared.

Sprawling underneath the ground floor, the Alexander Henry's bathrooms were bigger than many modern theaters altogether. To reach them, you descended a wide staircase covered with a once-red carpet now faded pinkish at its edges and in the middle worn down to mole-colored padding. Despite the clarity of her childhood Alexander Henry memories, Janie could not recall, no matter how hard she tried, ever entering these bathrooms before she became a popcorn girl. Some never-seen janitor cleaned the bathrooms in the mornings before the matinees, but then the popcorn girls were expected to do hourly checks. If you were appointed, you had to go down in the middle of the movies, when the fewest people would be using them. None of the other popcorn girls seemed to mind it. Janie pretended she didn't either.

Each pink-gray step deeper, her shoulders knitted tighter, her head drained lighter. Once you reached the bottom, before you even entered the rooms with the stalls, you had to pass through odd preliminaries, rooms random and with no apparent purpose, as though they'd been donated from other buildings. A room with nothing but sinks. A room with a gas fireplace and a mantle piled with broken bricks and musty couches that looked upholstered with shorthaired hounds. A tall, narrow, lightless room containing a single empty cot and three locked doors. By the time Janie got to the actual toilets, her panic had spread from her head and shoulders through her whole body, chilling even her fingers, her toes, but she still had the wherewithal to intone to herself, "You're eighteen years old, Janie. Janie, you're eighteen years old."

Then she was at the threshold of the stalls, stepping into the shock of fluorescent lights. The floor here was a vertiginous checkerboard of disintegrating black-and-white tiles the size of record albums, some chipped, some cracked, some missing completely and in their place what looked like earth coming up. And there wasn't simply one room of stalls. There were three, end to end. The closed stalls ran on and on to Janie's right, their wooden doors freshly painted the color of flesh, and to her left, the infinite mirrors, so many opportunities to find a dead body, everything resplendently lit. Janie quick-clicked down the broken tile floor in her cheap Heck's work loafers as fast as she could without breaking into a full run—because always, in a small corner of her huge vague fear, a specific little fear that she might run into a live person down here and all her infantile fears would be found out—her heart now surging like a body-big bellows, all of her, from guts to throat to ears, gorged with that bellowing heart. She kept her head turned slightly to the right, one eye on the tile, the other on the stall doors, all of her resisting the horrific pull-to of the mirrors. But now and again, in the far corner of her left eye, unavoidable, a flash of her red popcorn girl smock, her black popcorn girl pants, but Janie resisting, refusing, to look full-on, for fear of . . . what? She thought she knew. For fear of what she might see in the mirror with her.

Until she reached the end, whirled around, and did it all in reverse.

Then she'd burst back up into the relief of the mute lobby lights after the bathroom blare. She'd pause on the top step until her breathing evened. She straightened her smock and ran her fingers through her bangs. Then, when her hands stopped shaking, she'd initial the restroom check-sheet where it hung on a clipboard near the time clock.

It never did occur to her to cheat and not walk the whole thing.

RELAXED, NATHAN ALWAYS looked sleepy. This contrast made his outbursts even more electrifying, when they weren't directed at Janie, and they rarely were. Even so, now that he and she were a couple, her role in the tantrums changed from those early days in the garage when she and Uncle Bobby could just watch. Now Nathan's upset became in part her responsibility, to placate, to make right, an obligation not exactly imposed by Nathan, and not learned by Janie by having watched Melissa with him, but something Janie knew intuitively herself. Knew it was her job, but had almost no idea how to go about it. So that when he finally did calm, her relief was so profound it was intoxication on its own.

She met Nathan's friends, the languid, belt-thin pothead boys familiar to Janie from home. Nathan the shortest of them all, and it amazed her how he could be so small and at the same time the most cocksure in any group. She'd assumed growing up in the city would have made the friends more sophisticated, but that wasn't the case at all. Like it had with those boys back home, the weed fertilized their indifference and dulled their desires, so that they floated, day in, day out, in a complacent sag. This was another way Nathan stood out. The fuse in his belly, the periodic bombs—they also made him more alive.

Because he still slept in his childhood bed across the hall from his parents, they did it in his Chevrolet Scout. In his father's pickup camper shell. Once standing up along the wall in the clean concrete smell of the basement, his teeth clenching his bottom lip. They did it on the ground wherever the motorcycle stopped, in the blackberried brush between the river road and the Ohio dock, many times on a sheet of plastic in the head-high weeds at the base of one of the old factories, only yards away cars echoing in the metal ravine. Once, after a seven-hour partying marathon that included sneaking into the drive-in, crashing an outdoor party with a band playing some strain of violent country, and buying weed from a pothead friend's father (a man with the oil-slicked hair of the 1950s and who dealt while sitting in a barber chair he kept in his basement like a parodic throne), they ended up at 4 AM in a dew-soaked field beyond a couple tract homes. Janie without the remotest idea where they were and her obligated to be up, clean, and sober in time for 10 AM church. Nathan always came quick, she never did at all, and neither expected anything different.

The truth was, for Janie, the bodies were almost incidental. For her, sex enchanted for the same reasons as drugs and alcohol. The quick, easy intimacy, the crumbling of the barrier between herself and other people, the way during sex it was impossible to hold herself apart not only from him, but apart from herself. The mist of transcendence the sex showered over ordinary things, and later, Janie'd remember not the quick, hard thrusts, the skin on skin, but the little fog lifting off that field in the almost-dawn afterwards. She'd remember the scent of sycamores and river from the seat of the bike on the ride home, remember how the act drained both of them like an abscess, from him, his anger, his frustration, from her, her self-consciousness and anxiety. And also afterwards, a tenderness in him she never saw otherwise for longer than a few seconds, a vulnerability, and she knew it wasn't like that with many boys when they finished, but it was for him.

Once in a while among those pallid, droopy, dope-loving boys, Nathan might make a remark about her. Janie would flinch, and the boys would snicker, but only a little and usually uneasily, and after a few seconds, Janie would think, that wasn't what he meant, was it? Sometimes for a day or two he seemed to ignore her for no reason, then say he hadn't when she got up the nerve to ask him why he had, and then she'd have to replay the whole period in her head—so she'd just imagined it, right? She must have. Sometimes when she and Uncle Bobby hung around watching Nathan work in the basement, Nathan might not even acknowledge them, it all depended on his mood, but she knew he had to concentrate when he was working on the Harley and how exasperated it made him. Besides, his distractedness then and elsewhere meant she, too, could be by herself and with him at the same time. Meant she didn't have to think of things to say. And when he finally did come back, and touched her cheekbone, or sleepy-smiled with his eyes locked onto hers, or patted the back of his bike seat, his attentions radiated all the more brilliantly because of their absence before.

Janie's aunt came down to visit for a weekend. On Sunday afternoon, while Janie was helping her load the car, the aunt stopped Janie by the rosebushes, well out of earshot of Janie's grandmother and grandfather.

"Janie, Bobby can't handle drinking." She looked Janie in the eye, but not mean like her own mother would have. She looked worried and even awkward. She was only a year older than Uncle Bobby, much younger than Janie's mother, and she'd always been the cool aunt. Janie, her face warm, shifted her eyes to a dandelion in a driveway crack. "You understand that, right?" the aunt asked.

"Yeah," Janie said. Then mumbled, "But he loves it when we go out."

"And Nathan Simmons," her aunt went on, not responding to the Uncle Bobby excuse, "he doesn't treat you right." She looked hard at Janie again, and Janie thought she saw her mouth start to move, but then her aunt stopped.

As Janie, Uncle Bobby, and her grandparents waved to her aunt backing into the street, Janie hung back, a dark quaver in her chest. Then she reminded herself that her aunt was approaching forty and couldn't grasp the nuances of either the Uncle Bobby or the Nathan situation.

ONE HOT SATURDAY morning after two days of Nathan's keeping his distance, he called her and asked her to go with him to the lake. She hadn't known there was a lake.

She stepped cautious into the driveway where he was hitching the aluminum fishing boat to his father's truck. She paused there, uncertain whether he'd noticed her or not, him bent over the ball hitch and his white T-shirt riding up his back. The narrowness of his waist riding out of his Levi's, the gap between denim and skin. Janie raised her eyes and tried to read his mood from the side of his face, but then he finally turned, and his smile broke out full, and in the light off him, Janie lightened, too.

Then they were pulling away down Kentworth Drive, and the sky actually blue, exceptional for a late-morning July in Remington, West Virginia, where summer sky was usually the color of pale metal. Janie was drunk before they hit the city limits, as though the half-beer she put in herself as they headed out of town ignited the alcohol left in her body from the night before, and she dropped her head back and gazed into that uncommon blue sky. Over her eyes settled a kind of squishy glass, something that often happened when she got drunk in broad day, so that she saw everything, but saw it pleasantly distorted and at a padded distance. And all along, Nathan was talking to her, gentle-teasing, a mood almost as extraordinary as the sky, and Janie heard herself, more extraordinary, talking, and she understood Nathan was listening, and Janie thought, *this is how couples are. Couples who love each other. This is how couples are together.* Now they were winding through daylit hills that before they'd only ridden at night, and Janie, with the abysmal sense of direction of those who've lived their whole lives in one little place, became, as usual, completely disoriented, and that lostness, as usual, forced her to give over even more to Nathan, and she felt the savor of the fear in that giving over.

They finally reached the lake, not much more than a pond, Janie saw, its parking lot crawling with people like themselves. Then she and Nathan were putting in the aluminum boat with all the other people putting in their aluminum boats, all the others, too, with heavy loaded coolers and fishing poles like props, everyone else, too, drunk, but lazy drunk, not fighting drunk. Nathan was behind her now, his hand on the muted chuffing of the outboard, them moving just faster than a drift. And Janie bask-lazed in that similarity between themselves and the other couples, in the miracle of Nathan's contentment, in how he wanted her there in full light, how seldom they did anything together in the day. The two of them in a comfortable silence now, the kind that settles after you have had a conversation and followed it to its natural easy end. The squishy lens still padding her eyes, Janie leaned over the boat edge and towards the water, a second layer to look through. The grasses slimy waving under them and the algaed stones on the bottom, hypnotic.

It might have been fifteen minutes, it might have been forty, when she heard Nathan, his voice like ice water but with just a hint of taunt. "Miss Melissa Kendrick."

Janie's head snapped up. Sliding by, not ten feet distant, was another aluminum boat. A boat so like their own boat that if Janie had come up on them side by side in the parking lot, she wouldn't have been able to tell which from which. The other boat moving exactly parallel to theirs, but in the opposite direction, and in its bow, as Janie was in theirs, sat Melissa.

By the time Janie looked, Melissa was directly across from her. Melissa's blonde hair in drifts of perfectly executed curls clear to her shoulders, the hair immobile yet not stiff, her face meticulously, but not excessively, made up. Her features sharper than Janie's, Melissa had grown into them, they fit her, while Janie's face still floated in baby and beer fat. Melissa wore a bikini, her body big and small exactly where it should be, Janie in a one-piece with a pair of shorts pulled over to hide her thighs. Melissa was beautiful in the way favored by both Remington and McCloud County, so the way favored by Janie, too, and under the foundation, behind the mascara, Janie looked for surprise, anger, hurt, jealousy. But by the time Janie saw Melissa, the face had already been blocked off.

Janie registered all this in just a few seconds, both boats moving on their slow, opposed courses, and now Melissa was gone altogether and it was the man in the stern Janie faced. Him turned halfway, like Nathan was, with a hand on the tiller, his thick, earth-colored hair buckling out from under a black Walker cap. There was a heaviness to his body, to his bare torso, although he was not at all fat, his skin the kind of brown, layers deep, of men who work outside. His face was not as fine as Nathan's, the face had a heaviness to it, too, and a pair of grooves from the sides of his nose to the corners of his mouth. The face of a man. Which—it occurred to Janie for the first time, there'd been no reason for it to occur before—Nathan's was not.

After Nathan's "Miss Melissa Kendrick," the whole tableau unfolded in silence.

When stern had passed stern, the two boats completely clear of each other, Nathan gunned their motor. He straight-lined it back to the ramp, their wake wobbling and shaking the peacefully drunk others bobbing about, it all happening so quickly, Nathan moving so fast, that only a few even had time to muster a "Hey!" or give them the finger.

They drove all the way back to Kentworth Drive without exchanging a word, Nathan silent-screaming from every pore. Janie, tiny on her side of the seat, soberness fast overtaking her, and how she hated to go sober when she was still awake, and this in the worst of circumstances. The squishiness melted from her eyes, the sweet distance it imposed collapsed. And she knew Nathan's rage, his pain, had little to do with her, and she waited to feel pain herself, or jealous, or mad, but nothing came. Aside from a general miserableness, nothing came but the other man's face. That face she had read. Surprise, yes, but brighter than that, guilt. And she saw too, despite the bulky brown body, despite him being so much bigger than Nathan, you could tell that even when he sat, despite all that, Janie saw he was scared.

"YOU KNOW THOSE box seats they've got stuck up on the side walls?" It was late Sunday afternoon after the Saturday lake incident, that dead hour before her grandmother would call them to help her with supper. Janie lay on her stomach on Uncle Bobby's bed, her head at its foot, her bare feet on his pillows where Tina curled. Fresh from his shower after his shift, Uncle Bobby rocked in his recliner, Old Spice flavoring the room, and the air conditioner throbbed in the window, the sky outside cement-colored again. When her grandmother called them, Uncle Bobby would set the table, the napkin rings, the cloth napkins, the water pitcher. Janie would construct the salad, Jell-O squares in little nests of iceberg lettuce, or, her favorite, Seven Layer, with bacon and frozen peas. Napkins in their laps, they'd say the blessing before they ate, they'd please and they'd thank you, and every second, without looking, they'd feel the other's strain to be finished and go out.

"Yeah?" Uncle Bobby said.

"Well, they're fake. There's not even a door to get into them. That's just paint." She hadn't seen Nathan since he'd told her to go home when she tried to help him unhitch the boat. He'd left twice on the motorcycle after that. Once shortly after they'd returned from the lake. Again, Uncle Bobby had reported when she asked, while she was working Saturday night.

"I know that, Janie." It was the soft studiedly understated tone, both pitying and slightly embarrassed for her, that he used when she didn't know something he thought she should. When he knew more than she did, he was always sympathetic. "I thought you knew that. I thought you knew that, Janie."

"Also"—Janie pulled Tina down to where she could stroke her back—"Tommie Sue says the basement and the bathrooms aren't as deep as the Alexander Henry goes."

"What do you mean, Janie?"

"She says there are levels under the bathroom that run all under the whole city block." Janie hadn't believed this at first, but reliable Ronnie, with his rubber-band legs, his transparent moustache, who'd worked at the Alexander Henry for five years, said, yes, he went down there all the time to check the heating and air-conditioning.

"Do you think you could go down there, Janie?" Uncle Bobby rocked faster now, she could feel a little breeze off it. "What if you got to go down there?"

"And she says there are still dressing rooms somewhere behind the stage, and under those, a bunch more rooms that are caving in." Tommie Sue had spoken of snakes, which Janie didn't mind so much, and of rats, which she did. "Tommie Sue says sometimes the rats get so bad they have to shut the theater down for a few days and spread poisoned popcorn all over the floor."

"Ooooo, Janie! That's awful! That's just awful, now!"

Janie let go of Tina, turned her head to the side, and propped it on an elbow. That's when she noticed that the laundry E.T. no longer occupied the place of honor on the maiden aunt's jewelry box. That E.T. now sat on the surface of the dresser itself, and on the jewelry box sagged a second E.T., a cheaper version made of a smooth synthetic material, well-used, with shiny black streaks. An E.T. that had never seen the inside of a washing machine.

"Tell me about the cat shit," Uncle Bobby was saying, then pealing into giggles.

"Where'd you get that E.T.?"

"What?" The giggles collapsed.

"Where'd you get that new E.T.?"

"Oh." He paused. A cloak fell over his voice. "Friend of mind gave it to me."

"What friend?"

"Oh. Just a friend of mine." Now he'd recovered himself, retreated into exaggerated nonchalance. Janie watched his face. "You don't know 'em." He wasn't looking at her. "You don't know 'em, Janie." His brow furrowed. His lips moved. *Just a friend of mine. You don't know 'em.* The shadow say.

A place in Janie's chest twisted. She pulled the liner notes out of the album nearest at hand, *Tommy*, and pretended to read. Only once had she slept in this room, in Uncle Bobby's bed. She was ten years old, and her great-grandmother had died. The house was overfull with relatives home for the funeral, and Uncle Bobby had been moved to a couch because his bed would hold three children. Janie slept there with her two younger cousins, them five and six at the time. When she'd been told of this arrangement, she'd feigned annoyance, but she was secretly relieved because she suspected Great-grandmother's ghost might be coasting the house at night.

A generous and bony woman who'd grown skinnier and skinnier until there wasn't enough to her to hold her up, Great-grandmother had lived in a small brick house in the city and wore dresses like those the other old ladies in Remington wore, but Janie's mother had told Janie many times that Great-grandmother had grown up in "dire poverty." Up a dirt road out in the country, the daughter of a pipe-smoking woman and a half-Cherokee man with the un-Cherokee name "Alan." "Dire poverty," her mother would say. "Your great-grandmother would take me out there to visit them when I was little, but your grandmother was ashamed of them." "Your great-grandmother only went to the third grade," her mother also told her, this the most fascinating piece of all, especially because when Great-grandmother died, Janie was in fourth grade so had passed her.

After Janie's mother turned out the light the night she slept in Uncle Bobby's room, Janie drew as close to her little cousins as she could without raising suspicions. Then she prayed.

She hadn't known she'd fallen asleep when a rapping woke her. She snapped to, rigid in every digit and limb. At first she thought she'd imagined it, she'd been told since she could talk that her imagination was too big, but then the rapping began again. Against the window pane, an insistent, a confident *tack tack tack*. She had jerked the covers over her head and was reciting "God is Great" when she heard a call-hiss as loud as a voice can get and still be under breath: "Bobby!"

"Who's that?" blurted her cousin Ellie, her voice as clear as though she'd never been asleep, and then she was crawling over Janie towards the window.

Janie followed instinctively to protect her and so as not to appear more cowardly than a kindergartener. Ellie was now pulling back Uncle Bobby's plaid curtain and rising to her tiptoes, Janie huddled behind, both of them leaning forward. And then looking down into the upraised and shocked face—she could see one side of his face quite well in the light off the back porch next door—of a blotchy, tubby man with greasy graying red hair.

Before he wheeled and sprinted around the corner of the house, Janie saw he carried a yardstick.

The other cousin slept through the whole incident. Ellie did not mention it in the morning or ever again as far as Janie knew, which made her wonder if Ellie had really been awake after all.

Janie never told anyone either. Although she was even more naive about sex than other ten-year-olds in 1975, an unsettling part of her that occasionally knew things ahead of her mind, a part that felt like memory when Janie knew the things remembered had never happened in her life, that part seeped into her heart an unnameable and untraceable shame for Uncle Bobby and for herself. As she got older, that night at the window would sometimes resurface, and each time it did, she understood more with her brain and she shoved it harder away. But now, here on Uncle Bobby's bed, behind her a new curtain, still plaid, and Uncle Bobby and the shadow-say—

There came a tap on the door. Janie jumped.

"You all ready to help set the table?"

AFTER THE DAY at the lake, Nathan stopped varying their night rides. Now she only saw him very late, after her evening shift or after she and Uncle Bobby had already been out. On work nights, Uncle Bobby liked to be in bed by ten because he had to get up at five to walk to the hospital. Nathan would go out, too, during those earlier after-dinner hours, to where, she did not know and never asked. She'd lie, her body strung tight, on the porch swing, with Uncle Bobby before ten, without Uncle Bobby after, waiting while pretending not to wait, until she'd hear, a quarter-mile away, the Yamaha turn onto Kentworth Drive.

When it slid into the driveway across the street, Janie would lift up just far enough to glimpse through the hedges Nathan rip off his helmet and stalk into his house. Not long after, he'd resurface, float gray across his lawn, then hers—he who had to start work at 7:30 AM, almost as early as Uncle Bobby, but who never seemed to need sleep, as though the perpetually sleepy look he wore when he wasn't angry was rest enough for him—and fetch her. Sometimes he didn't even speak.

He'd hell-bend them out of Remington, using the back streets behind the art museum, past the extravagant turn-of-the-century mansions there, a neighborhood Janie's grandmother had showed her when she was little, and when she was little, they didn't even make her envious. The mansions were still what she could grow up into. Then, abruptly, they were in woods—how quick the city stopped and the country began—and then in fields, and then in woods again, it could almost have been McCloud County except these hills were smaller, growing gradual out of the Ohio Valley. Within minutes, Janie would be lost, and the first time and even the second, although she must have seen the little house in the corn, the impression didn't stick. But she must have registered it because the third time, when they actually stopped near the house, memories of passing it earlier returned. Still, even that third time, Janie believed it was because Nathan liked the ride. By the fourth, she knew different.

That night, she decided not to wrap her arms around him; she clutched the sissy bar instead, to punish him for his aloofness. If Nathan noticed, he didn't show it. By now, more than a week after the incident at the lake, Janie understood that whatever had been between her and Nathan—and she still couldn't name it; neither of them had ever said "girlfriend," much less "love"—had peaked, and there was nowhere to go but down. When she was anticipating being with him instead of actually with him, she could sometimes bury that understanding. When they were together, like now, the burying did not hold. As they sledded the hills, Janie pushed deeper into the sissy bar, made space between them, closed her eyes, and tried to be with only the smells. The smells so much louder in the night than in day, and Janie pulled them around her, envisioned them as a screen between her and Nathan. Eventually they surged up the highest hill of all, almost a mountain, then down into a straight along a creek, and finally up a smaller hill. At the crest of it, Nathan killed the engine.

They coasted down in the whine of the wheels, the after-roar of the engine still vibrating in Janie's ears. They coasted as far as momentum would carry them into a bottom full of hip-high green corn. The bike stopped well short of the house, but with the house in clear sight. Nathan didn't heel the kickstand. They stood there with their feet on the road holding the weight and the heat of the bike between their legs.

The house sat lonely in a tiny lot stamped out of the corn, a single outbuilding behind it. One-story, small, porchless, no white clapboard or aluminum siding, there was nothing farmhouse about it. Stucco, of all things, like a bewildered transplant from town. The hills bulked in the near distance. Janie inhaled the McCloud County odor of corn just beginning to tassel. Her thighs were starting to strain. In dogless silence, the house was lit on the outside only by a cloud-scarped moon, on the inside by one illuminated room. Two tall, pointed shrubs flanked the porchless front door.

Standing there in the humidity without the wind of the ride, she felt under her sweatshirt the perspiration bead in the small of her back. Nathan, still straddling the bike, reached into his inside jacket pocket and pulled out a joint. He pushed back his face shield, slipped the joint between his lips, and thumbed the lighter. Janie waited, suspended between outrage at his not admitting her existence and a heart-craning hope that he would. Nathan passed the joint over his shoulder. Janie took it, tasted the moisture of his mouth on it, and she drew deep and returned it. Nathan's face did not waver from the house. Janie stared, too. Wondering if she was coconspirator or afterthought.

She gulped the second drag, all the smoke her mouth and throat could hold. She knew it wasn't Melissa's house, Melissa lived in an apartment near Rees Park, Uncle Bobby had pointed it out one time, and Uncle Bobby was never wrong about that kind of thing. She looked for Melissa's car, she knew that, too, from before Nathan and Melissa broke up, but the only car was a newish Ford truck. She wondered was it something to do with one of the belt-thin boys, maybe a falling out or, more frightening, an argument with a dealer. And then an image bloomed in her mind, and as soon as it did, she felt so foolish her face flushed. The hard brown handsomeness. The grooves from his nose to his lip. His fear anyway.

They smoked the roach until it seared their fingernails. Nathan flipped the last of it onto the berm. He snapped down his face mask and turned the key. He rotated the bike, unrushed, his feet still on the ground. Then he leaned into it and they were smooth-moving, the corn, the flat, the stucco house falling fast behind.

THE NEXT TIME Uncle Bobby left without inviting her along, Janie waited ten minutes, then headed to the Coin Castle.

The Coin Castle had not a single castle attribute, not even a fake turret or a crenellated facade, was nothing but a cube squatting in a black asphalt lot. From the edge of that sun-fired lot, Janie squinted at the open door, the Coin Castle's interior as dark as a midday tavern. She hesitated again on the threshold. The games sizzled and flashed in that dark, they cheeped and sang, she recognized their voices, Centipede, Donkey Kong, Pac-Man and Ms., she'd played them all, always in bars, never sober. A pack of boys under fourteen jostled each other and the machines, the place ripe with the aroma of grape gum blended with the high, sour odor of prepubescent boy sweat. When she finally slipped in, she pulled off to the side and willed herself unnoticed. As soon as her eyes adjusted, she spotted Uncle Bobby.

He stood beside the counter where they got their tokens, bought their candy, complained when their money was lost. He was fresh from his after-work shower, and now that she saw him, she could detect Old Spice floating through the grape gum and boy smell. His thinning hair neatly combed, his polo shirt tucked into his too-tight shorts—in perpetual denial of his weight, he insisted on buying them one size too small—Uncle Bobby rocked on his heels. And beamed at the woman behind the counter.

A woman shaped like a planet with fine brown hair that fell straight to her shoulders like a thin fountain, making her face look rounder than it was. She wore over brown double-knit pants a smock top of Holly Hobbie fabric. And she was speaking, Uncle Bobby urging her on, "Mmmm-hmmm. Mmm-hmm." Uncle Bobby attentive, enthusiastic, close to euphoric, now he was convulsing into laughter over something she'd said—"Oh, c'mon, Tessa! C'mon, now! You're kidding me!"—and Janie shifted to where Uncle Bobby could see her.

When he did, not a trace of embarrassment invaded his face. Not a trace of shame. After a short surprise, his face held only pleasure, and not just pleasure, Janie saw, but also pride. He stuck out his arm towards Janie. "Tessa, this is my niece, Janie. She works at the thee-ay-ter."

Tessa turned to Janie, smiling, and extended her hand. Janie stepped towards her, and as she did, she was startled by how badly she wanted this for Uncle Bobby. Two boys slammed between her and the counter, slapped money down—"A pack of red hots!"—and Janie was reaching over them, taking the plump warm hand, saying, "Nice to meet you."

And while she was usually too nervous to look a stranger in the face for more than a few seconds, this time she looked longer. Because she wanted so urgently for it to be, even though right under that she knew someone like Uncle Bobby could never run a video arcade. Janie took the hand, looked in the face, and saw, first, tiredness. Then patient kindness. And finally, intelligence. Janie saw in Tessa everything was right there.

IT WAS THE very next day that her grandmother had arranged for her to pick up Uncle Bobby from work after lunch and take him to his dental appointment. She'd accidentally made it for an afternoon when she was teaching Bible study. "Thank you so much, honey," her grandmother had said. "You'll have to go in and get him. He won't know what time to come out."

Janie decided to drive the back way to the hospital, to follow Uncle Bobby's walking route, two and a half miles each morning, no matter the weather and in the dark in the winter. She imagined Uncle Bobby in his down-to-business get-there gait, his head pitched forward, his arms swinging, his shoulders and butt rocking side-to-side with so wide a sweep you feared he'd lose his balance. But he never did, Uncle Bobby borne upright by momentum. Once in a while her grandmother picked him up in the afternoons, Janie had ridden with her many times, and since she'd gotten her license two years before, Janie had picked him up a few times, too. So for years, Janie had waited in the alley outside the service employees' entrance until Uncle Bobby torpedoed through the door at 3:16. But this was the first time she'd been inside.

She slipped into an empty yellow hall splitting into other empty yellow halls and not a sign anywhere besides EXIT. Wandering right, she ran into a woman resting with a mop bucket in an alcove under the time clock. The woman's chin sloped long off her face like a scoop.

When Janie asked her for directions to the laundry room, the woman laughed, the scoop shimmying. She heaved herself out of the chair, Janie saying, "Oh, no, don't get up," the woman laughing at that, too, and the woman led her around corner after yellow corner to a set of solid double doors.

Janie thanked the woman, then pushed through them. And her breath stopped.

All these years (he'd been promoted from housekeeping to laundry a decade ago) when Janie thought of Uncle Bobby at work, which she often did, she saw—not imagined, but saw—a cheerful, clean, brightly lit room, a platonic ideal of a Laundromat. But now she stood on the edge of a sprawling, windowless dungeon, somehow both low-ceilinged and cavernous, lit only by intermittent yellow bulbs, and the light stopped before the room did, the room's edges running off into spaces she couldn't see. The giant machines thudded in her torso, tingled her hands, now all their beats at cross-purposes, now synching into harmony, now out again, just above her head a convolute of ducts and vents and tube, and she wondered if Uncle Bobby had to stoop. The humidity more tropical than outdoors—another characteristic of the platonic Laundromat, Janie realized, was that it was air-conditioned—and the damp heat clotted cottony in her mouth, a taste of lint and used soap and gray water, that already made her want to spit.

She strained to make out Uncle Bobby among the dim shapes pivoting between a row of mammoth front-loading washers and a row of mammoth front-loading dryers. The dryers emitted eerie light, brighter than the ceiling bulbs when the light wasn't obscured by the fabric the dim shapes pulled from the machines, scrubs, gowns, sheets, like fishermen hauling in nets, hand over hand, to find nothing at their ends. And for some reason she suddenly remembered another Uncle Bobby story the family told. How as a five-year-old, uncoordinated, he'd stumbled into a heater, and he still carried faded scars on his arms and hands.

Then she did see Uncle Bobby. Because he had seen her first and had pulled away from the others. He was fast-gathering his lunch bag from a shelf. She stepped towards him, and now Uncle Bobby was passing the metal manager's cage, hurrying like he always did, when a voice called from the cage over the din, "Hey, Bobby."

Janie turned to see inside the steel latticework the supervisor, his legs crossed at his ankles and propped on his desk, his left shoe almost touching the shredded lettuce protruding from a half-eaten sub. He was dangling from his hand what looked like a gold chain. "Ten days are up. I guess it's yours."

Uncle Bobby ducked in. He took the chain from the supervisor at a speed just short of a snatch and mumbled "Thank you"—Janie saw his mouth move, she could not hear it. Then he shoved it into the pocket of his skintight work pants.

In the car, after she turned on the ignition but before she put it in gear, Janie said, "Who you gonna give that necklace to?"

She'd asked him directly last night if Tessa had given him the black-streaked E.T. doll. He'd nodded. "It used to belong to one of her kids." Then he'd added, matter-of-factly, "Me and her might move in together."

"Oh," he said now. "A friend of mine."

Then, to Janie's surprise, he stretched out his leg and, squirming a little, wiggled the necklace out of his pocket. With great delicacy, his breath held, he laid it out across the yellow callouses of one palm.

The chain part was thickish, with large links, a little tarnished. Hanging from it was a large artificial red jewel like a screw-shaped tail.

"She's gonna like it," Janie finally said.

"Mmm-hmm," said Uncle Bobby. "I already know that."

THAT NIGHT WHEN she and Uncle Bobby got home at nine after riding around without even drinking, Nathan was sitting on the wall along his driveway. Janie pretended she didn't see him, and Uncle Bobby really didn't, but Nathan arced off the wall and strolled across the street. Without speaking, he took Janie's hand and laid it on his cheek. Her limbs loosened. Maybe he was done with the stucco house. Maybe after watching it like he had last time, they would move on to something else.

They did not. They stood again, bike between their legs, in that untraveled road between corn. The sky starless, the high summer clouds, invisible now, still pressing down heat. The house again with its single light, its single truck. She waited for Nathan to light a joint, but tonight he was so rapt he didn't even think of that. Then, as though Nathan had conjured it by his intensity, the front door opened. The door shielded by those high shrubs, Janie saw it open only by the light spilling out of it onto the grass. In front of her, inside Nathan, Janie felt the fuse ignite.

Two figures stepped out of the door, through the light, and towards the truck. All Janie could discern was that one was taller than the other. There was nothing else she could tell. Everything else was blotted, was drowned, by Nathan's body before her, the body dilating, taut as rock, the swelling strained, the high desperation, a shrill to it you could feel but not hear, the fuse flaring, and Janie saw again the unnerved face of the man in the boat, saw again the foam on Nathan's lips, saw again the banker's hand in the garage, cocking back.

Abruptly, Nathan arched his body like a wing and crashed all one hundred and fifty pounds down on the kick start. Janie lost her balance, grabbed his belt, and the engine roared, and at the same time, to Janie's disbelief, Nathan screamed, "Look!"

She never knew if they did look, because he'd already thrown the bike around, his body married to it low and tight as though he were injecting it with his fury, the better to charge the speed, the volume, and it was true, the bike was flying faster, screaming louder, than Janie could ever remember it before, and she had to wrap her arms around his waist despite herself or she would have toppled off, and she felt in her skin how she'd skid across the pavement, she felt the burn. The banks, the trees, spinning past, Nathan leaning into turns at an angle too deep, the bike canting to where she feared their hips would scrape ground, Nathan, who always drove fast, now driving dangerous, and Janie, whom Nathan's driving always scared a little, but in a thrilling way, realized she was scared for real. She was terrified. The bike just holding the curves like a marble in a low-rimmed slot, now them cresting the highest hill, and Janie saw the rusty guardrails, the dark-humped crown of trees under them, and Janie saw, too, the motorcycle sailing over those guardrails, her body, his, impaled on branches. Janie ricocheted between staring aghast over Nathan's shoulder, her eyes so wide they hurt, and squeezing her eyes shut and begging under her breath. Until finally she just balled all of herself into the very top of her chest, right under her throat, right under a scream, and held on and waited for the end. But she did not scream, not any more than she yelled, *What the fuck are you doing? Slow down! Are you crazy?* And why? Because her fear of appearing uncool was still more real to her than the fear of dying? Or was it fear of pissing him off that was more real? Or was it simply not wanting to call attention to herself?

Then suddenly, they rounded a curve, and there was a coal truck. Nathan did brake. But it was too late, Nathan had to pass on the right, the graveled shoulder, Janie felt the guardrail graze her ankle, and that Nathan kept it upright Janie could only attribute later to how hard her grandmother prayed for her each night, and the shoulder narrowed, them running out of space, and at the last possible moment, they cleared the truck, Nathan jerked the tires back onto the pavement, didn't even skid, and Nathan and Janie ripped on towards Remington.

WEDNESDAYS AT RAMELLA'S was happy hour all night long, and Janie ordered another tequila sunrise while Uncle Bobby complained about the lazy ways of the sub-eating laundry manager. "And he just sits in there talking on the phone to his girlfriend, Janie. Just sits in there talking to his girlfriend, and I'm telling you, I've never seen anyone so fat. She's as fat as those three ladies we saw climbing into that Volkswagen outside of Ponderosa all put together!" and him harr-ing, jungle roaring, she could hear all kinds of animals in it, and by the end of the second drink, Janie could shove away what had sickened her all day—that Nathan was more willing to kill himself and her than to confront Melissa's lover, yes, but also things even oozier than that. Now those things faded, and by the third drink, Janie was enveloped in glow, for Uncle Bobby, for the bartender, even for the Halloweenishly mascara'd woman in the Styx T-shirt the bartender was hitting on.

Then, at a distance from herself, Janie heard herself talking, the words coming easy as a creek running in her mouth, only when she was high and only with Uncle Bobby could she talk this way, and as she did, every bad feeling in her washed clear. She talked loose, with no regard for grammar, talked how almost everyone in McCloud County talked, including most of the teachers at school, and the way Janie talked when she wasn't at home or at her grandparents', and she heard her mother saying, "You keep talking like that, you'll never find a job away from here," then that, too, washed away. She was telling stories of college, all the wild parties, them wildening further in the telling, things she had actually done, and things she had heard other people had done that she wished she'd thought of, them now done by her in the telling, and Uncle Bobby howling with laughter and admiration at all the right places and then some. "Oh, I can't believe that, Janie! I can't believe it!" "Oh, I think that's so funny, Janie!" "Did you tell him, Janie? Did you tell him off?"

And then she let Uncle Bobby have his turn. He continued in the vein of the risky and the outrageous, repeating the story of the man at church who carried his wife's purse for her, a hilarious and unthinkable violation of Uncle Bobby's "ways." Next revisiting the time he came out of the liquor store, tripped, fell, but saved the Southern Comfort, and when he reached spots in his tellings where he had no words, he'd just improvise—"and so forth and so on and what have you"—Janie *mmm-hmmming* him right along. She glimpsed for an instant the pair they made in the mirror behind the bar, then jerked her gaze away and tossed back her head and crowed at the latest thing Uncle Bobby had said even though she hadn't really heard it.

Then he got into the keg party Nathan had thrown in high school while his parents were at Hilton Head and how Uncle Bobby had fallen in the bathroom and ripped off the shower curtain. Janie swallowed a gulp of tequila, the day's ruminations creeping back like bad light seeping under a door. But it was not just the mention of Nathan, Janie understood that. Something new was going on; it had happened the day at the lake and had been happening ever since. Earlier and earlier than it should, than it ever had, the liquor was dragging her down instead of raising her up. Leaving her even more unprotected than she was when she was sober. Uncle Bobby ordered another White Russian while Janie shook her head and picked at her coaster, as dread came witch-fingering into her. She felt herself pushing the time card into the clock tomorrow at 12:15, the tedium that would follow broken only by the cold sweat of the bathroom check and by Tommie Sue's monologue. The return to college, in just three weeks, and the loneliness there. Janie had graduated high school with two hundred other students—fewer than twenty had gone to college, and Janie knew that fewer than that would finish. Again, Janie caught sight of them in the speckled mirror, their faces broken by liquor bottles and beer logos. Uncle Bobby's enormous glasses, his mouth contorted in desperate glee. Janie dropped her eyes to the cocktail napkin on her lap.

And she realized—a paradoxical clarity the post-drunkenness carried—that it wasn't that she was simply tired of Tommie Sue's talking or even scared of her death stories. Janie understood, had all along, that under Tommie Sue's drone lived a secret knowledge that Janie was both horrified she would eventually pass to and, on the other hand, frightened of what might befall her if she didn't ever know. It was a secret knowing familiar to Janie because it was held by so many women of her childhood in McCloud County and by most older women she'd worked with in food service and on line jobs since she was fourteen. The Tommie Sue kind of secret knowing was more familiar to Janie than the sorority girls' secret knowing, but at this point, no more penetrable. One component of that secret knowing was an offhand disdain for the college-going and the college-educated, for manager types, for anybody who didn't work with their hands, but a disdain Tommie Sue and the others didn't bother to actively exercise because the objects of the disdain weren't worth it. And the disdain, Janie grasped, was borne of Tommie Sue and her people's matter-of-fact insight that they lived in reality while the others only believed themselves to do so. And while Janie feared ending up in Tommie Sue's reality, she also suspected that ignorance of that reality could expose a person to consequences more dangerous than those Janie could yet comprehend.

Now Uncle Bobby was saying, "Remember the time I took you and Ben to *Black Beauty* and Ben lost his mittens?" and fountaining into peals so shrill that even the bartender, who was accustomed to her and Uncle Bobby, looked away from the Styx fan to make sure all was well.

"Why don't you write a story about that, Janie? Why don't you write a story about that?"

And now, her glass squeezed between her hands, her mired in the blank, ground-bound sadness that always came after a drunk if she wasn't quick enough to fall asleep first, Janie understood one part of the Nathan ooze. That the drugs, the alcohol, had never really dissolved barriers, never brought her closer to others. They just generated an insulation whose padded distance made her feel safe enough to make believe intimacy.

TEN DAYS PASSED after that last drive to the stucco house without a word from Nathan, twice as long as he'd ever vanished before. Janie stayed off the porch this time. She watched from the window only. A Ferris wheel revolved through her head, each car pausing for her to sit in its feeling a while: rage at his ignoring her; relief that she possibly wouldn't ever talk to him again; pride that she did not reach out to him (she suppressed the fact that her not reaching out was more fear of rejection than anything noble); but, suffusing all of that, and this not suppressible, her desire for him anyway.

Only once did Uncle Bobby notice anything was amiss. "Wonder where Nathan's been keeping himself at these days?"

Then, a week before she was to return to college, when she and Uncle Bobby had already started saying good-bye to their places, she was upstairs pulling on her black popcorn girl pants for the evening shift when her grandmother called from downstairs, "Nathan's on the phone."

Janie held the receiver a little ways from her ear, as if this might help. She stared through her grandparents' living room window, at the brick walls across the street. But Janie could not picture him, invisible inside that near room.

He told her his parents had gone out of town.

"You and Bobby want to come over for dinner tomorrow night?"

No, a rigidness inside her hissed, say *no*. But that part was too brittle, too grown-up, to overcome the other. The seductive teasing in his voice, she heard it even in two sentences as bland as those. The nonchalant confidence, his wanting her and Uncle Bobby there. What's there to lose? Janie thought, and said, "What time?"

Nathan opened the front door, extended one arm, and pulled her to him. He turned his crotch into hers for a moment like a promise. In those ten days, he'd grown back the beard he'd shaved during the Melissa breakup, and she flinched at the prickliness. "Whatcha gonna put on the grill, Nathan?" Uncle Bobby was saying. "I could smell the coals clear in my bedroom. I could smell the coals clear in my bedroom, Nathan," and as they passed through to the kitchen, Janie was aware of the garage a story under their feet. How seldom she'd been in this part of the house except in secret, while his parents slept, she and Nathan tiptoeing up to his single bed.

"Sirloin, Bobby. Only the best," Nathan said. Uncle Bobby had dressed up, his nicest blue and green polo shirt, his new khaki shorts the requisite one size small, them riding high on his tree-trunk thighs. "You all want a beer or a rum and Coke?"

"Beer, please," said Uncle Bobby.

"Rum and Coke," said Janie.

"Yeah, that's what I want, too," Uncle Bobby said.

She saw right away that Nathan expected her to pull together most of the meal from groceries he'd bought—iceberg lettuce, baking potatoes, bacon bits—while he fretted over the three steaks on the grill. She set her drink on the windowsill and scrubbed potatoes while Uncle Bobby hovered between her in the kitchen and Nathan outside, Uncle Bobby knowing better than to help with hot things. All afternoon had been pumping up to storm, Janie could smell the lightning making, she didn't have to look at the sky, and the air-conditioning at Nathan's was a good five degrees cooler than her grandparents would run it, the chill lifting bumps on her upper arms. Each time Uncle Bobby opened the door, the humidity bulged in like a man-sized blister.

"It's gonna pour, huh, Janie? I hope he gets those steaks done before it pours, don't you, Janie?" She and Uncle Bobby had spent most of the day together, and the tag questions—*I am here, Tell me so*—were starting to get on her nerves. Janie poured herself another rum and Coke. Uncle Bobby wandered outside to "huh" Nathan awhile. Janie ripped the lettuce into a bowl.

Through the window, she watched Nathan's self-important fussing over the steaks. She felt the pressure of his groin against hers, and she was suddenly so angry her hands shook. She snapped the last leaf into the bowl and swallowed the second half of the rum and Coke. But it wasn't working. Like those tequila sunrises at Ramella's had not worked, the alcohol was plateauing. She looked at Nathan again, and again, her hands shook, her teeth clenched. But shot through that, complicating, confusing: the normalcy, the domesticity, of standing at this sink preparing food. That Nathan had invited them upstairs, invited them for a dinner he at least thought he was preparing, and he'd asked Uncle Bobby, too. For Nathan, there was nothing strange about having Uncle Bobby, too. And it dawned on her that this was the only event she or Uncle Bobby had been invited to all summer with the exception of church functions, and this flooded her with such embarrassment and desolation her fist went to her chest.

Shrieked giggles bugled from the patio, Uncle Bobby's high apparently escalating in inverse proportion to hers falling. Through the glass door she saw him doubled over, clenched hands pounding his shorts, his face forced purple, and she knew it was because he'd remembered her grandmother was right across the street and might hear. Janie knew he was trying to gulp down the laughter, flatten it into pressurized shrieks. And finally they were sitting down at the dining room table, famished and agitated, Nathan not having understood how long potatoes took to bake. Janie put her napkin in her lap and surveyed the room.

Its casual fineness made her small. The polished wood of the furniture, the paintings on the wall, the Oriental rugs under her feet, the dark gleaming bookcases evenly rowed with hardback books. Other things she didn't even have a name for, only knew that they were expensive. All of it, Janie understood, exactly what her grandparents' house wanted to grow up into. But almost certainly would not have time. And then Nathan at the head of the table in greasy cut-offs, bare feet, and a *Johnny's* T-shirt with its collar frayed, and two months ago Janie would have marveled at how hard it was to reconcile him with his house and that would have made her want him even more. Now she understood that his subversion was deliberate. The air-conditioning churned, the storm still had not broken, and Uncle Bobby commented three or four times how lucky they were the steaks had gotten done before the rain. They'd only eaten a few bites when the phone rang. Nathan sauntered into the kitchen and lifted it from the wall.

Janie strained to hear past Uncle Bobby—"And I told him, you should keep your dog tied up, German shepherds are mean dogs. And I was right, wasn't I, Janie? Wasn't I?"—but she could tell only that the exchange was muffled, sharp, and short. The clobber of receiver back on the wall. And the second she glimpsed Nathan's face again at the table, Janie winced in the base of her throat. It had something to do with Melissa.

Nathan pulled his plate right under his chin, wrapped one arm around it, and began spearing into his mouth bits of steak he'd already cut up. Every sane impulse in Janie screamed "stay quiet," but the part of her that had asked "What time?" on the phone instead of no, she heard that part softly inquire, "What's wrong?"

"Nothing!" Nathan jammed another chunk of meat into his mouth.

Uncle Bobby took him at his word.

"Man. It'd sure be nice to have a nice homegrown tomato with this dinner."

Nathan's jaws worked like an animal's. Janie could hear the cartilage, the hinge. She lifted a forkful of lettuce, Thousand Island, and bacon bits to her lip, then set the fork back down.

"Man, it'd be nice to have a nice fresh tomato. I just love homegrown tomatoes. Those store-bought tomatoes, they taste like plastic water. Huh, Janie? Huh?"

"Yeah," she said. Nathan smashed his baked potato with the back of his fork.

"This dinner would be perfect with a tomato. A nice, fresh, red tomato." Uncle Bobby demolished his food as he talked without choking on a word, his astounding skill at talking with his mouth full without anyone hearing the food, years of practice under her grandmother's vigilant ear and eye. "I know where there's a homegrown tomato, you know that, Nathan? You know that?"

Nathan tore off half a piece of garlic bread and thrust it into his mouth. Janie could see clear back to his molars before he started chewing. *Don't talk to him, Uncle Bobby*, she whispered in her head, *leave him be.*

"There's a nice ripe tomato on one of your dad's plants out back by the alley. I saw it when I was putting out the trash."

Uncle Bobby, and this time she just about said it out loud.

"I'd sure like to have a tomato now, that would be nice." Uncle Bobby looked at each of them in turn. "You know, if neither one of you all are gonna get it for me, I believe I'll just go out there and pick that tomato myself."

In a single motion, Nathan rammed his chair away from the table and hurled his knife, the blade glancing off an antique bureau and dropping, mute, on the Oriental rug. "You can't have that fucking tomato!"

Uncle Bobby looked down and away. Nathan bolted onto his feet, wheeled, and slammed an open hand against the arch between the kitchen and dining room.

"Goddammit!" he shouted. "Just get the fuck out of here!"

Janie stood up. Uncle Bobby stayed down.

"Not you! Him!"

Uncle Bobby gazed shut-mouthed and blank-faced off to the side. A dog who didn't do it. Upon Nathan's command, Janie had started to sit back down, but she stopped halfway, her hands on the chair arms, her knees slightly bent, paralyzed by emotion. Frustration with Uncle Bobby for never knowing when to stop, and embarrassment for him, too, and shame. But more impassioned than those, the instinct to defend Uncle Bobby against Nathan and the line he had crossed. Nathan was not family, only family was allowed to raise their voices at Uncle Bobby, and when they did, they never screamed, they did not cuss, there were rules for reacting to Uncle Bobby annoyance. But in that moment, overriding even her outrage at the injustice committed against Uncle Bobby, Janie felt most primally the urgency to calm Nathan down.

By now, of course, he'd blown himself up big, and this time he bellowed instead of screamed: "I said, get the fuck out of here!"

Uncle Bobby scooted away from the table. As he walked out, his napkin dropped from his lap to the floor.

Nathan flung himself into a living room chair, his heels on the seat, his knees pulled up to his face. Janie eased herself back down into her own chair. She looked at the torn food on her and Nathan's plates. At Uncle Bobby's almost empty one. After a few minutes, she started to clear the table.

Nathan entered the kitchen behind her, placed his soft hand on her arm right above her elbow, and pulled her, not roughly, outside. The clouds strained towards storm, dusk greenish with it, and he led her, him still barefoot, to his Scout on the street.

They'd just turned off Kentworth Drive and were passing the Coin Castle when the storm finally broke, instant and violent. Just like a movie, Janie thought. *Just like one of these old movies.* That too explained why everything felt at such a distance from her. Around them, cars pulled off to the sides of the streets to wait out the first blinding force of the rain, but Nathan forged head-on into it, and Janie had no room in her to be afraid. They were driving up the Ohio River on the West Virginia side this time, the rain exploding on the windshield like comic book firecrackers, and Nathan had not spoken a word. Soon the thunder and lightning started to divide so she couldn't tell which clap went with which flash, and the rain fell with less ferocity, and Nathan was pulling them into a field across the river from an Ohio country club. They'd been in the field before. They had rapid sex in the backseat while the rain continued to slack on the roof. Then Nathan passed out.

Janie disentangled herself. She pulled up her shorts, snapped them. She pushed her hair away from her face. She crawled into the front seat. She could see even in the dark how clumps of weeds in the field had been beaten into swaths laid low across the ground, and from a side window, she watched the lightning recede across the rest of West Virginia. The lightning cutting the sky to the east. Uncle Bobby would not turn on the TV until the thunder died completely away. He was terrified of the set blowing up, not to mention "ghosts" appearing on the screen, which he claimed he'd seen before during a storm, but Janie'd never understood if he meant actual spirits or some technical term he'd turned into a malaprop. In the morning, he would not mention the dinner. She also knew that no matter what else he felt about the evening, he'd still have some regret about missing dessert.

Suddenly, all the lights went out on their side of the river. The Ohio golf course continued to burn.

THOSE VERY LAST days before she left, she and Uncle Bobby made a final ritual sweep of their places, Uncle Bobby toasting the two of them in each one. To skip the Alexander Henry was unthinkable, but the only movie they hadn't seen was *Reds*, two years old and just reaching Remington. Predicting small crowds, Gus assigned it to the shoebox-shaped confines of the converted shoe store.

Despite there being only twelve rows, Uncle Bobby made them sit in the back, the EXIT sign's red glow almost near enough to touch. Janie used to think it was the color that made him think fire, but now she understood the fire fear was yet another suspicion he'd contracted from "one of these old movies." As soon as the lights lowered and the previews began, Janie eased the Southern Comfort into the Sprite, nudged Uncle Bobby with her elbow, passed him the drink, and toasted the waxed cup with her knuckles. Uncle Bobby hailed their naughtiness with a constricted cackle.

Almost immediately Janie regretted that they'd come, her unable to focus on the movie, and into the vacuum that inattention created surged the Nathan situation like a vomit. She glanced at her uncle to see how closely he was watching. She doubted *Reds* would have any scenes he found scary so at least she wouldn't have to suffer the laugh-shrieking when everyone else was silent. Again, the Nathan situation lifted into her throat. Janie swallowed on it hard. Then she remembered the time back in July when Uncle Bobby had stopped laughing halfway through a movie. She recalled it now even though she hadn't given it a thought after they walked out of the Alexander Henry that afternoon. That was *Mask*, the Eric Stoltz and Cher picture about the kid with the horrible degenerative disease they said made him look like a lion but that actually made him look like a lion with a horrible degenerative disease, and Janie hadn't even noticed when Uncle Bobby's laughing stopped. She realized it only when she heard instead a peculiar snuffling sound in the dark beside her, and when she did, she pretended not to hear it, picking up the Sprite to pull a few last sips of ice melt and alcohol. The cup was already drained. The second the lights came up, Uncle Bobby began convulsing with laughter again.

"I have to use the restroom," Uncle Bobby whispered now. He heaved himself up, and the whole row of seats shuddered at the loss of his weight.

The morning after the dinner at Nathan's, she and Uncle Bobby sat across from each other at the dining room table. She rotated in her fingers a piece of toast, Uncle Bobby behind his lineup of mixing bowl, Cheerios box, and gallon jug of milk. He would eat two mixing bowls of cereal because, he had explained to her several years ago, the holes in the Cheerios cut the serving in half. Uncle Bobby acted as if the night before hadn't happened, which gave away how profoundly it had, because if it had been a night during which nothing out of the ordinary had occurred, Uncle Bobby would be asking, "What happened after I left, Janie? What'd you all do?"

And as she sat there watching Uncle Bobby shuttle the Cheerios into his mouth with a gusto verging on ecstasy, she understood that forgiving her had not occurred to him because he had not registered any offense. And self-hatred and shame rushed through her in black-red waves so intense she felt vertigo.

She dropped her toast. Right then she decided, pulling her mind, heart, and groin into a single-steeled purpose. She was finished with Nathan. She was going to, as Uncle Bobby would put it, tell him off.

But how to do it? The phone was out of the question. Because the phone was nothing but voice; even in ideal circumstances with easy people, the phone made her anxious. After loading the dishwasher with the breakfast dishes, she threw herself on her bed where she scrawled a three-page-long letter to Nathan, but after she reread it, she shredded it and flushed it down the toilet, praying it did not clog her grandparents' pipes. No. She would have to tell him face-to-face. And because she knew he would vanish again, she'd have to march herself to his front door, firm up her voice, and ask his mother if he was in. Janie stood at her window and stared at that door across the street. The only arched door in the neighborhood, with dark woodwork and three small stained-glass panes. In her head, Janie began what became a three-day-long rehearsal of her telling-off-Nathan speech.

But Nathan didn't vanish. In the seventy-two hours following that dinner, Nathan was more visible than he'd been since before they started going out, Janie saw him from her upstairs post several times a day. Washing his motorcycle in his driveway. Spending half an hour on the curb with his head stuck inside the car window of a belt-thin boy. Striding back and forth between Scout and house, Scout and house, even cutting the grass when Nathan's father had taken care of that all summer long. And each time she spied him alone, Janie inhaled, braced, silently repeated her first rehearsed sentence, and made to approach. And each time, she exhaled, limpened, and told herself there'd be a better time. Then, just yesterday, she had run head-on into him. Her walking to her Chevette in her popcorn girl clothes for her last shift of the summer, and suddenly there was Nathan, ambling up the street on foot of all things, an absolute anomaly. There was no way to avoid him unless she turned and fled inside, which she considered, but she kept moving, her insides as roily dark as the Ohio, her dragging her practiced speech into her mouth. Then they were across from each other, and Nathan raised his eyes and looked at her as you would an acquaintance you met on the street, and with a chilly smile, part smirk, part faux polite, he remarked, with sarcasm gauged just subtle enough he could deny it later if anyone asked: "Miss Janie Lambert." And sauntered right on by.

She had slammed herself into the Chevette and gunned it down the street. By the time she reached the end of Kentworth Drive, rage tears were runneling down her cheeks. Rage at Nathan, yes, but rage at herself a hundredfold that, and as she drove, she actually lifted and bunched her fist, and if she hadn't had to downshift to avoid crashing into a truck, she would have punched herself in her chest. Her cowardice, her stupidity, her muteness, that she'd allowed him to dump her before she could say a word towards dumping him, even though she was certain she was the one who had decided to dump him first.

Now Uncle Bobby plopped back down beside her, and she shot a look along the row to see if the seat reverberations reached the couple on the other end. Uncle Bobby leaned into her ear again, his hygienic odor of Crest and Old Spice, and he whispered loudly, "Remember when Ben forgot his mittens in *Black Beauty*? If that'd been in this puny place, I'd have found 'em in three seconds."

The truth was, Janie did remember it. In scraps and from the narrow tilted perspective of someone looking up out of a box, which was how she remembered many of her pre-school experiences in Remington. She remembered at eye-level a glamourous brass door handle twice the length of her head that Uncle Bobby pushed with one hand while the other arm bundled Ben and her against him like packages. She remembered how he blocked them with his body the moment they reached the sidewalk in case they should take a notion to bolt into the street. She remembered the windless cold leaching into them as they stood just beyond the gold and scarlet splendor of the Alexander Henry marquee, its contrast with the monochrome vacancy of Remington's late afternoon winter light. Uncle Bobby was very tall and very wide, like grown-ups were, but Janie felt also, as charged as a mild shock, Uncle Bobby's anxiety. All the potential mistakes and mishaps lying in wait for Uncle Bobby entrusted with taking his little niece and nephew to the show. In the burr of that anxiety, Janie felt only half-safe herself, her understanding that Uncle Bobby was only a makeshift adult, but she knew also that he was the closest thing they had at the moment, and she had no option but to surrender to trusting him. And in that moment she trusted him utterly.

He had each of them by the hand then, Uncle Bobby craning his neck up and down Fourth Avenue. "Look for your granddaddy's car," he told them. It was then Ben mumbled, "I think I left my mittens in there."

Janie could remember Uncle Bobby's face: three seconds of naked shock, disintegrating into blinking confusion, eventually gelling to horror. Now, eighteen years old herself, Janie could translate: the horror of being the most responsible person present. Of having no choice but to take charge in a crisis.

And he had taken charge. All by himself he'd approached an usher—a trauma in itself since Uncle Bobby secretly feared all authority figures, which in Uncle Bobby's mind an usher was—and the four of them reentered the theater. While she and Ben stood in the aisle, Uncle Bobby and the usher searched under the back-row seats with flashlights. And the mittens were found.

They walked out of *Reds* two hours into it when Uncle Bobby's snoring got louder than the soundtrack. They found themselves swept into the exiting *Jedi* crowd and Janie glad of it, knowing Tommie Sue would ignore her when she passed and that would be less humiliating if she were veiled by a group. She and Uncle Bobby currented along with the others out the brass-handled doors, Janie groping in her purse for her keys, rooting among contraband and tampons, and she halted in the stream under the marquee lights, Uncle Bobby dutifully stopping with her. She finally shot a hand to her jeans pocket outside, and of course, there the keys rode, and at that moment, she heard Uncle Bobby shadow-say something, which struck her as strange because he'd said nothing first to make the echo. She looked at him. His expression was a déjà vu of the lost-mitten afternoon.

Janie followed his stare. Moving away from them, not twenty feet distant, clearly part of the *Jedi* crowd, waddled a globe-shaped woman. It was the large-print smock that gave Tessa away. She walked hand in hand with a squatty man in a purple tank top, his shoulders and neck a snarl of dark red hair the length and texture of granddaddy long-legs. Janie gawked, mesmerized by the repulsiveness of that thicket, vivid under the streetlights, and suddenly in the folds of the neck, she thought she glimpsed, although later she could not be sure, the glint of a gold chain.

The couple vanished into the alley shortcut to a parking lot.

For several seconds, she and Uncle Bobby stood silent. They were alone now, the crowd dispersed to cars and bars. And then her uncle threw back his head and exploded into laughter. His most crazed and out-of-control variety, the kind forbidden by her grandmother, the kind that made everyone within earshot turn with a "what on earth?" stare, the kind that had made Janie run away and duck behind the nearest object in mortification when she was a kid.

"WUUHHHHHH wuh wuh wuh, WUUHHHHH wuh wuh wuh." Uncle Bobby bent in half at his waist, his fist beating his thigh, his face the color of wine. "WUUHHHHH wuh wuh wuh, WUUHHHH wuh wuh wuh." Until finally, after depleting himself, he gasped for breath, caught it after a few strangled tries, and said, "I think that's so funny, Janie. I think that's just so funny."

ONE ESPECIALLY SLOW weekday afternoon in early August when Gus was gone for a funeral, Ronnie had volunteered to take them behind the screen and below the floors. Tommie Sue, in her single act of magnanimity that summer, said of course she could cover concessions and egged them on. Janie and two of the sorority girls trailed Ronnie and his flashlight down the side aisle of the big central *Jedi* theater, Hillary and Nicole deliberately bumping into each other with muffled chortling. Janie brought up the rear, breathless with disbelief that this was happening and already buzzing with the anticipation of telling Uncle Bobby when she got home.

Ronnie led them up a short set of steps at the corner of the stage and then behind the screen. Janie nearly tripped in astonishment.

And we were standing there with the Star Wars people right alongside us—

—What, Janie? What? I don't get what you mean.

You could see them on the screen, just we were behind it, Luke and Leia and the Ewoks, *they were the same size as us*, the characters' feet and Janie's feet on the same level so it was like walking among them, and Janie stopped, faced them, and gaped, but Ronnie was hissing, "Hurry! C'mon!" motioning them to the rear of the stage to what turned out to be a longer flight of stairs.

These dropped into a dark warren that under Ronnie's flashlight revealed itself as an elaborate skeleton-work of broken rooms. *It was pitch-black down there, a bunch of rooms with no walls*, naked beams, snapped lathes, heaped bricks—*Oh, Janie, I didn't know that*—and they were weaving around piles of dismembered tables and chairs and clambering over flattened doors and plaster piles, everything saturated in an odor both moldy and dry—*Were you scared, Janie? Were you scared?*—and Hillary and Nicole clung to each other for drama and screamed when one stepped on a board that kicked up a couple bricks at its other end, but to her bewilderment, Janie was not scared at all. Because it was too ruined to host ghosts? Because it was too real to? Then Nicole was asking, "Is this the basement that runs under the whole city block?" and Ronnie was saying, "No, there's a whole 'nother level yet below this one. I'm gonna take you all upstairs first."

And then we climbed two more flights of stairs—were you scared, Janie?—No, not yet. But by then, I tell you, I was completely turned around, I had no idea if we were on a side of the building, or in back, or even in front—I wouldn't have been scared, Janie. I would have laughed at it! Halfway up the second flight they were coming back into natural light, and finally they reached a shortish corridor. "The dressing rooms," Ronnie explained. "There's three levels of them. The best ones are on the top." So even higher they climbed, these stairs narrower and steep as loft ladders, the sorority girls quieter now, the light having sobered them. *And then we started peeking in the rooms.*

What were they like?

Dressing tables under a strange white dust as plush as felt and chairs painted in festive colors, aquas and limes and yellows. Decaying clothes looking like dead animal pelts tossed over their backs, and *their makeup in some rooms was still sitting open*, as though all the actors had leapt up to flee a disaster. *They weren't like dressing rooms on TV and in movies* because while every dressing room Janie had seen there had been windowless, insular, lit only by artificial light, these dressing rooms were open, spacious, every fourth wall a window that started below her waist and rose nearly to a ceiling twice as tall as she. *It was weird. It was really weird—Yeah, it sounds really weird, it sounds spooky, how come you weren't scared, Janie?*—and Janie knew these rooms were smack dab in the middle of downtown Remington, Janie knew she should be seeing out each window just another brick wall. But every last one, the spattered ones, the fractured ones, the ones missing panes, were flooded with the opaque glary white the sky took on all over West Virginia in the summer, but especially in Remington.

The other popcorn girls were giggling again, teasing each other, while Ronnie smiled shyly, uncomfortable in his authority. "Okay," he said. "The best for last. I'm gonna take you on down into the bottom basement now."

Janie turned to follow, then stopped. For some reason, she wanted that last dressing room for herself for a minute. Without even Uncle Bobby accompanying her in her head. She heard the other three voices receding and again she marveled at her lack of fear. If she'd been asked what she felt, she would have said just a little sad. On the dressing table's surface, a single open jar of face cream, yellowed and parched to cracks. In the ornate gold scroll framing the mirror, a wasp nest. And then Janie noticed the mirror itself.

In the other rooms, the mirrors had been fissured on walls or lay shattered on the floors. Two mirrors had been still in one piece, but reflectionless, just stippled black glass. This mirror looked back. It framed Janie's red-smocked torso. Cut her off at her neck.

Abruptly, Janie stooped. She seized either end of the dressing table with a hand. She scanned the mirror's whole surface. And finally the fear flared, but Janie didn't turn away. The mirror held just her. And to see one's face in such glass, in such light.

MOUSESKULL

I PUT MY HAND on it while shinnying down a wall in the barn, fleeing my sister Mavis in a game of Witch, and when I grab a side-running beam to slow my fall, my fingers graze it on a little ledge there.

I nest the skull in my hand. Drop the rest of the way down. Throw up my face to make sure no brothers or sisters saw, but they're still shrieking in the haymow, and only Mickey, the biggest and wisest dog, watches me. I tuck my mouseskull in my jacket pocket, stoop-run to a manger, and wiggle in.

There in the moldy dusk I study it with my fingers, with my nose. The flesh has rotted down to dry, bald bone, but the mouse is new-dead enough it exhales a corpsey odor still, an odor home to me, from all the creatures, tiny as mice, big as coons, who crawl into our house walls to die. I blow across it to unstink it some. Hear the kids rattling down the haymow stairs, hide the skull deep in my jacket. I jump out of the manger empty-handed and still make them scream.

An hour later, I'm in my bedroom unscrewing the lid of the only perfume I own, a bronze liquid labeled "1929" as nostril-shocking as a chemical sap. I cradle my mouseskull in my left palm while I daub it with a "1929"-soaked cotton ball, whispering apologies as I do, then blow on it again, this time to make it dry. I mount it on a pillow at the head of my bed.

It is the unbleached yellow of fresh-killed antlers or grown-up teeth. As thin-boned as locust shell it looks, but when my brother Sam tackled me at the end of Witch, it did not crack—my skull flawless right down to its exquisite tiny fangs. I press with my thumb the jagged place that used to wear the softness of nose. Peer into the bonery at the back where it dropped from its spine, a rough honeycomb that won't let my finger in. And suddenly I know exactly what to do.

I swing off my bed and rummage through a dresser drawer. I find a long white shoestring with just a bit of grime. I snap the shoestring like a little whip and moisten the frayed end with my mouth, then necklace my mouseskull through where its eyes used to be.

ON MONDAY, I decide to wear my necklace to school, and because there are five younger children to get ready, my mother either doesn't see it or doesn't care. I am deliciously hopeful that the other fourth-graders will notice its remarkableness. But desensitized to the unusual like my classmates are—after four years of exposure to the intricate spiralings of ringwormed hair, and Kevin with his shoebox-shaped run-over-as-a-toddler head, and tiny towhead Henry who speaks with the ravaged baritone of a drain-cleaner-swallowing old man, and the CPs and the Downs and the shiny house fire survivors—only two people comment on my necklace.

One is Ronnie Phillips, whose desk the teacher has recently pushed against mine so I can help him with his work, she says. Ronnie has fanged teeth and the manner of a forty-year-old man who after seeing it all has now put away his hard-living, wild-running days and mellowed to a gentle jadedness. Ronnie glances at my necklace and says, "Mouse that big, probably a rat."

The other is Michelle Livingstone. Who is not from here, who moved to West Virginia from Connecticut two years ago. She sees my necklace straightaway. "What's *that*? Who'd put it on a shoestring and wear it to school! You smell *gross*."

OUR HOUSE HAS twenty-one rooms, some heated, some not, a few less indoors than out. There are rooms that leak rain and rooms that hold, rooms with windows that peer into other rooms, rooms up two stairs, rooms down three. Rooms from the nineteen hundreds, rooms from the eighteen hundreds, two rooms from the seventeens. A few rooms that comfort, many that scare.

A basement with one room of coal, a pyramid of clinkers, and a squat cement furnace growing out of the ground. An attic I see only by standing in the yard and squinting up at high dormered windows for a glimpse of the blacksnakes Mrs. Dock says raise their families in there. Over top the kitchen a room called "the little study room," where no one studies. A rust-stained toilet. A rust-stained sink. A freckled aluminum pipe passing through from the old oil stove below.

The ghosts prefer the second floor. For a long time, they were only my grandfather. Then Ham died, too.

HAM, "WHO WORKED for your granddaddy," as my parents say, lived six miles upriver on our family farm in an unpainted cinderblock house a-foam in a blizzard of albino cats. Cats uncountable, unownable, unpettable, although when we were four, five years old, Sam and I tried. Crept close the house, froze-so-as-not-to-be-seen, crept close the house, froze-so-as-not-to-be-seen. Until we tripped some trigger line and the cat storm blew up, cats mashed themselves under the foundation, bolted silent-screaming into weed fields, warped through open window cracks, disintegrated under eaves and into culverts. Their ear insides, their toes, their tongues, all of that colored like ham, and my older cousins told me Ham ate them, but I knew better than that. Those cats would never have submitted to being meals.

The cat blizzard was a natural chapter in the snowy history of Ham, who, about the time I was born, passed out in a snowdrift while hitch-hiking home from the VFW and froze off the three smallest toes on his right foot. Ham never worked again and ever after had to lean on a three-toed cane and wear special shoes that looked hewn from a block of black rock. His real name was Raymond—we knew this from the collect calls from the county jail—and "Why do they call him Ham?" any new brother or sister would ask when old enough to wonder, and my father would weary-say, "Because he likes ham." But I knew better than that, too. Ham smaller in his hips than he was in his belly and chest, him tapered like a ham standing on end. A whole country ham in its grayish sack, propped upright on the tri-pronged aluminum cane.

After my granddaddy's estate was settled, the farm fell under the charge of my aunt's husband, who had an MBA. When I was eight, my granddaddy dead three years and Ham unable to work for way longer than that, this uncle had the cinderblock house bulldozed to the ground.

Many a night I lay in bed and visioned it, the cat bomb detonating the instant the dozer blade struck. The cat cloud suspended for long seconds in air before collapsing to flurry the valley, every one landing on its feet. The original cats fructified and multiplied, until within a year the whole countryside was aghost with Ham cats, them always just behind what you could see. In the meantime, Ham moved in with "some woman on the other side of town" and the jail calls kept coming. "Why is Ham put in jail?" some younger brother or sister would ask, and our father would explain again, "Drunk in public. They only keep him a few days."

Now and again I would be in the backseat of the station wagon when we picked Ham up and gave him a ride to the house of the woman on the other side of town. The whole way there, Ham would talk in his round, rivery voice—"Ham should have been a lawyer, the way that man can talk," my mother would say—and I kept an eye on the air because Ham, unlike everybody else I knew, sometimes talked about my granddaddy.

"Me and your dad," he'd sometimes say to my father, or, "Your dad used to," and, always, right before he did, there would be a change in the air. At first a warple . . . then it snapped cold-bright. "What a shame about your dad," he said just one time, and just one other time, "Why do you think he dropped that nail down that pipe?" "Your dad was one of the kindest men I ever knew"—Ham said that every other time—and "Uh-huh," my dad would say, his face shut tight as a jammed dresser drawer, then start talking about something else. And the air dulled back.

A year after the cats went refugee, it happened. We walked behind our barn, six miles north of the Ham-flattened house, and there in the broom sedge crouched a nightmare white tom. Fur spiked like he was outlet-plugged, asylum escapee eyes, and, most ghastly of all, a hairless pink tail. He invisibled himself the moment after we saw.

"We can call him Snowball," my little sister said. I stared at Mavis's naïveté. I both coveted it and was horrified at where it might end her up.

JESUS'S VOICE IS not in red in my new Living Word Children's Bible, on its cover a berobed Christ shepherding children in 1950s dungarees and dotted-Swiss dresses. My new Living Word Children's Bible was given me three weeks before I found my mouseskull by my normal grandparents, who live in another part of the state. The foreword in the Living

Word Children's Bible recommends that children read first the Gospel of John, so I am reading first the Gospel of John. Every night before sleep, and it is beginning to dawn on me that if I hadn't ever started this, I wouldn't have set myself up to disappoint God by stopping, so I cannot stop. I'm scripture-trapped. When I'm finished with my daily dose—the Old Testament has much better stories, I know, but I dare not say this even in my head—I fold in the bookmark ribbon, close the pages, and turn to my nightstand. I place my Living Word Children's Bible gingerly on top of a stack of books already there.

At the bottom of this stack lies squashed the true book about paranormal activity I ordered from *My Weekly Reader* in a fit of self-sabotaging curiosity, on *its* cover a photograph of an actual ghost: a smoke woman descending curved stairs. I have a second Bible, the oldest book I own, a white King James the size and shape of a Band-Aid box, presented to me the week I was born, with gilded pages and my name misspelled in that same gilt on the front. In this Bible, Jesus does speak in red. The King James Bible, I've placed strategically in the little bit of space between the bottom of the book stack and the edge of the nightstand, making sure the King James does not touch the true ghost book, but is near enough to throw against it an invisible protective steam.

That done, I lift my necklace over my head. I hold the skull between finger and thumb to gaze in the sockets of its eyes, stroke its nose, rub its forehead the way my horse books say horses like to be rubbed. I press it against my cheek and slip it under my own nose, and just when it seems the corpsey reek might have all the way disappeared, it flares back through the perfume like roadkill in a thaw. I rest my skull in the dead center of my new Living Word Children's Bible, right on Jesus's chest. Nothing else can touch the top of that Bible, nothing is allowed to obscure so much as a tuft of Galilean grass except the mouseskull.

I reach over my head and pull the bolt tied to the string that runs through eyes on the ceiling to the bulb in the middle of the room. The second the light snaps dark, I plunge under the covers and jerk them over my head. Recently it's occurred to me that such nightly oxygen deprivation might cause brain damage, but I figure if a turtle can survive it, I can too. I lie on my back as still as glass, willing my muscles, my bones, to melt towards the mattress. If not a lump of me shows under the bedspread, not the slightest rise of me in the sheets, no ghosts will bother me because they won't know I'm here. "Please, Lord," I pray in a whisper. "Make me flat."

WE GET THE Ouija board a few weeks before Christmas from Polly Sharon, the organist at our church. Every other week, we visit her so our father can buy eggs and we can gape at the Civil War bullet holes in the kitchen door and the Methuselahan dog with the cannonball-sized knot in his side, possibly a Civil War artifact himself. Polly Sharon loves us and gives us a present this year even though our father says, No, no, you don't have to do that, they don't need anything. When we unwrap the box at home, it has fewer parts than any board game we've played before, and I don't see how the pronunciation of it, which our mother can say, matches up with its letters. Distracted by the countdown to Christmas Day, only Sam gives the Ouija board any more attention until Mrs. Dock notices it.

Mrs. Dock, "who worked for your grandmother," now helps our mother once a week with the cleaning and will babysit us after dark. Before dark, it's me. Mrs. Dock lives down the railroad tracks, and her husband, Delvin, like Ham, drinks too much. Our mother doesn't drink at all. Our father drinks once or twice a year a wine called Christian Brothers, the word *Christian* evidently canceling out the sin. To reach my earliest memory of Mrs. Dock I must walk way back in my head, and there I see her laboring up the stairs with a tray bearing a cereal bowl, a small pitcher of milk, and a box of Special K. I asked my mother why, meaning why didn't Granddaddy eat downstairs with everybody else. My mother, misunderstanding, answered, "Your granddaddy thinks Special K will help him get better."

Mrs. Dock is a five-by-three-foot library of information our parents either haven't learned or don't believe: the "black man" who lives under our bridge and will get us if we're bad, the rats that gnaw through the soft spots in babies' heads, the cats who want to suck out their breaths. "Sugar tit" is what she calls a pacifier although she never, ever otherwise cusses, but the word "tit" is one we're forbidden to say, and we find "sugar tit" scandalous and hysterical. Mrs. Dock acquaints us with hoop snakes that roll up and chase you through fields, and black racer snakes that chase you flat, and milk snakes that slither into barn stalls to suck the cows' . . . yes, titties. She tells all this without a trace of melodrama, tells it like she tells you you'll catch a cold if you wade the creek in January. She almost never laughs, has no entertainer in her and no time to waste. The only game she will play is "school," and only if she can be a student named "Susie." It was Mrs. Dock alone in the house working for my grandmother when my granddaddy dropped the nail down the pipe.

When Mrs. Dock sees the Ouija board, she says, matter-of-fact, "That's a tool of the Devil, Lainey." Mrs. Dock just tells you how it is, you can take or you can leave it. "Do your mom and daddy know you have that?" Then she wobbles off to the kitchen. The second she shuts the door, I shove the Ouija board under all the other games in the closet.

Later, I tell my mother what Mrs. Dock said.

"Do you really think Polly Sharon would give you something from the Devil?"

I finger the shoestring around my neck, shake my head. But the question sounds like what my mother says when I call her in the middle of the night. "It was just a bad dream," she says. "Go back to sleep." And two or three times she's added, "Even if your granddaddy was a ghost, do you really think he'd do anything to hurt you?"

OUR HOUSE IS strewn round with outlier buildings, as though in decades past it shuffled around and shed parts of itself. The pump house, the icehouse, the garage, the barn, woodshed, chicken house, goat shed. There is also the old mill, not a splinter of it still standing, but its innards retired in unexpected places—grinding stones rupturing the yard to stun mower blades, the giant wooden gear shaft in the barn I was shinnying down when I put my hand on the skull. Each building at a different stage of fall-down, and every one bulging with dead people's or dead animals' stuff.

In these outpost buildings we are seldom grown-up-watched. The animal places, now animal-less, are musty and mote-choked with what used to go into creatures and more of what used to come out—hillocks of stale unbaled hay, moldy sacks of oats and corn, and everywhere the desiccated turds you can throw at people, churn with a broom handle into a witch's brew, build into wigwams and lean-tos for Indian and pioneer elves. In the buildings where people's things are cached, we mole through dry-rotted cardboard boxes and peculiar-odored trunks and plain old uncrated piles, Mickey and Bingo always busy alongside us, raptured by two centuries of scent.

Oddly, none of these places feels haunted, as though all the castaway junk and belongings left behind have absorbed any ghosts or sated them. We unbury ice skates and child-sized boxing gloves, saddles we throw over nail kegs and ride, box traps and arrowheads and a snake in a jar of formaldehyde. We flip through ledger books and photo albums, the corner tabs unsticking and the pictures shuffling down—most of them boring, old-timey people we don't know, but in a few I recognize our father and our aunts and uncles. Once, I uncovered one of my granddaddy.

I leaned back with my behind on my heels and stared at it there. He was outside. My granddaddy was outside the house—I recognized the barn wall behind him, he stood in the part of the garden that still came up rhubarb, and there was even an unfamiliar beaglish dog pushing his nose into Granddaddy's hand. I had seen my granddaddy outside one time, and that was in his green recliner, an inside chair my uncle pulled out onto the front porch. In the picture his hair was already white, but he stood outside, a hundred yards from the house, not in pajamas, but wearing regular clothes.

I looked behind me at the kids fighting over the nail-keg horse. I felt a ping of responsibility to show them the picture—or at least to show Sam, who remembered him. But a peculiar protectiveness—of them? of him?—smothered the ping. I found a spot in the album with a photo slot still sound, and I pressed the outside Granddaddy carefully into its corners. I closed the covers and stashed it away.

"COLLECT CALL FROM Raymond Clinster. Do you accept the charges?"

"Something happened between him and the woman on the other side of town," our father tells our mother when he returns to the supper table, paper napkin flapping from his belt. "He's got nowhere to go."

While my granddaddy and grandmother had Ham and Mrs. Dock to work for them, our father has us. He's decided the icehouse will be the most livable outbuilding and the easiest to clean up. Bundled up against the New Year's cold, we restack bed frames and canning jar boxes and cobweb-filmed kitchen chairs and who-knows-what's-in-them garbage bags high against the icehouse walls to make a clearing in the middle. We sweep, we mop, we wipe. We duct tape the slits in the walls where the sawdust insulation leaks out. We haul in a space heater, a mattress on a cot.

At first, our father carries Ham's supper out to him, but then has to go to Charleston for a meeting, so my mother hands the foil-covered plates to me or to Sam and tells us come right back. By the time my father gets home, he and my mother have been spoiled by our help, and Sam and I end up feeding Ham most of the time.

I am not afraid of outside places, not even in the dark, at least I wasn't before Ham moved in. And now I am afraid not because of Ham, who, alive, scares me not at all, but because I can't help but believe that if Ham is here, that white naked-tailed cat cannot be far away. I learn to run fast without spilling the plate, even with a dinner-smell-bewitched dog or two thrashing through my legs. I race between kitchen window light and icehouse window light with my face held down so I won't risk glancing at a lunatic cat at the edge of the yard. I skid short right outside Ham's door, settle myself, rap on it twice, and push dogs back with one foot. Ham hollers, "C'mon in," and I step into the whir of the space heater fan.

Ham is lying always on his side on the cot, and he will eat that way, too, elbow-propped, the space heater aimed at his feet. Always—I do not think it and cannot help it—my eyes are sucked first to those feet, and always the no-toes are hidden in a sock. I lean forward to hand him the plate, my mouseskull necklace swinging out a little—I never bother to put on a coat—and he says, "Tell your mother thanks." Then I back off a few steps, Ham peeling away the foil, and even though I'm supposed to "come right back," I can't help the longer look my eyes must take next.

Down that Ham undershirt, the gray of a blood-swoled tick. Across the sack of his belly. Along the length of the work-pantsed legs that no longer work. Then I take in the smell of Ham, in that close space-heatered clearing, smell familiar to me and not unpleasant to me, the contained unwashedness of grown-up poor people with no water inside. A dry vinegar. Something to do with rising bread if rising bread could smell old and stale. My stare is clothespinned to the gray socks, but no matter how big I bug my eyeballs, how hard I push, I never discern the slightest sign of where those toes are not. Ronnie Phillips told me his brother ordered the X-ray glasses from the back of a Flintstones comic. When they didn't work, he busted open a lens and found something that looked like a little feather inside.

Often, me standing there with my eyes dangling out, Ham'll start talking in that tuneful river-flow voice, the beat just right between sentences and chews. When Ham talks to me, it's like I'm not a kid. Not like he's a sometimes drunk who used to work for my granddaddy. We're the same. Not like I'm peculiar and so shy I've been mistaken for deaf. Not like he's a Mrs. Dock kind of poor person whose eyes, even when their outsides stand still, dart around behind themselves. Never expecting or receiving a word in return, Ham talks, all of him right there in his face—the way Ronnie Phillips is, I realize, just like Ronnie Phillips, no gap between who's inside and who's out.

"I cut ice for this icehouse when I was a boy. Cut it up on Stump's Eddy and dragged it out with horses. Them was different winters then. River never freezes that thick that long anymore."

Or, "Bought me some mousetraps in town today. You all had a few cats around, keep down the mice."

Or, "I do miss seeing your grandma. I reckon it's nice and warm for her, though, down in Florida."

And one evening I fasten on the foot longer than usual because, lo and behold, it's got a new sock, a white one, no less, which might be easier to see through. I'm beaming into that sock, and I half-hear

Ham say something about running into Mrs. Dock today, but I'm not really listening when, suddenly, the air changes. Just like how when Ham talks to my father in the car, I recognize it right away, suddenly everything—Ham, cot, me, sock, space heater—fades to background for the new air, cold like on your teeth, bright that hurts your eyes.

"Now I know Mrs. Dock don't like to talk about it. But I asked her, early on, just oncet. And she said she knew as soon as she heard that nail what was going on, she didn't have to hear the other. But then she did hear the other. And after that said she went out to that little back stoop and just set there, trying to think what to do."

Ham pauses there, forks up another fish stick bite, and sees my face. He lays the fork down.

"Now your granddaddy," he says, "was one of the kindest men I ever knew." He holds my eyes to his. "Don't you let nobody ever tell you anything different than that."

THE IRON WATER in our house puts rust in our sinks, in our toilet bowls. Rust in the shower, rust in our clothes. We drink rusty water, chomp rusty ice cubes, eat potatoes, macaroni, and rice boiled in a rusty brew. Is it the iron water, I wonder, puts the copper hue in our blonde hair? Our dinner plates dull a mild orange, same color as our underwear. Our father says it is good for us, that it builds up our blood. During a 4-H meeting at our house, Becky Weelis goes to the bathroom, looks in the commode, and screams.

While our father's at his meetings in Charleston, Sam and I must keep the coal furnace fed. In our house, ghosts rise, not fall, so the basement is less a scary place than a curious one, the place where the house starts to end and the outside to begin, a laboratory for experiments in science class bread mold. Our mother doesn't like us stoking the hopper alone, so Sam and I descend together to the boardwalk over the coal-watery floor, usually in our pajamas because it's a right-before-bed and right-after-you-wake-up kind of job. We take turns stepping into our father's enormous rubber overshoes, then wading puddles to the coal bin, choking up on our shovel handle, and scooping a load. This is where we are, a month after Christmas, when Sam tells me again what he's going to do.

"No," I command. "You can't. You can't."

Sam heaves a shovelful over the hopper rim, waits until the skattle sounds end. "Yeah." Nonchalant. Resigned. Melodramatic. Sam can emanate all three at the same time. "I'm going to." He hands the shovel to me.

It was ordering I tried last time, so this time I switch to beg. "Please, Sam. Please. Please don't."

"I've already made up my mind." He walks out of the overshoes, pivots regally, and his Pufnstuf pajamas retire up the wooden stairs.

That afternoon I don't *have* to go in there. No one's sent me after anything. Usually I dare not enter even the room we must pass through to get to the little study room, but today, I cup my mouseskull in my hand, turn the knob, and step down in.

The little study room is unheated but brilliant. Winter sun. Dazzling motes. A sink and a toilet along one wall from the days, I've been told, when a "servant" stayed here. The floor tilts a little from every corner, all of it running down to a slight center sag. I stand against the wall on an uphill edge, and I look around. At the clutter of the rolltop desk that gives the little study its name. The joint of pipe running up from the old oil stove in the kitchen below. The spider dust, the insect husks, the fly crusts over every place the room lies flat.

Then I brace for the terror, I wait. Until I realize that I am less scared than separated. My eyes not touching my mind, my heart not touching my guts, not touching my legs and arms, and my iron-thickened blood standing still. Nothing touching nothing, so there is no channel for the scared to move through. I already know, from errands past, that there is no box of bullets. No box of nails.

There is rust in the toilet, rust in the sink, but no rust in the sag of that varnishless floor.

BINGO HAS PUPS. Mickey does, too—the only time in my life or theirs such a coincidence occurs, and I know it's because of Ham in the ice-house. Blizzard of cats. Downpour of dogs. Early February wet false thaw, and Bingo has hers in the garage like she always does, under a wobbly old table, and like always, she has three girls and one boy. Mickey, with her significantly higher IQ, shifts her birthing places, and we have to sleuth a little before we find her under the front porch. I lie on the steps in a cold drizzle, angling a flashlight through the crack, and finally I count eight. Because we still have three pups—now dogs, actually—from earlier litters, this makes our total seventeen.

It takes a while to think up twelve new names, and "Taffy" is not one of my best. But Taffy's Sugar Daddy–colored hair is the softest of all, and it is Taffy Ham chooses. As soon as she is weaned, and without Ham saying a word to any of us, to my parents or to hers, there Taffy is one evening when I carry in Ham's plate. She's curled up against Ham's sideways belly on the cot.

We are forbidden to bring animals inside, but Ham is a grown-up and a guest. Taffy turns quickly snobblish and prematurely mature, like a little girl gone beauty contestant too young. Never does she leap off the cot and clamor at my legs like a normal dog would do, choosing instead to tuck in closer to Ham, haughty under his palm. By now it is April, still light when I carry out the plate, and the space heater less often turned on. With each warming day, my anticipation builds. Surely the sock must soon come off.

One unseasonably warm evening I burst in, but right after I see the same old sock, my attention is snatched by something else. The icehouse is tumbly with a sharp glassy smell, like the prisms in Polly Sharon's chandelier let loose to somersault through air. Smell of the old men on the Rexall steps. Smell of Delvin Dock when we give him rides to town. And the truth is, always in Ham's complicated aroma lies a liquor layer, but since he's come to live with us, that smell is smothered down under others, and I've already figured out it's part of the deal he's made with my father. Then I'm reaching his plate to him, and he's reaching back, when something happens. I let go the plate too soon, he grabs hold too late, and the food falls to the floor.

I hear myself gasp. There are no more leftovers in the house. But Ham just laughs, louder than usual, looser than usual, picks the plate—the meatloaf, the boiled potato—off the floor, and sets Taffy down in the green beans. He begins eating the meatloaf with his fingers while I, even though it's past time to leave, can't help staring at the undogly Taffy who hesitates before picking at a bean.

"Lord, I reckon that was a mess. Now that would have been a mess to clean up."

I whip my eyes back to Ham. I can hear the mush of meatloaf in his mouth, see his own eyes on his feeding fingers. He shakes his head.

"Before he got to where he didn't hardly leave his bed, he'd pace the upstairs floors at night. Sleep in a different room every night, carrying that pistol with him." Ham pushes more potato in. "Scared people were after him, you know. He told me that."

I feel myself nod like I already know this, because if I can trick myself into believing that, the now-knowing might not overtake me. It might stay stuck at my ears. But the truth is, although I've never heard this, didn't I know it anyway?

"He was," Ham says, and then he swallows and even wipes his mouth on his sleeve, and I can tell he's talking to himself and not to me, "one of the kindest men you'd ever know."

THE OUIJA BOARD tells Sam 1976. Three years from now, he'll be twelve, I'll be thirteen.

I'm in my room where I've been sent for thumping Mavis in the head with a rolled-up *Good Housekeeping* magazine. The only way into my room is through my youngest brothers' bedroom, which has not only a window that looks outside but also one that opens onto the back hall, a window left over from a house addition fifty years ago, when they didn't bother to seal up the old exterior wall. No one is allowed to come in or talk to me when I've been sent to my room. When I hear Sam whisper-calling my name, I crack my door and lean around, making sure my feet never technically leave my floor. Sam's opened that interior window just enough to squeeze his face through.

"1976," he says.

A drain falls open between my throat and my guts. It foams a cold green fizz.

"You're sure?" I hiss.

He nods. "I asked it twice."

The truth is, before we got the Ouija board I didn't give much thought to Sam living or dying. Now that I have him for only three more years, his dorky glasses, his lopsided cloud of dark hair, his genius for picking at people for hours without ever crossing the line where he'll be spanked or sent to his room . . . all of it takes on the precious temporariness of captured lightning bugs or the perfect birthday. I swear to myself I'll never tease him again, and I mean it. But even as I'm making the pledge, I overhear a frantic calculating in some closet of my head. How on earth, in heaven, and everyplace in between am I going to evade two ghosts in the house?

Sam, however, doesn't look frightened at all, there in his Snoopy sweatshirt and his gigantic smudged glasses. Sam's face is goldly lit with the purpose of tragedy, a radiant poignancy and, yes, self-pity, but he's entitled to that. He pushes his glasses back up his nose, steps away, and shuts the window, firm. I hear the latch. Behind its dusty chiffon curtains I imagine him recessing down the hall, stoic, resigned, and above all brave.

THE SHEET OVER my head blinds me good, but it does not help much with sound. Me flat, my Living Word Children's Bible two hand-lengths from my head, my mouseskull necklace standing sentry on its cover, but still I hear. I hear the usual, the inevitable, although that doesn't make it less terrifying. The stuff of scary movies and scary books: floorboards creaking, shutters banging, maple limbs scraping gutters. I also hear the peculiar-to-our-house sounds of leaks dripping into plastic buckets, space-age pings of the nineteenth-century radiators, Mavis's snoring. But the winter and spring of the mouseskull necklace, I hear sounds I never ever imagined, and this means I couldn't have made them up, irrefutable evidence of how real they must be.

One night I hear the record player in the dining room switch on. For only a few seconds, not long enough for me to identify the song but long enough that I know it's not a dream. Another night I hear a cascade of keys, bottom octave to top, across the out-of-tune piano in the living room under me. And another night I hear a ruckus in the chimney that I realize, after a baffled moment, has to be the sound of knives and forks dropped down.

Mrs. Dock does not believe in ghosts except the Holy One. She'll tell you. There are no such things. Mrs. Dock does not talk about my granddaddy: he is a missing volume in her library, I know this, and I know she won't answer questions even though I never ask. But I remember. Mrs. Dock's chapped hand on my shoulder, ushering me through the door and under water. Walls green, blinds green and filtering the summer light green, so that the chest of drawers, the bedside tables, the mirror, my granddaddy—all of them rippled under river water. Mrs. Dock gave me a small push. "Go on, Lainey. Say hi to your granddaddy."

I went on. The mattress pushed against the collar of my dress. My granddaddy lay in immaculate white pajamas with trim blue piping, his bedspread folded in a straight line across his chest, his fingernails round and pink and white. He smiled at me, said, "What beautiful eyes."

That was what he always said, then he always smiled, and then he would say nothing else. Under his river water. But the smile, I saw, was real, not an automatic smile or a nervous smile or a smile hiding something else. It was a real smile. Lying across a cave mouth of sad.

Flattened under my own sheets, I wait, I hold off. I do. I am ten years old, humiliated by my babyness, and I don't want to wake my mother. But eventually I hear myself at a distance from myself, moaning, "Maaa-maawwww." Wait. "Maaa-maawwww." Wait. Until she finally wafts into my room in an aura of Shower-to-Shower and foamy green gown, and she does not touch me, but says, sleep-husky and a little impatiently but not without kindness: "Shhhh. Go back to sleep. It was just a bad dream."

One of those nights, me pleading Jesus for invisibility, something occurs to me that goose pimples me first, then thickens my throat with despair. The clattering silverware, especially the piano keys, even the spontaneous record player: weren't those exactly the gestures an unhappy and restless mouse ghost would make?

FANGS ARE SOMETHING everybody has four of, but Ronnie Phillips's fangs are the longest I've ever seen on a human, and then he has more than that. Some of his front supposed-to-be-blunt teeth are pointed, too. Within a few weeks of the teacher pushing our desks together so I can help him with his work, Ronnie started helping me with life, like an older brother or a different kind of dad. "Don't stoop," he'd soft-chide. "My aunt's shoulders got stuck that way." And, "You've gotta speak up for yourself. Don't be so shy." And, "Why do you worry so much? Smile." Like Ham's, Ronnie's smartness sits unself-conscious and raw in his face—a confidence without pretense or arrogance. Like Ham, Ronnie has no fear and no memory of fear, has never even had to jump over scared. About the Ouija board I decide to try Ronnie out.

Without looking up from the eighteen-wheeler he is sketching, Ronnie says, "My brother burnt up his Ouija board with his records when he got saved. It flew up out of the fire and scorched his eyebrows off."

Everybody in town knows what happened to my grandfather. It was five years ago, but only Ham ever says. A few weeks after my Ouija board question, Ronnie is copying how I labeled parts of speech, his head cocked to the far right and that eye almost touching his worksheet, the way he does.

"Where were you when your granddaddy shot himself?"

His pencil doesn't stop moving. I let close the book I'm reading hidden in my desk. "We didn't live in that house then."

Ronnie keeps copying. I pull my mouseskull out away from my chest, tuck in my chin so I can study it better. Within the soup of classroom aromas, keenest near me Ronnie's skin smell of eraser leavings, the mouseskull stink is faint. I have to touch it under my nose and inhale sharp.

My hair prickles. I turn and catch Michelle Livingstone spying on me. She wrinkles her nose so her own fangs show, then shakes her head as she wheels her finger around her ear.

I'VE JUST GOTTEN my jeans zipped when Sam crashes through my open bedroom door, catches himself with a hand on each jamb, and sags in and over, panting even though the dash from his room to mine might be thirty steps. He lifts his face, ablaze with illicit thrill. "I think Ham's dead."

Then we are both stealth-racing past the bathroom where my father showers, past the bedroom where my mother dresses, and down the stairs. I gather from Sam as we go that he glanced out his window a few minutes ago and spotted a long gray bundle on the lawn. I'm levitating, stretched between the revolting terror of seeing a real dead person and the overpowering magnetism of seeing a real dead person, and once we're running barefoot through the dew-cold grass, the magnetism is boosted by my realization that the dead are usually barefoot, too—aren't they? By now Bingo is chasing alongside us, and she keeps right on going when Sam and I halt a few yards from where Ham lies. Sprawled on his side, fully dressed right down to his shoes, one arm cocked up at its elbow and shielding his face. Now I can smell the tumbling prisms, but before I can contemplate the corpse, Bingo pokes Ham's head with her nose. The arm swings out and swipes Bingo away just as we hear the back screen slam behind our father.

Not long after this, Sam and I are pressed into helping our father with his annual attempts to patch leaks in the roof. Today the three of us are doing the very top of the house, which means scaling a bobbly ladder two stories, being tied by ropes to the central chimney, then creeping around on a slant with a bucket of gray tarry goop and long-handled brushes. Even though right under us is the attic and, according to Mrs. Dock, generations of mammal-digesting blacksnakes, I much prefer tarring the top of the house to tarring the flatter porch roofs, because when you're padding around on those, you have beside you always the second-story windows, and who knows what might decide to look out.

We're taking a break before sealing the last seam when Sam asks, "Where did Granddaddy shoot himself?"

The air warples on "Granddaddy." Sam doesn't even have to get to "shoot." I don't look at our father, but I hear his jaw tighten in his voice. "You know where. The little study room."

"No," Sam says. "I mean what part of his body."

I slide one hand down to the rope around my waist. I look up at the chimney, and I wonder where the mouse ghost found the silverware that it dropped.

"Why do you want to know that?" our father asks.

Sam shrugs. "I always figured it was in the head, but Ham said it was in the stomach. So he could have an open coffin."

Now I do look at our father. He's turned off his face. "When did Ham tell you that?"

"Once when I took him dinner." Sam grabs the bottom of his T-shirt and tugs it down around his hips. "Just so you'll know," he says. "I want an open coffin, too."

MAY SETTLES IN blue and mild, and Ham takes to watching us play behind the house. Him on a stove log he's uprighted into a stool, the wrist cuff of his cane leaning against his thigh, his no-toes boxed in his special shoes, Taffy luxuriating in his lap. The day it happens we are playing chase, and a porch pole directly in front of Ham is our base. Ham seems sleepy, now and again slapping his knee like he's remembering a joke, laugh-talking to himself or to Taffy. But we're all a little giddy, us kids laugh-talking, too, chattering to each other or taunting "it," which I just then am. Mavis has one tennis shoe against the porch pole base, her other leg extended, poised, me hovering in front of her like she's prey. Then she darts, and I leap after her, but from the side of my face I glimpse the ruckus behind her, and I freeze, Ham lunging off his stool, the stove log toppling, Taffy paw-pedaling air, and Ham charges after my seven-year-old sister with his arms outstretched before falling hard on his knees and then on his face, right at the instant our mother reaches the back door to call us for supper.

"Ham can't be that way around you kids."

The verdict comes down later that evening. They don't even sleep on it. After the cinderblock cat house, the woman on the other side of town, jail, and the icehouse, there is just one place, my father learns after a week of phone calls, for Ham to go: the old folks' home for poor people up in Terra Alta.

On the last day of school, we walk into the yard from the bus and everything—the outlier buildings, the woodpile, the house windows, even the grass—lies a little stiller. I drop my stuff and sprint to the icehouse, Sam right behind. But when I stop outside the door, I know not to bother to knock. I hear Sam open it, but I'm already running back to our house, calling for Taffy. All the not-yet-given-away pups swarm my legs, tongues flopping joyful out their mouths, but Taffy is not among them, and then I'm on my hands and knees, shouting and then crooning under the porch.

Lord knows where Terra Alta is. We only know it's up, and what kind of place is a nursing home for a pup just starting to grow? "That's not what he meant," I said to my parents the minute I realized they were saying Ham had to go, but then I was unable to say what I meant: that Ham was just playing, like Mrs. Dock and school, and worse, he was not only just playing, he was trying to help me catch my sister, trying to help me out. But a question thistles in me under everything else: did I truly want Ham to stay or not, and was that why I couldn't explain what I meant?

Suddenly I see Ham, a gray clash in the white old-folks'-home sheets. I see Taffy looking on from a dresser top as a stranger changes Ham's socks. Ham's face intelligent, his smell out of tune, his toes hidden by the stranger's hands. A half-dozen albino cats mist through the weeds beyond the old-folks'-home yard, stalking baby's breaths to suck, and I hear Ham say to the sock-changer, "I used to work for a man down in Romney . . . "

A few weeks after Ham leaves, our father visits him. He comes home quiet, the curtain pulled over his face. "He's not going to last up there," I hear him tell our mother. "He can't get outside and they won't let him drink anything at all." I know better than to ask about Taffy.

I SMUGGLE THE Ouija board to the goat shed, the outlier building farthest from the house, back behind the barn, where it teeters smotherwebbed in honeysuckle vine. So furtive am I that not only no brothers or sisters follow me, but no dogs either, except Mickey, who God couldn't outsmart. I smuggle it to the goat shed even though to get there I must pass the rodent-tailed electric-furred tom spot. I smuggle it to the goat house even though to get in I must wiggle and rip through honeysuckle, multiflora rose, and two violent-thorned locust saplings that grow right in the open door.

Mickey's too wise to trail me in. I stow the Ouija board box facedown in the darkest corner, then stand in a sun stripe with a splinter-handled spade in one hand and look for the softest place in the dirt floor. When I think I have it, I set my spade, aim my foot, and hammer down on the blade. It sinks an inch. I move it and try again. Again the floor gives an inch. I move and try, move and try, pocking my way across the floor, sweat-soaked already in the small of my back and under my arms from frustrated panic more than the June humidity, and the Ouija board gloats from its corner. I reach a wall and stop. I'm going to have to try another way, but apparently goats don't poop as much as some animals, or if they do, it doesn't last as long.

So then I'm shredding back through the thorns, praying past the tomcat spot, to the barn where, as Mickey looks on apologetically for not being able to help, I fill a burlap feed sack with horse and cow turds, marveling as I pick them up at how long the animals' poop has outlived them. Finally I'm back in the goat shed, frantic now, crumbling the manure with my fingers to make it fine like regular dirt, which I use to bury the Ouija board until not a spot of the box shows, and then I add a layer on top of that. Last, for good measure, I mound over everything whole patties and hard fist-shaped plops in a pyramid almost as high as my knees.

Then I plunge through the thorns and the vines and sprint to the house, sheltering my eyebrows with my hands.

THE OUIJA BOARD got the name one letter wrong. It was Ham, not Sam, who died in 1976, three years after he moved into the old folks' home. Our father went to the funeral up in Terra Alta and reported that no one else showed except a woman who claimed to be Ham's sister, which my father was sure Ham never had.

We continued to sight an occasional white Ham cat, one degree above optical illusion, one degree below peripheral vision, usually when we were in the back of the station wagon coiling along some country road. The naked-tailed tom with the asylum eyes, we never did spy again.

By 1976, I was thirteen. Too old to call "Maaa-maawwww." Too self-conscious to wear mouseskulls. Too cynical to depend on my Children's Living Word Bible, which I stopped reading the summer of the Ouija board burial and had not a moment of retribution befall me. But I still slept with my head under the covers and still prayed to be flat. I still braced, heart chuttering, for that now double haunting: the ghost of Ham working for the ghost of my grandfather, both of them hovering through the house.

But although I didn't move out until 1981, I never saw a soul and, far as I know, a soul never saw me.

What I still see decades later is that nail—I see it more than hear it. Flipping end over end down the oil-stove pipe. I see Mrs. Dock, her head flushed up from the dishes in the sink, her mouth falling open and her wet hand flying to her throat. I see her on the back stoop, knees spread in her apron, a fist kneading one thigh. I see her eyes a-dart with what to do.

"AND WHY DO you reckon he'd do that?" Ham says to me "Before he pulled the trigger, drop a nail down that pipe to warn Mrs. Dock?" He has a chicken leg in his fingers, Taffy balled up against his belt. Outside, it's April dusk, but the sky so vague it could be any season, any time of day. Inside, air glitters like lit ice.

"I'll tell you why"—Ham nods—"same reason he waited to do it until your grandma was out of town for that church ladies' meeting. Same reason he picked that little back room instead of messing up the nice room where he slept."

Ham lays down the bone. I've got my gaze fastened to the floor, but Ham stares at my head until I have to look his eyes right back.

His voice comes tender as baby skin and resolute as rock.

"He done it out of kindness," he says. "He done it out of care."

And for a minute, pinned in that hard, cold bright, I feel the truth of what he says. Then I open the icehouse door, step onto dull grass, and hear again the shot that follows the nail.

ARSONISTS

THE PHONE RINGS just as he's zipping his suitcase shut, even though he hasn't seeped a word to anyone in town, but Dell is not surprised. Kenny always knows. Five years ago, Dell would have let it ring; ten, he would have cussed it, too. Now he cups the back of his head with one hand, shuts his eyes, and says hello.

The first call is Becky, gobbling desperate—"Dell, you got to get up here, get him to himself"—before the receiver is grabbed, Dell hears the scuffle, and the connection thumbed off. Within fifteen seconds, it rings again, Kenny this time—"You just stay where you're at, boy, I don't need nothing from you"—before that call goes dead, too. Dell waits until the glow of the number pad darkens in his hand, then calls them back.

"Listen, Becky." He says his words like flat creek rocks laid. "I'm sorry. I am. But it's my little granddaughter's birthday. I'm just out the door to northern Virginia."

"Oh, Dell, I'm sorry, too, I'm just as sorry as I can be, but I've been trying to talk sense to him for two hours. It's the them-coming-to-burn-us-out again, only now he's saying he's got a bomb strapped to his wheelchair and's gonna blow us all up when they get here, Dell, I don't know where else to turn."

Dell tips the receiver away from his mouth. The birthday present lies beside him on the bed. "Can't you at least try?"

"He don't want me in that bathroom, you know that better'n I do, *please*, Dell."

The wrapping is twisted sloppy, the white undersides of the birthday paper showing. It was Carol always took care of that. Dell shuts his eyes again, middle and first fingers forked below his brows. "All right," he says. "I'll be up."

"Oh, I thank ye, Dell," the gobbling again, "I thank ye, if it weren't—"

"Put him on first."

He waits. When enough time has passed for Kenny to lift the phone to his ear, Dell speaks to the silence. "They ain't yet burned one with people still in it, Kenny."

The nothing on the other end lasts so long Dell wonders if Kenny hasn't hung up and he's just not heard. Then a mutter comes.

"Boy. You just don't get it." The voice rasps to whisper. "This house is worth so much they don't got the money to put an offer on it."

ALTHOUGH IT'LL TAKE at least a half hour to crawl the busted-to-pieces road to Kenny's place, Dell does not rush. Kenny'll never touch Becky, and anything Kenny's ever owned that can shoot or blow up is locked in Jason's old room in the upstairs of Dell's house. He gets Carol's Geo Metro started, his truck sitting with a bad alternator, and goes to scraping the windshield with a spatula. He had called Jason as soon as Kenny hung up on him the second time.

"I don't suppose you could hold it a day, could you, son?" He winced at his selfishness soon as he spoke so it was mostly relief he felt when Jason said no.

"All her little friends are coming over. I'm sorry, Dad."

"I understand," Dell cut in quick. "Don't you worry, I understand." And while Jason talked on, Dell felt, as he always does, the surprise and then the pride, his youngest son, at twenty-four, speaking into his own phone, sitting in his own condo, surrounded by things he's provided for his wife and two kids. Jason already that kind of man. He built houses in northern Virginia, went up there at first thinking the job was temporary and then found himself plunged happy over his head in the construction boom, earning overtime every week and sometimes even more than that.

"We'll do something, too, when you get here, Dad," Jason was saying. "Manda'll like that. Make her birthday two days long."

He's forgotten to turn on the defrost, and the coffee he stowed on the dash has steamed the windows good. Dell smears holes where he needs them. Then he is stuttering past the padlocked beige trailer that was the Tout post office, past the old gas station/grocery store, with its window shattered into webs, and here and there—rotten teeth among the sound ones—the burned-down homes. Dell sips his coffee careful, his eyes narrowed on the road. Some of the houses are just scorched, their windows like blackened eyes. Others went full-blaze, gaping open now, their charred rooms exposed—a pitiful vulgar to it, Dell can't help but feel. Others are nothing but steps climbing to rubble-cluttered concrete slabs. The kudzu already covering. Overhead, the flattened hills roll in dead slumps, like men's bodies cold-cocked, Dell sees them when he brings himself to look, like men knocked out. The humps of their twisted shoulders, their arms and legs drunk-flung. Them sprouting their sharp foreign grass.

The company is finished with Tout, West Virginia, now.

SOMEBODY STARTED BURNING houses within a year after they blew up the first mountain. More than a decade ago, Jason still a boy, Carol still with them. In the worst of the blasting, dust stormed the hollow so thick Dell couldn't see Sam Sears's house across the road, and everybody'd had to burn their headlights, their houselights, right through the middle of the day. A few people'd even videotaped it—Lorenzo Mast had, and Sibyl Miller—back when some believed bearing witness could make a difference. That year, there was no summer green, no autumn red. Everything evergray and velvet.

Sam got him and his wife gas masks from an army surplus store, but Dell made do with a scarf. Standing on his front porch, a winter muffler wound round his face, watching the horizon dissolve in linked eruptions like the firecracker strings him and Kenny'd a couple times got hold of as kids. Blasts thunderclapped the wishbone of his chest, and the rock dust taste familiar in his mouth. Dell looked on at first in disbelief and even awe—it was nothing fancy they used, ammonium nitrate and fuel oil, exactly how Tim McVeigh bombed Oklahoma City at about the same time—but quick that turned to outrage and frustration and, finally, helplessness and grief. Which was at last, Dell understood now, a different kind of awe. Brimstone. The word would come to Dell, he couldn't help it. It came on its own in the taste of the rocks. And through it all, the hole opening in him. The hole small at its mouth, but boring deeper, deeper. Craving always to be filled.

Six months into that gray blizzard, the company started offering the buyouts. By then, a lot of the properties were good and blast-busted, with walls cracked, ceilings dropping, foundations split. Wells knocked dry. By the time the offers came, the homeowners had been told by the Department of Environmental Protection that they couldn't prove the damage hadn't been there before the blasting started, and no one had the lawyer money to argue with them, so many people sold, even at the pathetic prices offered them. If their houses weren't shot, their nerves were, and those who could start over, did.

Dell and Carol talked about it, too. Discussed it, argued it, full-on fought. Lying in bed of a night in the silver glitter of the lights on the mine, Carol crumpling Dell's hand under her chin. Pressing her lips there. Shouting at each other once while they were power-washing the dirt crust off their house—that comes back to Dell too often now, the splatty roar of the spray, the expense of the rental and still the dust sticking like paint. How hard it was when you got nowhere else to put it not to take it out on who you loved. Sometimes Dell'd take the leave side and Carol'd take the stay, then by next time, they'd have traded places on it. Bottom line was, Dell was pushing sixty, had taken early retirement, and where were their life savings? Right there in the house. Like a big pile of money blowing away littler and littler with every explosion, every dust cloud, every coal truck crashing through town.

They reached the final decision one afternoon while they were reframing family photos and Carol's needlepoint, fixing them sturdier to the walls. They simply couldn't begin again on what the house would fetch now. Dell remembers how they weren't even sitting when they decided it, they were standing in the living room, finished with rehanging the last picture. He remembers the gray cast to Carol's face, the afternoon having just reached that moment when it's time to turn on the lights. The minute they made it definite, there came in Dell a peculiar painful rightness that he recalled from when he was a kid, back when he used to bang his head against his bed frame, against walls, usually out of anger, occasionally to salve a shame. And for a day or two, the little hole hushed its yearning.

In the meantime, the other houses were bought up; the families packed; the homes darkened. And then, when the machines finally began to retreat, still blowing up ridges but farther away, and just when Dell and Carol thought the dust might lay . . . the smoke came.

The Williamses' house went first. They'd been gone for several months, and it sat there at the far end of town, no neighbors on its one side, and Dell and Carol and Jason slept right through the fire. Woke in the morning to the odor of smolder. Slept through because although everyone left in that end of Tout had called it in, no fire trucks showed. The second fire came about three weeks later, then the third, both in abandoned company-bought houses. Then they burned regular, about once a month, the glows of the closer fires quavering Dell and Carol's window, choking them awake on their trash smoke stink. Sometimes the firefighters came. Other times Dell rushed out with the neighbors and their sorry garden hoses, trying to contain the flames. But what has stayed with him tightest, longest, is not the panic or the odor or the colors of blaze. It's the noises. The pops of little things blowing up in the houses, the whoosh-roar of bigger, the shuddering wrenching cracks, then the crashes as roof parts cave in. It is the ripple sound of flames moving good. The "I'm coming" like sheets of canvas flapping in wind.

For over a year, they burned. Still, even living in the middle of it, no one, no matter how close they watched, could figure out how the fires were lit or by whom. The arsonists couldn't be caught, even though there was a clear design, never did a lived-in house ignite, always the deserted company-owned ones, and usually those houses targeted were some distance from inhabited homes; only once did a fire jump to a place where people lived. The mysteriousness of it all terrorized everyone even worse, and more people sold, just like the company wanted. If they couldn't shake them out, they'd burn them out—Dell suspicioned this at the first one, and by the third one, he knew. But every house burned was company property, just like county law was company property, just like state law was. When some official finally arrived to investigate, the company was behind that, too.

They pronounced it vandalism. Local boys. The locals, the officials reminded them, had a long history of vandalizing company property.

By this time, the holdouts were patrolling with shotguns in pairs. Kenny came down off the mountain to help, him and Dell doing their turns together. Jason begged in on it, too, and for nonschool nights, Carol finally said yes, although Dell never let him go farther off than reaching distance. They'd stake out the houses most likely marked, and if they had enough people, post two men at each one. If they didn't, they rotated between them. Houses burned anyway, but never on Kenny and Dell's watch.

"I know what's going on," Kenny started grinding. "Somebody ain't got the balls to hang in there, face who it is. Or else somebody's lazying off. Sneaking home for a nap."

"I believe you're right," Dell eventually agreed. "I believe you're right."

After August, they didn't say that anymore.

Five men were on duty that night, Dell and Kenny and Jason covering the low rancher that had been Lorenzo Mast's, Charlie Blizzard and his cousin Burl on the other house across town. Dell and Jason were hunkered down in lawn chairs in the brush behind the Masts' backyard, Kenny guarding the front from his own chair in the blackened house frame across the road.

Dell pulled his undershirt away from his skin, him sticky with sweat and Off and the bugs still biting. Beside him, Jason slept in an upright slump would have left a six-day crick in Dell's neck. The Coke can was already warm and slippery in Dell's hand, and he wrangled a colder one from the stash in his old lunch cooler, his fifth of the night, its sizzle like another layer of locust shriek. The core of his body was pulling down hard towards sleep, but his skin and his mind rode the caffeine current, memories and images, roiling up like drift. First him and Carol, at their beginning, and that led further back to a wild girl who'd been his high school love. And then the pictures were of him and Kenny, who'd come before any woman, those images, too, moving in reverse: the first day of their first real job, working underground; the night they got arrested, running the roads drunk at seventeen; the shared frustration of second-string in junior high basketball. Then clear back to a time in grade school Dell had almost forgot, both of them sent to Mr. Dickens's office for a paddling. Dell couldn't remember for what, and the paddling hurt, but being watched by each other was worse, which is what Mr. Dickens made them do. Dell didn't cry. Kenny did. At least that's how it comes to him now.

He drained the last of that Coke and shoved the can under his chair. Stepped deeper into the weeds to take a piss. When he turned back around, he saw the light.

At first he didn't believe it, but quick it went from a winking glimmer to a blaze, ripply but constant. Dell snatched up his twelve-gauge, thumbed off the safety, jerked Jason awake. And then he was straining on the balls of his feet, every inch of him taut, him twenty years younger, thirty pounds lighter, not an achy place in him save the effort of his eyes. The loud part of his body hollering, *Go*, Dell, *Run*, close in and *grab* him, while his head hissed, *Hold* your place, *hold* it, you take off now and you'll never see him if he flies out the other end. Dell's eyes searing the overgrown juniper bushes against the house, the single back door over its three-stepped stoop, the five shutterless windows in their neat row. The fire was accelerating now, furying from the middle of the house into both ends until the whole building was puking flame, every window sheeted with it, flames battering out the roof, and Dell knew the burner had to have been flushed. Couldn't no one survive that hot, that high.

"Kenny's got him!" he yelled at Jason, and his boy took off so fast he slipped down on one knee. Then they were tearing through the yard towards the side of the house, Dell as fast as Jason was, not feeling his body, not feeling the house heat, all the while knowing—Dell did not expect, he *knew*—that Kenny'd either be chasing the arsonist or have him at gunpoint.

When Dell careened around the corner and into the front, he at first couldn't find Kenny, what with the neighbors streaming in, faces red-lit, them still in the commotion of what to do. Dell finally spotted Kenny because he was the only person standing still. Kenny paralyzed in the road, taut-frozen, a mirror of how Dell'd been out back, Kenny's gun stock in his armpit, the barrel resting in his left hand, and not a soul at the end of it. Dell rushed up to his side, and as Kenny recognized him, a realization rolled over his face. Dell saw that just as much as Dell'd expected to see two there, Kenny'd expected them to come as three.

Kenny slammed his shotgun to the ground. Dell jumped back, pushing Jason behind him. "Goddamn you, Kenny," he heard somebody yell even though the gun didn't trigger. "Watch yourself! Watch yourself!"

Not long after that, Carol got diagnosed and Dell turned his attention there. A couple more abandoned houses were torched that year, but as the machines gutted the mountains in the middle distance and then pulled even farther away, the fires stopped, too. After Dell quit, Kenny only kept it up a month or two more. By then, they were closing in on his own place.

It had been on one of those watch nights before the Mast house burned, Jason not with them, that Kenny had said it. Coming on towards dawn, and them meeting up to share a cigarette after guarding separate houses all night, the clunk of the monster bucket in the distance overhead, the hish of dead earth poured over the hillside. Kenny said it just once, and in the dark. Said it not as a question, didn't risk contradiction or conversation. "What we did, Dell," he said. "It wasn't like this here."

Through Dell, a cold gust flashed, from his groin to the top of his chest. He wet his mouth to speak back, to agree. Then he stopped and let it go.

NOW HE TAKES the turnoff to Kenny's leery and slow, the road cratered dirt with asphalt stumps rearing up out of it until it breaks down to no pavement at all. Dell straddles the worst of it best he can, eases the car into the holes when he has to, the jolts up his body so bad he can't tell if his bones are scraping together or pulling apart. Used to be a creek run down along this road, the same creek that used to run by Kenny's house. They played in it as boys, back when both him and Kenny lived down in Tout and it was Kenny's grandma on the place. When Kenny got too worked up—oh, that temper, how he'd beet like a redhead, windmilling punches at air—his grandma'd screech, "You all get outta here! Go getcha in the creek!" And she was right. Even back then, water worked.

He drives by the barred haul road to the shutdown part of the mine, the guard shack plywooded over, the sign beside it peppered with pellets: COAL KEEPS THE LIGHTS ON. The last couple places him and Kenny worked, they passed every shift a sign that said that, too. Right beyond that fork, the road returns to mostly hardtop, and Dell leans into the gas. Not long after, he hits the first of the NO TRESPASSING signs Kenny's hung all along the borders of his property and right up to his front door, some store-bought, some homemade, and finally, Kenny's house swings into view.

It's a big four-bedroom. Single-story, but rangy and imposing, built against the steep hill with a grand high deck on two sides. Painted a two-tone blue, baby for the walls, navy for the trim, and a full basement, a two-car garage. It makes the house that was up here before, the one Kenny's grandma lived in, look like a goat shed. Makes the houses him and Kenny grew up in down in Tout in the forties and fifties look that way, too. But Dell can see, if he squints through the half-leaved autumn trees, the mine, crunching away to horizon like Satan's gravel pit. The house, the bit of woodland around it, the sweep of yard that Becky cuts with the ride mower, Becky and Kenny themselves—they are surrounded on three sides. Living inside a nutcracker's vee.

Dell pulls up beside Becky's Blazer on the parking pad Kenny poured and jerks his brake. He reaches for his door, then stops. Sets his hands back on the wheel. Kenny crows tirelessly about how nothing nor nobody in the world will ever make him sell his place, but the truth is—nobody's offered to buy it.

Becky meets him at the bottom of the deck steps. "Oh, Dell, I thank ye. I thank ye, and I'm sorry, I am so sorry." She has an old denim coat of Kenny's thrown over her shoulders, and she rubs her fists on her thighs in fret. "I feel so bad about you missing your little Amanda's birthday, but where else can I turn? Where else can I turn?"

Dell knows sorry for him is about the least of her worries right now. "It's all right," he says. Kenny found her at a church function a while back, and she is fifteen, twenty years younger, and not real bright. His sensible wife, Doria, left back at the beginning of this mess. Now Becky is blocking the front door, her hand on the knob. "He says he's gonna roll that wheelchair up on the mountain and suicide bomb em, and he's already tried to get out on the deck twicet."

"We'll get him settled down," Dell says. "We'll get him settled down."

He works his shoes off in the little entrance hall. Kenny always insisted on that, and it used to annoy the hell out of Dell. The ancient poodle with the stained under-eyes slingshots out of somewhere to harass his pants-cuffs until she recognizes him and retreats, snuffling, to one of the big floral-patterned armchairs. Dell takes a breath. Then he follows the dog into the living room.

Kenny sits at attention in his wheelchair. Ironed jeans, steel-toed boots, a paisley pajama top. The chair is pulled up to the picture window, and under Kenny's right arm is snugged the black plastic case of a student-model guitar. The neck of it follows Kenny's forearm. The tip is pointed at the pane. Dell clears his throat.

"Hey, buddy." The bellow in his own voice catches Dell off guard, even though it's how he usually talks to Kenny now. "What's going on up here?"

Kenny snaps his head around. As if he's not watched Dell all the way up the drive, didn't have him and Becky at the end of the guitar case when they stepped up onto the deck. Kenny stares at Dell a hard five seconds, working a little his mouth. His eyes ringed dark, his face caved so the bones stand in peaks, and his silver hair slicked, he reminds Dell of a chicken-coon cross. The eyes slide off Dell's. Kenny pivots back to his vigil.

"Done got that side." He swings his free hand to the left. "Done got that side." Flings it past his face to the right. "Done got all that behind, and now they're coming after the front side, too. Gonna burn me and her out and blast right up under the house."

Behind Kenny's back, Becky raises her eyebrows and nods, See? Dell ignores her. He saunters across the persimmon-colored carpet into the kitchen, where he takes a place at the table so he can watch Kenny across the living room. Everything Dell does, he does noisier than usual, including an exaggerated sigh of contentment when he settles into the chair. Kenny does not turn around.

"Can I get you a cup of coffee, Dell?" Becky asks, like she always does, her overloud too. At least she's quick enough to remember her lines.

"Oh, yes, please," Dell booms. "Don't mind if I do."

"Black, right?" Becky asks.

"Black's right," says Dell. "Like my pap always said, 'Drink it black, or don't drink it at all.'"

On the little TV next to the microwave, Rachael Ray is whipping up some kind of Mexican dish. Dell thanks Becky for his coffee, and she sits across the table with her own, sugaring it heavy enough for a cake. Then they commence the pretending-to-watch the show, each sipping slow, now and again making a comment to each other for normalcy's sake. Both with an ear, an eye, constant-cocked to Kenny.

Dell can remember when Kenny's whole family had to live in this one room, the kids doing their homework on sawhorses. How Doria'd hung Christmas decorations on the insulation the December before they got the drywall up. Kenny built the house little by little, whenever he had the money, and Dell'd helped him off and on until he'd get sick of being bossed and take a break for a while. He always came back, usually after Kenny called and asked him to drive up and see some new tool or piece of equipment he'd got, which was as close as Kenny could come to an apology. Dell sneaks a full-on look at Kenny. He can feel that it's still too soon.

Becky refills his cup. He'd had to ask Jason many times to show him the houses that he built before Jason finally did, one time about a year ago. A subdivision, Jason explained, an old horse farm split up. He and Jason glided in Jason's new Ford Explorer over fresh-paved streets through acre after acre of immaculate vacant homes, bulked up and bulging on undersized lots. The streets deliberately unstraight, snake-tailing into dead ends that made no sense, everywhere treeless, hill-less. Until Dell, despite how he'd looked forward to this, despite his pride in what his boy did—build things—started to get carsick for the first time in sixty years. He had to ask Jason to stop. By this time, they'd reached the outermost ring of the maze, where houses still under construction stood half-naked in their pressed woodchip skins, their Tyvek wraps. Dell stepped out and breathed deep: odor of raw lumber, fresh-poured concrete, and something chemical he could not name. He looked over his shoulder, expecting Jason behind him. Jason sat in the Explorer, fooling with his cell phone.

Dell hits the bottom of his second cup. Usually that signals that the wait's been long enough. He glances at Becky. She opens her hands in an I-don't-know. So Dell reaches towards Kenny, not with his body, not with his hands, but with the how-long-he's-known-Kenny, that's what he uses to catch where Kenny's at. But still Dell can't tell, and if he starts too early, Kenny won't play. Dell goes on and risks it.

"Hey, Kenny," he calls, forcing a casualness in his tone. "I hear you all been getting some real bad shakes up here." Dell waits. Kenny does not move. Dell swallows. "I don't see no cracks, though."

He waits again. The poodle tumbles off the chair and disappears. Then Dell does feel it off Kenny—a stiff ripple up his back, a prickling above Kenny's ears. Without turning from the window, without the slightest stir of his head, Kenny sneers, "Ha. Look there. Above the refrigerator. See there?"

Dell lifts his face, squints, and frowns, even though the cracks are as visible as the grandchildren's coloring book pages on the freezer door. "Huh. I can't see nothing," Dell says.

For some seconds, the only sound is Becky's fist, a hishing against the denim of her thigh. Then Kenny blurts breath in disgust. He thrusts the wheelchair back and heaves himself to his feet, hobbles a step or two, unstiffening. Then he stomps across the living room without a limp.

"Right there, you blind ole sumbitch. Right there. See where I tried to patch it up, bought that stuff from Lowe's? See what a sorry job I did, trying to patch it together?"

Becky vanishes like the poodle. Dell squints deeper. "Oh. Okay. Yeah." He nods slowly. "I see it." He gets to his feet, Kenny right up beside him now, wagging the guitar case back and forth from his waist, and Dell can smell the aftershave heavy on him. Dell reaches up on tiptoe, gritting his teeth against the old pain that lightnings down his right leg, and runs his fingers along the splits. "That is sorry."

"You never seen such shaking, buddy, the night that ceiling busted open." And now Kenny is going. "Here we was, just setting eating supper, had a big pitcher of ice tea there in the middle, and they set one off"—he leaps back, throws out his arms, the guitar case slamming into the door frame—"blew that pitcher clear up off the table. And she didn't tip, boys, she didn't tip, but tea sloshed out all over ever'thing. Spoilt our spaghetti." He swings the guitar case at the back wall. "Got them windows, too, that time. But I done replaced those."

"It's terrible." Dell shakes his head, freshly mournful and shocked, as though they've not already had this exchange eight times, ten. "It's just terrible." Then he cocks his head, studies the cracks more intently. He spreads his thumb and first finger to take the measure of one. "Huh. But I think I seen bigger cracks than these down at Charlie's." He nods thoughtfully. "Yeah. Believe I did. And over at Miz Reynolds', too, come to think of it."

Kenny starts working his mouth, his teeth rabbitting his bottom lip. The eyes seem to steam, Dell can see the wet glow. Finally Kenny snorts. "You did, huh? You did?" He reels away, the case grazing Dell's arm, and marches into the hall. "Well, you follow me. You just follow me."

Dell does. Kenny is heading for the fractures behind the photos in the hall, skipping both the living room and the garage. The tour is going so fast that Dell wonders—like he did last time, that tour shortened, too—how much Kenny is truly led on and how much he's performing, exactly like Dell and Becky are. "See here? My Sheetrock?" Kenny has unhooked the picture of his son Roger in his high school football uniform and the one of him and Becky getting married, and he thumps the wall with his palm. "Here how I tried to paper it back over?" "Yeah," Dell is commiserating, "I see what you mean, them ones are deeper than Charlie's," and as he says that, he's cramming down the other, what he dares not think in words but what boils up anyway: that maybe, just maybe, the tour will shorten and shorten, until . . .

Then Kenny speaks again, his voice dropping to a husk: "And I got something else to show you, buddy. Here in the bedroom." He twitches his shoulder back towards the kitchen, and for the first time all morning, he grins. "Not even she don't know yet."

The half hope drops out of Dell like a trapdoor in his gut. His face heats, his fists curl—he did think it, did jinx—but still he follows. He tails Kenny into the room, the air close and slept-in, Dell cringing with the queasiness he always feels in other people's rooms with beds unmade. Kenny is already in the closet, the guitar case tossed on the mattress, Kenny thrusting aside clothes on their hangers, and he calls, "Lookee there, Dell."

Dell looks. A dim, cream-colored wall.

"I don't see nothing, Kenny." He says it in his normal voice. Not the pumped-up playacting one. Not the one that goes along.

Kenny whips his free arm up and jerks a cord. A bare bulb in the ceiling snaps on. "See there?" Kenny's voice is both soft and shrill. He is looking past Dell, to make sure, Dell knows, that Becky has not sneaked in. "Them scorch marks on the wall."

The walls shines bare in the harsh light. Dell does not speak.

"That's where they got it set. They test-runned her the other night, just to see how it worked. Left them marks there." Kenny drops his arm, the hangers clashing back into place, and shuts the door, gently.

He leans forward from his hips towards Dell's ear. Dell's arms pimple. "They got a three-mile-long fuse, Dell. End of it laid right under my bedroom."

Dell feels himself falling away. Kenny shrinking before him, although neither of them has moved, the distance widening, a rushing noise come in. Kenny seen across a featureless gray field. For twenty years, they strip-mined together—contour jobs, peeling the sides off hills. They'd both worked underground first. And after years in tunnels, what it meant to get up on top, nothing about to fall on you, the machines doing all the heavy work, no more black dust. To be up out of the dark. And they'd been proud of what they did, they made America's electricity, they kept on the lights. The money they earned raised their kids comfortable, like they deserved, way beyond how him and Kenny'd come up, refurbished Dell's old company house to modern, built Kenny's from the foundation up.

But to blow the top off a mountain. *It wasn't like this here.* Still, by now, Dell understands the little hole inside him, boring down, down, farther than he knew he went, yearning always to be plugged. And all Dell can do is pull a screen across it.

Then the distance dissolves, and Kenny is regular-sized before him again. Dell hears himself speak.

"How's your bathroom holding up, buddy?"

Dell closes the door at the end of the hall behind them. He squeezes past Kenny and sags down onto the lip of the tub, twists on the spigots and lets the water run hard, his hand in the gush. Kenny has clapped the commode shut and dropped his guitar case, which skitters into the metal trash can and drives it into Dell's leg. The temperature right, Dell stops the drain and sits, studying the vinyl tile on the wall. He can feel Kenny behind him almost as certain as a touch, sitting on the toilet unlacing his boots—thinking what, Dell never knows. Only when the tub's full and Dell cuts off the water does Kenny stand and start to fumble with his clothes. The soft plomp on the floor, the clank of the belt buckle. Like he always does, he comes to the tub edge with his boxers still on.

Dell rises and takes Kenny's upper arm, a little rough. A helping hand, not a petting hand, not a comforting one. Kenny gets his leg over the rim and Dell eases him down until he sits slumped in the water, his arms around his knees. All the muscle in his back has fled to a pile of sags at his waist. His skin is colored like a speckled cold grease.

That time Dell'd visited Jason a year ago, the time they'd gone out to the construction site, Kenny hadn't stopped him before he left, but Dell'd had to cut a five-day stay two days short. Becky'd called at eleven at night, swearing she'd spent since noon trying to get Kenny to himself, oh, she was terribly sorry, but where else could she turn? Dell had to sleep first. He was way too old to make an eight-hour drive in the middle of the night after playing with his grandbabies all day. He had set his alarm for four.

When he woke, he feared at first he'd overslept, light as it was outside, until he understood it was the condo complex's security lights. He'd never driven in northern Virginia before dawn, and as he loaded the Metro under floodlights, there stirred in him an uneasiness mingled with awe. Then he was passing under the streetlights that canopied the suburb's four-lane main drag; the gas stations, office buildings, stores, sidewalks, and the street itself were completely people-less, him the single car, and all of it, everywhere, lit bright as an emergency room.

Dell's shoulders were hunched, the wheel was dampening under his hand. Then, suddenly, and to his total surprise—the light turned to sound. The strip malls first—they burst into roar, a crowd in his head—then the box stores, Target and Home Depot and Sam's, them louder yet, squalling and hollering bald blares of light. Among them the fast-food places, Wendy's, Burger King, Taco Bell, Sonic, each shrieking light, and then the quaint and quietful places—coffee shops, boutiques—Dell heard them, too, hissing their squander of light.

He was speeding now, his eyes cramped to just enough pavement to let him safely drive, his body braced, his heart held. And then he was out and onto the highway, hurtling south and west, towards home, his body easing, his breath coming catch-up in his chest—when he heard, from the near distance in what used to be fields, the wailing flare of subdivisions, each one, he knew, either uninhabited or asleep. Yet each one haloed in a great conflagration of light.

In the corner of the tub sits a tall plastic Go-Mart cup Becky keeps there for the purpose. Dell reaches for it. He sinks it into the bath and lifts it full, water dribbling into his pushed-up sleeve. He looks at Kenny's back, and for a second, Dell knows the chill of Kenny's bare skin, and for that second, a tenderness spears him. Dell banks it down. He tips the cup. Water sluices over Kenny's spine. Dell dips again, lifts, and pours. Again. And again. Sloshed water dabbling his knees, an old hurt wrenching his shoulder. Until Kenny starts to come back to himself.

DOG SONG

HIM. HELLING UP a hillside in a thin snow won't melt, rock-broke, brush-broke, crust-cracking snow throat felt, the winter a cold one, but a dry one, kind of winter makes them tell about the old ones, and him helling up that hill towards her. To where he sees her tree-tied, black trunk piercing snow hide, and the dog, roped, leashed, chained, he can't tell which, but something not right about the dog he can tell, but he can't see, can't see quite full, and him helling. Him helling. His eyes knocking in his head, breath punching out of him in a hole, hah. Hah. Hah. Hah, and the dog, her haunch sat ear cocked waiting for him, and him helling. And him helling. And him helling. But he does not ever reach her.

This is his dream.

HIS DOGS STARTED disappearing around the fifteenth of July, near as he could pinpoint it looking back, because it wasn't until a week after that and he recognized it as a pattern that he started marking when they went. Parchy vanished first. The ugliest dog he ever owned, coated in this close-napped pink-brown hair, his outsides colored like the insides of his mouth, and at first, Matley just figured he'd run off. Matley always had a few who'd run off because he couldn't bear to keep them tied, but then Buck followed Parchy a week later. But he'd only had Buck a few months, so he figured maybe he'd headed back to where he'd come from, at times they did that, too. Until Missy went, because Matley knew Missy would never stray. She was one of the six dogs he camper-kept, lovely mutt Missy, beautiful patches of twenty different dogs, no, Missy'd been with him seven years and was not one to travel. So on July 22, when Missy didn't show up for supper, Matley saw a pattern and started keeping track on his funeral home calendar. Randolph went on August 1. Yeah, Matley'd always lost a few dogs. But this was different.

HE'D HEARD WHAT they said down in town, how he had seventy-five dogs back in there, but they did not know. Dog Man, they called him. Beagle Boy. Muttie. Mr. Hound. A few called him Cat. Stayed in a Winnebago camper beside a househole that had been his family home-place before it was carried off in the '85 flood, an identical Winnebago behind the lived-in one so he could take from the second one parts and pieces as they broke in the first, him economical, savvy, keen, no, Matley was not dumb. He lived off a check he got for something nobody knew what, the youngest of four boys fathered by an old landowner back in farm times, and the other three left out and sold off their inheritance in nibbles and crumbs, acre, lot, gate, and tree, leaving only Matley anchored in there with the dogs and the househole along the tracks. Where a tourist train passed four times a day on summer weekends and even more days a week during leaf colors in fall, the cars bellied full of outsiders come to see the mountain sights—"farm children playing in the fields," the brochure said, "a land that time forgot"—and there sits Matley on a lawn chair between Winnebagos and househole. He knew what they said in town, the only person they talked about near as often as Matley was ole Johnby, and Johnby they discussed only half as much. They said Mr. Hound had seventy-five dogs back in there, nobody had ever seen anything like it, half of them living outside in barrels, the other half right there in the camper with him. It was surely a health hazard, but what could you do about it? That's what they said.

But Matley never had seventy-five dogs. Before they started disappearing, he had twenty-two, and only six he kept in the camper, and one of those six was Guinea, who fit in his sweatshirt pocket, so didn't hardly count. And he looked after them well, wasn't like that one woman kept six Pomeranians in a Jayco pop-up while she stayed in her house and they all got burned up in a camper fire. Space heater. The outside dogs he built shelters for, terraced the houses up the side of the hill, and, yes, some of them were barrels on their sides braced with two-by-four struts, but others he fashioned out of scrap lumber, plenty of that on the place, and depending on what mood took him, sometimes he'd build them square and sometimes he'd build them like those lean-to teepees where people keep fighting cocks. Some dogs, like Parchy, slept in cut-out cable spools, a cable spool was the only structure in which Parchy would sleep, Matley could find cable spools and other almost doghouses along the river after the spring floods. And he never had seventy-five dogs.

Parchy, Buck, Missy, Randolph, Ghostdog, Blackie, Ed. Those went first. That left Tick, Hickory, Cese, Muddy Gut, Carmel, Big Girl, Leesburg, Honey, Smartie, Ray Junior, Junior Junior, Louise, Fella, Meredith, and Guinea. Junior Junior was only a pup at the time, Smartie was just a part-time dog, stayed two or three nights a week across the river with his Rottweiler girlfriend, and Meredith was pregnant. Guinea goes at the end of the list because Guinea was barely dog at all.

THEY COULD TELL you in town that Matley was born old, born with the past squeezing on him, and he was supposed to grow up in that? How? There was no place to go but backwards. His parents were old by the time he came, his brothers gone by the time he could remember, his father dead by the time he was eight. Then the flood, on his twenty-third birthday. In town they might spot Matley in his '86 Chevette loaded from floorboards to dome light with twenty-five pound bags of Joy Dog food, and one ole boy would say, "Well, there he goes. That ruint runt of Revie's four boys. End piece didn't come right."

Another: "I heard he was kinda retarded."

"No, not retarded exactly . . . but he wasn't born until Revie was close to fifty. And that explains a few things. Far as I'm concerned. Old egg, old sperm, old baby."

"Hell, weren't none of them right," observes a third.

"There's something about those hills back in there. You know Johnby's from up there, too."

"Well," says the last. "People are different."

Matley. His ageless, colorless, changeless self. Dressed always in baggy river-colored pants and a selection of pocketed sweatshirts he collected at yard sales. His bill-busted, sweat-mapped, river-colored cap, and the face between sweatshirt and cap as common and unmemorable as the pattern on a sofa. Matley had to have such a face, given what went on under and behind it. The bland face, the constant clothes, they had to balance out what rode behind them, or Matley might be so loose as to fall. Because Matley had inherited from his parents not just the oldness, and not just the past (that gaping loss), and not just the irrational stick to the land, even land that you hated, and not just scraps of the land itself, and the collapsed buildings, and the house-hole, but also the loose part, he knew. Worst of all, he'd inherited the loose part inside (you got to hold on tight).

NOW IT WAS a couple years before the dogs started disappearing that things had gotten interesting from the point of view of them in town.

They told. Matley's brother Charles sold off yet another plat on the ridge above the househole, there on what had always been called High Boy until the developers got to it, renamed it Oaken Acre Estates, and the out-of-staters who moved in there started complaining about the barking and the odor, and then the story got even better. One of Dog Man's Beagle Boy's Cat's mixed-breed who-knows-what's got up in there and impregnated some purebred something-or-other one of the imports owned, "and I heard they had ever last one of them pups put to sleep. That's the kind of people they are, now," taking Matley's side for once. Insider versus outsider, even Muttie didn't look too bad that way.

Matley knew. At first those pureblood-dog old people on High Boy appeared only on an occasional weekend, but then they returned to live there all the time, which was when the trouble started. They sent down a delegation of two women one summer, and when that didn't work, they sent two men. Matley could tell they were away from here from a distance, could tell from how they carried themselves before they even got close and confirmed it with their clothes. "This county has no leash ordinance," he told that second bunch because by that time he had checked, learned the lingo, but they went on to tell him how they'd paid money to mate this pureblood dog of some type Matley'd never heard of to another of its kind, but a mongrel got to her before the stud, and they were blaming it on one of his. Said it wasn't the first time, either. "How many unneutered dogs do you have down here?" they asked, and, well, Matley never could stand to have them cut. So. But it wasn't until a whole year after the encounter that his dogs started disappearing, and Matley, of course, had been raised to respect the old.

The calendar was a free one from Berger's Funeral Home, kind of calendar has just one picture to cover all the months, usually a picture of a blonde child in a nightgown praying beside a bed, and this calendar had that picture, too. Blonde curls praying over lost dog marks, Matley almost made them crosses, but he changed them to question marks, and he kept every calendar page he tore off. He kept track, and for each one, he carried a half eulogy, half epitaph in his head:

Ed. Kind of dog you looked at and knew he was a boy, didn't have to glimpse his privates. You knew from the jog-prance of those stumpy legs, cock-of-the-walk strut, all the time swinging his head from side to side so not to miss anything, tongue flopping out and a big grin in his eyes. Essence of little boy, he was, core, heart, whatever you want to call it. There it sat in a dog. Ed would try anything once and had to get hurt pretty bad before he'd give up, and he'd eat anything twice. That one time, cold night, Matley let him in the camper, and Ed gagged and puked up a deer liver on Matley's carpet remnant, the liver intact, though a little rotty. There it came. Out. Ed's equipment was hung too close to the ground, that's how Mr. Mitchell explained it, "his dick's hung too close to the ground, way it almost scrapes stuff, would make you crazy or stupid, and he's stupid," Mr. Mitchell'd say. Ed went on August 10.

Ghostdog. The most mysterious of the lot, even more so than Guinea, Ghostdog never made a sound; not a whimper, not a grunt, not a snore. A whitish ripple, Ghostdog was steam moving in skin, the way she'd ghost-coast around the place, a glow-in-the-dark angel cast to her, so that to sit by the househole of a summer night and watch that dog move across the field, a luminous padding, it was to learn how a nocturnal animal sees. Ghostdog'd give Matley that vision, she would make him understand, raccoon eyes, cat eyes, deer. And not only did Ghostdog show Matley night sight, through Ghostdog he could see also smells. He learned to see the shape of a smell, watching her with her head tilted, an odor entering nostrils on breeze, he could see the smell shape, "shape" being the only word he had for how the odors were, but "shape" not it at all. Still. She showed him. Ghostdog went on August 19.

Blackie was the only one who ever came home. He returned a strange and horrid sick, raspy purr to his breath like a locust. Kept crawling places to die, but Matley, for a while, just couldn't let him go, even though he knew it was terribly selfish. Blackie'd crawl in a place, and Matley'd pull him back out, gentle, until Matley finally fell asleep despite himself, which gave Blackie time to get under the bed and pass on. September 2. But Blackie was the only one who came home like that. The others just went away.

BEFORE MOM REVIE died, he could only keep one dog at a time. She was too cheap to feed more, and she wouldn't let a dog inside the house until the late 1970s; she was country people, and that was how they did their dogs, left them outside like pigs or sheep. For many years, Matley made do with his collection, dogs of ceramic and pewter, plastic and fake fur, and when he was little, Revie's rules didn't matter so much, because if he shone on the little dogs his heart and mind, Matley made them live. Then he grew up and couldn't do that anymore.

When he first started collecting live dogs after Mom Revie was gone, he got them out of the paper, and if pickings there were slim, he drove around and scooped up strays. Pretty soon, people caught on, and he didn't have to go anywhere for them; folks just started dumping unwanteds along the road above his place. Not usually pups, no, they were mostly dogs who'd hit that ornery stage between cooey-cute puppyhood and mellow you-don't-have-to-pay-them-much-mind adult. That in-between stage was the dumping stage. The only humans Matley talked to much were the Mitchells, and more than once, before the dogs started disappearing, Mrs. Mitchell to Matley would gentle say, "Now, you know, Matley, I like dogs myself. But I never did want to have more than two or three at a time." And Matley, maybe him sitting across the table from her with a cup of instant coffee, maybe them in the yard down at his place with a couple of dogs nosing her legs, a couple peeing on her tires, Matley'd nod, he'd hear the question in what she said, but he does not, could not, never out loud say . . .

How he was always a little loose inside, but looser always in the nights. The daylight makes it scurry down, but come darkness, nothing tamps it, you never know (hold on tight). So even before Matley lost a single dog, many nights he'd wake, not out of nightmare, but worse. Out of nothing. Matley would wake, a hard sock in his chest, his lungs aflutter, his body not knowing where it was, it not knowing, and Matley's eyes'd ball open in the dark, and behind the eyes: a galaxy of empty. Matley would gasp. *Why be alive?* This was what it told him. *Why be alive?*

There Matley would lie in peril. The loose part in him. Matley opened to emptiness, that bottomless gasp. Matley falling, Matley down-swirling (you got to hold), Matley understanding how the loose part had give, and if he wasn't to drop all the way out, he'd have to find something to hold on tight (yeah boy. Tight. Tight. Tighty tight tight.). Matley on the all-out plummet, Matley tumbling head over butt down, Matley going almost gone, his arms outspread, him reaching, flailing, whopping. . . . Until, finally. Matley hits dog. Matley's arms drop over the bunk side and hit dog. And right there Matley stops, he grabs hold, and Matley . . . stroke. Stroke, stroke. There, Matley. There.

Yeah, the loose part Matley held with dog. He packed the emptiness with pup. Took comfort in their scents, nose-buried in their coats, he inhaled their different smells, corn chips, chicken stock, meekish skunk. He'd listen to their breathing, march his breath in step with theirs, he'd hear them live, alive, their sleeping songs, them lapping themselves and recurling themselves, snoring and dreaming, settle and sigh. The dogs a soft putty, the loose part, sticking. There, Matley. There. He'd stroke their stomachs, finger-comb their flanks, knead their chests, Matley would hold on, and finally he'd get to the only true pleasure he'd ever known that wasn't also a sin. Rubbing the deep velvet of a dog's underthroat.

BY LATE AUGUST, Matley had broke down and paid for ads in the paper, and he got calls, most of the calls people trying to give him dogs they wanted to get rid of, but some people thinking they'd found dogs he'd lost. Matley'd get in his car and run out to wherever the caller said the dog was, but it was never his dog. And, yeah, he had his local suspicions, but soft old people like the ones on the ridge, it was hard to believe they'd do such a thing. So first he just ran the road. Matley beetling his rain-colored Chevette up and down the twelve-mile-long road that connected the highway and his once-was farm. Holding the wheels to the road entirely through habit, wasn't no sight to it, sight he couldn't spare, Matley squinting into trees, fields, brush, until he'd enter the realm of dog mirage. Every rock, dirt mound, deer, piece of trash, he'd see it at first and think "Dog!" his heart bulging big with the hope. Crushed like an egg when he recognized the mistake. And all the while, the little dog haunts scampered the corners of his eyes, dissolving as soon as he turned to see. Every now and then he'd slam out and yell, try Revie's different calling songs, call, "Here, Ghostdog, here! Come, girl, come!" Call, "Yah, Ed, yah! Yah! Yah! Yah!" Whistle and clap, cluck and whoop. But the only live thing he'd see besides groundhogs and deer was that ole boy Johnby, hulking along.

Matley didn't usually pay Johnby much mind, he was used to him, had gone to school with him even though Johnby was a good bit older. Johnby was one of those kids who comes every year but don't graduate until they're so old the board gives them a certificate and throws them out. But today Matley watched ole Johnby lurching along, pretend-hunting, the gun, everyone had to assume, unloaded, and why the family let him out with guns, knives, Matley wasn't sure, but figured it was just nobody wanted to watch him. Throughout late summer, Mrs. Mitchell'd bring Matley deer parts from the ones they'd shot with crop damage permits, oh how the dogs loved those deer legs, and the rib cages, and the hearts. One day she'd brought Johnby along, Johnby'd catch a ride anywhere you'd take him, and Matley'd looked at Johnby, how his face'd gone old while the mind behind it never would, Johnby flipping through his wallet scraps, what he did when he got nervous. He flipped through the wallet while he stared gape-jawed at the dogs, gnawing those deer legs from hipbone to hoof. "I'm just as sorry as I can be," Mrs. Mitchell was saying, talking about the loss of the dogs. "Just as sorry as I can be." "If there's *any*thing," Mrs. Mitchell would say, "*any*thing we can do. And you know I always keep an eye out."

Matley fondled Guinea in his pocket, felt her quiver and live. You got to keep everything else in you soldered tight to make stay in place the loose part that wasn't. You got to grip. Matley looked at Johnby, shuffling through his wallet scraps, and Matley said to him, "You got a dog, Johnby?" and Johnby said, "I got a dog," he said. "I got a dog with a white eye turns red when you shine a flashlight in it," Johnby said. "You ever hearda that kinda dog?"

WHAT MADE IT so awful, if awfuller it could be, was Matley never got a chance to heal. Dogs just kept going, so right about the time the wound scabbed a little, he'd get another slash. He'd scab a little, then it would get knocked off, the deep gash deeper, while the eulogies piled higher in his head:

Cese. Something got hold his head when he was wee little. Matley never knew if it was a big dog or a bear or a panther or what it was, but it happened. Didn't kill him, but left him forever after wobbling around like a stroke victim with a stiff right front leg and the eye on the same side wouldn't open all the way, matter always crusted in that eye, although he didn't drool. Cese'd only eat soft food, canned, favored Luck's pinto beans when he could get them, yeah, Matley gave him the deluxe treatment, fed him on top an old chest of drawers against the propane tank so nobody could steal his supper. Cese went on September 9.

Leesburg. Called so because Matley found him dumped on a Virginia map that must have fallen out of the car by accident. Two pups on a map of Virginia and a crushed McDonald's bag, one pup dead, the other live, still teeny enough to suck Matley's little finger, and he decided on the name Leesburg over Big Mac, more dignity there. When that train first started running, Leesburg would storm the wheels, never fooled with the chickenfeed freight train, he knew where the trouble was. Fire himself at the wheels, snarling and barking, chasing and snap, and he scared some of the sightseers, who slammed their windows shut. Although a few threw food at him from the dining coach. Then one afternoon Matley was coming down the tracks after scavenging spikes, and he spotted a big wad of fur between two ties and thought, "That Missy's really shedding," because Missy was the longest-haired dog he had at the time, and this was a sizable hair hunk. But when he got home, here came Leesburg wagging a piece of bloody bone sheathed in a shredded tail. Train'd took it, bone sticking out that bloody hair like a half-shucked ear of corn, and Matley had to haul him off to Dr. Simmons, who'd docked it down like a Doberman. Leesburg went on the thirtieth of September.

That sweet, sweet Carmel. Bless her heart. Sure, most of them, you tender them and they'll tender you back, but Carmel, she'd not just reciprocate, she'd soak up the littlest love piece you gave her and return it tenfold power. She would. Swan her neck back and around, reach to Matley's ear with her tiny front teeth and air-nibble as for fleas. Love solidified in a dog suit. Sometimes Matley'd break down and buy her a little bacon, feed it to her with one hand while he rump-scratched with his other, oh, Carmel curling into U-shaped bliss. That was what happiness looked like, purity, good. Matley knew. Carmel disappeared five days after Cese.

Guinea he held even closer, that Guinea a solder, a plug, a glue. Guinea he could not lose. Now Guinea wasn't one he found, she came from up at Mitchell's, he got her as a pup. Her mother was a slick-skinned beaglish creature, real nervous little dog, Matley saw the whole litter. Two pups came out normal, two did not, seemed the genes leaked around in the mother's belly and swapped birth bags, ended up making one enormous lumbery, retarded pup, twice the size the normal ones, and then, like an afterbirth with fur and feet, came Guinea. A scrap of leftover animal material, looked more like a possum than a dog, and more like a guinea pig than either one, the scrap as bright as the big pup was dumb, yes, she was a genius if you factored in her being a dog, but Matley was the only one who'd take her. "Nobody else even believes what she *is*!" Mrs. Mitchell said. From the start, Guinea craved pockets, and that was when Matley started going about in sweatshirts with big muff-like pockets in front, cut-off sleeves for the heat, and little Guinea with him always, in the pocket sling, like a baby possum or a baby roo or, hell, like a baby baby. Guinea luxuring in those pockets. Pretending it was back before she was born and came out to realize there wasn't another creature like her on earth. Matley understood. Guinea he kept close.

COLUMBUS DAY WEEKEND. Nine dogs down. Matley collapsed in his lawn chair by the househole. Matley spent quite a bit of time in his lawn chair by the househole, didn't own a TV and didn't read much besides *Coonhound Bloodlines* and *Better Beagling* magazines, Matley would sit there and knuckle little Guinea's head. Fifteen years it had been since the house swam off, the household now slow-filling with the hardy plants, locust and cockaburs and briar, the old coal furnace a-crawl with poison ivy. Fifteen years, and across the tracks, what had been the most fertile piece of bottom in the valley, now smothered with the every-year-denser ragweed and stickweed and mock orange and puny too-many sycamore saplings. Matley could feel the loose part slipping, the emptiness pitting, he held Guinea close in his pocket. Way up the tracks, the tourist train, mumbling. Matley shifted a little and gritted his teeth.

The Mitchells had ridden the train once, when they had a special price for locals, they said the train people told a story for every sight. Seemed if there wasn't something real to tell, the train people made something up, and if there was something to tell, but it wasn't good enough, they stretched it. Said they told that the goats that had run off from Revie decades ago and gone feral up in the Trough were wild mountain goats, like you'd see out West. Said they told how George Washington's brother had stayed at the Puffinburger place and choked to death on a country ham sandwich. Said they pointed to this tree in the Malcolms' yard and told how a Confederate spy had been hanged from it, and Mr. Mitchell said, "That oak tree's old, but even if it was around a hundred and forty years ago, wasn't big enough to hang a spy. Not to mention around here they'd be more likely to hang a Yankee." Matley couldn't help wondering what they told on him, but he didn't ask. He'd never thought much about how his place looked until he had all the time these train people looking at him. He was afraid to ask. And he considered those mutt puppies, sleeping forever.

By that time, he'd made more than a few trips to Oaken Acre Estates despite himself (how old soft people could do such a thing). He'd sneak up in there and spy around, never following the new road on top the ridge, but by another way he knew. A path you picked up behind where the sheep barn used to be, the barn now collapsed into a quarter-acre sprawl of buckled rusty tin, but if you skirted it careful, leery of the snakes, there was a game path above the kudzu patch. He usually took four or five dogs, Hickory and Tick, they liked to travel, and Guinea in his pocket, of course Guinea went. They'd scramble up into the stand of woods between househole and subdivision, Matley scuttling the path on the edges of his feet, steep in there, his one leg higher than the other, steadying Guinea with one hand. Matley tended towards clumsy and worried about falling and squashing Guinea dead. This little piece of woods was still Matley's piece of woods, had been deeded to him, and Matley, when he moved on that little land, could feel beyond him, on his bare shoulders and arms, how far the land went before. Matley angled along, keen for any dog sign, dog sound, dog sight, yeah, even dead dog odor. But there was nothing to see, hear, stink.

Then they'd come out of the woods to the bottoms of the slopey backyards, shaley and dry with the struggling grass where the outsiders played at recreating those Washington suburbs they'd so desperately fled. Gated-off, security-systemed, empty yard after empty yard after empty, everything stripped down past stump, no sign of a living thing up in there, nor even a once-live thing dead. Hickory and Tick and whoever else had come would sniff, then piss, the lawns, been here, yeah, me, while Matley kept to the woods edge, kept to shelter, kept to shade. Guinea breathing under his chest. He had no idea where the pureblood-dog people lived, and they left no sign, no dogs, no pens, no fences, and although the ridge was full, of lookalike houses garages gazebos utility sheds a swimming pool, it was the emptiest place he'd ever felt. How you could kill a piece of ground without moving it anywhere. And Matley'd watch, he'd listen, he'd sniff best he could. But no dog sights, no dog sounds, no smells, and nothing to feel but his own sticky sweat. Matley'd never discover a thing.

Matley tensed in his lawn chair, nine dogs gone, Guinea in his pocket, Junior Junior cranky in his lap. He listened to that train creak and come, the train was coming and coming it was always coming and you would never get away. The train slunk around the turn and into sight, its bad music an earbeat, a gutbeat, *ta TA ta TA ta TA*, locomotive slow-pulling for the sightseers to better see the sights, and how did they explain Matley? Plopped between Winnebagos and household with some eighteen doghouses up his yard. How did he fit into this land that time forgot? *ta TA ta TA ta TA*, the beat when it passed the joints in the rails, and the *screee* sound over the rail beat, and even over top that, a squealing, that ear-twisting song, a sorry mean ear-paining song. Starers shouldered up in open cars with cameras bouncing off golf-shirted bellies, and from the enclosed cars, some would wave. They would only wave if they were behind glass. And Matley would never wave back.

HE COMES TO know. In the dream, he is a younger man than young he ever was, younger than he was born, and the hillside he hell-heaves, it's hill without end. The leaves loud under snow crust, his boots busting, ground cracking, the whole earth moanering, and him, him helling. Snow lying in dapples, mottles, over hillside, ridgeside, dog-marked like that, saddles, white snow saddles, see, his side seizing, breath in a blade, and the dog. Who he dream-knows is a girl dog, he knows that, the dog haunch-sat waiting pant, pant, pant. His hill pant, her dog pant, the blade in his ribs, who pants? say good dog "good dog" good, him helling and the dog roped leashed tethered to a cat-faced red oak black against the snow blank, dog a darker white than the snow white and. He cannot ever reach her.

EVENTUALLY IT TRINKLED down to them in town. A few had seen. The fuel oil man. The UPS. Gilbert who drove the school bus to the turnaround where the road went from gravel to dirt. Dog Man blundering in bushes, whistling and yodeling some chint-chant dog-call, when few people besides the Mitchells had ever heard Muttie speak beyond shopping grunts. Of course, there were the lost ads, too, and although Matley wouldn't spend the extra dollar to print his name, just put a phone number there, well, the swifter ones put it together for those who were slow. Then somebody cornered Mr. Mitchell in the Super Fresh, and he confirmed it, yeah, they were vanishing off, and right away the story went around that Muttie was down twenty-seven dogs to a lean forty-eight. The UPS driver said he didn't think those old people out in Oaken Acre Estates were hard enough for such a slaughter, but then somebody pointed out the possibilities of poison, "people like that, scared of guns, they'll just use poison," a quiet violence you didn't have to see or touch. Yeah. A few speculated that the dogs just wised up, figured out Cat was crazy and left, and others blamed it on out-of-work chicken catchers from Hardy County. One (it was Mr. Puffinburger, he didn't appreciate the ham sandwich story) suspected the train people. Who knew to what lengths they'd go, Mr. Puffinburger said, the househole, the campers, the doghouses and Mr. Hound, that scenery so out of line with the presentation, so far from the scheme of decoration. Who knew how they might fix ole Beagle Boy and his colony of dog. He'd heard they tried to organize the 4-H-ers for a big trash cleanup. Then a sizable and committed contingent swore Matley had done it himself and ate em, and afterwards either forgot about it or was trying to trick people into pity: "I wouldn't put anything past that boy."

"I wouldn't, either, now. He's right, buddy. Buddy, he. is. right."

"Hell, they were all of them crazy, you could see it in their eyes."

"And I heard Charles lives out in Washington State now, but he won't work. Say he sits around all day in a toolshed reading up on the Indians."

"Well," the last one said. "People are different."

MATLEY STANDING AT his little sink washing up supper dishes, skillet-sized pancakes and gravy from a can. His dogs have took up a dusk-time song. An I'm gonna bark because I just want to song, a song different from an I'm barking at something I wanna catch song or I'm barking at somebody trying to sneak up song or I'm howling because I catch a contagion of the volunteer fire department siren-wailing different from I'm barking at a trainful of gawkers song. A sad sad song. The loose parts in him. Daylight puts a little hold down on it, but with the dark, nothing tamps it, you never know. You got to hold tight. He'd seen Johnby again that morning, humping along through the ditch by the road, and now, behind his eyes, crept Johnby, hulking and hunching to the time of the song. Dogs sought Johnby because Johnby wasn't one to bathe much and dogs liked to pull in his scents, Johnby could no doubt bait dogs to him, Matley is thinking. The way Johnby's lip would lift and twitch. Muscles in a dead snake moving. Tic.

Matley stepped out, pulled Guinea from his pocket, and took a look. As sometimes happened, for a second he was surprised to see her tail. The dog song made a fog around them, from sad to eerie, Matley heard the music go, while Matley counted those dog voices, one two three to twelve. Matley hollowing under his heart (the part slipping), the fear pimpling his skin, and then he called, moany, a whisper in his head: *come out come out come out come out.*

He breathed the odor the place made of an evening, a brew of dropping temperature, darkness, and househole seep. A familiar odor. The odor of how things fail. Odor of ruin in progress, of must and stale hay, spoiling silage, familiar, and mildew and rotting wood and flaked paint; twenty-year-old manure, stagnant water, decaying animal hides, odor of the househole and what falls in it, the loss smell, familiar, the odor of the inside of his head. And Matley stroked little Guinea, in full dark now, the dog song dimming, and he heard Mrs. Mitchell again ("but I never did want to have more than two or three"), the not-question she used to ask, him not thinking directly on it, but thinking under thinking's place, and he knows if you get a good one, you can feel their spirits in them from several feet away, right under their fur, glassy and clear and dew-grass smelling. If you get a good one. You can feel it. No blurriness to the spirit of a dog, no haze, they're unpolluted by the thinking, by memories, by motives, you can feel that spirit raw, naked bare against your own. And dogs are themselves and aren't nothing else, just there they are, full in their skins and moving on the world. Like they came right out of it, which they did, which people did, too, but then people forget, while dogs never do. And when Matley was very young he used to think, if you love them hard enough, they might turn into people, but then he grew up a little and knew, what good would that be? So then he started wishing, if you loved one hard enough, it might speak to you. But then he grew up even more and knew that wasn't good either, unless they spoke dog, and not just dog language, but dog ideas, things people'd never thought before in sounds people'd never heard, Matley knew. And Matley had studied the way a dog loved, the ones that had it in them to love right, it was true, not every dog did, but the ones that loved right, Matley stroking, cup, cradle, and hold, gaze in dog eyes, the gentle passing. Back and forth, enter and return, the gentle passing, passing between them, and Matley saw this love surpass what they preached at church, surpass any romance he'd heard of or seen, surpass motherlove loverlove babylove, he saw that doglove simple. Solid. And absolutely clear. Good dog. Good dog, now. Good. Good.

MEREDITH. WAS JUST a couple weeks shy of dropping her pups, no mystery there, she was puffed out like a nail keg, and who in their right mind would steal a pregnant lab-Dalmatian mix? It could only be because they were killing them, if Matley'd ever doubted that, which he had. Which he'd had to. Meredith'd been a little on the unbrightish side, it was true, had fallen into the household more than once in broad day, the spots on her head had soaked through and affected her brain, but still. And it was her first litter, might have made some nice pups, further you got from the purebloods, Matley had learned, better off you'll be. Meredith went on October 17.

Muddy Gut. A black boy with a soft gold belly, and gold hair sprouting around his ears like broom sedge, soft grasses like that, he had the heaviest and most beautiful coat on the place, but the coat's beauty the world constantly marred, in envy or spite. Muddy Gut drew burrs, beggar's lice, devil's pitchforks, ticks, and Matley'd work tirelessly at the clobbed-up fur, using an old currycomb, his own hairbrush, a fork. Muddy Gut patient and sad, aware of his glory he could not keep, while Matley held a match to a tick's behind until it pulled out its head to see what was wrong. A constant grooming Matley lavished over Muddy Gut, Matley forever untangling that lovely spoiled fur, oh sad sullied Muddy, dog tears bright in his deep gold eyes. Muddy Gut went on October 21.

Junior Junior. Matley'd known it was bound to happen, Ray Junior or Junior Junior one. Although they were both a bit ill tempered, they were different from the rest, they were Raymond descendants several generations down. Junior Junior was Ray Junior's son, and Ray Junior was mothered by a dog across the river called Ray Ray, and Ray Ray,

Mr. Mitchell swore, was fathered by the original Raymond. In Junior Junior there was Raymond resemblance, well, a little anyway, in temperament for sure, and Matley didn't stop to think too hard about how a dog as inert as Raymond might swim the river to sow his oats. Raymond was the dog who came when Matley could no longer make the toy dogs live and who stayed until after the flood, and for a long time, he was the only dog Matley had to love. They'd found Raymond during a Sunday dinner at Mrs. Fox's Homestead Restaurant when Matley had stretched out his leg and hit something soft under the table, which surprised him. Was a big black dog, bloodied around his head, and come to find out it was a stray Mrs. Fox had been keeping for a few weeks, he'd been hit out on 50 that very morning and had holed up under the table to heal himself. Later, Revie liked to tell, "Well, you started begging and carrying on about this hit dog, and Mrs. Fox gave him up fast—I don't believe she much wanted to fool with him anyway—and here he's laid ever since, hateful and stubborn and foul-smelling. Then after we got done eating, Mrs. Fox came out of the kitchen, and she looked at our plates, and she said, 'You would of thought finding that hit dog under your table would of put a damper on your appetites. But I see it didn't!' It was a compliment to her cooking, you see." Junior Junior was Raymond's great-great-grandson, and he disappeared on Halloween.

Matley in the bunk at night. He'd wake without the knowledge. He'd lose the loss in his sleep, and the moments right after waking were the worst he'd ever have: finding the loss again and freshly knowing. The black surge over his head, hot wash of saw-sided pain, then the bottom would drop out. Raw socket. Through the weeks, the loss rolling, compounding, just when he'd think it couldn't get worse, think a body couldn't hold more hurt, another dog would go, the loss an infinity inside him. Like how many times you can bisect a line. They call it heartbreak, but not Matley, Matley learned it was not that clean, nowhere near that quick, he learned it was a heartgrating, this forever loss in slow motion, forever loss without diminishment of loss, without recession, without ease, the grating. And Matley having had in him always the love, it pulsing, his whole life, reaching, for a big enough object to hold this love, back long before this crippling mess, he reached, and now, the only end for that love he'd ever found being taken from him, too, and what to do with this love? Pummeling at air. Reaching, where to put this throat-stobbing surge, where, what? the beloved grating away. His spirit in his chest a single wing that opens and folds, opens and folds. Closing on nothing. Nothing there. And no, he says, no, he says, no, he says, no.

COME NOVEMBER, MATLEY was still running his ads, and he got a call from a woman out at Shanks, and though he doubted a dog of his would travel that far, he went anyway. The month was overly warm, seasons misplaced like they'd got in recent years, and coming home right around dusk, he crested High Boy with his windows half-down. At first, he wasn't paying much mind to anything except rattling the Chevette over that rutty road, only certain ways you could take the road without tearing off the muffler. But suddenly it came to him he didn't see no dogs. No dogs lounging around their houses, and no dogs prancing out to meet him. No dogs squirting out the far corners of the clearings at the sound of the car, even though it was dog-feeding time. No Guinea under the camper, no Hickory and Tick fighting over stripped-down deer legs, no welcome-home dog bustle. Not a dog on the place. None.

A panic began in the back of Matley's belly. Fizzing. He pushed it down by holding his breath. He parked the car, swung out slow, and when he stood up (hold on tight) there between the car seat and door, he felt his parts loosen. A rush of opening inside. He panic-scanned Winnebago and househole, sunken barns and swaying sheds, his head cocked to listen. Doghouses, tracks, bottom, and trees, his eyes spinning, a vacuum coring his chest, and then he heard himself holler. He hollered "Here!" and he hollered "Come!" and he hollered "Yah! Yah! Yah!" still swiveling his head to take in every place. Him hollering "Here Fella! Tick, C'mon now! Yah, Big Girl, Yah," his voice squalling higher while the loose part slipped. Matley hollered, and then he screamed, he clapped and hooed, he whistled until his mouth dried up. And then, from the direction of the sheep barn, way up the hill, he spied the shape of Guinea.

Little Guinea, gusting over the ground like a blown plastic bag. Matley ran to meet her. Guinea, talking and crying in her little Guinea voice, shuttling hysterical around his shins and trying to jump, and Matley scooped her up and in his pocket, stroking and trembling, and there, Guinea. There. And once she stilled, and he stilled, Matley heard the other.

Dog cries at a distance. Not steady, not belling or chopping, not like something trailed or treed. No, this song was a dissonant song. Out of beat and out of tune. A snarling brutal song.

Matley wheeled. He charged up the pasture to the sheep barn there, grass tearing under his boots. He leaned into the path towards the subdivision, despite dark fast dropping and him with no light. He pounded that game path crazy, land tilted under his feet, his sight swinging in the unfocus of darkened trees, and the one hand held Guinea while the dead leaves roared. He was slipping and catching his balance, he was leaping logs when he had to, his legs bendy and the pinwheel of his head, and the parts inside him, unsoldering fast, he could feel his insides spilling out of him, Matley could no longer grip, he was falling. This land, this land under him, you got to grip, tight, Guinea crying, and now, over top the dry leaves' shout, he heard not only yelping, but nipping and growling and brush cracking, and Matley was close.

It was then that it came to him. He dreamed the dream end awake. Him helling up that endless hillslope, but the slope finally ends, and he sees the white dog tree-tied ear-cocked patient waiting, but still, Matley knows, something not right he can't tell. Black trees unplummetting out of white snow skiff, and Matley helling. Him helling. Him. Helling. He reaches, at last he reaches her, a nightmare rainbow's end, and he's known all along what he has to do, he thrusts his hand behind her to unleash her, free her, and then he understands, sees: behind the live dog front, she is bone. Her front part, her skin and face, a dog mask, body mask, and behind that, the not right he's always sensed but could not see, bone, and not even skeleton bone, but chunky bone, crumbled and granular and fragrant, the blood globbed up in chunks and clots, dry like snow cold day skiff and Matley moaning, he'd broke free of the woods and into a little clearing below the subdivision, ground rampant with sumac and dormant honeysuckle and grape and briar. It truly darkening now, and the way it's harder to see in near dark than it is in full dark, how your eyes don't know what to do with it, and Matley was stopped, trembling, loose, but he could hear. A house-sized mass of brush, a huge tangle of it making like a hill itself, dense looped and layered, crowned with the burgundy sumac spears. That whole clump a-sound with dog, and Matley felt himself tore raw inside, the flesh strips in him, and Matley started to yell.

He stood at a short distance and yelled at them to come out, come out of there, he knew inside himself not to dare go in, he knew before seeing what he couldn't bear to see. But nary a dog so much as poked its head out and looked at Matley, he could hear them snarling, hear bones cracking, see the brush rattle and sway, but to the dogs Matley wasn't there, and then he smelled it. Now the smell of it curled to him on that weird warm wind, as it had no doubt curled down to the household and lured the dogs up, and he was screaming now, his voice scraping skin off his throat, ripping, and Matley, with the single ounce of gentle still left in his hand, pulled out Guinea and set her down. Then he stooped and plunged in.

Now he was with them, blundering through this confusion of plant, and he could see his dogs, saw them down through vine branch and briar. Louise, the biggest, hunkered over and tearing at it, growling if another dog got close, she held her ground, and Ray Junior writhing in it on her back, and Honey lavering his neck in dried guts. Big Girl drawn off to the side crunching spine, while Hickory and Tick battled over a big chunk, rared up on their hind legs and wrestling with their fronts, and Matley pitched deeper, thorns tearing his hands. Matley tangled in vine and slim trunk, the sumac tips, that odor gusting all over his head, and he reached for Tick's tail to break up the fight. But when he touched Tick, Tick turned on him. Tick spun around gone in his eyes, and he drew back his lips on Matley and he bared his teeth to bite, and Matley, his heart cleaved in half, dropped the tail and sprung back. And the moment he did, he saw what he'd been terrified he'd see all along. Or did he see? A sodden collar still buckled around a rotting neck, did he? The live dogs eating the dead dogs there, what he'd suspected horrified all along, did he? And then Matley was whacking, flailing, windmilling looney, beating with his hands and arms and feet and legs the live dogs off the dead things because he had nothing else to beat with, he was not even screaming any longer, he was beyond sound, Matley beyond himself, Matley reeling, dropping dropped down.

Until Guinea was there. Against him. Hurtling up to be held. And Matley took her, did hold her. He stroked her long guinea hair, whispering, good girl, Guinea. Good.

Matley stood in the midst of the slaughter, shaking and panting, palming little Guinea's head. Most of the beat dogs had slunk off a ways to wait, but the bolder ones were already sneaking back. And finally Matley slowed enough, he was spent enough, to squint again through the dim and gradual understand.

There were no collars there.

Slowly.

These colors of fur, these shapes and sizes of bones. Were not dogs. No.

Groundhogs, squirrels, possums, deer.

Then he felt something and turned and saw: Johnby crouched in the dead grass, rifle stock stabbed in the ground and the barrel grooving his cheek. Johnby was watching.

SOMEHOW IT GOT going around in town that it had been a pile of dead dogs, and some said it served Muttie right, that many dogs should be illegal anyway. But others felt sad. Still other people had heard it was just a bunch of dead animals that ole Johnby had collected, lord knows if he'd even shot them, was the gun loaded? His family said not; could have been roadkill. Then there were the poison believers, claimed it was wild animals and dogs both, poisoned by the retirees in Oaken Acre Estates, and Bill Bates swore his brother-in-law'd been hired by the imports to gather a mess of carcasses and burn em up in a brush pile, he just hadn't got to the fire yet. Mr. Puffinburger held his ground, he felt vindicated, at least to himself, because this here was the lengths to which those train people would go, this here was how far they'd alter the landscape to suit themselves. What no one was ever certain about was just how many'd been lost. Were they all gone? had any come back? was he finding new ones? how many were out there now? Fred at the feed store reported that Muttie wasn't buying any dog food, but the UPS truck had spied him along a creek bed with a dog galloping to him in some hillbilly Lassie-come-home.

Despite all the rumors, it must be said that after that, they didn't talk about Dog Man much anymore. Even for the skeptics and the critics, the subject of Matley lost its fun. And they still saw Muttie, although he came into town less often now, and when they did see him, they looked more closely, and a few even sidled up to him in the store in case he would speak. But the dogless Matley, to all appearances, was exactly like the dogful one.

THESE DAYS, SOME mornings, in the lost-dog aftermath, Matley wakes in his camper having forgot the place, the year, his age. He's always had such spells occasionally, losses of space and time, but now it's more than ever. Even though when he was a kid, Mom Revie'd only allow one live dog at a time and never inside, they did have for some years a real dog named Blanchey, some kind of wiener-beagle mix. And now, these mornings, when Matley wakes, believing himself eight in the flood-gone house, he hears Mom Revie's dog-calling song.

Oh, the way that woman could call a dog, it was bluegrass operatic. "Heeeeeere, Blanchey! Heeeeeere, Blanchey, Blanchey, Blanchey," she'd yodel off the back porch, the "here" pulled taut to eight solid seconds, the "Blanchey" a squeaky two-beat yip. Then "You, Blanchey! C'mere, girl! 'mon!" fall from high-octave "here's" to a businesslike burr, and when Blanchey'd still not come, Revie'd switch from cajole to command. "Yah, Blanchey, Yah! Yah! Yah! Yah!" a belly-deep bass; while the "here's" seduced, the "yah's" insist, oh, it plunged down your ear and shivered your blood, ole Mom Revie's dog-calling song. And for some minutes, Matley lets himself hover in that time, he just lies abed and pleasures in the tones. Until she cuts loose in frustration with a two-string riff—"comeoutcomeoutcomeoutcomeout"—rapid banjo plinkplunk wild, and Matley wakes enough to know ain't no dogs coming. To remember all the dogs are gone but one.

He crawls out of the bunk and hobbles outside. Guinea pokes her head from his pocket, doesn't like what she sniffs, pulls back in. It is March, the train season is long over, but Matley hears it anyway. Hears it coming closer, moaning and sagging like it's about to split. Hears the haunty music that train plays, haunty like a tawdry carnival ride. Train moving slow and overfull, passing the joints in the rails, beat beat, and the *scree* sound over the railbeat, he hears it shriek-squeal over steel. And Matley stands there between household and Winnebago, the morning without fog and the air like glass, and he understands he is blighted landscape. He is disruption of scenery. Understands he is the last one left, and nothing but a sight. A sight. Sight, wheel on rail click it on home, Sight. Sight. Sight. Then Matley does not hear a thing.

COOP

THEY BUNKED IN old chicken houses jammed with older iron beds, lumpy-ticked, stained, summers and summers of homesick child urine, then the rat and the swallow dirt all empty winter. The beds pressed so tight the girls who brought suitcases had to sleep with them, so tight Carly could shift an elbow and touch the girl beside her. Feel the girl's night breath on her own cheek. Carly held her pee as long as she could before she dared the dark walk down the splintery floor past forty-three sleepers and their forty-three dreams. After, kneeling on her bed, she peered at the cousins from Honeyvine heaped alongside her. Found the face of the littlest one and wondered again about what the bigger ones said.

The camp was six miles off the highway down a dirt road, an old farm donated to the county by a dead bachelor. School buses carried them there, the road so narrow, the woods so close, in places leaves crushed against the windows. It was a free camp for girls, with sweaty surplus cheese in the dining hall and gallon tins of peanuts. The milk always this side of turning, and the raisins. Some girls brought their things in plastic bags, and some brought nothing at all, and behind the ruined piano on the dining hall porch were piled big garbage bags of donated clothes. The littlest Honeyvine found an ankle-length football jersey she wore like a gown until it tripped her in a kickball game, pitching her on her face. Carly watched her struggling there. Live thing in a sack. And a girl named Izzie came every year, a retarded kid with a finger missing, hard to tell if it was the second or third. She'd lie with her head at the foot of the bed and seize through the bars at the little girls passing. And if she was mad at somebody, which she generally was, she'd throw that stump like a middle finger. Only the finger wasn't there.

Community Action had a hard time recruiting counselors, but for the three years Carly had come, they'd always got Debbie and Royal. Both had been campers themselves at one time, and Debbie was the darker, her skin pillowy, Carly saw, calling you to touch it. Like it needed your finger pressed into it. But then, underneath, Carly understood, a hardness harder than bone. Royal was leaner, lighter, a high fine freckled, berries or seeds, her beauty more boy than Deb's beauty was. They were a kind of girl Carly had never seen outside of camp, you felt it the second they stepped off the bus, and you could not help but watch them. Carly watched.

Mrs. Junkins, the camp director who was often tired, always called Debbie and Royal her right-hand women. Mrs. Junkins, with her plum-mottled calves under floppy dresses, and how the hug-thirsty little ones would climb all over her, poking in her pockets, palming her cheeks. How the older ones would have to remind her about the next thing on the schedule. That year, though, Mrs. Junkins didn't come. *Died*, the older girls whispered. Just plain wore out, said the cook. Instead, they brought in a woman called Dr. Maxine from someplace else, Carly heard that right away in her voice. And the second thing Carly noticed was how she smiled, tight, all the time over nothing. Like she knew something to smile about none of them ever would.

That year, Carly wasn't in Debbie and Royal's bunkhouse. Her coop's counselors were 4-H volunteers, motherly, placid. She landed in a bed beside that bunch from up in Honeyvine, their first time at camp, and sisters or cousins they all claimed to be. They pushed their beds even closer and puppy-slept in a pile. They admitted they had no running water in their Honeyvine houses, and right away, they showered every chance they got, their hair all the time wet and the parts in it crooked. Them streaming naked, two, three, at a time in those slimy concrete stalls, and it was there Carly saw, the first afternoon, how the littlest had a caved place in her chest. Like someone had struck a rock to her wishbone.

"Her," one of the older Honeyvines said when she caught Carly looking, "she'll leave every night."

Carly looked back into the Honeyvine's glasses. Saw two of her own face. The campers were forbidden to cross the bunkhouse stoop after lights out.

"She won't use the door," the Honeyvine said.

Carly stretched her borrowed garment bag along the edge of her mattress. She slept with the bag between her and them.

Turned out Dr. Maxine was not just a doctor, but a lifeguard, too, and all day long she wore a little robe over a strange bathing suit of jagged colors, her navy-veined thighs something any woman Carly'd ever known would have scrambled to cover up. When Debbie and Royal started to lead the songs at assembly, Dr. Maxine motioned them back to their seats with a smile and led the songs herself, swaying at her knees and strumming a guitar, her voice a high pinch in her nose. After crafts, Dr. Maxine asked all the girls to stay at the long tables, and then she passed out multiple-choice questions and number two pencils. *This*, she promised, *is not a test.* When I grow up, I want to A, B, C, D. The number of people who live in my house is A, B, C, D. *There are no right answers*, Dr. Maxine assured. While they filled ovals, Dr. Maxine strode around behind them and patted girls' shoulders with a stiff hand. She lifted a strand of Izzie's hair. Carly watched Izzie's eyes flare, her neck stiffen. But Izzie kept her stump in her fist.

The harder it was to like Dr. Maxine, the harder Carly watched Debbie and Royal. Royal's sharp white hair, prickly even in its length, and the tight bow of her back when she bent down to pull socks over long leg muscles. Debbie's tough quieter, it turned in while Royal's turned out, and how little she smiled. How little she ever smiled, so when she did smile at you. When she did. The tough girls Carly had seen outside of camp were a scrabbling, desperate, seedy tough, a tough that made you shamed or scared. This tough made you want to be. And everybody watched them. The little girls scribbling notes on the backs of mimeographed sheets they stole from Vespers, True Friends Always and check the box, will you be my best? The fourteen-year-olds, after lights out, whispering, and the middle girls, like Carly, shy and achy, changing their underwear under the covers. They watched.

It was swimming they all looked forward to the most, the release into cool and clean blue water, and at first, even Dr. Maxine on her lifeguard throne could not dampen the escape. Girls burst squealing through the gate, the bravest cannonballing off the sides, while the ones who couldn't swim, like Carly, dropped into the shallow end, flung open their arms and pretended, then saved themselves with their feet. Carly stood still a minute, chin lifted, and scanned the deep end, where Royal's body shimmer-ran through water. Carly's eyes following, her heart knocking, sun flash skin, water, skin, water, which? moving. That's, Carly thought, why they call her Royal.

Then Royal hauled herself up the ladder, calling over her shoulder to Debbie, a dark head only. Carly hung on the shallow-end side, watching through splash and spray. Royal doubled on herself on the ladder, halter top to knees, water sluicing off the arc of her back. Royal climbed out, pounded her cocked head to drive water out her ear, and sauntered towards the shallow end. The nonswimmers shrieked.

Royal dropped into the middle of them, while the small ones reached, famished for touch, and Royal picked a couple up, then chose a tiny one and lifted her lengthwise in water. Royal steadied her, one hand on her back and the other hand underneath, Royal slid her, balanced her, the others hollering, look, look, you can swim, my turn! my turn! Then the second chosen one, lifted, the small of her back, her stomach, her swimming between Royal's two big hands.

Carly, too old to be picked, felt someone else watching Royal. Carly swung her head. Dr. Maxine in the lifeguard chair, her whistle squeezed between her fingers, fingers poised between her breasts. Then the littlest Honeyvine was right there. Shivering on the pool edge, her feet almost on Carly's hands, water streaming down to make a puddle like a shadow at her feet. Her bathing suit drooped around her rock-struck ribs, the tiny nipples pecking out. She left every night, they all said it. She didn't use windows, didn't use doors. Carly pushed off to run away through water, the weight of it against her a quicksand dream.

That was Wednesday. Soon the black girls from Piedmont were calling Dr. Maxine Mrs. Reagan because of all the speeches she made. Although she'd said she was a doctor, when Rhonda Funkhouser sprained her ankle, it was the cook had to wrap it. That night at campfire, a puny nick in the heavy heavy woods, Dr. Maxine and her guitar led the songs again, Izzie howling the refrains, while Royal sat on the front bleacher with a stick in her hand, drilling the end into ground. "Amazing Grace" and "Almost Heaven," and what did Dr. Maxine know of Jesus and West Virginia? Debbie crouched a few girls away from Carly where Carly could see only the waves of her hair. Carly had overheard the older girls before Vespers, something about Dr. Maxine and Royal and the pool, and the darkness rose behind Carly like a hood. After the fire, the campers walked in scattered clumps back to the coops, the Honeyvines moving in a huddle under a shared blanket, Carly at their edge, near enough but far enough. Overhead, ridges drew closer together. *You don't touch them there.* That's what the big girls had whispered Dr. Maxine said.

Maybe the last night would have gone differently if nobody had told on the Honeyvine girls. Carly's bunkhouse was the one the boys used when boys came, and on Thursday morning, the two littlest Honeyvines washed their hair in a urinal, just seeing they were shiny things, porcelain and white. Somehow Dr. Maxine heard, and when she did, she blew her whistle and assembled the whole camp into that bathroom and gave them a lesson on what urinals were. Then she went further.

Smiling, she told a 4-H girl to fetch a washcloth, and when the girl got back, Dr. Maxine used her as a model for how to take a proper shower. Dr. Maxine instructing the counselor, fully clothed, to scrape the soap in the washcloth, then run the washcloth over different body parts. The milk-blue counselor, obedient, shamed horror in her rabbit eyes, rubbed the dry washcloth under her arms, and Carly's stomach curled. In the front of the crowd leaned the Honeyvines. Shadows like thumb-pressed bruises under their eyes.

After lunch, the Piedmont girls, lounging on top a picnic table, smoothing lotion in their knees, started telling about the special soap.

Got in that robe pocket a plastic box with a germ-killer soap, said one.

It's green, said another.

Every time she gets too close to one of us, sneaks back in her cabin and scrubs herself.

Carly remembered the feel of Dr. Maxine's hand on her upper arm at lunch the day before.

Then it was afternoon rest period, everyone back in their coops. The aroma of antiperspirant over teenage girl sweat, and Izzie lying in wait like some lunatic zoo animal, working terrible her green-apple gum. At the end of the building, the oldest girls held counsel on three pushed-together beds, their voices like bees, each painting all twenty nails the color of blood. Carly slid off her bed. Slipped towards that climate of tampons and turquoise eye shadow, the bed bars cool in Carly's hands. If Izzie really wanted to scare you, she'd sit and stroke her stub. Shaping the air where the finger was not. Carly sidled up on the older girls before they could see. Heard something dirty about Dr. Maxine. Something about Debbie and Royal she couldn't quite make out.

Carly. How old are you?

'Leven.

Go on. You're too young to hear this.

Back beside Carly's bed, the Honeyvines knelt on their mattresses in a train and brushed each other's long slick hair, that hair no color at all but dark.

"Guess where she went last night?" The one with the glasses pushed them back up her nose.

Carly shook her head. "What do you mean?"

"She don't just have dreams," the glasses said. "She is one."

Carly climbed onto her own bed and pulled her sleeping bag around her shoulders. Cowled it over her head.

After supper, Carly and the next-to-the-biggest Honeyvine leaned against the propane tank across from the director's cabin. The Honeyvine pulling petals off a daisy in a he-loves-me, he-loves-me-not, the mildest rise in her tube top where the breasts would come. Then Debbie and Royal burst out of Dr. Maxine's cabin door, stumbled down the steps, Royal bent forward with her hands fisted, her skin blaring red from her forehead to her chest, and when Debbie touched her shoulder, Royal swung. But it wasn't at Deb.

Then Carly felt herself creeping. Felt herself slinking past the cabin steps, into the ivy and weeds strangling up the cabin wall. Stealthing back to where she knew the director's bathroom would be, and although the window was above her head, Carly could hear the sink. It gushing hard, and the squeal in the pipes when the spigots turned high, and Carly saw the soap. A green turning in Dr. Maxine's hands. But then she was just against the propane tank again, the Honeyvine still beside her mumbling love and not. Carly only brave enough to make the trip in her head.

It was tradition to stay up late that last night and have a dance. "We Will Rock You" and the Bee Gees and "Desperado." The slow songs, little girls dancing with little girls, Izzie dancing with herself, and the Honeyvines wallflowered up in the folding chairs. But it was the fast songs that counted. Knee-pitching, arm-cocking, they danced like they were skewered on wires, frantic windup and hurtle their bodies just short of relief, their bangs matting on their foreheads and kids punching each other in the water fountain line. Royal and Debbie danced with a half-dozen girls at a time, more girls circling off those girls like moons off moons, they hammered the floor with the soles of their feet like they could make the building split. Until, drenched, Carly threw herself outside, felt the night air on her, and twanged in her chest.

Not long after Dr. Maxine's lights-out whistle, they heard a strange noise not from the woods. Carly raised up on her elbows to listen. Dozens of dull ringings, muffled, and girls started to murmur. At least one started to cry. But not until the howling started did Carly understand what the ringing was: the beating of sticks on bed-frame bars. Now girls surged to the door to see, Carly swept along, the howls an orange funneling, a come-here and a fright, and Carly heard them not people, people, not people, people, and all along, the underbeat of sticks on bars. Big girls, the counselors, too, jammed the doorway, suspended over the stoop they were forbidden to cross, and a couple littlest kids crawled through their legs to see, but Carly could not. Izzie plunged up and down on her mattress, intent and twirling, her eyes run off someplace else. Carly wheeled back to her bed and hung out the window, the Honeyvines at her heels, *what? what? what?* and then she saw the orange flame in the howling, the flame tattered and thready and thin. The girls throbbed in the doorway, four or five deep, the girls throbbing, the howl a blood-orange come-here spiral, the girls piled, arms thrown across backs, heads over shoulders, and everyone quivering against the rule. Throbbing. They never broke it.

Come morning, they found that the other coop had tried to burn their bunkhouse down. Got it going with toilet paper, empty half-pint milk cartons, and a poster of Peter Frampton. It didn't amount to much, though, but a couple scorched mattresses and a whole lot of hollering. But Debbie and Royal were gone. Dr. Maxine, no longer smiling, ordered everyone to sit cross-legged in a pack on the front field while the sheriff's department searched the woods. They got Debbie by noon, but when the school buses showed up at 2:30 to take the campers home, Royal was still missing.

It was an hour later, on the bus, most kids nodding off after all the excitement, that the littlest Honeyvine told. She was curled up in the lap of a bigger Honeyvine and all of them such a tangle, arms, legs, heads, you couldn't tell what or whose. But she told.

Told how she'd been there, around 4 AM, when Royal fell asleep in wet grass. Told how she stepped through a door into Royal's head, then she felt a changing. Said she watched her own hands stiffen and web, felt her back hump. Saw the hair on her arms glisten into scale. Then she flashed up on her tail, struck out with a fin. She punctured the dream, and she fish-flew away.

THE FOLLOWING

I CROSSED THE PARKING lot in one of those Northwest drizzles so fine I could see it only as beads on my sleeve. Ducked into the cedars, the hemlocks and firs, of the forty-acre city park where I went almost daily for its little bit of raw. Once I got under those limbs, got my feet off asphalt and on dirt, I knew now I was not just knowing, but following. I knew it was carrying me, the sweet eerie draw. I knew, too, what lay at its end, so that the following, the finding, at least when I was in the middle of it, had nothing to do with me and had nothing at stake. And if for a second my head broke in and a stake did rise, the lightness of the following extinguished it like wind on a match.

That was the March day before I flew to Pittsburgh. I'd felt it as soon as I stepped out of the car. The knowing that was not mind-knowing, that had been the single knowing I could remember before this other knowing had arrived six months before. The new knowing came through my chest and I could describe only in paradox: weightless presence. Silent thrumming. Untethered balance. And if I tried to name the emotion of the knowing, the closest I could come was paradox again. Uncharged euphoria. Ecstasy without edge.

Now I was clipping along a muddy side path, scrambling over trees fresh-fallen from the weekend storm. Straddling puddles as wide as the trail, and once, on a rain-slicked slope, my right boot skidded, but I did not fall, buoyed by the blunt bliss of the following. I stopped under a leafless big-leaf maple, the moss humps along it like blind animal heads, and I knew to veer onto an even lesser-used trail. Although arced licorice ferns wet me to my chest, still, when earlier than I expected, the over-here tugged, I nearly held back, not wanting the feel of the following finished so soon.

But I did leave the trail. Plunged into drenched salal, English ivy, Oregon grape. It led me around a nurse log high as my waist, pushing up seedlings, sloughing off rot. And, finally, with one hand in the chill of the log's soaked moss, I spotted what I'd known all along. The tiny bones of a bird. Its skeleton intact as a cage.

At the confirmation, as always, my eyes filled with tears. And just as the chest-knowing was something unknown to me before this year, these tears were, too. Just as this felt more right to me than anything had in my life, yet lacked sharp emotion, these tears were peculiarly neutral, too. After the tears, as always, the spontaneous upgush of gratitude, not exactly for the bone, but for the reassurance that the following had once again been right. And on the heels of the gratitude—this hardest of all for me to accept, to understand, yet also less ambiguous than anything else—love.

I touched the skeleton on the log with one finger. I held my finger there for a while. Then I waded back through the brush and towards the main path, the knowing already asleep again, but leaving an exquisite equilibrium as its trace. Still, later that night, balance unsettled, elation dissolved, I wondered again. What did it mean to always find bone at the end?

FOR SEVEN MONTHS now in this way, I'd been finding them. The knowing and following given me right after I lost more at one time than I'd lost in my life. Last June, I'd been laid off just weeks after I'd had to put down my old lab-collie mix, Shea. Shea's death nearly coincided with the end of a five-year relationship, and while losing Shea hurt sharper, I was forty-eight, and that I'd blundered at love again ignited a scarier grief.

That same spring my life was being dismantled, BP annihilated the Gulf and a coal company with a criminal environmental record slaughtered twenty-nine miners in the hills not far from where I'd lived as a child. These two disasters, of course, just the latest and most spectacular of what I shorthand-called the Great Losses of These Times—the atmosphere boiling, the Arctic thawing, oceans rising, species dying—and on my most desolate days, no matter how my conscience recoiled, I couldn't help but see my own disintegration as a microcosm of the Earth's. The world unraveling in sympathetic backdrop to my own misery—then I'd hate myself for such analogy even occurring to me.

It was the September after the layoff, in this state of mind, that I found my first bone. True, by then I was outside more often than I'd been since I was a little girl. Now I had no one to answer to but Unemployment and nothing but filling out applications to take up my time. But I'd always spent hours upon hours in woods and canyons, on mountains and beaches; I'd grown up roaming Appalachian hills and needed wild like a nutrient even as an adult. And nothing remotely like this had ever happened before.

It was hard to mark the very first one because only later, of course, did I see it as a pattern. The long, slender wing bone I found by the lake? The vertebra dropped in my yard by a crow? Most of those first bones were small; in the city, they usually were, rat or bird or squirrel, I'd only know for sure when there was enough skeleton to tell. A couple times in that early period, the bones turned up in urban coyote scat, bones shorter than my fingernails and gut-polished to delicate pins. Once—I was standing on them before I knew—salt and pepper ashes, sloppy-scattered and clumped by rain, fragments big enough, unburned enough, I had to pray they belonged to a pet.

For as long as I could, of course, I called it coincidence. I was a practical person, reasonable, no New Ager, never a looker for signs. And I probably could have gone on dismissing it as coincidence—the beaver jaw I found near the Columbia River, the raccoon ribs behind my compost bin—except for one thing: the consistent bizarreness of how the finding of them felt.

I'd be striding along, minding my own business; if I were looking for something, anticipating something, it was not what I'd later find. When suddenly, but lightly, no heaviness in it ever, the knowing would settle over me like a transparent veil.

From that second forward, it was like I was following an invisible current already laid. Tracking without any senses I knew, leading with my chest, the whole experience completely feinting past mind. And upon finding the bone, always, the strange tears, me, always, despite myself, caught off guard. Because no emotion preceded the tears and with them came only a softening in my chest, the tears just a few degrees more personal than wind watering my eyes. And lastly, paradox again, the dead thing at my feet, while love—I simply couldn't call it anything else, I'd tried—enveloped me.

I lay down my pen. Gazed out the kitchen window where my moss-topped bird feeder rocked in rainy December wind. The following excluded all examination of itself during itself, so I'd started writing up what I could reconjure of it once I got home, and now, after two months of trying, I believed I was getting it almost right. Around my cramped kitchen and living room, bones nested wherever I could clear a spot—the raccoon skull sharing the windowsill with a salt shaker, a crow shin on a low bookshelf right above Shea's bed, a shard I'd just picked up buried in the mail. Now that I'd mastered the description of the following, there was nothing left but to confront the meaning. And here the real trouble always began.

I flipped pages backwards to the day in October I'd first put questions on paper: *How much of this am I making up? Is there a rational explanation, and if so, what? Why is it always bones I find at the end?* I thumbed forward, the questions set apart from other ruminations by marginal asterisks and bold underlines. *How is the knowing related to the Great Losses of These Times? And why is it coming to **me**?* Finally, the question that when I was honest with myself, actually frightened me: *What in the world is driving this? What's underneath it all?* But I could only point to the place in my chest where the sensor hovered. What the sensor was guided by, I could not fathom at all.

Four o'clock dusk was pushing in, and as the room dimmed, the desk lamp on my kitchen table illuminated just a corner of my notebook, the frayed edges of my long-sleeved T-shirt. The age in my hands. As I sat there, confounded, drifting farther from the following itself, the nearer all those outside world torrents—wars and hurricanes, radiation leaks and man made earthquakes, the end of unemployment checks and the endlessness of loneliness—hurtled past. All crises I should be battling head-on instead of sneaking around diddling with bones.

I SAW MY friends less and less. Some had disappeared as collateral damage from the breakup, and when I did see others, it seemed I no longer had much to say. Faithful Terri kept close tabs on me, but she mostly wanted to discuss how I was "healing," and although I did mention three or four times what I was finding, leaving out, of course, the knowing part, she would express polite interest, then not remember from one report to the next, so never even noticed I was talking about a series of events. Shockingly soon, I lost touch with most of my co-workers, connections I'd thought were substantial exposed as hollow without enforced meeting and shared projects.

I kept following. Spent longer and longer hours in the old-growth city park in every degree of winter rain from palpable fog to Gore-Tex–penetrating downpour. Sometimes what I found was not exactly bone. Was cousin-to-bone, used-to-be-bone, going-to-be-bone, replica of bone. The broken pin-stripped shaft of an eagle's feather. A fallen but uncracked pileated woodpecker's egg. A baby's black sock stamped with a pirate crossbones and skull.

A single other person haunted the park as often as I did, a gentle mutterer in an immense vole-colored coat, all his belongings in a duffle on his curved spine. I greeted him always. The man never made eye contact back. More than once, after passing him, and even more often upon waking in the night, I asked myself if I was losing my own mind, but the *no* came as easy as the following did. Because—the paradox again—as deranged as my experiences seemed if I looked at them from the perspective of my one-year-ago self, the actual following shifted me into an alignment with a force so grounded that I knew it was the essence of sanity. From beginning to end and then beyond, until the final fading of the wake, the following was suffused with a simple matter-of-factness—no disembodied voices, no light orbs, no dizziness or daze—that made the bone-finding as natural as shoots leafing, as down-to-earth as molehills under foot. And no strain, either, never any groping or trying too hard. Until I'd return to my notebook and ask questions again.

After New Year's, I decided to spend a few days on the other side of the Cascades, hike the sunlit canyons there. I'd held off out of respect for Shea, who loved that place best, but I thought enough time had passed that she'd forgive me now. The first morning, I found deer antlers. A coyote mouth with most of its teeth. The second day, the leg of an elk.

I'd known of the elk bone from two miles away. It was my longest following. From the mouth of that basalt canyon to the draw at its end, a following so sustained it wore an imprint on my insides I could easily call up afterwards, inoculation against between-followings doubt. Me led in that weird, neutral ecstasy past bone-trunked young aspens, through the vibrant grays, the scouring scent, of sage. The beat of my breathing, the arch of turquoise sky, and what I'd find at the end so certain it was like time had folded up in pleated paper strips, me standing simultaneously on the first square and the last and seeing straight through.

When the trail tapered out where the canyon pulled in, I knew to drift left and scale the wall. I knew where to place my hands and feet, what saplings and roots, what rocks and nooks would hold. Until I put my fingers on the bone itself. I touched it before I saw. A leg bone longer than my forearm. Bleached white but not yet a trace of pock or gray.

Instantly, those tears that had so little to do with me. As though my heart were speaking directly with what moves the world, and me registering the profundity of that communication in my eyes, but the communication so far beyond my ken that my self could touch only its rim. Next, the wash of gratitude, spreading and deepening the gratitude already laid. And finally, love. Me, as always, unable to discern if it was from me for it or from it for me and, as always, dumbfounded over what "it" might be anyway.

I eased down cross-legged on the lip of the bluff. I held the elk bone close to my face, then pressed its joint against my own bone where all my ribs met. When I was ten years old, in West Virginia, I'd seen a water dowser work. A silo of a woman, her legs like bridge abutments, her face full and firm. Someone handed the woman a branch. As soon as she held it, it dwarfed in her hands. I watched that branch, forked like a wishbone. Like an armless stick man. I watched that woman grip a fork in each hand. Her moving like the day was dark or she was blind, she let the straight piece lead, me near enough to see the cold pimpling her arms. At least I'd thought it was the cold back then.

I'd started picturing the vee of my rib cage as a dowsing fork. My two bottom ribs as where the dowser hands held, the nub of bone at solar plexus the part that led. Divination, they called it. "Divine." Into the canyon, I said it out loud. Unlike most people I'd met after childhood, I'd never felt obligated to insist there was nothing beyond—above, alongside, behind—this world you could measure and touch. I had always been open to the existence of something else for the right type of soul. But ultimately, its possibility had mattered little to me because that type of soul, I'd known, was not mine. For all kinds of reasons—era, culture, too much of the wrong kind of education, my white skin—I'd accepted without regret or even much thought that the other place was for me forever sealed shut.

Up and down the ruddy cliffs, swallows sprinted in and out their keyhole nests. Shivering, I pulled the elk leg into my coat and laid it long ways from my throat to my waist. But it was water that dowsers found. How could the knowing feel more right to me than anything had in my life, yet always arrive at dead bone in the end?

I lay back on the ground. I opened my eyes straight into the sky. And in that moment, my body understood that mind just murkies it. Keep it clean, I heard. Love your mute chest.

WALKING INTO THE airport in March after nearly a year of isolation was like blundering against a volume knob. The world rushed in like flood-stage rapids, the hyperglare of the concourse lighting, the overlapping loudspeakers' blare. I jostled past glistening-skinned soldiers in clean camouflage, dodged children bunkered in giant gadget-bulged strollers.

Television monitors, never fewer than two in view, regurgitated footage of the Japanese tsunami two weeks earlier, of the towers at Fukushima, of tornadoes juggernauting swaths of the American South.

The invitation to a job interview outside Pittsburgh had come just ten days before. Pittsburgh was not a place I wanted to live, but I'd had not a single other serious offer. But I still might not have gone—many days I felt so feral I'd choose homelessness over that sense of living inside a speeding car I'd had while working full time—except for this: Pittsburgh was a five-hour drive from the small town in West Virginia where I'd spent the first twelve years of my life.

I'd been born in West Virginia and did not leave until my parents divorced. We left some relatives behind, aunts, uncles, but within a decade, everybody else had either died or moved away, too. I had not been back in over twenty-five years. Yet once I started finding bones, the land back there roiled up in my mind more often. The water-dowser memory just one of many surfacing with greater frequency and vividness. My family had lived on the edge of a small neighborhood on the edge of a very small town, no border between our yard and woods unfolding over mountains stretching farther than I ever reached the end of, even though I wandered them almost every day. I figured I was thinking of back there, back then, more often because it was the only other period in my life I'd spent so much unfettered time outside. But I also knew that the visitations from West Virginia were more than that.

So when the interview came with a free flight to the top of Appalachia, a part of me read it like another bone. How might the following play out in mountains so much more ancient than the Olympics, the Cascades? And on land that had suffered greater hurt, land being destroyed faster and more spectacularly than almost anywhere else in the besieged United States, land that was itself a Great Loss of These

Times? Given the place's age, the level of loss, and my child connection to it, maybe—I almost dared not say it even in my head—whatever was behind the bone following would speak a little louder in Appalachia than it had so far.

Now we were airborne. The jet bellowing, my seat vibrating, the sides of my eyes polluted by images darting on neighbors' handheld screens. After three hours of reimmersion in most people's reality, my plan had started to fray. A little part of me was starting to see my hopes for West Virginia as far-fetched as most of my seatmates would. On repeating screens up and down the plane aisle, yet another film version of Armageddon. Terrified people in business attire charged at the camera down skyscrapered streets. My friend Terri had stopped by after work the evening before to wish me luck. I hadn't seen her in two months. In her presence I felt, sharp, my isolation like I had not in some time, and for a second, I considered blurting it, the knowing, the following, all of it out. Then between my stomach and my heart came a sensation like sand sucking over feet when a wave draws back. I knew I shouldn't go on.

After she had left and I was rinsing out our beer bottles, I thought of the first time Shea, maybe eight months old, had seen a horse. We'd been on the outskirts of the city on a trail that surprised us when it passed a paddock holding three placid mares.

"Look, Shea! Look!" I had hissed, excited to see her reaction, and Shea did look, but up at me. I gestured towards the horses, pushed Shea in their direction with my knee, and then she turned her eyes to them, but with no more interest than if they'd been a parked car.

Then, abruptly, she went rigid. Stared so intently for a full minute that later I imagined I could see the new circuit plowing through her brain. And, finally, she lunged, she barked, entranced, until I had to drag her away and out of their sight.

As we kept walking, Shea prancing and pulling, I understood: in those first minutes, Shea had not seen the horses at all. Even though the mares were moving a little, tails swishing, a fetlock cocked. Shea had not at first seen them because she had no shape in her brain to receive "horse." So the horses, until her mind laid new track, did not exist.

I SPENT THE night near the Pittsburgh airport, slept poorly, woke at six, found I-79, and turned south. These Pennsylvania hills shorter, rounder, more pastoral, than the ones I remembered in West Virginia, and I hoped my remembering was right. In fifty miles, I passed no fewer than four billboards exalting natural gas, including one where solemn steelworkers photographed in 1950s black-and-white passed a metal baton to fully colorized, grinning hydrofrackers. Then I crossed the state line, and the land did get steeper, closer, but otherwise the place looked like nothing I remembered, these chain restaurants and gas stations, the strip malls hacked into hillsides. The edge of my first mountaintop-removal mine I glimpsed outside Morgantown. Mistook my first drilling rig, spearing through trees in the near distance, for a cell tower. West Virginia had billboard love songs to gas and coal both: "clean," "keeping the lights on," the fuel of patriots. The poorest state in the nation, I knew, the saddest too, they had studies confirming that.

I grubbed down into my own history for happier images. I found my child hand turning over rocks to flush crawdads, squeezing puffballs between my finger and thumb. I brought back me lodging my head into a hollow log to discover, finally, my dog's new pups. But none of these, not even the puppies, returned fleshed, real, and I felt again the shame of absurdity I'd felt on the plane. That the past seven months were a fantasy I'd frothed up out of loneliness and idleness and the desperation to remedy despair, and on top of that, my noble-savaging of West

Virginia'd made me waste time and money on a detour that would only despoil my childhood sense of the place I could have otherwise carried forever undefiled.

I left the interstate for a two-lane highway before I reached Charleston. My plan—and for now I was sticking to it—was to visit our old neighborhood tomorrow. Because the woods around that neighborhood were private, if they were still woods at all, today my destination was a state park my family had often visited. I didn't know of any better place to place myself for the bone following.

The lone motel near the park was a Holiday Inn Express, its only trace of Appalachia the older clerk's accent. The younger clerk spoke just like I did now. They allowed me an early check-in, and I stumbled into the noon darkness of a second-floor room, slung my suitcase on a bed, and jerked open the rubbery drapes. My view was a high ocher bank, the skinned end of a hill half-sacrificed to make a flat place for the building. I bent down, angled up my eyes. On the bank's top, a brushy border of thick woods.

The approach to the park finally looked like something I'd known. The close-ranked deciduous trees, smaller than the ones out West, and at this highish altitude, still leafless in late March. The sensation of being girded by hills so close they couldn't be directly seen. My mind slowed, my breathing did. Possibilities, first tingling in my arms then tiptoeing closer, crept back again. I pulled into a parking lot with a single other car, swung open my door, and stood up. And had to catch myself with both hands on the window top. The smell of the place. It'd near rolled me. A smell foreign to anything I'd scented as an adult—water on limestone? Appalachian dirt? acorn rot?—but one sniff. And I was eight years old again.

The first few steps felt like dream-walking. I turned a slow circle under the clouded sky. It all came back, everything in its place—the primitive elegance of the WPA stonework, the damp coolness of the restroom insides, the softball field, the split-rail fence—but miniaturized. Everything at half the scale my little girl memory had saved it, and I broke into a smile. I discovered in a wooden pocket on the shuttered concession stand a map. I chose the longest path.

It was paved at first and over-signed. I hurried deeper. The air, of course, was dryer than the Northwest, but somehow more dense. Stiller, but a stillness that had nothing to do with presence or absence of wind. The trail turned to dirt now, but it still felt too domesticated. Yet, somehow also the enchantment that I'd touched earlier darkened into eeriness here. Was it just the emptiness of the place on this weekday afternoon? The vacancy of the sky, the way the high clouds simply erased it? And with the exception of an occasional rhododendron, almost all the vegetation was still black and brown, white and gray, a sobering contrast to the Pacific Northwest's winter-long green—salal and fir and fern—and for the first time, I saw the green as deceptive. This place told you. Look. Understand. Half the time, I am dead.

I walked faster to get ahead of my mind. I reached from my chest. But of course, I could not conjure it. The knowing, the following, never answered when asked. Yet another sign pointed to an overlook down a spur trail, and now I recalled it, the splintery roughness on my chest from the wooden rail topping the stone barrier wall. And then I was standing behind that wall again, the rail along my waist.

Soft-topped mountains bound me every way my eye could reach. Abruptly, my body remembered these mountains, too, remembered almost as sharp as it had remembered the smell. Mountains brooding, embracing. Radiant. Suffocant. I could see white water no wider than my two fingers in the gorge hundreds of feet under me, and between me and that river, two buzzards tilting, close enough it seemed I could reach out and graze their backs. Railroad tracks ran along a narrow wainscoting right above the river, hauling coal to power plants, I knew, and the single other man-made things in my view were the mammoth metal towers, stringing over the mountains through a clear-cut swath, giant skeletal metal men walking the electricity away. And how, I wondered, could this place feel more wild than the West when it had been so much more used, so much more lived in by European people? When it felt millennia tireder than land out West? Then I realized it was not wilder it felt. It was more primal. No. More elemental? Once again, I had no words to name what I knew.

I turned back to the main trail, tuned again for the following. When, without warning, I passed out of the woods and into a field. I stopped short, then choked out a laugh. I was right back at the concession stand, had walked the entire perimeter in twenty minutes. I'd completely overlooked that the scale of my little girl memory would include the hike, too. And, naturally, I understood now, this was a park more for picnicking than hiking, a working people's park.

I walked the loop twice more. With each diminishing circuit, my hope for the following withered. By the fourth lap, I'd given up altogether; I barged on out of a stubbornness that verged on spite. But the last time I stepped into that brown field, my anger had been smothered by a disappointment so penetrating my own bones ached.

Evening was shading in. The car of the other park visitor, whom I'd never seen, was gone. I plodded to a picnic table and climbed onto its top. I pulled my notebook from my pack. The temperature was falling fast, and I huddled deeper into my jacket. I couldn't help but recall the months-ago elk bone in my coat.

Bone, I scrawled at the top of a page. *What's left last.* I paused. My intellect stealthed in. My gut pushed it back. *Things supposed to be buried. Pushing up through graveyard grass.* Maybe its meaning was simply that it did not mean. Maybe the meaning was emancipation from that. *Feel it in your bones. Bred in the bone. Fishbone caught in your throat.* My throat had stobbed up, the pressure that comes before tears. Desperation tears. Not finding ones.

I closed my notebook. I thought again of the day in the canyon, the following to the elk bone. Me bereft of the following now cast into even more brilliant relief the memory of the following then. My sternum pulled to that leg loosed from its body, body loosed from spirit, bone drawn to bone. And next I knew, knew not with my mind, knew only because my mind had given up, that the point of the following was the feeling itself. There was no further, no deeper, understanding. That such a phenomenon could happen to one—that it had happened to me—was enough. Even if where I always landed was bone.

THE NEXT MORNING, I showered, grabbed a mealy bagel from the breakfast bar, and wheeled my suitcase to my car. During the night, I'd lectured myself to push the bone business aside; I needed to gird myself for this interview, face reality and the end of unemployment checks. As I lifted my bag into the trunk, my eyes snagged on that scabbed orange bank behind the motel. I looked away from its ruinedness, reached for the door handle instead. But unlocking the trunk had not freed the door, so I had to pull out the key, struggle with the button on that. And right then, light as a net. The knowing settled over me again.

I swiveled my head. The lot was empty except for me. I scanned the whole bank. I hesitated a long second, the keys still in my hand. Then I stuffed them into my jacket pocket and trotted to where the bank looked the least sheer. Then I was climbing it, using my hands, too. Shale crumbling under my shoes, me scrambling to get ahead of the ground's dissolve, I was helped, I was held. And then I was at the top in sparse sharp grass, and past that and into woods.

Now the following filled me, I knew how to move. Now I was traveling in the flat elation, never mind that these woods were more beaten-down than the park's, third-growth, fourth-growth, never mind the gash of fresh-dozed road I had to cross, never mind the NO TRESPASSING signs. I'd slipped out of mind joint and into soul joint, the buoyancy amplified because I'd abandoned all expectation of the following finding me here. And after a half-mile, it magneted me, I knew exactly where to turn. Into a thicket of scrubby, head-high pine.

Right away, the trees got too dense for me to burrow through them standing up. I wiggled on, bent at the waist, until I was forced down into a crawl. And spied, not five feet from my splayed fingers, a skull. Recognized next that the teeth were canine.

I could put it together in increments only, my eyes moving faster than my understanding could keep up. The long curve of spine, the serrated snake of tail, my sight widening to take in pelvis, to take in toes. The collar without tags.

I crouched paralyzed. Never had I found a full skeleton of a large animal, but worse than that, never had I found one of a pet. Grief for Shea vised my heart, grief for this dog's suffering, grief for the suffering of anyone who had loved this dog. Grief for the possibility no one had. But, exactly concurrent with the grief, with the horror, simultaneous with those and just as potent, the transcendent gratitude. I gritted my teeth in revulsion, in confusion—the uncharged euphoria—I twisted but could not pull away. And yet embracing, containing, the entire welter: the love. The love came, too.

Then I was sprinting. Thrashing out of the pines, losing all sense of direction, scuttling over rocks and logs, I tore across the road-marred ridge and dropped to the mountain's other side. Where I slipped, arms windmilling, on those decades-deep slick leaves, and fell, my cheek crushed into the acorn-rot smell. I rolled over, grabbed a spindly trunk, and hauled myself to my feet. Brushing away duff, I wheeled in what I thought was the motel direction and set off. But the following—my heart quivered—still held me. And the following tugged the other way.

I shook my head. Took two emphatic strides towards the car, then broke into a slow jog. But because the running was easier here, I couldn't help but notice how beautiful was this long flat where I'd landed, the trees here less recently timbered, the trunks bigger around and more space between them so it felt almost like a park. Despite myself, I couldn't help savoring that oaky dirt odor, thick again, the one that returned me to eight years old. And suddenly I knew the following would not just leave me with that dead dog. To move in the following direction, I felt sure, must lead to some compensation, some antidote. Why else would it feel so right?

When I turned, I was drenched immediately in the grounded rapture. Immediately my legs, my back, they glided, so easy was the way. I slipped through sassafras and hickory, maple and beech, me throbbing with the radiance of that bench. The smell changed. A tiny warning flared inside me. I'd never scented, not with my nose, a bone before. But the following insisted, I did not slow. Then just downhill ahead of me, I spied the high vault of rib cage—the following tugging—I saw the buck's head still in its skin, it still had a face. Me towed closer, the stench pulsing over me in ebb and flow of breeze, the deer's fur dun-gray dead, the hide splotchy in riddled decay, the eye sockets empty—and I wrenched myself away and was sprinting again.

Straight down the mountain to get farthest fastest, I did not think, I did not fall. The white belly of a big bird winged out over me, and I heard other crashings, other things flushed, but I did not stop. Then I hit the bottom, hard in my knees, a hollow no wider than my body was long, and without breaking my pace, I swung in the direction I had to pray was the car. And this time, I nearly stepped on it. The body of a red-tail hawk.

I staggered back. The bird perfect except for its stripped-off head. I couldn't pass. The corpse too fresh for odor, the torn flesh at the neck so clean it looked, I realized, then blanched, like something you could eat. I crept closer. The faultless yellow of the scaled feet, air-scoured. The hard grace of the muscled flanks. Her tail a red I'd never imagined, dusky red, an earth red, yet this red went in the sky. Something flashed in the leaf litter. I squinted. A glassy-backed beetle making for the meat. I was witnessing the very first one.

And wrapping me, the odd objective love. I stood over the hawk, my palms open at my sides, my cheeks sticky with tears. This time, I held. The revulsion and the tenderness, the grotesque and the gift. The numinous and the dismemberment, the terror, the bliss. My heart dilating to accommodate the paradox, the contraries interpenetrating, I felt them, until what they made together burst free of me, and I hovered inside of that. The hawk blurred below me, the ground around me, the trees, the sky. I didn't end at my skin.

Eventually, softly, the knowing seeped away. I turned from the hawk. I gazed down the hollow. In the grounded peace the following left behind, I trusted I'd take the right way.

I'd walked maybe a quarter-mile when a mild unsettling prickled me. I stopped and lay my hand on a young sycamore trunk. Every realization I'd had about the bone following, I remembered, had always been temporary. Had always eventually been overturned. I pressed my whole body along the tree, but the uneasiness did not wane. I understood I would not lose anything that had already come to me. But I knew also I'd found no final word.

SAID

SAID THAT WHEN them boys jumped out, ours was already loaded, safety off, and cocked. Said nobody thought. Said who could of lived through that close of range, what the hell we gonna do now? Said it was the other two fired first, but ours aimed best, what the hell? Said only one of them got up afterwards, the least hurt dragging the most hurt away. Said it'll be all over town by evening, all over the county by morning, what? Said get our goddamned story straight, that's what they said.

They come off the mountain with their own boy in a purple-lipped panic. Eyes frogged out and reared back both, horse at a snake, and shiny with a crazy crying, at first I thought it was just a crazy crying, only later did I hear the guilt. And him a big boy, at least fifteen, you'd thought it was him'd got hit, but although it was him they wanted, he wasn't so much as grazed. I just went on a-peeling my potatoes, licked my finger on a nick.

First I thought it was an accident, then I started hearing how on the other side it must of been planned. First I thought it was only our boy pulled the our-side trigger, then started hearing I was at least half wrong. Heat off that woodstove, heat off fourteen scared men, and already five different stories were fighting for what would be said. I was getting my taters going in some grease out a cup, when the oldest one, Franklin's first son, Bunk, come up on my back. I shifted my head and I looked at him there. "Chester. Ches." Was all he said.

Aside from Bunk, they brung me only because they could stand my cooking and was always short on people to drive, I knowed that. And because, at sixty-nine, I was still my father's son, them theirs. And because they knowed I couldn't talk good when I could talk at all, and most people thinks what comes out your mouth is one and the same with what runs in your head. Which works against you most of the time, but with them, it usually worked for. Hunting places around here have shrunkt up smaller every year, I needed fresh meat in my freezer. Now Bunk had slumped away from it, into a back-cracked chair between the cookstove and wall, and he dropped that gray chin in his hand.

I got to slicing my onions, the sharp of that odor a-stamping at theirs. Boots and blaze orange and gun cases and guns, they was a-raising a steam with what they thought should be said. Closest to my age were Franklin's three sons—Bunk, Gordon, and Kenny Lee—and them three'd had five sons, and out of their son-in-laws, two who would hunt. And then that bunch had a whole slew of boys, Franklin's great-grands, but only four with us now because a few was too little, and more only hunted on video screens. And some of them argued nasty, and some argued reasonable, and some argued crazy, and some argued half-sweet, but only Ryan, the one the other side'd been after, showed any hurt for them two shot kids. Kids, I heard them say, he knew from school. And other things. He was the youngest with us, Rusty's son, Gordon's grand, Franklin's great, I'd never paid him much mind, him a-surlying around under stringy red hair, fingering spots on his face. But now he was carrying on like a just-cut calf, snotting and bawling where he curled on a cot, until one of em said, "Get out there in that johnnyhouse til you get hold yourself!" Then another one said, "No, just go out there sit in Uncle Kenny's truck." I poked the rings out my onions. Felt the thin curl of trigger in the middle of a finger. Before pot, before cocaine, before crack, oxycontin, and crystal metholatum . . . My daddy wasn't a drinking man. Franklin, he wasn't neither.

Started my onions in the skillet next the taters, and they said the boys was a-waiting for theirs, couldn't have known how this family hunts. Because most people these days still-hunt, which would have made the Ryan alone, but this bunch did it the old way, drive and watch, which meant there was all kind of family along that them boys didn't expect. Now Frankie, Bunk's boy, was a-stepping out his coveralls, and he drop-spilled a whole box of cartridges on the floor, and if that didn't rattle em higher. They was big men, I tell you, they got fatter as they went the generations down. They was bear-chested and bullheaded and they knowed more about guns than they did people, woods, or sense. My daddy talked good, walked tall, stood right alongside Franklin even if he never did own not one acre of land. But Chester, he told me, you watch his boys, and that was before the grands come along, and long before the greats.

Now Bunk'd got up, he was trying to talk sense to the younger ones, his brother Gordon was, too. Me with my back to em, moving onions, moving taters, I was hearing more than I could see and smelling more than either. The heat of em was beading water on the winders, water a-starting to drip, and it'd already come to me I was smelling em when before I couldn't, but then it come to me that I couldn't before, because before, they'd smelled like me. I flopped a liver out a bread bag and onto the heat, stepped back when the bacon grease popped high.

"Oh, he won't say nothing."

And there it was. Me the only one not related by marriage or blood.

"Course he won't say nothing, but he can still tell!" Hothead Rusty talking, even fireder up than usual with the Ryan being his.

"You know what I mean," that was Bunk again, we'd come up together, him just two years younger. But although Bunk had always wanted different, wanted us to be like Franklin and Daddy, me and Bunk could never be.

"Well, we got to know for sure, and he's got to keep it straight," another grandson, I couldn't tell which, but I could hear the walleye scare of his eyes.

"Hell, I don't even know if he can remember something for that long," and one or two snickered despite everything else.

"He's ever bit as bright as any one of you!" That was Kenny, the third and last son. I saw how the liver was colored like the boy's shivery lips, jerking in the pan. Like its nerves not yet shut down.

Then somebody's chair legs went a-scudding crosst the boards, and "Make em write it down!" and then they was thrusting for paper. Slamming through kitchen drawers and outturning dirty pockets, and they ripped off part of the tater bag, but decided that was too small. Bunk fell back into the chair, I seed him. I seed his gray face spider-held in his hands. My back still to em, water dribbling down the winder insides, and guess drug dealin' and deer huntin' don't mix too good, I wanted to say, but never did.

Finally one fished a doughnut box out the garbage, and another grandson took a knife to it, and that gave them some room. Somebody grabbed my arm, "Write it down!" and I heard my spatula hit the floor. He turned me around, and then I seed them all, but their faces had done run away, they was stubble, they was glasses, they was orange and camouflage caps, and I could feel in his arm he was still holding back. He slammed my hand on the box piece, and one stubble-cap turned into Gordon and turned away, and with a nub of a pencil out of somebody's pocket I wrote, "I won't say nothing." That's what I said.

"Naw! Naw! Put, 'I'll say exactly like they want'!"

I felt me swaver a little on my feet. Them winders was a-swimming, they took no reflection, they let in no night. I steadied myself with my left hand on the table edge, pressed down hard to keep the mark from wiggling, and how little you all are a-knowing, I said in my head. Then it got so quiet, all of them watching my hand, you could hear the sugar crust crunch under the tip. Quiet enough you could hear Kenny or Gordon a-walking away up the stairs, I could tell it was a son by the slow in the step. Then I laid the pencil down, stepped back best I could with them all around, when Rusty yapped out "Put 'I swear'!" How little you all are a-knowing. I pulled the pencil to the very edge. I squinched the "I swear" in. How little you are knowing, and nothing about said.

Rusty grabbed the scrap, jammed it in the thigh pocket of his canvas pants. And for about three seconds, they all of them looked at me there. For about three seconds, all of them's faces come back, each one clear, and dark, and at a great far away. And I seed Franklin, Gordon, Kenny, I seed Bunk, even in the by-marriage ones, I seed. Then they turned from me and back on themselves. A-arguing again over what would be said.

I picked my spatula up off the floor. I lifted that liver out, still bleeding a little, and I laid it on a plate. Shoved the taters on a back burner, figured if they scorched, the eaters wouldn't notice much. Then I walked to the door and out of the said.

My daddy'd been a few years older than Franklin; I was older than all his sons. Old enough to listen. Old enough to not have said. Franklin called that an accident, too, but only one man pulled the trigger then. And that story didn't have to get made and straight, because the woman didn't just get winged and she couldn't run away, and she was from back in the hills anyway, her good looks didn't save her there. And no one seed it happen but Franklin hisself, and just one man, Franklin's tenant farmer, my daddy, seed it after, as he helped to clean and cover up.

My daddy told only me. Me a wee little boy, but already understanding way ahead of where my mouth would ever get. Somehow Daddy knowed that then. He said to me just oncet what happened, but he said to me the other many times more. That he never knowed forever afterwards if he was a friend or a debt.

I grabbed me a broom, dropped Kenny Lee's tailgate, felt it sharp in my knees when I swung up in. I waited a second for the pain to ease. Then I walked the bed to the cab.

The Ryan laid crumpled on the bench seat there. Teary face part up and his hands between his legs. He looked at me out of an eye and a half, and I looked at him. Then I turned, set my broom between the liner ridges, and swept the deer blood out. Nothing yet said.

SUGAR'S UP

THE SAUSAGE BISCUIT at McDonald's was supposed to cost ninety-nine cents, but Calvin Bergdoll saw they'd raised it to a dollar twenty nine. He knew they were using the county's Bygone Days celebration as an excuse for the hike, and he knew, too, that they thought nobody would notice when it stayed upped afterwards.

"They got their prices up so high now I don't know if we can eat here anymore," Calvin said in a stern voice to Theodore Munney, putting enough loud in it that not only the cashiers would hear, but also the day manager Eddie Sloan, there in his saggy McDonald's pants juggling the drive-through headset, two sleeves of hash browns, and a drink cup the girth of a steer's neck. Theodore Munney already had his biscuit bit into and was grinding along as they walked to their table, bearing down hard on the sausage's gristly parts. Theodore was fifty-six, and his back teeth were eroding, but Calvin Bergdoll knew from a career as a mental health social worker that you'd be surprised what all people could eat without teeth. *Took that one boy out of Weston, and he ate a whole pizza first stop we made.* Cal toured his own teeth with his tongue, all but two in their places despite their daily labors, and he flashbacked to the second Italian sub he'd taken on while the boy he was ferrying home from the state mental institution polished off that twenty-two-inch pepperoni and mushroom.

After they slid into the booth, Calvin eyed the McDonald's receipt with indignation, but also with a calculating concern. The truth was, if Calvin could no longer eat at McDonald's, he was out of breakfast places in town. He'd gotten into a tussle with Irene, the head lady at the Hilltop Truck Stop, when he marched behind the counter and turned down the music she was playing too loud, and he'd been banned from Rita's Diner for ordering Rita to reheat for him a couple bacon strips abandoned on a plate by a departed customer. *Well, I hate to waste.* Such skirmishes had become more and more common for Calvin in the past couple years. Times and tides had changed, people on edge and quick to seize the upper hand with tender-hearted types like him. *I am no fighter.* He underscored this proclamation with a throat-clogging swallow of biscuit. Yet the second the proclamation came, there whirlpooled to the top layer of the sediment he carried in his brain a sentence he'd overheard his wife say on the phone the other day: "When his sugar's up, there's no telling what he might do."

From within his biscuit absorption, Calvin half-noticed hobbling towards them the well-dressed midriff of an elderly woman. "Well, hello Cal."

Cal looked up. Miss Dola Wysapple, an esteemed Presbyterian lady and one of his late mother's younger cronies. This recognition brought with it the taste of Miss Dola's covered-dish-dinner-famous Mississippi Mud Pie. Calvin cleared his mouth and wiped his hand on his napkin, gathering himself for what might come next. He carried within the cylinder of himself a half dozen smaller cylinders, reminiscent of chambers in a handgun. Each cylinder housed a different personality, and Calvin was never entirely sure which personality would present itself, making moments like these a kind of character roulette.

"Good morning, Miss Dola!"

The tone was solicitous and grand all at once: the Courtly Gentleman. A fortuitous appearance. Struggling to his feet, Calvin took Miss Dola's cold hand, and Miss Dola, wedging her cane between her knees, placed her other spotted hand on top of his. Now she was gazing at Theodore Munney with the small, quizzical smile a person offers when waiting to be introduced. The Courtly Gentleman took a step back and swept his free arm towards the booth.

"This, Miss Dola, is Theodore O. Munney," Calvin announced, and although at that point his mind stopped, his mouth kept going. "My gun-bearer."

Miss Dola's friendly smile passed into one of bepuzzlement. She nodded, lifted her free hand, and gave her cane a trial tap. "You and Theodore have a good Bygone Days," she said, and she clapped Cal lightly on the shoulder before she staggered on.

Calvin sidled back into his yolk-colored seat, took up his sandwich, and smiled at Theodore Munney, who immediately averted his gaze. *Gingerly, gingerly.* "Well, Theodore," he began in a tone one might use to suggest a joint business venture. "Would you like to cut a little grass today?"

Theodore Munney squashed a few biscuit crumbs on his fingertip and popped the finger into his mouth.

"Looks like nice grass-cutting weather," Calvin tried again. "And we'll stop down at the trailer and pick up your laundry."

"RealbadwreckupSlanesvillelastnight." Theodore wiped his mouth with the back of his sleeve.

Based on the absence of sour in Theodore Munney's response, Cal decided to interpret it as a "possibly," which was more than Theodore had given up in several days. Calvin had a good acre of lawn that needed mowing weekly in the early part of the season, and since his children had mostly moved away, finding a reasonably priced grass cutter had been a trial. In past summers, Theodore had seemed to enjoy the tranquilizing orbits of the riding mower, but recently, something had been afoot in Theodore Munney, something that had caught Calvin off guard. This complicated even further the diagnosis he'd been trying to pin on Theodore since he'd taken him into his oversight two years ago after his former charge, Nutley Randalpin, had died on him. Suddenly Theodore jerked to his feet, tray in hand, and dumped biscuit wrappers and senior-sized coffee cups down the garbage chute. Calvin scrabbled after him—*learning initiative, yes, he's maturing*—and then the two of them were snarling the Bygone Days traffic in the parking lot on their way to Cal's eighteen-year-old Blazer, Blackie.

It was early May, still cool in the mornings. Theodore Munney wore his usual work clothes, both his shirt and his pants the color of grass when it gets gobbed up around lawnmower blades, a timeless outfit no one in the town of Berker would have looked at twice in 1953 and one no one looked at twice now in 2003. Calvin Bergdoll, in contrast, dressed like an onion, in layers he could subtract and add depending on temperature. The deepest strata were T-shirts with frayed necklines, thin as Saran Wrap, and over those, several layers of plaid in varied styles, colors, and check schemes, including always at least one pajama top. On his pate rested his current favorite cap, one he had paid for, gold mesh ventilation in the back and a navy blue front with the words Almost Heaven and a silhouette of the state of West Virginia. Noticing an out-of-state car waiting for Blackie's parking space, Calvin stopped, stretched his back, and ran his hand over the slight push-out of his belly, the only interruption in his otherwise svelte figure. This mystery, he knew, was the talk of many in the town of Berker, how could anyone eat like Calvin Bergdoll did and still preserve such slimness? Package that and you'll be a millionaire, one of his daughters had told him once. *Just good genes.* Calvin humbly smiled.

To avoid the hubbub of the Bygone Days setup on Main Street, Calvin cut behind the Coke plant, skirted the Little League field, and then shuttled the sidewalkless backstreets on the rump side of Berker. Theodore Munney rode in silence, his face turned out the open window. Was Bygone Days a good thing or a bad? The biscuit travesty forced the question again. Now they were passing the house where Calvin had lived until he was eight, Cal scowling over how they'd let the porch screen shred, and three blocks later, the little house his mother had occupied in her final years, the two big water maples out front violated to stumps by the current owner whose name Calvin would not deign to mention. Bygone Days did generate civic pride, something sorely diminished over Cal's lifetime in the town of Berker, once a proud little village named by young surveyor George Washington himself, in honor of the county's fine Berkshire swine. But Bygone Days meant his bride of forty years was away all weekend helping at the Fine Arts Room, and it lured hordes of gawkers to town and threw off Calvin's schedule. Further, almost all the food at Bygone Days was out of his price range, and he couldn't help but suspect that the overstimulation of the celebration was at least partly responsible for Theodore Munney's recent behaviors.

As they neared Theodore Munney's trailer, the houses got narrower, the dogs grouchier, until the pavement gave up altogether and they were rutting through the potholes of Roundhouse Hollow. "Take your time, my boy, take your time," the Benevolent Landowner offered as Theodore Munney dropped out the door, but Cal kept the engine running. Growing grass did not wait. Yes, the only Bygone Days food Calvin could afford were the Cub Scout hot dogs, and those upset his stomach. He did, however, look forward to the pancake breakfast at the Fire Hall on Saturday morning, reasonably priced, all-you-can-eat, and a fund-raiser, satisfying Cal's stomach, pocketbook, and liberal leanings all at once. And over the past couple years, as Calvin was aging into a county elder, Bygone Days held one other allure—the anointing of the Knight of Olde Berker.

Theodore Munney recrossed his yard with his distinctive gait of an unconfident chicken. He swung into his seat, the stuffed pillowcase of dirty laundry perched in his lap like a chubby beheaded child. "Now that's a good lad," lauded the Benevolent Landowner.

"WreckupatSlanesville. Themboysdealindrugs."

As they neared Main Street again, Calvin directed Blackie down a parallel detour. Despite the seduction of the Bygone Days setup—no, not even Cal was immune—he could risk not even a peek. Not with the matter of the Lions Club booth. But Calvin could feel Theodore Munney's eyes straining to penetrate through the intervening block, and at each intersection, Cal fought the urge himself. Then, at the corner of Bluebonnet and Shute, Blackie took his own wheels, veered left. And spilled them plop into the brouha.

Stout women poled up canopies for the crafts fair while apprentice volunteer firemen pushed brooms through gutters and veterans speared American flags into parking meter tubes. Those storeowners who'd weathered Wal-Mart wheeled wares out of doors, portapotties were wrestled off trucks, and overhead, cousins Tick and Carroll Might dangled from ladders, precarious cupids in camouflage pants, stringing the Bygone Days banner. Roland, the little man who lived daytimes on the bench in front of the courthouse and nighttimes in the courthouse furnace room, oversaw it all from his seat at the stoplight. Theodore Munney thrust his head and shoulders into the stir, someone shouted his name, he pretended not to hear, and the Lions Club booth loomed.

Calvin Bergdoll's sugar squirted up. He yanked his eyes to the opposite side of the street. Where, yes, a lone Cub Scout towed a red wagon piled with hot dog buns, *Truant!* Cal's guts soured—

"Gonnashootoutupthetracks." Theodore Munney's machine-gun stutter bumped Calvin from his demons. He glanced out the windshield on Theodore Munney's side. In the field beside the grade school milled men in blue and gray, the uniforms baggy in peculiar places and clingy as long underwear in others. Cal's face tightened. *Republican stuff.* A few were pitching canvas pup tents the color of putty, and a copper cauldron already dangled from a tripod of sticks. Here was another bad side of Bygone, and Theodore Munney needed no such influence, having just a few weeks ago asked Calvin to drive him to the high school to talk to the recruiter who trolled the halls as a kind of Republican-funded guidance counselor.

"Gonnashootoutupthetracks," Theodore Munney fired again.

By now the tents were behind them, Blackie rolling down Town Hill and into the valley where Calvin lived. In Cal's head jarred something he'd overheard at the Senior Center then chosen to forget. This year, along with their usual encampment and marching in the parade, the Civil War reenactors were to perform some kind of fake battle for the benefit of the tourist train gawkers. The battle would be staged in a defunct cornfield a mile up the river behind Calvin's house.

Cal cleared his throat. "Yes, I did hear that." His voice was measured now, at once autocratic and compassionate. The Progressive Mental Health Worker seasoned with a strand of Stern Father. "I never did understand why people would want to be involved in something like that, and I know you don't either." But in the darkest levels of Calvin's brain sediment slurked a knowledge Cal was not even aware he was about to speak from: that his own family had favored the Confederacy. That Roland, the little man on the bench, who used to show up at Calvin's mother's asking for odd jobs or money, was, according to family legend, a descendant of Calvin's family's slaves.

"But if you had to take a side," the Progressive Mental Health Worker continued, and now he was addressing a more general audience—a meeting of mental health workers, or a collection of handicapped people, or his six children—than he was Theodore Munney, "you'd want the Union." His eyes flicked to the side of the road where a black and brown dog rump vanished into the cocklebururs and broom sedge. "That's the blue clothes," he said.

THEODORE MUNNEY HAD only wanted to cut grass for fifteen minutes. After that, Calvin had generously and patiently driven him the two miles back into town where he dropped him at Theodore's second-favorite hangout spot, the BP station, even though Cal had reason to suspect that the back room of the BP was one place Theodore was absorbing inspiration for his insubordination. Now, with Theodore Munney's chopped-grass-colored clothes spinning in the washer and Cal's wife in town setting up the Bygone Days' Fine Arts Room, Calvin was having his quiet time.

He took it in the TV room with his deer heads, First Buck and Biggest Rack, looking on from their mounts as Cal watched the Arts Channel, a commercial-free station that aired segments of ballets and operas and symphonies often backdropped with beautiful scenery from European ruins. The Arts Channel not only permitted Calvin to exercise his cultivated side, not easy in a county that had just gotten its second stoplight, but also lowered his blood pressure and his sugar, too. He was enjoying a concoction of leftover beef stew, a can of peas, a can of sardines, and some past-due milk he'd picked up for a very reasonable price at the County Pride supermarket. He dipped two chunks of old Italian bread into his creation to soften them. His daughters insisted that people with diabetes shouldn't eat white bread. Even though it didn't taste sweet, they said, it somehow turned to sugar in your body. An interesting but suspect fact.

As Cal chewed, he eyed the carry-around phone he'd placed within reach before he'd sunk into the bog of the couch. He'd already checked the answering machine—although he had no idea how you retrieved messages, he knew a blinking light signaled one—but it had been blank. He took a long swallow of his SunnyD orange drink. Well, with the anointing of the Knight of Olde Berker not until tomorrow night, they'd probably make the nomination calls this afternoon or evening. He pictured the committee cloistered in the bowels of the courthouse, possibly in the room beside the one where Roland slept, possibly throwing their arms up in relief and in disbelief that here they'd sat for hours and had only now thought of the obvious choice. *Doughnuts all around!*

Someone struck the floor bottom under Calvin's feet hard enough to vibrate his left slipper. He chose to ignore this in favor of a Wagnerian opera snippet featuring Brunhild. "I don't think my tarn helmet covers me completely," the subtitle read. Cal squinted. *Tarn helmet. Now that's one you don't often see.* Under the floor, someone snarled. Someone snarled back. "A woman's anger passes quickly." *Huh.* Calvin started to wag his head in agreement as he often did to demonstrate his intellectual compatibility with the Arts Channel, then stopped mid-nod.

The under-floor exploded into squeals and thrashes, concussion-hard *thwacks* and fratricidal growls. Calvin bared his bottom teeth in frustration, set his saucepan on the couch beside him, spread his knees, and glared into the carpet. "Quit that! You all quit that!" *Growing pains.* They fought down there as fiercely as his own children had fought up here, this litter of possums coming of age under the TV room, never mind how easy he'd made their lives, weaning them himself with cookie sheets of cat food they gorged on after dark. "Quit that!" the Stern Father ordered once more, stomping his slippers. The cat food was left over from his own cats, now all dead or run away. *Cat food.* He'd tasted it a couple times. *Kind of fishy.* Now the possums were obeying, or they'd run themselves down, and Calvin moved his saucepan back onto his lap. *But a whole lot better than dog food.*

At that moment, the back door opened and shut. Calvin thumbed the mute.

A body blurred past the TV room door. Calvin tautened under his plaid.

Raising his hand slowly, as one would not to startle an animal, Cal tugged down his Almost Heaven cap and retracted like a turtle, and his beard helped, too, along with large glasses so light-sensitive an outsider could see through them only in semidarkness. His tinnitus, as it did in moments of crisis, admitted a thin laser of clear sound, and, the deer heads listening with him, Calvin detected the soft pop and hiss of the refrigerator seal.

It was his thirty-three-year-old son. The one who never left West Virginia, the one who never left town, the one who had only recently left the house. The son who used to have a few problems.

The son stepped into the TV room balancing a sandwich that looked to be baloney on a paper napkin, in his other hand a 7-Eleven coffee cup the size of a two-liter pop bottle. He settled into the dog-hair-ridden easy chair, threw a leg over the chair's arm, fixed his eyes on the television, and slurped. "Got any jobs for me, Dad?"

Calvin released the mute and feigned reimmersion in the Arts Channel. Using his hat bill as a sort of blind, he studied his son who used to have a few problems. Recently his son's oil-splattered jeans had been hanging slack on his hips and even his elbows looked sharper than usual. His cheekbones knobbed against his skin and his eyeballs bulged, but the son had a hat bill blind of his own. Plus he almost always kept enough distance between himself and Calvin that Cal couldn't discern if there was blood in the whites. *That skinny . . . when it's just liquor he's into, he gets kind of fattish* . . . Calvin entombed that thought in his brain soil in favor of something he'd heard his bride say to a friend on the phone the other day. "He's just happier than he's ever been!" And, "He looks better than he has in years!"

"You can finish up that grass Theodore didn't get to." Calvin plugged his mouth with beef stew and sardines.

"Okay." The son unfolded onto his feet, already moving towards the door, taking his sandwich with him. "I can do it this afternoon. Could you pay me now?"

"And how am I to know how many hours it will take?" Cal asked peevishly. The Savvy Businessman, a legacy from his departed father. He would not be taken advantage of.

"It'll be worth at least ten dollars," the son said.

Calvin spooned more concoction into his mouth, his eyes trained on a string ensemble performing Vivaldi's "Summer" in the National Botanical Garden of Wales. The son who used to have a few problems waited in the doorway. Cal reached the bottom of the saucepan and diligently scraped its sides. A second possum skirmish broke out, this one shorter-lived, but concluding with a squeal of acute injury, possibly death. The son leaned comfortably in the doorframe, also watching the National Botanical Garden of Wales.

Calvin set aside his saucepan. He shifted his hips and extracted a faded rump-shapen wallet. Shielding it from his son's eyes, he thumbed through bills until he crossed a ten. He worked it out of the wallet and laid it on the couch beside him without looking at it or at the son as he picked it up.

The back door slammed. *Probably has some work in town.* A starter shrieked, the familiar cry of Floodie, a burgundy Chevy Ciera who had gone through the '96 flood and, seven years later, still had river silt drifted in the bottom of her gas gauge and speedometer. Most of her engine had had to be replaced part by part, but Floodie ran. *That Floodie.* Calvin nodded and rotated his legs onto the couch for a rest. *She's a survivor.*

ON HIS WAY back to the house two hours later after a disappointing Senior Center lunch of shriveled Salisbury steak and hefty chunks of white cake he'd had to decline on account of his sugar—and quite proud of himself he was for declining—Calvin decided he had no choice. A clandestine inspection of the Lions Club booth was his duty as a lifelong, if currently boycotting, Lion himself. Inhaling stiffly through his nose, he positioned his cap over his face. Yes, they'd recognize his vehicle, but, with luck, mistake its driver as his bride or his son. "All right, Blackie," Cal whispered. "Gee haw."

Main Street's metamorphosis was complete, craft booth canopies erect, the Bygone Days banner rippling in the spring breeze, porta-potties neatly twinned in opportune alleys. Cal and Blackie wheeled by the Athletic Boosters' dunking booth, a funnel cake truck rushing by in the opposite lane, more truant Cub Scouts with buns—and there it was. Calvin's heart twisted.

Lion Halsted was wrestling the used-eyeglass barrel into position, Lion Stephens tacking a price sign over the fund-raiser brooms, and they were going to sell chili this year, Cal remembered. Blackie tugged towards the curb where Calvin could at least throw out a few encouraging words to his fellow Lions if he couldn't pitch in with the setting up himself—and he couldn't, he had no stamina for such anymore, not with this sugar—and now was certainly the time to stop, if ever. Before Helen Smithster got off work from her secretary's job and arrived to boss and cow her aging Lion man-slaves.

Calvin Bergdoll gritted his molars. *Helen Smithster.* He plunged the name into his mind muck and gave it a punch for good measure *Helen Smithster Helen Smithster* it bobbed back to the surface, *Helen Smithster*, he swatted, it scooted, *Helen Smithster Helen—*

A bawl-mouthed mad-eyed Republican woman with a last name no one had heard of, who, on the tide of out-of-state imports seeking the peace of West Virginia, then infecting it with their hyperactive hubbub (and worse), had moved to Berker County from New Jersey thirty years ago. At first she'd meddled in others' business, Calvin had been spared, but then she'd set her improvement sights on the Lions Club, *and what does she think the Lionesses are for?* Cal couldn't resist a last glimpse in his rearview, Lion Stephens' price sign already gusting away. The sleepy, unsuspecting Lions had, to Calvin's horror, fallen under Helen Smithster's spell, and Miss Machiavelli had risen through the ranks like a house afire, seizing the offices of secretary, tail twister, finally president, at which point Cal, his heart heavy, had no choice but to go on strike. After forty years of every-other Thursday meetings, Calvin only attended now when the club met at Grassy Creek Chapel, to remind himself of how bad things had got and because the Grassy Creek Chapel women-of-the-church baked the best hot rolls he'd ever eaten.

But there was Theodore Munney, a half-block away, hen-pacing in front of the video store. Brightening, Calvin punched a little honk that Theodore Munney pretended not to hear. *Backwards.* This time Calvin let Blackie pull all the way over.

Theodore Munney was staring at the courthouse across the street. When Cal called to him through the open passenger window, Theodore spasmed his head like he'd not known Blackie was there. After a few seconds, he pullet-jerked to the window, still not making eye contact, his face as serious as a funeral home.

"Hello, Theodore," Calvin offered cheerily. In his rearview mirror he could see Theodore Munney's ostensible girlfriend, Nicole, arranging an armload of history-flavored videos on a rack she'd pushed outdoors. And then—Cal twinged—Floodie swelled in the mirror; escaped it; and passed Blackie at a good ten miles over the speed limit. The son who used to have a few problems tossed Calvin a nonchalant two-finger wave. Theodore Munney's gaze was tracking a ring of coffee stain on Blackie's dash.

"Well, now," continued Calvin. "How about we finish cutting that grass?"

Theodore Munney rotated his head at a right angle so Cal was looking into the gray-brown bristle tracks in the hollow of his cheek. It occurred to Cal that Theodore Munney had not simply missed a spot but had chosen not to shave.

"Cottonpickindruggieshithervan." Theodore glowered.

An unpromising reply. Calvin set his teeth. *Good thing I didn't eat that cake.* He'd spent hours of his limited free time attempting to diagnose Theodore Munney using, despite how hard the Progressive Mental Health Worker had tried to keep up with the trends, terminology in vogue during his mental health heyday, the 1970s. Theodore was sharper than Trainable MR, this Cal knew, but to call him duller than Educable MR, even though Theodore couldn't read, was also inaccurate. Theodore Munney functioned on a plane not just outside of, but on a tilt to, all these. Some days Calvin felt optimistic that Theodore was of average intelligence and just needed to be coaxed out of his shell, a shell that had thickened and hardened during Theodore Munney's childhood up on Salem Orchard under the heavy, calloused hand of his father. Other days, especially lately, Calvin was arriving at just plain stubborn. Nutley Randalpin had been a more cut-and-dried case, predictable and tractable, if less interesting. But one thing you had to say about Theodore Munney was that he had a robust sense of justice. At times admirable. At others, obstacle.

"Now Theodore. I'm beginning to lose my patience." Calvin closed his eyes for a second and envisioned the National Botanical Garden of Wales. "I'm only going to ask one more time: do you want to finish your job?" Although the Garden didn't come, the violins did. Cal's irritation ebbed one degree. "I'll pay you when you're done, and we'll pick up your laundry while we're at the house."

"Cottonpickindruggieshithervan."

Calvin sighed. He turned his own head towards the courthouse. Roland, keeper of the stoplight, sat on his bench, one ankle cocked across his knee, his stubby arms winged out along the bench back, his mouth arrested in its permanent at-no-one smile.

"Gottatakebackthecounty. Gottatakerback."

"All right. All right. We'll finish it tomorrow." Cal flipped the ignition and sat a few seconds longer, Theodore Munney not moving either. "Now you behave yourself."

Theodore Munney gave no sign he had heard.

THIS TIME CALVIN spied Silas for certain, loping across a just-planted soybean field. He tapped the horn again, just in case Silas would pause long enough to recognize Blackie's distinctive exhaust system and then sprint back, but Silas was already an eel-colored streak evaporating over the riverbank. A hundred-pound Rott-Doberman cross who misunderstood himself as a lap dog, Silas had been acquired five years ago, by the son who used to have a few problems, and was dumped on Cal and his bride a few months later. Silas, like all Calvin's children, was a vagabond, a wanderer. He spent most of his time running off to eat cast-off hamburgers behind McDonald's and to have sex. On porches and in yards within a six-mile radius of Cal's house, Calvin often spotted little Silases, or even big ones. *Powerful genes*. Cal nodded to himself.

He pulled into the driveway to find his wife's car snugged up near the back door. The riding mower moped in the uncut yard. Stepping into the house, Calvin made his daily stop at the gun cabinet, where he counted aloud through its glass door.

"One. Two. Three. Four." He nodded to Biggest Rack. The same number the gun cabinet had held for the past couple months, these four survivors of the original eleven, all hunting rifles, most of them heirlooms. The one that had dropped First Buck when Cal was just twelve years old had been the first stolen, almost a decade ago, and for that disappearance and the next one, Calvin had marched into the pawn shop and demanded their return. Slope Hines had said somebody'd have to pay for them. Calvin knew that the somebody was not him. Now for a second, little mud spouts of rage at the son spurted up in Cal's mind, but then frantic, busy hands buried them like a cat in a litter box. Calvin kicked behind himself and ran.

He could hear the staccato peck of his bride holed up in her office on her laptop, no doubt doing computer mail to his children, receiving news he'd never hear about, dispatching reports on his bad behaviors. *Computers. Secret stuff*. Calvin had never learned to type. He drifted into the doorway behind her. His wife, he had always known, was smarter than he was. She, however, had not come from a well-established family like his. That made them even. He had just separated his lips to ask her if she'd checked the answering machine when she said, without turning away from her screen, "Are those Theodore Munney's clothes in the washer?"

Calvin gently cleared his throat. "Yes, my dear." The Courtly Gentleman. Perhaps not even a West Virginian gentleman, perhaps not even Southern. Perhaps Russian. A Russian gentleman.

"Well, move them into the dryer. I have a load to do myself."

The Russian Gentleman transcended this. "Any phone messages for me?"

This time she did turn around. "Who were you expecting to call you?"

His bride. At moments like these, it was best to perceive her as a vague presence with temperature, an ambulatory heat. It was when she rippled into focus like she was under the influence of tracking on a VCR that he and she got into trouble. He backed away to hobble up the stairs for his afternoon nap. If his wife had time to fool around with computer mail, she had time to move Theodore Munney's clothes.

On the way to the room where he'd slept alone for ten years, he passed the door to hers. A pink and white quilt was pulled square over the bed, her dresser orderly, the fragrance of powder and face lotion tendrilling out the door. She complained she could smell his room from all the way down the hall. Calvin understood. Women's sense of smell was overly developed, they were overly evolved in that way and in others, which made it harder for them on this earth. Cal eyed the answering machine she kept hostage on the far side of the bed.

With his best ear tuned to his bride's little office beneath him, Calvin placed a foot over the threshold. He leaned onto it. It held his weight without a creak. Emboldened, he swung his other leg in. Still silence. In studied slow motion, he lurched across the room, resisting the roll of butterscotch Life Savers on her dressing table, until at last he stood over the answering machine.

0 Messages.

Calvin didn't bother to sneak as he left.

In his room, the mattress and box springs squatted directly on the floor so that Cal had to crawl down instead of up to get into bed, and once there, the frame rose around him like the bed rails in the mental hospitals he'd visited so often in his work. The enamel pot with a wire handle that he'd kept under the bed until the mattress fell through stood off in a corner. When nature called in the middle of the night, that was where the call came from. Calvin peeled off shoes, jeans, and two layers of plaid shirts, draping them over the bed frame, lastly swapping his Almost Heaven hat for his nightcap, a blaze-orange toboggan he kept on the bedpost. Stepping down onto the mattress, he stretched his envied physique full-length, folded his hands over his breast, and sighed.

His view from here was the dresser top across the room. On it Calvin'd propped a photo of his late mother and departed father in a frame of metal ivy, and he'd scattered around that small pictures of his kids at younger and more controllable ages. All of them except the son who used to have a few problems had moved away and found good jobs. They returned to Berker less and less often with every year that passed. *Busy.* He'd scrunched up and folded into the edge of the mirror the newspaper announcement of his election as Lions Club Tail Twister a decade ago, a final golden era before Helen Smithster. Tallest among the photos was a card featuring a buxom tom turkey that Theodore Munney had given him for his birthday last summer. Over top the turkey glittered the words "For a Special Grandpa on Thanksgiving." Inside it read "Thanks, Grandpa, for all the happiness, joy, and special memories you've given to our family."

Calvin rolled over to forage in the stale twist of covers for his book on the Russian royal family, found first a Donner Party book he'd completely forgotten and saw was nine months overdue at the library, plus two slices of Italian bread of the same brand he'd had earlier that morning but apparently from a much older loaf. At the foot of the bed, strangled in a T-shirt, he did unearth the Russian book, one of his all-time favorites and the source of his concept of the gun-bearer, a notion both he and Theodore Munney liked a lot.

He propped the book on his chest and thumbed to the chapter he'd been savoring since April. His wife, who zipped through five murder mysteries a week, ridiculed Cal's reading pace of two or so pages a day. *If you move slowly, you'll notice more things.* Calvin's eyebrows raised, and he tipped his toboggan to a personality he hadn't seen in a while. The Seasoned Woodsman. He polished off the first piece of found Italian bread, half-consciously patting himself on the back—a lesser roof-of-the-mouth would have needed stitches—and motored into the second.

When exactly the words "Catherine the Great" became "The Great Muppet Caper" Cal could not have said. "A Muppet Family Christmas," "Elmo's Adventures in Grouchland," "Big Bird in China," the phrases scrolled by, until the fruity odor of Theodore Munney pooled into Calvin's sinuses, and *oh no, uh-oh, oh no, uh-oh,* Calvin clutched at the bed frame, but it was too late. He'd been snatched into another daydream.

The daydreams had been coming with more frequency lately, day-dreams unpleasant, daydreams as uncontrollable or more than night dreams, and now Cal's perspective was enlarging. He could see the black gridwork of more video racks, Theodore Munney's back immediately in front of the rack Cal floated behind. To Theodore's right the glass candy case, its microwave popcorn packets and Raisinets, to his left the sooty path through the gray-blue carpet, route of heaviest video-renter traffic. Calvin saw all this with a lucidity so exquisite he might be peering through God-burnished eyeballs and through tinnitus so amplified he wouldn't have heard the fire siren if it blew, and *oooohhh. Oooohhh,*

Cal reached for the rack to steady himself, but his hand passed through. Because, most unsettling of all, in the daydreams, Calvin could see and feel himself, but nothing there could see, hear, feel, him.

Behind the counter, blonde Nicole, attractive as always if a bit wide, was narrating with dramatic gesticulation and a heart-wringing expression of been-done-wrong a story to young Deputy Sheriff Justin Ripper. Theodore Munney jackhammered his fist in his hand, while Deputy Justin shook his head and shifted his holster, and suddenly the three of them took off for the rear of the store, Calvin towed behind Theodore like a helpless balloon.

The shock of sunlight in the grubby parking lot might have felled Cal if there'd been body to fell, and there among dandelions and Frito bags squatted Nicole's green Dodge Caravan, the passenger side scraped, creased, and well-stove in. Nicole set to demonstrating the unopenability of the sliding door, and Theodore Munney, Calvin could discern by the hen-bob of his head, stuttered along as indignant backup chorus, while Justin put his pen to paperwork on the van's snubbed hood. Then Nicole pointed towards the unattended cash register, the trio hustled back into the store, Cal again dragged after.

Here Justin undertook his report on the microwave popcorn counter, and Nicole retold her story to a customer. Theodore Munney had halted at a respectable distance from young Deputy Sheriff Justin Ripper, Calvin hover-trapped behind Theodore. But very soon, Cal felt the sensation as though it were his own, Theodore Munney could no longer resist the uniform, holster, badge. And nearer to young Justin Theodore sidled, nearer on light baby-chick feet, nearly imperceptibly nearer and nearer. Until Deputy Justin Ripper began eyeing the approaching Theodore Munney with a touch of discomfort.

Finally Justin laid down his pen. He stepped away from the counter and from Theodore Munney, and he reached into the deep pocket of his bear-brown deputy pants. As Theodore Munney's eyes widened, Young Justin pulled out his palm and opened it. Theodore Munney leaned closer, so Calvin did, too. At first Cal identified the objects—there were four—as edibles. Then he understood there were not misshapen malt balls. They were miniés. Civil War reenactor rifle ammunition.

Gentle Justin Ripper dropped two into Theodore Munney's fist.

"It is unlikely Zubov felt any strong attraction to sixty-one-year-old Catherine although she was a well-preserved lady with sound white teeth."

Cautiously, Calvin lowered his book and darted his eyes about his room. Black-and-white parents, 2-by-3 children, chamber pot, bed frame like asylum rails—each stood in its appointed place. Cal brushed bread crumbs from his collar and forced a smile. *Those ole daydreams! Symptoms of genius. Ha-ha.* But Calvin's heart beat harder than it should. He blinked rapidly and drew a few faux-emphysemic breaths, the ones that brought back memories of his late cigarette-favoring mother. This settled him some. Calvin turned over. He arranged his limbs into a napping position. When he closed his overworked eyes and saw only darkness, his relief carried him instantly into sleep.

He was awakened at 4 PM by a summons from the refrigerator. *Right on schedule.* Calvin's stomach growled. He lifted his book off his hip, pausing to nod at the cover photo of Czar Nicholas and his doomed family, then folded in the jacket flap to secure his place. He'd started on page 272. He closed it on page 272. There was a kind of symmetry to it. *Always learning. Always learning.*

He staggered down the stairs, mouth watering. Through the dining room, around the kitchen table, the refrigerator drew its pilgrim on. Its sanctimonious whiteness. Its dependable hum. Its chrome handle like a ritual instrument, and now, it stood before him, its skin pimpled with magnets and coloring book pages, this suffering at the hands of his bride making it all the more precious. Calvin reached behind him and scraped a chair across the floor. He extended his right hand and pulled, bathing his belly in light. Tugging the chair closer, he sat down, his thighs spread, his back bent, his torso stretched into the refrigerator's bosom. From somewhere he overheard a pleasure grunt.

And then he was sorting and shuffling, lid-lifting and poking. He was sniffing, he was tasting. After Russian history books, Calvin favored tales of explorers and adventurers, Shackleton, Cook, Everest toppers from Hillary to Krakauer. In the refrigerator, Calvin had encountered heretofore undocumented hues and textures, had discovered exotic molds and Ice Age fungus. In the refrigerator, Calvin had observed fantastic patterns of shrinkings and separations, swellings and discolorations, in this very refrigerator, he had stumbled upon odors that eluded the English language. Odors perhaps only expressible in Olde Russian. Here anonymous paper bags and Styrofoam boxes gave up their secrets, today drumsticks as desiccated as shrunken heads, a broccoli and cheese that seemed to have reproduced like a yogurt culture. Today blue sour cream and germinating meatballs, and now Calvin hailed a banana as black as a St. Petersburg winter night, next a tiny wedge of cheese grits one generation removed from the Confederacy. Refrigerator as mapless territory, unbagged summit, sacred grotto. Refrigerator as archive, antique auction, refrigerator as mausoleum. At last, Calvin settled on a green Jell-O salad left over from Easter. He shut the door to conserve electricity and dignity, leaned back in his chair, pulled a spoon from his breast pocket, and slurped.

His wife passed behind him like a shade. "You know you're not supposed to eat that."

"I don't guess anybody called while I was taking my nap?" Calvin asked in a jaunty tone as his wife gathered her pocketbook and other mysterious satchels for her return to the Fine Arts Room. Like she had earlier, she stopped and looked directly at him.

"Who were you expecting?"

Calvin continued to sip his collapsed green salad. Then his wife, so much shrewder than she needed to be, understood. "Oh!" Her eyebrows pulled to a vee. "You were waiting for them to call about the Knight of Olde Berker, weren't you?"

Never had the VCR tracking been so clear. In this moment, Calvin Bergdoll hated his wife.

"Cal, they announced those nominations two weeks ago. Didn't you see it in the paper?"

Calvin's organs turned to stone.

He stood, cast the bowl into the sink, and swung open the refrigerator. "I don't have time to read the paper. I have too much work to do," he muttered into the leftovers to conceal his face.

"Well, I'll tell you this: if you're ever going to be nominated, you're going to have to behave better around town. Finding a commode to pee in instead of a camellia bush would be a start. And if you think I haven't heard about what happened in County Pride last week just because I haven't mentioned it, you couldn't be more wrong." Bags rustled, car keys jingled, and the kitchen door hinges squealed shut behind her.

Calvin snatched the meatballs, dumped them into the broccoli and cheese, and slammed it all into the microwave. His innards burst from fossil to flame. Who in God's name had been on that committee? What in God's brain had they been thinking? Who in this county was a worthier candidate for Knight of Olde Berker than he? His family had settled in this valley seven generations ago, he'd been born here and had lived here his entire life except for the last two years of college in Morgantown, and then he'd come home every weekend. His father had been an esteemed leading citizen and a landowner, and Calvin Bergdoll had been respected as well, had even served for one term on the school board, never mind that his wife believed he'd won only because the photo on his campaign poster triggered rumors that he was terminally ill (*bad lighting*), there were worse reasons people got elected to things. The microwave beeped, the startle of it ratcheting his rage, and Calvin seized the softened Tupperware and lurched to the TV room. If not a nomination for Knight of Olde Berker, they should at least make him an honored exhibit, a representative of living history. And if not that, surely someone should interview him. An unsolicited voice broke in. *If you want to be part of Bygone Days, why don't you volunteer? Nobody calls me up and begs me to help, you know*. Well, his wife wasn't even from here.

He dropped heavily into her newish red recliner, the one he was forbidden to sit in unless he was wearing clean clothes and had recently showered. Grabbing the remote—*focus! focus!*—he streamlined his brain to where he could punch the buttons for the Arts Channel. The County Pride incident hadn't been his fault, he had not started it, he was a peaceable creature, he never did. A German choir. Medieval hymns. Calvin expelled a strangled breath and crouched over his meatballs. Next a three-minute excerpt from a play, *The Cherry Orchard*, Cal'd not seen this one before, and, oh, it was Russian, he pricked up, a Russian play. Calvin's sugar considered tiptoeing back to the nether regions of his digestive tract or wherever it was that it belonged. And after the play, a Gregorian chant while the camera panned statues of stone saints in some Old Country crypt.

That was when the revelation struck. As Calvin watched the second slow survey of the gallery of saints, certain granite faces assumed the features of—Cal squinted—of former . . . was it so? Former Knights of Old Berker? Calvin leaned forward and stared. And now, yes, entire statues dissolved into Knights, a kind of psychic palimpsest, Calvin transfixed, the white heads, the gnarled limbs. The canes, one wheelchair, a toupee, and a glass eye. And by the time ballerinas replaced the crypt, Calvin Bergdoll understood.

To the number, the Knights of Bygone Days past had been older than he. Calvin loosed an epiphanic grunt. Although Cal had many health problems and was probably soon to die, had been at the risk of death for twenty years, he was actually just sixty-eight and looked even younger than he was.

That was it. They were postponing his nomination because of his age.

He must be patient. Let those who appeared nearer death than he take their turn.

Calvin swallowed his last broccoli spear, then lay back in the recliner, removed his cap, and set it on his knee facing him where he could see the Almost Heaven. First Buck and Biggest Rack radiated their assent. The floor underneath lay silent, the possums at truce. And then Calvin remembered something else, and he only had to launch himself out of the recliner and swing a few feet to the left to reach it. On the bookshelf, cached behind a framed finger-painting by his little grandson, a fist-sized chunk of deer baloney.

FRIDAY MORNING FOUND Calvin Bergdoll, Theodore Munney, and Blackie on the street in front of Rita's Diner. Calvin was not sure how long Rita's ban was in effect, and with the price hikes at McDonald's, he'd decided he'd just show up and see if anyone said anything. He'd made sure they arrived after 8:30 AM to prevent any chance of running into Helen Smithster, who worked a few storefronts away and occasionally frequented Rita's on the early shift. As they walked in, Cal forwent his usual hearty and undirected greetings. The restaurant, the size of a two-car garage, was half full, a couple Calvin didn't know, probably Bygone Days gawkers, in intense conversation under the broken cuckoo clock, others, whom Cal did know, hypnotized by *Fox News* on a television mounted in the front corner. A few old men nodded at Calvin, but Rita just looked up through the slot into the kitchen, then looked away. Calvin and Theodore took their favorite booth near the front window.

"Anything you want, Theodore my lad. Anything you want. As long as it's not over a dollar fifty. Ha-ha."

Before he'd left the house that morning, Cal'd checked the dryer, found it full of his wife's clothes, and flipped open the washer to see the sodden heap of Theodore Munney's. She must have pulled them out long enough to wash hers, then dumped them back. *A clever one.* The lawn mower, beaded with dew, squatted forlorn in the mostly uncut yard. *Him and Floodie'll probably be over to finish it once the grass dries.* Now a high school student named Tasha Haggerty carried over two tiny plastic water glasses. Calvin unfurled his arm towards her.

"This is Miss Tasha, a Russian lady from Purgitsville," the Courtly Gentleman announced. Tasha rolled her eyes. "And this, Miss Tasha"—the arm now gestured towards Theodore Munney—"is Theodore O. Munney, my gun-bearer."

"Do you all want anything to drink besides water?" Tasha said.

Cal scanned the menu. Somehow during the ban, he'd forgotten the outrageousness of Rita's coffee prices. "Just water," he said, the Courtly Gentleman doused. "And a sausage biscuit for Theodore Munney and a bowl of oatmeal with brown sugar for myself." Tasha scribbled on her pad, unsmiling. "And"—a mute button went off in his brain, but the signal didn't reach his mouth in time—"for a dollar fifty, it better be a big bowl of oatmeal."

Tasha swished off without comment.

Calvin settled back in the booth and tucked his napkin in his collar. "Well, Theodore," he began in his most expansive patronly tone, "would you like to cut a little grass today?" No sooner had "little grass" crossed his lips than a flash of Floodie flitted by. Cal swiveled to the window and watched Floodie slow for an instant at the stop sign. *Ten dollars would buy you a lot bigger breakfast than a bowl of oatmeal and a cup of water.*

"D-d-d-d-d-didchahearwhathappenedatthedumpyesterday?"

"What?" asked Calvin.

"Bigpilecinderblocksblewup."

"Hmmm," said Cal. He had spied, on a table that two of his acquaintances had just vacated, a piece of scrapple the dimensions of a Gideon New Testament. He said nothing. *I'm on my best behavior today.* Lou Seaton walked in, followed by his daughter, a friend of Calvin's youngest daughter's. Cal withdrew into his cap. His own children were very busy these days. They didn't often come home. It was hard to get to Berker. The nearest airport was a hundred miles away. The last time they'd come for Bygone Days, the son who had a few problems exercised poor judgment and forged three checks with Calvin's name. The other children were unhappy when Calvin refused to press charges, and their spirits were only moderately lifted when the son was arrested that weekend anyway for a gas driveaway at the 7-Eleven.

Cal surfaced from his cap to address Theodore Munney about the matter of grass. But Theodore Munney was gone.

Theodore was sprint-strutting out Rita's front door where a motley squadron of reenactors trudged down the center of Shute Street. Centuries and wars collapsed into four rows across and six down, their ranks including not only Confederates and Federals, but a few representatives from World Wars I and II and one musket-bearing

French and Indian remnant, Vietnam notable by its absence. A largely bedraggled and spiritless bunch, especially for the very first morning of Bygone Days, but Theodore Munney and now a couple of regulars from the VFW next door stood at attention on the sidewalk, one VFW denizen cocking a hand in salute. Lou Seaton was remarking to Tasha, "I hear they're actually going to reenact a battle this year. For the train."

Calvin shook a packet of Sweet'n Low into his ice water. The Republicans held a real allure for the mentally deficient. He frowned. He was fairly certain the comment about the cinder blocks was not an unequivocal yes to the grass-cutting.

Theodore scooted back into the booth, his eyes directed inside his head.

"I need you to cut some grass today, Theodore," the Stern Father pronounced.

Theodore Munney spit an ice cube back into his cup.

Now Tasha was setting Theodore Munney's biscuit on the table, the oatmeal nowhere to be seen, and Calvin glared. *Not coordinated enough to carry both at one time, shouldn't even be a waitress.* Theodore powered into his biscuit like he hadn't eaten since the dollar-twenty-nine one at McDonald's yesterday morning when Cal knew Nicole fed him Nip-Chee crackers and Sun Chips at the video store and that there was usually a pot of beans going in the back of the BP. But now Tasha was returning, bearing a gigantic orange tray possibly stolen from an all-you-can-eat buffet. Calvin unturtled an inch out of his hat. Tasha placed the tray on the table from which she'd recently cleared the enticing scrapple, then painstakingly transferred to Calvin—her effort not to spill so momentous she had to hold her breath—a bowl the size of the pan he used to feed Silas brimming with oatmeal and brown sugar.

Calvin Bergdoll sat back. Blinked. He mumbled thank you. But Tasha was already gone, and he hadn't even had the wherewithal to make his obligatory demand for more napkins. He leaned over the oatmeal to confirm it was real, his brain layers bubbling and burping, and through the mire beamed a ray of suspicion that some kind of joke was being played on him or revenge taken. But a bowl of oatmeal this big? For a dollar fifty? As revenge? Nothing made any sense.

Calvin saw no choice but to stir the sugar in good and eat.

As he did, a conversation from six months ago roiled up. He and a visiting daughter, the two of them sitting in this very booth, and Calvin, because he considered the morning a special occasion, spooning extra brown sugar on a much smaller bowl of oatmeal, and his daughter, shaking her head, saying, "I don't think you should eat that brown sugar. It might make you crazy."

Suddenly, everything went dark. A cool sogginess settled in the seat of Calvin's pants. And then, from the odor and the specific strain of clamminess, Cal deduced that he sat in Floodie's passenger seat, whose cushions still held a reservoir of floodwater, and now Calvin could see, with cornea-polished clarity, his son who used to have a few problems swinging out the driver's door, and Cal's heart sank to his belt. Son daydreams were the worst of the lot.

Calvin bobbed behind the son, at a slightly greater distance than the gap between him and Theodore Munney in the daydreams that featured Theodore, but his hearing just as obliterated—he might as well be standing on a Newfoundland bluff in a nor'easter—while the son slunk up a short sidewalk, hands in pockets, shoulders hunched, his legs and rear end lost in the once well-fitting billows of the belt-cinched jeans. They halted in front of a door with a torn screen, and there Calvin's vision broadened. It was the threshold of Berker's Unwed Mother HUD housing. No, no, that wasn't it, it was Single

Mother Housing now, but no, the Progressive Mental Health Worker scrambled to keep up. They had arrived at Berker County's Alternative Family Apartments.

The son pushed an arm through the ripped screen and knocked. After he dropped the arm, both hands quivered against his thighs. "Shakes," the son's contemporaries called him, and the first time Cal had answered the phone and "Shakes" had been requested, Cal had turned and shouted it into the upstairs without even thinking, so natural the nickname was. The door swung open by apparent remote control until Calvin dropped his eyes and spied behind it a heavy-browed boy of about six with a strange growing-out haircut that made his head look shingled.

Here his son's stride transmogrified from a slink to a cool side-of-the-foot-rolling amble, a nonchalant stroll down a hall with tile identical to the grade school cafeteria's. Calvin floated behind, the odor of burnt frozen-pizza cheese jumbling his appetite. At the end of this hall the son stopped, Cal did, too, before a monstrous easy chair. In this chair lounged not a single mother, but an aged boy.

At the son's entrance, the old boy in the chair smiled as broad and as false as a jack-o'-lantern, and he did not rise. Something about this gnome put Calvin in mind of a certain hyperactive eighth-grader on the son's junior high basketball team. But the present face looked as if a flash flood had gulched it and left the long hair permanently wet. The son eased over and clapped his hand right below the other's elbow, a kind of one-sided arm shake, and the shingle-headed child dropped on the floor a nose-length from a chalkboard-sized television to observe robots killing each other in metal compactors.

From a vantage point now to the side of his son, Calvin could see his mouth moving, the flood-faced boy's moving back, the old boy never shedding the smile and never desisting in shaking his head. The son who used to have a few problems extracted the ten-dollar bill that had so recently slept in Cal's wallet along with a fan of soggy ones, and he offered, too, an expression he'd offered Calvin infinite times. A face that had never told a lie, a face chagrined that it needed a favor at all, just this time and I'll never ask again, the son not yet unhandsome despite his decay, his eyes blue and baby-big, and into those eyes swam the son at fourteen, *everybody in my whole class is going, please Dad, Danny's mom will be there the whole time,* then the son at six, *please Daddy, will you buy me a milkshake, please Daddy, can I have a milkshake?* and lastly a chubby wailing infant, clenching in and out its trembling fists, a younger Cal trying to dam the noise with a pacifier. But the old boy, pumpkin grin fixed, never stopped shaking his head.

And then Calvin's vision held only his own hands, scraping oatmeal remains into a big Styrofoam cup. The hands began to shake. *Like father, like*—Calvin nudged the cup away and pressed his fingers on the table rim. Across from him, Theodore Munney was staring out the window as though he could see leftover imprints of the disheveled reenactors, apparently oblivious to both Cal's absence and his return.

Calvin squeezed his eyes open and shut a few times and repositioned his glasses. *Oh, the mature brain.* He emitted a chuckle that petered out in a cluck. The crazy tricks his mind played anymore, no doubt because it had so few outlets for his creativity, intellect, and spiritual proclivities. Just two weeks ago, his daughter in Colorado had called, and before thinking, he'd asked, "How's your hip?" For a moment, she'd been silent. Then: "How on earth did you know about that?" Calvin had swallowed. He remembered in yet another daydream following her up a mountain trail, granite and aspen, no West Virginia hill, then watching her boot slip and her fall hard on her hip. He'd stayed long enough to see her pick herself up and limp on.

His temperature had risen. He removed one layer of plaid and laid it across his arm. No time to wallow in mystery with his charge a half-arm's-length away. The Benevolent Landowner cleared his throat.

"Okay, my fine-feathered friend. Let's get to that grass."

HIS WIFE'S CAR was gone, and on the kitchen table, a note: "Cal. Please move TM's clothes to dryer." He'd enticed Theodore onto the Cub Cadet by mentioning how often and loudly it had been backfiring lately—"lately" applied loosely, but no harm—and now Calvin was stowing his oatmeal safely in the refrigerator. He paused. The landscape had shifted. A fresh take-home box his wife must have carried in last night. Calvin fumbled with the lid—onion rings, a real find, ideal for his midmorning snack in thirty minutes. Smiling and stroking the small hump of his belly, Cal was halfway to the TV room when he picked up the reek of river algae and faint cow manure, another happy surprise. Silas had come home.

"Oh. You decided to come home?" Calvin said gruffly as he dropped into the couch. Silas was spiraled up in his chair, his big head hanging over the chair's front so that he resembled a sedated python. He wagged his wrapped-around tail as best he could while Cal took the remote into confident hand, whispered a prayer, and—the third sign in five minutes that this day would go so much better than yesterday, oatmeal daydream aside—conjured "The Dance of the Sugar Plum Fairies," of all things. In May, of all times.

Much to be grateful for. Much, much, indeed. The pleasure of the oatmeal. Of Russian tutus and Christmas. Silas un-run-over and home. The grass shortening under Theodore Munney's rotations, onion rings in the kitchen. And the greatest blessing of all, his revelation about the median age of past Knights of Olde Berker. Quite proud of himself he was for that mathematical insight. Now whenever the Knight pierced his thoughts, Calvin felt only a short sharp twinge before wisdom salved it. And then there were the gratitudes to come, tomorrow's pancake breakfast, and a mere thirty-six hours after that, Bygone Days would be bygone. Calvin would recover his routine, and his bride hers, and without the bad influence of the reenactors and the general overstimulation of the celebration, Theodore Munney would return to tractability.

The back door slammed.

Calvin Bergdoll stiffened like a doe at a branch snap.

He tilted forward, his concentration searing a tunnel through the eternal ring in his ears. The lawn mower still throbbed in the near distance, and then a branch did snap, or rather, Theodore Munney ran over a rock. The footsteps to the kitchen had been too quick for his wife's. The refrigerator unsealed with a lip-smacking suck, and Calvin collapsed back into the couch, his sugar galloping, and affixed his gaze on the Prague Symphony. His son with a few problems swung open the TV room door, the onion ring box in his hand.

"I was just coming to finish up the grass. How come you got Theodore doing it?"

Calvin concentrated on Prague. "You were supposed to finish it yesterday." His ears flinched. In his head, it had been a growl, but somehow the TV room air ironed it into a whine.

The son rested the onion ring container on top of the television. No sign of onion ring protruded over its rim. The son rubbed Silas behind his ears, Silas responding with pre-orgasmic groans, the decimated onion rings a mocking crown over Czech cellos and violins.

"Got any other jobs?" said the son.

At that moment Theodore Munney stumbled-strutted in—"Busted eightathemdruggiesupSeymourHoller"—and Silas broke into maudlin whines meant to seduce Theodore Munney near enough that the dog could bury his muzzle in Theodore's rich aromas. Theodore didn't take the hint. Silas didn't give up the chair. An elf was striking Calvin's eardrum with the end of a baton.

"I'll finish up the grass, and then I'll weed the hedges."

"EightathemtheybustedupSeymourHoller."

"Can you pay me up front for the hedges? You'll be gone to lunch by the time I get back."

A skull smacked under Cal's feet and the Prague Symphony faded, now the son massaging Silas's chest, Silas rubberized, his limbs gangling out of the chair, and the head-smacking doubled, while Theodore Munney poked two fingers into the onion ring box and came up with a scrap of breading. Red splotches swam across Calvin's eyes while the Arts Channel began its three-minute-long plea for donations. Calvin clenched his butt cheeks, a fort around the wallet. One hand gripped the couch arm and the other a pillow embroidered with AS FOR ME AND MY HOUSE, WE SHALL SERVE THE LORD. But up from his mind sediment reeled an image of the son, in the striped shirt, black pants, and mask of a cat burglar, crawling through a window belonging to the wealthiest lawyer in town, the one with the penile implant, and behind the window image, a dimmer one, but distinct: the aged boy, his flood-face bisected by a pistol in his hand. A deer head nodded.

Calvin Bergdoll shifted his hip. He turned away and hunched over the wallet, drawing the Serve the Lord pillow closer to serve as shield, too. *None of any of their businesses*, not the son's, not Theodore's, not Silas's, not the possums with the knots on their heads. Two ones. Three twenties. He thumbed through again. No tens. No fives.

Pulling out the twenty was as painful as extracting a tooth. Calvin laid it on the couch beside him. The son departed, taking the bill but leaving the onion ring box.

Cal slumped back. He lifted his face to Biggest Rack, then First Buck. Both avoided his gaze. Silas squirmed out of his chair, stretched, padded to Calvin, and pushed his front paws, head, and sixty pounds' worth of his body into Cal's lap.

"Any of those onion rings left, Theodore?"

"Takebackthecounty," saidTheodoreMunney. "We'retakingerback."

BEFORE THEY REACHED the BP station, Calvin pulled Blackie over into the Baptist Church parking lot. He parted his lips to begin his talk with Theodore Munney, then prudently closed them against the pot of words boiling over in his throat. He noticed a potentially comforting Little Chug of chocolate milk resting in Blackie's cup holder. He tasted it. *Keeps better in winter.*

"Theodore, I'm losing my patience with you." Blackie shed another of the several hundred staples that held his headliner in place and a new sag drooped onto Cal's cap.

"If you work for me, you have to finish your job." Still the Stern Father, whom Calvin knew would fail with Theodore in this mood, but the appropriate personality would not present.

Theodore Munney feigned fascination with a pair of elderly women, their dress marking them as out-of-staters as distinctly as if they'd been in tribal costume, forging fearlessly into traffic towards a yard sale. Calvin Bergdoll's children were very busy. They didn't often come home. When they were growing up, he'd had a whole stable of yard tenders, Calvin had taught them the value of work. That accounted for why they were so successful now.

Theodore made a muffled noise about a flue fire.

"I pay you four dollars an hour and buy you breakfasts." Theodore Munney opened the glove box, toppling out a roll of toilet paper and a Baggie containing a half-eaten peanut butter sandwich.

"Now, Theodore. Does that sandwich belong to you?"

Theodore shoved the sandwich back into the glove and slammed it shut. Then he straightened at the waist, stretching his legs as far as they could go, and dug into his pocket. He wrenched out his fist. Calvin peered without turning his head. Theodore spread his fingers.

The two musket balls Justin Ripper had given him.

Theodore Munney snapped his palm over them, dropped out of Blackie's door, and pulleted to the BP without looking back.

Within Calvin's brain sludge rose a spiraling funnel cloud, the musket balls dancing on top it like plastic popcorn in a lottery bubble machine. Cal jiggled his head, then cocked it to one side and thumped it as though he were clearing water from an ear. *Happy thoughts. Happy thoughts.* He gripped the steering wheel and narrowed his eyes.

Friday. This is Friday. Calvin reset his cap, shoved some headliner fabric into a slit, and left the lot.

Because the Senior Center didn't serve lunches on Friday—*and whose idea was that, and was it laziness or stinge?*—Calvin usually visited his stroke victim friend to see what his helper had fixed. From the street where he parked, Cal could see Petie and his wife and the helper all sitting in the carport around the hood of Petie's Cavalier taking in the fresh May air. Petie's little terrier dog, Picky, sprung from lap to lap, darting his tongue at lips, and when he spied Calvin, he raced to him as well, scrabbling at his pants cuffs. The wife and the helper hailed Cal's approach with less enthusiasm.

"Oh. How are you, Cal?" *Well, it's not them I'm here to see.*

He stood behind Petie's wheelchair and placed a hand on Petie's shoulder. Petie smelled like baby powder. He did not turn around. The ladies continued their conversation, ignoring Calvin, although he noticed that the helper was carrying on her half of the dialogue as she backed towards the kitchen inside the sliding glass door. Cal patted Petie, a scraping motion across the top of his back. Petie didn't respond. In Lions Club, he and Petie had shot napkin spitwads at each other during speakers, catapulted butter pats off forks like the other Lions with healthy senses of humor. All that had ended with the finality of . . . yes, with the finality of a stroke, at the arrival of Helen Smithster.

"Here you go, Cal." Petie's helper placed a plastic picnic plate before him on the hood. Calvin squinted. A tuna sandwich. *And why hasn't she prepared something hot?* The Petulant Cousin from the City. *What pleasure does Petie have besides food anymore, and why does she think she's drawing a paycheck?* The helper, Peggy used-to-be Powell—Calvin couldn't recall who she was married to this time—had graduated from high school with Cal but now seemed a good bit younger than himself. *Well. Hasn't gone through half of what I have.* Now a female neighbor dog on the loose was sniffing with gusto the shrunken privates of the neutered Picky. Peggy looked at her kindly. "Honey," she told her, "he can't have no intersection."

I'd like to introduce that young lady to Mr. Silas.

"I think Helen has a real good chance," Nonie was saying.

Calvin's ears iced over. "Of what?"

Nonie looked a little surprised. "Getting Knight of Olde Berker."

Calvin's plastic plate collided with the fender.

"Oh, I don't even know who the nominees are," said Peggy formerly Powell.

"I didn't tell you? Lloyd Hines, and Maribel Summers, and Randolph McDouglas, Helen, of course," Nonie ticked them off on her fingers, "and . . . let's see, I'm forgetting someone . . . But I think Helen has the best chance of winning, everything she's done for this community. Especially after the Lions Club highway cleanup, all the organization and work that took." Nonie wagged an awestruck head. "They say almost every child in the county participated in that."

Peggy nodded. "Yes, she's made a real contribution. She certainly has. Why, Bygone Days itself might not even happen if she wasn't on the steering committee. Are you gonna get to the knighting this evening?"

Nonie shook her head, tipping her eyes towards Petie. "No, but we're gonna try to make the parade this afternoon."

From a great distance, Calvin Bergdoll sensed his legs unfolding. His joints as stiff as crusted sugar, his hands the temperature of freezer trays. His plastic plate slid to the carport floor with a spin and a ring. Picky vaulted from Nonie's lap to snuffle up bread crumbs and tuna seepage while Calvin's feet floundered off concrete and onto a softer green substance, Blackie now looming larger and larger before him.

"Leaving Cal?" Peggy called after him.

Helen Smithster, Knight of Olde Berker? Helen Smithster, Knight of Olde Berker? Helen Smithster, Knight of Olde Berker. Helen Smithster, Knight of Olde Berker. How could they, how could anyone, how could—her not over sixty years old and having moved to Berker County only thirty years ago when his genes had been here for generations and his body for sixty-eight years, Helen Smithster, who talked like her tongue lived in her nose, how could someone with an accent be Knight of Olde Berker? *A Frozen Child* . . . what was that phrase in the published diary of local Civil War hero Lt. Samuel White regarding an enemy he'd encountered during a watch? "A Frozen Child of the North," yes, that was it exactly, A Frozen Child of the North and a Republican as Knight of Olde Berker, Calvin Bergdoll visioned the surface of Indian Bluff cemetery ripple like an earthquake and his late mother and departed father each thrust an arm through their respective coffins and clasp hands in grief.

Now Blackie was cruising the streets of Berker at a pointed fifteen miles an hour, Calvin reveling in the frustration of the tailgaters, gunning the engine and spurting ahead when one tried to pass him on Bluebonnet Lane. *Helen Smithster, Knight of Olde Berker? Helen Smithster, Knight of Olde Berker?* He aimed Blackie's right front tire at an errant balloon and its explosion startled a family of four back to the curb like a covey of quail. He crept onto Main Street, its banners and its craft booths, its overpriced food stalls, nothing for him, stray reenactors comparing rifles and facial hair, and there was the spitting image of Floodie parked at the Moose, but that could not be, not this early in the day and with grass to be cut and hedges to be weeded. *Helen Smithster, Knight of Olde Berker. Helen Smithster, Knight of Olde Berker.* Blackie leaked a few more staples, and more fabric swagged down on Cal's Almost Heaven cap; he swiped it away, it drooped back, he swiped it away. He was an old man, it was true, with less energy now for civic contributions, yet he still cared for Theodore Munney and other county less fortunates, he still visited shut-ins, he was just coming from one now. *Fifty-five years old. I bet she's not yet fifty-five years old.* Gawkers choked the sidewalks, and this a Friday afternoon, where did out-of-staters get their money and time anyway, was West Virginia the only state that had to work?

He found himself steering towards the community building where his wife tended the Fine Arts Room instead of him. He would slip in and surprise her, reap a little relief from picking at her, just a bit, her anger and resentment better than nothing. Actually, better than a whole lot of things, plus they sometimes had little eats at such exhibits. But now he saw that the community building parking lot had been converted into a full-blown food court, every space occupied with some prohibitively expensive delectable, kettle corn, apple dumplings, Italian sausage sandwiches. A car that had been stalled behind Blackie roared past on Calvin's right, trying to teach him a lesson with his muffler, but Calvin did not care because he'd taught his lesson first.

And then Blackie must have taken the helm because before Calvin could plan it, they swung into the library's small parking lot where Calvin took the single spot left, handicapped, well, he'd earned it. He reeled through the automatic doors and into the reference section where, to his bewilderment and then his fury, he discovered an interloping antique exhibit a-crawl with even more gawkers, this, this, what Berker was coming to, not even the library a place of peace, and he charged on, ignoring the two or three antique fans who greeted him, and into the empty preschoolers' section. There in a darkish back corner Calvin Bergdoll collapsed across three beanbag chairs.

HE WAS AWAKENED by the whispers of children.

"Is he dead?"

Under his lowered Almost Heaven bill, Calvin raised his eyelids just enough that he could see through his lashes but no one could see through them.

"I don't know. Is his chest moving?"

A head dropped down towards Cal's plaid torso, the hair in a peculiar patches. Shingles. The boy he'd seen only a few hours ago at single-mother apartments.

"I don't think so," he whispered.

The other child waved in front of Calvin's face a damp palm creased with black, the tiny nails on the back of that palm a chipped purple. When she stepped back, Calvin saw that she was even younger than the shingle-headed boy.

"Let's see what's in his pockets!"

The boy, beyond Calvin's view, mumbled, "Uhhh. I don't . . ."

"C'mon, Aiven! Funnel cakes!"

Calvin held his breath, commanded every muscle still. *This* was the future of Berker County, *this* the fallout of a Frozen Child of the North as Knight of Olde Berker—child pickpockets in public libraries, along with dollar-twenty-nine sausage biscuits and nobody capable of cutting grass, and limp across his beanbags Calvin played long-suffering possum, sacrificing himself for the confirmation of ruin.

The girl knelt beside him; he could smell the vinegary scent of her child sweat, as the little chip-polished hand began tickling towards his hip pocket. Suddenly, the boy's hiss. "Raven!" Then the scuffling of tennis shoes across wall-to-wall carpet.

"What are you all doing back in here?" It was Kathy Taylor, librarian.

The girl genius Raven answered. "Aiven's looking for something to do his book report on."

Through the veil of his lashes, Calvin watched Kathy Taylor's green pants cuffs as she paused over his body before turning back to the children. "You know the parade's almost here?" The tennis shoes wheeled and pounded away.

Calvin waited until he heard Kathy Taylor talking quietly behind the circulation desk before he launched his struggle out of the beanbags. Except for Kathy's one-sided phone conversation, the library was finally silent. *As it should be*. Cal braced himself with a hand on a bookcase, a teddy bear leering at him from the shelf. The "as it should be" had sounded puny and neutral, as though the righteous-oriented personality cylinders were shooting blanks. And in truth, Calvin did feel peculiarly vacant inside. *Helen Smithster, Knight of Olde* . . . the curse tapered out in a muffle.

He'd had a shock. *I've had a shock*. Cal cradled his belly. *Must get . . . The refrig* . . . .

Calvin lurched away from the bookcase and out of the children's section, tottering towards the front door with both hands frankensteined before himself in case he took a sudden spill. He spied through the glass front of the library an ATV pulling a cart advertising a computer repair service. The Bygone Days parade had indeed gotten there. Knowing from experience that if he took the library side door he'd detonate an alarm, Calvin had no choice but to take the front one.

An avalanche of noise. Retina-searing light. Butt-to-butt lawn chairs lining the curb, other spectators on their feet and craning forward, arms windmilling, to better see and shout and wave, everyone watching the parade knowing everyone in it and vice versa, and kids and more than a few adults with their plastic Rite Aid and County Pride bags sprinting into the street after cascades of Smarties and Tootsie Rolls, their faces focus-frozen on their quarry, then bursting into triumph, focus-frozen, then bursting into triumph. A Dum-Dum glanced across Cal's shoulder, he ducked and threw up his hands, Calvin charged on, head tucked, towards the refuge of Blackie, and now the high school band bore down in arrhythmic drum roar, marchers in mismatched blue pants and white shirts to publicize their eternal uniform fund-raising drive, and Calvin slammed Blackie's door behind him, muting the drum section by four decibels. Not until he'd gathered enough wit to get the key in the ignition and then throw Blackie into reverse did Calvin see: the leaning and darting parade oglers, the bulging lawn chairs, the parade itself—Blackie was triply blocked in.

And what was he supposed to do?—the band now blattering into the "Battle Hymn of the Republic," his blood pressure high enough to accelerate hair growth—sit out the parade with nothing to eat while sugar showered the streets? Ronald McDonald deliberately dropped his juggling pins for a laugh, but slow-headed Clancy Myers and a little girl rushed out to his aid. Calvin grabbed the Little Chug, knew at first sniff it was too far gone even for his digestive system, and then he recalled the baggie Theodore Munney had found and punched open the glove box, devouring the bag's innards though they were but crust. What was he supposed to do, sit here and wait while the Knight nominees tooled by on their anointed fire engine, smirking and waving dismissively?

Blackie's door swung open. Calvin tumbled back into the parking lot. He wobbled there a moment, and then Cal was forging up the narrow sidewalk lane between booths and parade watchers. His legs churning along independent of his volition, Calvin even clapped a hand on his Almost Heaven cap to prevent its spinning off in his wake, it was as though his body were being hauled by a rope embedded in his chest and no telling what held the other end. And then, Calvin glimpsed the reenactors, and he could not resist, he turned his head and pedaled in place. The reenactors had little more spring in their step than they'd had yesterday during their dress rehearsal, post-traumatized, trench-mouthed, jungle-rot-footed, Calvin knew not which. And there—Calvin continued to step in place, pulling against the rope—zigzagging alongside the rear row, making it the only one with seven members instead of six, un-uniformed and unarmed and not yet bearded: Theodore Munney.

At that moment, Calvin was plucked off Main Street and tossed down Shute Place. He flew past the post office and Rita's, both deserted, he coasted along the meticulously landscaped lawn of the lawyer with the penile implant, he ran the stop sign and crossed Bluebonnet Lane. And there, under a pair of pin oak trees, Calvin halted. And found himself, hat in hand, gazing up at the brick front of the First Presbyterian Church.

His own church. The church his family had attended for generations. The church where his parents had been married, his head had been baptized, where he'd served through the years as Sunday School teacher, lay reader, usher, deacon, elder. And then Calvin Bergdoll knew why he'd been pulled and by Whom.

What he needed was in the basement. He'd replace it tomorrow.

The only unlocked door would be the sanctuary's, available to those prayer-famished and otherwise. Calvin leaned heavily on the metal rail as he mounted the steps. At the top, he straightened and thumbed the clasp on the ornate handle of one double door, terrified for a second that it'd be locked after all. It was not. As he slipped into the vestibule, the heavy doors clocked into place behind him, obliterating every trace of Bygone Days pandemonium.

Calvin wheezed several mock-emphysemic breaths: *Here I am. I'm still here. I'm still here.* He stepped into the rear of the sanctuary.

The stained glass gentled the clamorous afternoon light. Soothed by the hymnals snuggled up in their racks, by the chart on the front wall announcing last week's attendance and offering amount, by the trunk-sized Bible on the pulpit, Cal's sugar began creeping back into the runnels where it was supposed to run. He gripped the top of the nearest dark walnut pew, and through that hand, his back felt the back of the bench, contoured exactly opposite a human spine. *Little time to linger here.* God understood. On Calvin processed down the aisle, overtaking the baptismal font, the pulpit, the organ, and finally the door into the choir room.

Here he nodded to a thicket of hanging robes and was momentarily startled by an old man in plaid before he registered the mirror. Then yet another door and into the warren of Sunday School rooms. Their weeklong shut-up scents, he could have traced his way with eyes closed, the old ladies class, a warple of artificial rose perfume, the nursery, pee muffled with milk. When he finally reached the stairs to the basement, he stopped to mentally prepare himself. Behind his eyes crossed a vision of the Miss Dola Wysapple's Mississippi Mud Pie. Calvin took the bannister and descended one stair at a time, a pace at once dignified and safety-conscious.

From the fellowship hall, dimly lit by ground-level windows, Cal could see that the kitchen's serving window had been rolled down shut, and when he stepped through the kitchen door, he floundered around the wall for some time before landing on a light switch. In the startle of fluorescent blaze, the refrigerator showed itself first.

Calvin set his cap on a metal table and smoothed what was left of his hair. He whispered a thanksgiving prayer. Under his respectful clasp, the door's seal unsucked with a *smuck* more refined than his refrigerator's at home. Its light shone more boldly. Calvin tipped forward, head bowed. At first survey, he saw that the refrigerator sheltered six half-gallon jugs of Welch's grape juice. On second survey, he saw the refrigerator sheltered little else. He stooped into the sanctum, almost losing his footing, and trained his explorer's eye over every nook, including the vegetable crispers and the drawer meant for baloney and cheese. The search yielded one tiny jar of Miracle Whip.

Calvin Bergdoll was not rattled. He withdrew a single juice jug and set it on the counter. Then he closed the refrigerator, pressing his hand on its front for a moment in a gesture of thank-you-anyway before reaching up and opening a cupboard door. He found the bread, two loaves, in the second one he checked. He kept going. The third cupboard empty, the fourth. Calvin kept going. The fifth, now the drawers, going and going, the lower cupboards, faster, frantic, until, no telling how much time had passed, Cal spun in a circle and could find nothing else shut, and he had unearthed only three partially full cans of Maxwell House and a cottage cheese container crammed with little sugar packets.

Calvin did not flinch. In one hand he gripped the twisted ends of the bread bags and in the other he carried the juice. He placed them at the end of a long table in the fellowship hall and unfolded a metal chair.

The loaves were Stroehmann's whitest. Into his brain spurted his daughter's warning about the conversion of bread into sugar. Well, the body of Christ was not whole wheat. Calvin folded his hands, bowed his head, and said the blessing.

Soft as it was, especially after his recent encounters with old Italian bread and glove box crusts, the slice nearly melted on Cal's tongue. He tilted his chin in rapture. At the third slice, he dispensed with ceremony and devoured it in three bites. Midway through the loaf, his stomach finally began filling. But as Cal's cavity topped up, the personality cylinders, silent since the library nap, rumbled. The brain sediment heaved.

Calvin swept his eyes over the whole fellowship hall. All the wedding receptions he'd attended here, with their mints and nuts and white-iced cakes, all the covered-dish dinners, their deviled eggs and fried chicken, scalloped potatoes and bacon-grease-delectable green beans. The hymn sings, the missionary slideshows, hot chocolate and cookies after trick-or-treating for UNICEF. The meetings of the Lions.

Calvin stiffened.

He crammed down the next slice in two bites. It didn't help. His eyes fixed on a cross in a corner, nailed off-kilter to a base like a Christmas tree stand. *Helen Smithster, Knight*—still it came. Cal wrinkled up his eyes, *Helen Smith*—, he flapped his head to rattle out his brain, *Helen Smithster, Knight of Olde Berker. Helen Smithster, Knight of Olde*—

And he saw Main Street again, the candy chaos, fire trucks from a five-county area, perspiring politicians on foot regardless of obesity to illustrate their everyman-ness. Helen Smithster's broad monobreast—Calvin shoved the second bread loaf out of his immediate view—straining against her butterfly-print blouse, her teeth bared in that domineering smile that had spellbound the unbright of Berker. Cal's hands were shuddering now, or maybe they had them in convertibles this year, some years Johnny Bell and Hal McCauley and Reed Johnson drove their convertibles, the incipient knights perched on top the backseats, their hands turning in slow waves, *Helen Smithster, Knight of Olde Berker, Helen Smithster, Knight of Olde Berker*, and Calvin grabbed the juice jug, tipped it, and the glass slipped in his hand. Grape juice splashed over his plaid front and into his khaki lap.

Calvin looked down. Across his pants spread a stain the color of deer blood.

Calvin stared.

Or royal blood.

Calvin fluttered his eyelids.

Purple vestments.

"King." Calvin Bergdoll said it out loud. He swept his eyes across the room, pausing again on the cross. "Lord." *Father, Son, and Holy Ghost.* He dropped to the wooden X at the cross's base, then trolled his gaze over the checkerboard tile of the floor. King. Queen, Bishop, Rook. *And the least of these is the Knight.*

"King. Emperor." *And the least of these.* "Your Majesty Monarch Highest Highness Sovereign Sultan—"

Czar.

Czar?

Czar.

"Calvin Bergdoll." Cal moistened his mouth with his tongue. He placed his hand on his belly to support his diaphragm.

"Czar of Olde Berker."

The title thundered across the long bare tables, the racks of folded chairs, the gaping cupboards and cockeyed drawers, the flags of the United States and West Virginia. "Calvin Bergdoll. Czar of Olde Berker." *And the Knight is the least of these.*

"CAL-vin BERG-doll, CZAR of Olde BERK-ERRRR," he roared the last "r." CAL-vin BERG-doll, CZAR of Olde BERK-ERRRR," the appellation pealed past the room, resounded through every Presbyterian Church reach. "CAL-vin BERG-doll, CZAR of Olde BERK-ER," it bombinated beyond the windows, it boomed into the streets where the Knight nominees twitched at a vibration in each ear. "CAL-vin BERG-doll, CZAR of Olde BERK-ERR," and Cal's insides filled, his outsides swelled, he was already bigger than his seat, his shoulders as broad as the Winter Palace, his hips could straddle the Baltic Sea.

It was at that moment the Czar caught a movement in one of the ground-level basement windows. "CAL-vin BERG-doll, CZAR of Olde BERK-ER. CAL-vin BERG-doll, CZAR—" The motion again. The Czar closed his mouth. He laid down his bread.

For just an instant, the movement constellated into what the Czar could not deny was a face. Just a flash, and no beard, no hair at all in fact, but the Czar knew immediately Whose face it was. What he couldn't tell, after the eyes moved, was whether The face had blinked or winked.

ON SATURDAY MORNING, the Czar of Olde Berker and Blackie glided to a stop under the locust trees outside Theodore Munney's trailer. The Czar did not honk. He drew himself tall in his seat and beamed at the grizzled pit bull who approached from the house across the road, sniffed Blackie's tires, and peed. "You just help yourself," the Czar permitted through the window.

The Czar had awakened in fine fritter, full of oil and vinegar, right as ravioli, even the faux Christmas icicles dangling from Theodore Munney's trailer eaves dazzled on this day. *Calvin Bergdoll, Czar of Olde Berker. And the least of these.* His mouth watering a little, he smoothed his hands over the mostly clean yard-sale corduroy pants he'd donned for the all-you-can-eat pancake breakfast. Theodore Munney would not be taken to the all-you-can-eat pancake breakfast; five-dollar all-you-can-eat pancake breakfasts were reserved for more loyal subjects, but once Calvin got Theodore Munney circling on the Cub Cadet, Cal would pick up a sausage biscuit for him—or could the Czar pocket a pancake and patty at the all-you-can-eat?

Then Theodore Munney was on the porch, his tensed arms radiating an impression of flapping even though they did not move. His legs rushed him to the passenger window, his eyes panicked. "Gottagivemetimetobrushmyteeth."

"Surely!" granted the Czar. "You just take your time. Take your time, my sage serf." Patience came easily to gentility. That's why their blood ran blue instead of red. The plastic watch taped to Blackie's dash indicated that the doors to the all-you-can-eat pancake breakfast would not open for another thirty minutes. *Calvin Bergdoll, Czar of Olde Berker.* The saliva welled up again in the Czar's mouth.

Theodore Munney was clambering into Blackie's passenger seat. The Czar noticed that for the third day, he had not shaved, whiskers sprouting in irregular scraps across his face, Theodore Munney's odor one degree richer than it had been yesterday. *Signs of spring.* A washing machine agitator plugged with wet grass swirled up into Cal's brain, but the Czar extinguished the image with a rap of his scepter.

"Shshshshshotoffthecannonatthegradeschoolthismorning," said Theodore Munney.

"Now, Theodore." The Czar adopted a tone both authoritative and benign, gentle and firm. "Today I expect you to finish what you've started. You're more than halfway through." Not exactly true, but *positive, positive.* "I'm going to get you started, and I'll bring you back some breakfast. And that four dollars an hour will give you a little spending money for the rest of Bygone Days."

"Shshshshshotoffacannonatthegradeschool."

Early this morning, at exactly the moment the Czar had been scattering cat food in the possum pan, several pickups wearing rail adapters on their axles had passed the house. Reenactors on their way up the railroad tracks towards the defunct cornfield where they'd fake-kill each other for the pleasure of the tourist train. That this occurred before Theodore Munney had witnessed it from his orbit on the lawnmower was yet another blessing endowed upon the Czar, and the Czar had every reason to believe more were forthcoming.

Soon the Czar of Olde Berker was striding across the gravel lot to the Fire Hall, having left Theodore Munney contentedly circling on the Cub Cadet. The Czar tripped on the step up to the door but caught himself with regal aplomb. *Still nimble.* He took his place behind a family of five waiting to pay their pancake fee. Beyond them, the high-ceilinged fire hall thrummed with conversations around long tables covered with white paper, and eaters already padded back and forth for seconds, maybe thirds, while the fire trucks, consigned to the darkened half of the building, looked on through headlights and gape-mouthed grills. Calvin felt a twinge of panic that the cakes might all be gone before he had seconds himself, and how'd they all get in here so fast? The doors had opened just twenty minutes ago; there must have been a line outside before then; *note for next year.* And now the Czar was at the money-taking table, and the folded tent of cardboard in front of the cash box read $5.50.

The Fire Department had raised the price.

"I see the Fire Department has raised the price," the Czar remarked primly, pretending not to recognize the lady collecting the cash although she was a friend of his youngest sister's whom he'd known since grade school. The Czar took two deep breaths, repressing a sugar rise with a quiet grit of his molars.

The money lady smiled. "Yes, well, this is the first increase since Bygone Days began in 1982. They just have—"

"Should get extra for that," Calvin snapped unmajestically, his mind whipping out in several directions to identify what extra a person might get from an all-you-can-eat.

He received his first round in silence at the serving window, but the aroma of fried pork restored his luster as he carried his tray to the end of a table near the fire engines where no one else yet sat. The Czar did not want to be eaten with or talked at, he wanted to treasure his all-you-can-eat pancakes in peace, he hitched down his cap bill and retreated behind his glasses, fading into the gray specter featured on his school board campaign poster. He looked around for a bottle of syrup. All the condiments huddled in a small thicket several yards away in the inconvenient middle of the table. The Czar exhaled loudly. He levered himself off his bench and shuffled towards them.

The Czar plucked up each and strained at its label through his darkened bifocals. His stomach fluttered. He ran through the thicket again. Spinning around, he called to the nearest bunch of happy all-you-can-eaters clustered around syrup bottles at the next row of tables, "You all got any sugar-free over there?"

Cousins Tick and Carroll Might, eager to help, twirled each syrup in their hands. "Sorry, Mr. Bergdoll! It's all regular." Their buddy Bradley went so far as to research a third condiment station at a table behind him.

"None here either!"

Calvin crept back to his seat. Upon his nearly bald cakes melted margarine already coagulated. He shot the sugar-full Aunt Jemima a look that should have pierced a leak. This moment he'd been anticipating for weeks, there was nothing else for him to eat at Bygone Days, *I've paid my $5.50 and that includes a right to sugar-free syrup*. The effects of regular syrup were such that not even the Czar would risk them, especially after the brown-sugar daydream yesterday, those were the types of experiences Calvin could very well do without. If he'd brought Theodore Munney with him, he could have dispatched him to the kitchen to ask the cooks *bite off your nose to spite* Cal punted that one away, and he was just about to struggle to his feet and make the kitchen journey himself, leaving his plate undefended to who knew what, a loose dog, a slick-fingered child, marauding fire engine grills, when—

"Hello, Cal!" The volume and pitch stung through Calvin's tinnitus like a copperhead. A voice cheerful, boisterous, and hypercountrified. A campaign voice. A hand clapped Cal's shoulder. The Czar winced to his toes. It was George Callahan, a young local attorney, the one without the implant, a rampant Republican running for county commission. "How are your cakes?" *Calvin Bergdoll, Czar of Olde Berker.* George swung a leg over the bench and slopped his heaping plate next to Cal's.

"Not so good." The Czar glowered and Calvin cringed at this undignified mewl, but it had been as unstoppable as a hiccup.

George speared half a sausage into his mouth and while swallowing boomed, "And why is that?"

"There isn't any sugar-free syrup." The whine again, as if the Czar were possessed.

George licked the back of his fork. "Why don't you try the gravy?"

I don't want gravy on my pancakes. I want syrup. I want sugar-free Aunt Jemima's syrup. Calvin Bergdoll, Czar of Olde Berker, wants Aunt Jemima's Sugar-Free Syrup. His Majesty, Calvin Bergdoll, Czar of Olde Berker, has waited all year, there is nothing else to eat—

"Oh, she was just thrilled. Just thrilled to death."

A pair of gray-curly-haired women were settling in across from each other a few feet up the table.

"Yes, were you close enough to the stage to see? She was just a-crying!"

"And I can't think of a soul in Berker County who deserves Knight more!" bellowed George. "Miz Helen Smithster!"

Calvin Bergdoll's mouth went numb.

"George, I certainly agree with you. I'da thought it might of been Lloyd Hines, old as he is, but Helen, by golly, all the things she's done for this—"

The Knight? The Knight? The Least of These! The Least of These! The Czar, the Sugar-Free, Calvin Bergdoll, Czar of Olde Berker, Ole Cal Czar of Ole Berker, Calvin Bergdoll, Czar of Olde West Virginia, His Honorable Majesty and Lord Calvin Bergdoll, Czar of Almost Heaven and North America, Venerated Emperor of the Symphonies of Vienna and Prague—

An elbow whacked Calvin's bicep. "You should give it a try, Cal! It's some mighty good gravy!"

The Czar snatched a bottle of regular syrup the women had fetched and drowned his pancakes and then his sausage. He plunged the entire top pancake into his mouth, and once he got it chewed compact enough, forced a second one behind it.

Abruptly, Calvin was staring into the forsythia bush at the side of his own house, his sight scoured to ultraclarity. The tang of fresh urine steamed in his honed nostrils, and then he saw he was hovering right behind Theodore Munney's left shoulder while Theodore finished up with his zipper. When Theodore stepped back, Calvin stepped with him. Theodore turned in the direction of the waiting mower in the backyard, then stopped. He cocked his head, nearly imperceptibly, but Cal's vision detected it, and Calvin strained, but caught nothing but inner-ear bedlam.

After several seconds, Theodore jerked to the corner of the house, Calvin yanked along behind. There Floodie sat in the driveway catching her breath. Along the path to the back door hustled the son who used to have a few problems, his head swiveling, his eyes a-dart, but the watchfulness was all hollow habit, the son so preoccupied that he did not notice Theodore Munney at the corner of the house although Theodore didn't hide.

The back door slammed. Theodore and Cal slipped to its window. Now past the creases that made long X's on Theodore's sunburned neck, Calvin was studying the son's back, him in the same sag-seated Levi's as yesterday and in a white hooded sweatshirt that had been washed, at least twice, with something bright red. The son, in turn, studied the glass door of Calvin's gun cabinet.

The son snugged his cap tighter on his head. Scratching his ribs under his sweatshirt, he sidled towards Biggest Rack.

Calvin Bergdoll's skin went cold. It was the key. The one Calvin'd made sure Theodore Munney had never seen the hiding place of, not even during those times he and Theodore Munney had taken out a rifle or a shotgun and cleaned it or even enjoyed a little target practice. Scooting aside Biggest Rack's mount, the son plucked the key from the tack behind it.

Theodore Munney emitted a chokey "oh oh." He pitched backwards a step. The son lifted out one of the four remaining guns, Cal's favorite, a .30-30 his departed father had left him. The son held it lengthwise across his palms, examined it, returned it to the case, and reached for another. Twice the son glanced over his shoulder, and twice he did not discern Theodore Munney, who, after the key revelation, had skittered to a more discreet peeping angle, his back heaving with rapid breath, his mouth ajar. After the son had made his choice, relocked the cabinet and rehid the key, Theodore Munney scrambled back around the corner of the house and squatted in the side yard, Calvin still appended helplessly to his shoulder. From his hyperlucid proximity, Calvin could detect a quiver in Theodore Munney's ears, until, Cal had to surmise, Theodore Munney heard Floodie's engine flare full-bore upon hitting the smooth asphalt of Route 50.

At which moment Theodore surged back to the door, Calvin in tandem. Theodore rushed across the floor, his head in anticipatory full-blown chicken bob, Theodore Munney almost knocking Biggest Rack off the wall in key-fumbling enthusiasm, and Theodore Munney unlocked the gun cabinet.

Theodore Munney hesitated. Calvin could feel Theodore's body heat rise. Then Theodore Munney was reaching for the very rifle the son had decided against stealing, Cal's favorite deer rifle, the one Theodore Munney and Calvin had handled most often, the one Theodore Munney had most often watched Cal clean and had on occasion seen Cal load. Theodore dropped to his knees on the floor and, after some trial, some error, broke open the barrel. He pulled out the ammunition drawer in the cabinet's bottom. He sampled three boxes before he found cartridges that fit.

Boosting the rifle to his shoulder, Theodore rose, then pivoted so smartly Calvin nearly lost his hat in the spiral. Theodore Munney marched three steps towards the back door. He halted. He dropped his chin and mused upon his vegetation-hued clothes. Then, leaning the .30-30 gingerly against the wall, Theodore turned to the coat closet.

After a moment's survey, he plunged in both hands. Garment after garment he shoved aside, passing over a blaze-orange vest, a gray overcoat, several flannels of plaid, the grubby old letter jacket from the time the son was just starting his problems. Until he arrived at Calvin's bride's navy blue windbreaker.

The jacket choice confirmed Calvin's horrified suspicions. His invisible mouth reared open in inaudible yell. Into his blue uniform,

Theodore Munney wiggled, the fabric straining a little across his shoulders, and with a deep breath, Theodore puffed his breast, brushed phantom epaulets, and reshouldered his gun. Then Theodore Munney and Calvin were slamming out the screen door.

The blue jacket rooster-stepped across the yard, Calvin towed behind like a hobo bundle. Past the possum pans, the Cub Cadet, past the dingy white blossom of the Arts Channel–snagging satellite dish. Theodore Munney scrambled up the railroad embankment, dropping the .30-30 diagonally across his hands the way the Seasoned Woodsman had instructed him to carry it when crossing fences. Through the roar in Calvin's ears penetrated the report of an upriver cannon. The battle reenactment was well under way. Facing calamity, Calvin's brain shimmered with an acuity it hadn't had since 1979, but Theodore could not hear Calvin's desperate shouts, could not see his flailing hands. Once they reached the railroad ties, they pivoted again, to face upriver. Another cannon boomed. And Theodore Munney, Calvin Bergdoll tethered to his collar, marched to the cornfield to defend the Union.

ROCKHOUNDS

JOS HAD FOUND it first. Went out early that morning to the flat place by the creek where she practiced and saw straightaway the orange dirt they'd laid over the hole ripped up and sprayed. Without getting close enough to tell if the little body was gone, she wheeled and ran to the house to fetch her uncle. If they had to break more bad news to her grandfather, they could break it slow. But she and Uncle Derek weren't halfway back to the grave when they heard the door whine open behind them. Granddad had sniffered it without being told.

When they saw for sure the hole was empty, Uncle Derek shook his head. "Must have been coyotes." He said it "kai oats," which was how Granddad would say it, not how Uncle Derek, who had been to college, did. Joslin held her soccer ball between her elbow and ribs. She looked up at her grandfather, saw on his cheek the red webs brightening, and she pulled her head, just a little, back into her hood.

"Yep. Coyotes dug er up and drug er off." And that was all Granddad said.

They'd buried the little dog just the afternoon before, her granddad praying over her for a long time when they did. They'd waited until Jos got home from school, but not because she'd asked them to. It wasn't a funeralish day. Late bright October and the kind of blue like if you struck the sky with a pipe it would ring. "That curly dog," her grandma called Goldy; her grandma didn't much care one way or another, but her granddad doted on her. "Cuddle Dog" was Granddad's nickname, and Goldy was the only thing Joslin'd ever seen her grandfather hug. When she'd first come to stay with her grandparents five years ago while her mother got her life together, Goldy slept with Joslin every night until Granddad's bedtime. Then Granddad would shuffle into Jos's room, trying so hard to keep quiet he'd wake Jos with the effort. He'd pull Cuddle Dog by her armpits out from under Jos's covers and stow her in his own bed, where she slept on a pillow beside his head. Grizzled gold against grizzled black.

A little over a week ago, Goldy had looked at her food and looked away. Grandma said leave her be, she'll eat when she's hungry, but Granddad slipped her Penrose sausages and tuna until Goldy cared not even for those. By the fourth day, there was talk of taking her to the vet, but as usual, the consensus was wait and see. Mentioning cost would have been like saying there was dirt in the yard. Her uncle, when things became clear, at least to him, took hold the bigger younger dog, a lab mix named Bunker, and chained him to a pin oak behind the house. "It was the creek water got Goldy," Uncle Derek told Jos. "We don't keep Bunker tied, we'll lose him, too."

Anytime a person stepped out of the house, Bunker bolted to his chain end and danced on hind legs, baffled, but optimistic and eager to forgive. He spent the rest of his time wrapping himself around the tree and knocking his water pan dry. Every time Derek drove away from the house, Granddad unclasped the chain. Every time her uncle got home and found Bunker loose, he'd catch him and tie him back up. Neither her granddad nor her uncle said a word to the other about it. Joslin tried to keep the water pan full.

Still in her school clothes for the funeral, Jos'd stood behind the dug-up dirt pile while Uncle Derek carried Goldy to her grave wrapped in a bleach-splotched blue towel. Jos kept her head bowed, scared to look, then guilty that she felt more afraid than sad. Granddad wore the pressed red-checked shirt that reminded her of a cowboy, his hands clasped reverently below his dress belt buckle, a steel rope lasso that looked also like a snake. When Goldy'd first vanished, Granddad immediately named the pony shed, and when Uncle Derek found Goldy stiff behind a pile of pallets there, Joslin wasn't surprised. Granddad's snifters were almost always right. From the edge of her eye, Jos watched Derek lay the blue towel bundle down.

"Open it up," Granddad said.

Uncle Derek hesitated. Jos could see Bunker watching, stock-still on his haunches at the end of his chain. Then Derek unfolded the top like giving Goldy a breath before she went under, and as he did, Jos finally felt it. A sharp high ache in her fingers. An unswallowable stone lodged in her throat. She forced her gaze to Goldy's head, Goldy's tongue poking out the side of her teeth in a way Goldy never did, but when she reached Goldy's eyes, the shock took her breath. They had no more Goldy in them than a black beetle's back. Instantly the sadness dissolved, leaving Jos a little stunned by its going. Her unable to cry for what was left, and weirdly unable to recall, though it'd been just three days, what had gone.

After the hole was filled and Granddad said the prayers, her uncle turned back to the house. Jos did, too.

"Help me pretty it up with some rocks, Jos."

Her grandfather was already shambling towards the creek bank. These days even on level ground he walked always like he was stepping out of something sticky, and Jos followed behind. He made it safely to the rock bar, where he squatted himself like a stubborn folding chair and began to sort, culling rocks round and smooth, about the size, Jos noticed, of Goldy's paws. He'd collected rocks that caught his fancy since he was a boy, and when Jos was younger and his body sounder, they'd look for them on their walks. "I'm just an old rockhound," he often said. Most of his finds he stored in shoeboxes, but his favorites he displayed in the twins' old room where he now slept, the rocks on the blotter of their homework desk. When she was littler, Jos visited the rocks often. Tiptoed in and pressed her chest against the desk, placed her fingers in the fossil prints and stroked the ridges shells had left.

Now she filled her hoodie pockets. The cool rolling out the hollow mouth called the smells from the ground, rotting oak leaves, groundhog shale. She pressed a rock under her nose. Odor of creek water on it, so different from the smell of a rock in the woods. Twice they clambered up to the grave where Jos did like Granddad did, working each stone carefully into the dirt until the grave was ringed all around.

Finally Granddad wiped his hands on the seat of his pants. Jos brushed hers. She looked back at the creek, reflecting like aluminum in what little light was left. The creek water looked the same as it always had.

IT'D BEEN SIX months since her uncle'd come back in a Honda Civic that'd been wrecked at least twice but still ran. Wisconsin tags. Montana bumper stickers. He'd come back with a ring in his nose that he'd since taken out, but Jos couldn't help staring at the hole, especially during meals, when it turned her stomach a little. A good bit younger than her mother, he'd been born when her grandparents were almost old, and that was part of why he'd been so spoiled, her mother'd told her. All of Joslin's nine years he'd been away, appearing only at Christmas and now and again for a week in the summer. Most of those years, he'd been "out West," and before that he'd been to college, the second in the family to go and the first to finish, Joslin knew because now she was expected to go and finish, too.

"Although you wouldn't know it to look at him," her grandma'd say about the college. Him in jeans that looked slick from lack of washing, worn out around the hip pockets with his underwear showing through. Coffee-stained thermal shirts and floppy black hair without direction unless he rubberbanded it back in the tiniest of ponytails. Sometimes he'd not bathe for a solid week, and this outraged her grandma, who'd grown up without plumbing and kept herself and her house vengefully clean. But Joslin thought she understood. A group of college kids had driven down from Massachusetts last spring to work in Booker Hollow, where poor people lived. Jos's church had sponsored them for a dinner. The college kids came looking and smelling much like Uncle Derek, and her grandma's friends were still talking about one girl who appeared to have half-dried pee dribbling down her leg.

Like Grandma, Uncle Derek was no smiler, and like Granddad, he angered quick as a yellow jacket, but unlike Granddad, Derek carried inside some kind of reservoir that could fuel a fury forever. At first Jos figured he was mean and kept her distance, but soon she learned he'd also gotten Grandma's give-you-the-shirt-off-her-back. A little longer, and she saw he had too Granddad's mushiness under the crust, although Joslin had lived with that long enough to be far more leery of it than of Grandma's steady hard. Uncle Derek knew nothing about soccer; they didn't have that here when he was a kid, but he'd play it with her anyway even though she was better at it than him. Once he got used to her, he'd sometimes take her with him to town, where she'd fool with the library computers while he keyboarded furiously on his laptop. He helped her find soccer sites and soccer books, and it was Uncle Derek bought her the first pack of animal wristbands to be seen in her school after he learned about them from the son of a friend in Pittsburgh. In the evenings, especially when it started getting cool, the old people monopolizing the television, Joslin took to doing her homework on his bed, him busy on the laptop or with his magazines and flyers and books.

It was there in his childhood room in early September not long after school started that he'd explained it to her. Before that, of course, Joslin understood he was in an ongoing, unspoken rage at her grandparents, but her mother was angry at them always too and never with a reason that made sense, so Jos thought little of it. What did unsettle her was his bitterness towards the Hackerts, who had two girls younger than Joslin and lived on the mountain above. She and Sylvie Hackert played on the same soccer team. The Hackerts gave her rides to practices and games. Usually when their name came up he'd just snake-spit under his breath, but that afternoon, he'd blown. By the time Joslin got down to the kitchen to hear better what was going on, her grandma'd shut him down.

"Now don't you be badmouthing the Hackerts!" Her voice with the tremolo it got when she really meant business. "As good as they've been to Joslin. Me and your daddy can't be doing all that running around anymore." But Derek was already slamming the front door so hard the photos on the TV toppled, then Joslin heard the Honda throwing gravel behind it.

Shortly after, Addley from down the road dropped in like he often did, always right around time to refuse supper. He'd sit back along the wall with his chair tipped forward while her grandma'd beg him to eat, and just when they were ready to clear the table, Addley'd inevitably give in.

"You know the business sense Gary Hackert's got," her granddad was saying to him. Granddad's jaws worked his chicken patty twice as hard as they had to and Jos could see the red webs showing themselves on his cheek and the one side of his nose. "If he thinks it's the smart thing to do. . . . Why not have the property bring in a little income for a change?"

"You're right, Lloyd. You're exactly right," said Addley. Jos prodded a green bean, dull as straw, her grandma having left out the bacon grease because Uncle Derek wouldn't eat meat. The land man had come while she was at school, two years ago, but she did know now, after overhearing Granddad and Addley at dinners before Derek'd come home, that the Hackerts had come to the house with the land man. The land company wanted every acre they leased to touch. The Hackerts' hundreds. Her grandparents' twenty-seven.

"We can no longer be dependent on foreign oil," her granddad went on in the tone he used to quote TV news and the Bible. "The country needs natural gas. Energy independence."

Addley made his whole chair nod. "You're right, Lloyd. You're exactly right."

"Our young men and women being sent overseas to die for oil. It's a tragedy."

"You're right, Lloyd. Buddy, you are right."

Jos took a long look at Addley. The bottom half of his face was twice as long as the top, out of balance even by horse standards. Although Derek's name was never spoken, Addley knew it was against Derek Granddad was defending himself. Because Addley could not stand Derek, an arrogant enigma, and because Granddad wouldn't abide Addley speaking outright against his son, Addley was savoring this conversation like a pup rolling in a dead deer.

"He needs to find himself a woman and settle down," Addley declared. Granddad ignored this.

"I can show you the lease, Addley. It talks about the United States' energy independence right on it." Joslin had seen the lease herself, a photocopy Derek had made at the library after sneaking the original out of Granddad's files. In the upper right-hand corner was stamped a small American flag in a frozen ripple. "And it's not like they're gonna strip-mine it or something. This ain't southern West Virginia."

"It's your land, Lloyd. You can do whatever you want with it. It's your business."

"Besides," Granddad said, and now Jos could hear his indignation running down as it always did. He had a fraction of the fury reserve Derek did. "If we hadn't leased, they probably wouldn't of signed the Hackerts." He pushed his plate back. "It was the neighborly thing to do."

LATER, ON DEREK'S bed, Joslin tried to study for her social studies quiz. Her uncle'd snuck back in right before dark, and now he hammered away on his laptop like usual. All around them hung his childhood relics, things he never seemed to notice were still there, his sports trophies, his 4-H ribbons, photos of him with his teams, football, basketball, track, Derek's dark hair cut neat, him skinnier, but even back then, Derek didn't smile. Jos plucked at the rubber bluejay band on her wrist with her thumbnail. Every time she looked at Uncle Derek's hunched back, anger tightened between her eyes, anger over what he'd said about the Hackerts, anger at herself for wanting to be near him anyway.

Although you could start soccer when you were five, Jos had never played on any sports team before this season, this year the first Granddad and Grandma would pay for the uniform and league fees, and only after the Hackerts offered the rides. The next game was Saturday, three days away, and looking towards it opened a little blossom in her chest. To be on that field and moving, her body knowing exactly where and how to go without any mind thinking to it, it had always been that way, her body smarter than she was, but before soccer, no one cared about that. She looked back at her textbook. The dirty-clothes air of Derek's room was cottoning in her mouth. She slid off the bed and slipped through the floor clutter towards the door.

Derek turned in his chair. "What's wrong?" He pushed his hair back out of his face and held it to his head with his fingers the way he did when he really looked at her and expected her to look back.

Joslin shrugged.

Derek continued to hold her eyes. "It's because I don't like your friends." Jos said nothing. She pulled her gaze away from his and towards the door.

"Do you understand what your granddad and Hackert have done?"

She looked sideways at him and nodded, knowing as she did that he wouldn't be fooled.

He still didn't move, so Jos couldn't either, suspended just a step from the door and freedom. Then, so abruptly that she flinched, he dropped his hair and shuddered his head, reaching for his laptop. "You need to understand," he muttered. "You do. Especially for after I leave." He rammed his chair against the side of the bed, computer in his lap, and lay his hand on the mattress. Jos knew that meant sit. She did.

Not until later that night, when she was in her own bed, unable to fall back asleep, did she unnumb enough to feel what he'd said. She lay on her side, looking towards the window across the room. The house was tucked tight against the hollow side, and her second-floor view, if there'd been light enough to see, was a groundhog shale bank. No, Uncle Derek had said, it wasn't groundhog shale that they wanted. It was Marcellus shale. Darker, older, so deep under the ground they ran a drill for a mile before they blasted the water and the secret chemicals sideways into the earth. Besides, he said, I already told you. Groundhog shale isn't shale at all. It's pressed clay.

But groundhog shale was what Granddad called it, and he and Jos both loved it for the fossils layered there. The rock so scaly you could nearly dig them with your fingernails, but she and her granddad would bring a trowel, a never-painted-with paintbrush, and an old tackle box. Joslin squatted while Granddad gentle-scraped, and almost all the fossils they found were shells, no matter where they looked, in the groundhog shale, in the chunky creek rocks, in the slatey woods ones. Different sizes, different shapes, but shells all, and despite how hard Joslin stretched her brain, she could never quite believe it. The impossibility of ocean ever over where she and Granddad stood now.

Then she found herself leaving her room, floating it felt like, and in the dark hallway her nightgown seemed to glow against the leftover summer brown of her arms and her legs. She flowed down the hall and into Granddad's room, past the humpled bed where Granddad and Goldy burred their separate snores. The desk caught Jos right at her hipbones. The rocks a startling distance from her face, how much she'd grown since she'd visited last. She reached out a hand and pressed one finger in a small fossil print.

"Not every place has fossils all over like here," her grandfather'd told her many times. Another reason their place was special. Another reason to be proud of their state. She paused and tuned again to the snoring, made certain both of them still slept. Then she laid her whole left hand on the rock that used to awe her deepest, a slab shell-tracked densely as a tablet that reminded her of the Ten Commandments. She hefted in her right hand a blocky creek rock. Then with both hands full of rock she closed her eyes and waited for the old feeling to come. A funneling of her down from her mind to gather, solid, in her chest. And eventually it did come. At least some and for a little bit.

Not until a few years before had it dawned on her that she and Granddad had never found the original shell that created a print. All the creatures left were shadows of themselves. Had the way she felt about them changed between now and back when she hadn't known anything was missing? A little, she thought. A little of the feeling had.

SHE SAT CROSS-LEGGED on the living room floor, her animal bands spread out on the carpet in front of her. After Granddad and Derek had agreed on the coyotes, they'd all three spent a good half hour searching for Goldy, first up the hollow behind the house, then in the field on the other side of the road. No one had more than scant faith the coyotes would have given up the body, especially so near the house. Still, it seemed the respectful thing to do, at least to look a while. Jos untangled the bands for the three she always wore for luck at soccer games: Cardinal, the state bird. Eagle, the American bird. Blue jay, their team name, and the most potent of the three.

"I'm going in town to check my email. You all need anything?" It was Derek, in the kitchen.

"Kickoff's at noon," her granddad reminded.

"You could pick up some milk," Grandma said. "Get you five dollars out of my pocketbook."

"Don't worry about it," Derek mumbled.

The old people continued banging around in the kitchen, revving up for the Mountaineer game. More spirited than they'd been in weeks, they'd splurged on pepperoni rolls for a special game-day lunch, and they'd want both her and Derek there, at least for when the team rampaged out of the tunnel. Jos felt glad for them, but she felt gladder for herself, her own game starting a little late today, the Hackerts picking her up at 2:15. She smiled. Sylvie and her little sister Madison had been on teams since they were five, most of the kids had, but Jos had outplayed Sylvie by the end of the first game, outplayed everyone else, including the boys, by the end of the second. She had "a way with the game," all the grown-ups said it, although she'd told her grandparents none of this. She knew how they felt about bragging. She rolled the good luck bands onto her right wrist, then picked up a couple others to trade with Sylvie and Madison on the long ride to the fields.

It was when she slipped out to practice again that she saw Bunker's chain slack. Her heart cramped quick, and her lips already going to "B" when she remembered it'd be best Granddad not hear her call. "Wasn't no creek water got Cuddle Dog," her grandfather'd told her several times, including twice when she'd caught Granddad in the liberating act. "She just got into something somewhere." Jos nudged the chain clasp with her foot. When Granddad had pressed the tuna to Goldy's lips, the dog'd cringed away like it hurt. If Bunker was fresh let loose and not in sight, Jos knew pretty well where he'd be. She lobbed her soccer ball underhanded back to the porch.

She jogged directly behind the house, towards the pony shed and then on past it. The quickest way to the big bottom hollow was over the ridge above the pony shed, and the fastest way to the ridge was straight up the groundhog shale outcrop. So then Jos was scrambling it, the scabby earth colored the dullest butterscotch, her cutting footholds with the sides of her tennis shoes and using her hands, too, and she thought of her cleats—Mr. Hackert had given them to her after that third game—but she dare not use them on something not soccer, and besides, the damage they could do to the fossils right under the surface. Then she was passing through the oaks and hickories on the ridge, heave-breathing a little, a breeze driving leaves towards her, them glancing off her head and shoulders like slow unshy birds. When she got to where she could see down into the hollow's broad bottom, she stopped to quiet the leaves under her feet so she could hear the leaves under Bunker's. This was another place she and Granddad had little by little stopped going as his legs got worse.

"Bunker!" she shouted. "Bunker! Here, boy!" She went still and listened again. As she did, she couldn't help but listen not only for Bunker, but also for the other. But what would the other sound like? Engines idling? A boom underground? A giant hish like a thumb-blocked garden hose? She heard only a pileated woodpecker laugh.

She launched herself over the hollow side, slippery with a decade, with more, of dead brown leaves, the bank so steep that when she was little she would lie against it and still be standing up. She slide-angled down, using again the sides of her feet, the thinking part of her hiding to let her body do its knowing, how quick to move, how far to slant, where to step, her strong hips, her calves, even her stomach muscles helping. "I'm a deer, I'm a deer," she whispered like she'd done when she was small as though the saying it itself kept her from falling, and she never did fall. Granddad would be behind her, far more cautious, but still nearly magical in his balance, him catching himself from tree to tree, whooping sometimes after a near miss. Now she landed heavy at the bottom in a leaf drift higher than her knees.

"Bunker!" she shouted again. She whistled. The woodpecker *ha-ha-ha-ha-ha'd*. She started wading leaves towards the place where the hollow forked, passing right away the boundary between their land and the Hackerts', white paint slashes fading on trees. She dropped into the bed of a wet-weather stream parched waterless after the summer drought and she followed that. The run was choked with flat, dark, slatey rocks, sharp under her feet where they stood on end. Of all the things Uncle Derek had told her, this was the one she could not put away. How the poisons came not only from the stuff they pumped down in. How they came out of the rocks themselves. Things held safe by the earth until the rocks were shattered and the private things unlocked, and then they became poisons, too. "Then they pull back up out of the well that poison water and they have to do something with it. Where do you think they dump it, Jos?"

Suddenly she heard the chussle sound of a big animal moving in leaves, and she knew it was not a deer, because it was not explosive and then away. And right after she spotted Bunker in the hollow fork, panting and loose-limbed with happiness, Jos saw at her foot a buckle-sized rock with a deep imprint.

She knelt. Almost the entire surface of the rock was stamped with shell, a perfect cast. Like a flower floating in a squarish bowl. "Now I don't got no education," Granddad would say. "But all of history is in these rocks. Them's the oldest things that are." Joslin picked up the fossil and slipped it into her sweatshirt pocket.

SHE HAD TO stop and tie the sweatshirt around her waist on their climb back up. Midday rising summer warm, and she knew it must be close to noon, kickoff, and she climbed faster. Then she and Bunker were moving through the trees on the ridgetop, dropping towards the groundhog shale outcrop, when Joslin grabbed Bunker's collar and jerked him back.

Uncle Derek's Honda sat behind the pony shed, where cars never went. Uncle Derek himself was just stepping out of the shed carrying with two hands the biggest plastic bag Wal-Mart gave out, a weight swinging in the bottom of it. Jos tucked herself low. Without taking her eyes off Derek, she reached one hand to Bunker's stomach and rubbed. He collapsed onto his back and stayed still.

Uncle Derek laid the bag on the ground behind the car and unlocked the hatch. Joslin rose to a crouch to better see. Her uncle wedged the lid off a big white Styrofoam cooler and dropped the lid beside the Wal-Mart bag. Then he knelt, and peeling the bag back more than pulling something out, exposed the blue towel bundle. Jos shot an arm to the ground for balance. Uncle Derek lifted the bundle into the cooler, and she watched him shove and shift to make it fit.

Next he dragged a bag of ice from the front seat and set it on the hood. Seizing it at the top on both sides, he jerked at the staples, but Jos saw they wouldn't give, and then he was tearing at it, she heard the "Fuck!" Then he spun around, spotted something, and snatched up what she knew was an old piece of barbed wire that had once topped the corral. He punctured and ripped the plastic with that and dumped the contents in the cooler.

After replacing the lid, he pulled across the cooler the sleeping bag he kept in his car, and over and around that he arranged a casual heap—jumper cables, cloth grocery bags, his CD case, the grimy green backpack he called his survival kit. Then Uncle Derek lowered himself into the front seat and gentled the car back to the house, where it was parked in its usual spot when Joslin got there and tied Bunker back up.

THE MOUNTAINEERS WERE down by ten two minutes before the half. They'd all four ended up watching the whole thing so far, the old people decked out in their WVU sweatshirts and hats, and even Uncle Derek seemed taken in, hollering at the screen right along with Granddad. He'd brought back from town as a treat everybody's favorite pop to go along with the pepperoni rolls, and Jos, tucked up in the chair farthest from the TV, rationed her Orange Crush until the bottom went warm. She watched Uncle Derek as much as the game. Had he dug Goldy up or just found her where the coyotes left her? Just finding her was what she wanted to believe, but the older part of her knew how unlikely that was, especially with Goldy still in her towel. But why would Uncle Derek not have filled back in the hole, make it look like nothing happened at all? Because any messing in dirt Granddad would catch, especially since Derek had no idea how they'd placed the pretty stones.

And what secret something could he possibly want that little body for? Every time she got to that, her face flashed hot before the anger collapsed, too quick, into a pity close to tears. Goldy dead dragged around in a Wal-Mart bag. The choke of not just groundhog shale but also ice in Goldy's mouth, and the taste on the terrible stuck-out tongue.

"Well," Derek announced when they cut to the commentators at the half. "I'm heading out to Morgantown right after the game. Talked to Casey this morning. I'll be going against traffic."

"Defense don't wake up, I guess you won't be burning any couches," Granddad said. Uncle Derek left regularly, to Morgantown, to Pittsburgh, to Elkins. When he was gone, the taut rushed out the house a little like from an overinflated ball. Joslin was not sad he'd be going now.

She sprang up the steps two at a time to her room. The Hackerts would be by within twenty minutes. To put on the uniform earlier than right before the game felt to her a disrespect even though she knew some kids, like Madison, wore theirs around the house for fun. Into her shorts, she ran her hands a few times over their blue and black silkiness, and then she bent and fastened the Velcro straps on the shin guards, which she loved most of all because they made her legs look the way they always felt. She tugged her jersey over her head, "Blue Jays" in cursive over the back, and the uniform complete, a lightness rushed from her chest, carrying her along after it, her moving without thinking across that green field. She hugged her right wrist with her left hand, a good-luck embrace of the good-luck bands, and picked up her cleats by their tied-together laces. Then she remembered the fossil.

She pulled it from the pocket of the sweatshirt she'd hung in her closet and eased it into the toe of one cleat. Granddad would be out in the yard "getting some air," shuffling off his ire at the unraveling game. She'd give the fossil to him now, before she left. A little salve for both Goldy and the football loss.

But when she reached the porch, she stopped short. Granddad was hobbling towards the ripped-up grave and she didn't want to interrupt. Then her heart ducked. He was pausing at Derek's car.

For several seconds he stood as though paralyzed, his head thrust forward on his neck like a turtle's, his fingers spread open where they hung. And Jos, blood beating in her throat, heat rushing in her face—Jos understood it was a sniffer.

He cupped his hands around his face against the filthy rear window as though that'd cut the dirt like a reflection. Then he charged up the driver's side, clawing the roof for support, opened the door, dipped, and jerked the hatch lever, Jos heard it unclock. He jag-legged back to the rear, threw up the hatch, stared for a second, and then he pitched onto the ground behind him, using both hands, the cloth bags, the jumper cables, the survival kit, the CD case cracking open and the disks spooling out.

"Derek!" Granddad shrieked. "You get out here! Right now!"

Jos held her breath. Behind her, the door whined open. She could hear a crunching in Uncle Derek's mouth.

"Right now, boy!"

Jos dared not turn around. She heard a swallow. And she heard, too, heard this with her body, a rumbling right under the air, the rumble rising to mute roar, until Uncle Derek exploded, "I'm taking her in for tests!"

He screamed it with the passion of someone announcing the end of the world, but also with the humiliated fury of a little kid caught, and under all that, she heard, too, heard this with as much surprise as she'd felt when the blue towel came out of the Wal-Mart bag, the quiver that comes right before tears.

"Get out here lift this lid off!" Granddad bellowed.

"I'm taking her in for tests! Taking that goddamned creek water, too!"

Jos saw Granddad's lip lift, his top teeth bare, saw the red lace on the side of his nose, one cheek. He whipped around, jerked the lid off the cooler, and snapped it in two across his knee. He plunged both arms in, muddy ice erupting up and over the sides, and then Granddad was raising the blue towel bundle, matted with ice melt and grave dirt, and cradling it to his chest.

When she heard the thump she finally broke, turned to see that Uncle Derek had hurtled off the side of the porch and, although the drop was not waist-high, had fallen on his knees. He pushed himself up and crashed away, zigzagging like a rabbit, and she tore her eyes from him and back to Granddad, hovered over Cuddle Dog, an orange-brown mud stain spreading across his blue and gold front. Jos felt her legs step towards Granddad, then stammer, the trespass of breaking in on him and his dog, the pity she felt for Uncle Derek too, beaten near tears. And then she was moving to where Derek had gone, at first her knees locking and jolting her shins, her glancing over her shoulder at Granddad, but soon trotting, and at last breaking into a full-on run.

She found him in the dusky pony shed between a broken-down rototiller and the stack of old pallets. His back against the wall, his arms sprawled limp across his raised knees, his face flung down and his hair screening it. She stood before him on the pulverized manure and decades-old dirt, her understanding only, and that not even in a thought, that at least something could be right if he would just speak. She waited. He did not push his hair up and pin it clear of his forehead. He did not lift his face. She heard no sound at all, not even his breath, certainly not tears, and she wondered if he knew she was there. She took a step closer.

Back at the house, the Hackerts' big Suburban crunched into the drive. A half-minute later, its door slammed.

"Go on, Jos. Your ride's here."

His voice came empty as a broken bucket, barren even of anger. Jos bit her bottom lip, her expectation dissolving into panic. Her eyes darted, the top of a stall where the long-gone pony had left chew marks, the dry soil crusted in the rototiller blades. The place on the crown of Derek's head where the scalp showed white.

"Josss-linnn!" It came from behind the house, a piping. They'd sent Madison to fetch her.

"Go on, Joslin. You want to miss your game?"

The gap between her and Uncle Derek widened despite the step she'd taken closer, and every muscle in Jos's legs was rising to run, but her still rooted to the floor, her heart a barbed anchor reaching all the way to the ground. Madison called again. And suddenly, it came to Jos. If she left him something, she could go.

On reflex, she tipped the shoe, her palm out to catch the fossil, but before it shook loose, she stopped. Despite everything, she knew Granddad loved rocks more than Uncle Derek did. She dropped the cleat toe-down and pushed the tied-together shoestrings back into her elbow crook. Her mind flashed to the next most valuable thing she had. The blue jay band. She rolled it off her wrist. Kneeling, she rested it in the fine dirt right at the toe of his boots where he could not miss it when he finally looked up.

Outside, she had to pause a second for her eyes to take the light. Against the faded copper of the shale hollow side, the blond broom sedge, Madison in her green and black uniform shimmered like a toy hummingbird. "Jos!" she squealed. But behind Madison, a form shot out of the yard and towards the outcrop, an animal too low and dark to be a deer. In her own hand, Joslin could feel the pressed clasp under Granddad's thumb. She could feel Bunker's chest bloom as he vaulted free.

SAB

SULL, I FEEL the hurt of you. I feel you run. Air catch in your throat, not enough lung, all that land breathing on you. Breathing. Cucumber smell, skunk smell, rich rotty punk, I see you moving over ground, sinking into hollows, deer flushing all around. The bugs choiring like rattles, swell rattle, ebb rattle, Sull, they feel you, too. And you stop on a ridgespine, you brace your hands on your thighs until your breathing calms down. Then you listen. You listen hard. Hear only acorns dropping. A buck grunt-squeal, whinny wilder than a horse.

What can I tell you? Sometimes it comes easier if your body's on the run, your mind closing so your insides catch it, hills' channels, your channels, currenting as one. What I can tell you is it's not going to reach you through how you usually hear. It speaks in your throat like fingers spelling in a deaf-blind hand, you listen by a feel where you swallow. It feels like swallowing ground.

What I can tell you is your instincts are right. These hills, if you can open, will carry past your pain. But I know, too, they never talk in words or lines or tones. The thing you have to learn is to hear unsingable song.

WE WERE COUSINS just a year apart. Grew up in here together, then Sull left out. Gone thirty years, though at first she'd now and then come back. A family reunion, Christmas, when an old person passed. Eventually she stopped that, too, and the less we saw her, the more stories got told. Her obscenely rich husbands, outlandish mansions in outlandish places, uncountable affairs. Or they'd turn it and tell that Sull earned the money herself, in some just-this-side-of-legal way, and she not only seduced and discarded men, but had a taste for women as well. Then, in the last decade, the telling overturned. Became parable of the woman who got too big for her britches and lost everything she had. Drugs, bankruptcy, embezzlement, some said she'd even spent time in jail.

For years, I didn't just listen to those stories. I retold them myself, even though I knew they were at best half-truths, and so did everyone else. We craved the balm the stories gave, the way they spun our envy into smugness. Handed us our moral superiority and let us gloat. Then came my forties, and that all changed, along with everything else. You go through what I did, most of your judgment of others gets scoured right out.

When Sull called, I hadn't heard her voice in fifteen years. I was so surprised at first I couldn't talk back. She said she had to come home and didn't think a week would be enough. Said with her parents moved to South Carolina, she had no place to stay. Said she really just needed to get out in the woods, she'd be gone all day.

She drove up in a car that had never seen a road like mine and sat for five minutes behind closed doors. I saw how her profile'd gone from robin to hawk. By the time she got out, she wore a company face, cheerful, blithe, but right away I found it hard to look at her because no Sull I knew was there. We talked for an hour in the living room, sticking to the distant past. I asked after nothing recent. She offered even less.

My kids were long gone to places like where Sull went and worse. My son's room had the better view, but I put her in my daughter's, the farthest one from mine. My house backed right up against the woods, so my yard wasn't even really grass. Virginia pine, reindeer moss, old barbed-wire fence line. The next morning, Sull ducked her rubbed-down body through the wire. Stood still some seconds on the edge of it all. Then disappeared over the hill.

SUMMER FORTY YEARS ago. Grandmother's house. Sull's mom and dad, mine, most all the family back then lived no more than eight miles apart. We'd come together for Saturday suppers, and when the sweet corn was on, me and Sull'd carry to the pasture afterwards heaps of husks and cobs. Passing the old people on the porch, we'd always hear one call, "You all going down there? Daub some sab on that horse."

How wide apart a year seems when you're that young, and Sull always seemed way older than she was. Headstrong defiant from the beginning, and my mother'd shake a warning into me before she'd let us play. And Sull, being outside of an evening, did it settle you down like it did me? Deer shaping themselves in the wild end of the pasture. The way the cool coaxed the smell out the sycamore tree. Did we hear it then and just not know it, because at that age we'd never stopped hearing it yet? How else could you be gone so long and live the way you did, yet somehow get called back?

Brownboy'd nicker when he saw us, swim through chest-high Johnson grass. By evening he'd be free of flies except for the mob around each eye. While he crunched shucks, we ran hands across his hide, raised places, pus-running sores, pink and gray scabs. From a tree crook down there, we'd pull the dry cob and the pine tar salve we called sab. We'd daub it on fly bites gone bitter, gone bad.

MOST DAYS THAT first week Sull came back, we sat on my concrete stoop at night. Warm, dry, early September, sill between summer and fall. The lightning bugs were finished, but the haze was, too, the stars at their nearest, cream of Milky Way. We'd only been kids together, so we'd only ever played together. It's not like we had a history of sitting down to talk. And now, when we did, it was like that evening Sull arrived. Only light things, slight things, things anybody could have said.

I'm not sure what I expected, but I guess, given your ruin, some chink into your heart. The vacancy of your voice seemed a fog you threw around yourself. The vagueness a softness to cloud how hard you'd got. By the end of that week, I still had no idea why you'd come. Probably just wishful thinking that you'd returned to reach for what, after my own wreckage, I found. More likely it was "peace and quiet" as it was for most who came here from outside. The "beauty of the landscape." The myth that we had no crime.

Or—this occurred to me one night I couldn't sleep—were you in worse trouble than I knew? Was my house a hiding place from somebody or something? Did you really spend all day in the mountain? Or did you slink back inside after I left?

You answered that question the day I came home early and you stayed gone 'til dusk. And during—I'm ashamed to admit it, Sull—I tiptoed into your room. I could not resist, a photo, a note, a list, even a book you were reading. Anything to open you a slit. But, closet closed, suitcase zipped, laptop shut, the room felt more barren than it had before you settled in.

I went no farther than a step inside the threshold, which is why I almost missed the single thing that spoke. A handful of white oak acorns. Pooled in the seat of the cherry wood chair. Without touching, I felt the polleny dust on their peel. I tasted the pucker inside. They'd moved you enough to take them. Something slipped in my chest.

LATER THAT WEEK, I passed a fallow field with buzzards in the hunched dozens. Eating something small and scattered, like carrion sown. Having Sull in my house made my son walk my mind even more than he already did, Jesse also gone from his face last time I saw him, and doubtless buried deeper now. But it was on the night of the buzzards that Sull finally said something real. Said it into the dark, not looking at me. Said she was frustrated—frustrated she said, not afraid—that too many years gone had numbed her forever to what was in woods. "How long do you think it'll take?"—and she laughed at herself, but for the first time, I heard a fragileness there—"before I'll get all the city out of me?"

I drew a sharp breath. So it wasn't just peace and quiet you'd come for. Maybe I'd been right at the start, you did crave what I'd found. "Well, you just have to be patient," I said. Those vultures had lifted in a chorus. Lofted off in their slow-flop buzzard way. "It'll come," I said, praying that time didn't make a liar of me.

Because truth is, Sull—you'd gone to bed, I didn't say it out loud—now city is everywhere. There is no place it doesn't mute and dull and pad. It comes in trucks and on screens, city people carry it when they move in, and whatever is loudest trumps everything. Truth is, Sull, for decades I could not feel it myself, even though I never left this place. I never heard a thing between being little, when you hear it unconscious, like animals do, and my middle age. Only after I'd been torn down and drained did it enter, only then did it find holes to pass through. Even in the Bible, it says it takes an empty vessel. You only have room when loss lightens you.

BROWNBOY'D SUFFER MOST in the days, grazing in a cape of flies. Houseflies, bottleflies, horseflies, deerflies, feeding on panels of sorrel sweat, drinking from the pools of his eyes. The deerflies we dreaded most, playing in the creek in sagging swimsuits and tennis shoes against broken glass. The deerflies were the stealthiest and had a bee-sting bite.

I remember yelping and slapping my hand over my shoulder, the welt already on the rise. I remember shame over the tears in my eyes. I remember you taking my arms from behind and leaning in to find the place. You filled up your lungs. You salved it with breath.

YOUR PHONE DIDN'T ring at the beginning. The person on the other end waited to see if you'd call first. The single spot you got reception was the drive out front, so while I never eavesdropped, you'd pass me in the aftermath. Only a lover or a child, I knew, could light a fire of hurt that hot. Your bedroom door slammed behind you. My mouth went dry.

As Jesse forged on from liquor to pills, from lying to stealing, to probation to jail, Rick started dosing himself to survive our son. Overwork and television, denial and Internet. I swung between panic and talking myself out of what I knew to be true, between foolish hope and despair. Our life had turned a nightmare wait, for the knock, the call, the shot. Our marriage shrunk to scorekeeping, was it more him or me had made Jesse this way?

The afternoon I finally climbed in Clinton's truck, I'd been faithful for twenty-two years. I undid that not once, but over and over for four months. Like you, Sull, I learned that if you savage others far enough, you end up savaging yourself.

Every morning you still crossed the wire and sloped down over the bank. Walked out of an evening with your empty water bottle, the lines rawer in your face. I watched your frustration cinch to fear, your fear ferment to doubt. And one night, from the bathroom window, I caught a glimpse and startled back. You in the front yard, standing still between sky and ground. I saw how they cupped you like a bird who'd been stunned.

Sull, the next morning, I couldn't help myself again. After an hour, I pulled on my boots and crawled through the fence. It was easy to pick up your path, a scuffed rut in shin-deep leaves, and then you were following a deer trail. I would have done that, too. This time I wasn't spying on you or even checking on you. It was something else I only got to once I'd been moving through the trees a while. I'd come to listen for it *for* you. Maybe if I got it speaking for me, you'd happen into it as well.

I climbed a hollowside on a slant, rested against a shagbark trunk on top. Heard a doe bound down one steep then up the other, dead leaves unbend in her wake. You'd told me you'd tried in those mountains out West, but nothing at all would come. But I knew our throats weren't fit for out there, our bodies not tuned. You and me made from this land here.

Like I said, for thirty years, I didn't go in the woods, despite living on their edge. I only went in after chemo, when I was told to "exercise." Makes me smile to think of me then, winded in minutes, struggling up those shaley ridges, stumbling along dry runs. And of course, it wasn't really exercise that sent me. Like you, it was the pressure of needing, and, like you, no idea what lay at that need's other end.

But after a week, I understood how I could pull on the breathlessness of the climb to clear out the mess in my mind. I learned how the trees, if you move between them long enough, will eventually rub off your dirt. I'd fumbled around in here for a month when I turned a bend and the hollow came into my throat. All of it, the brittle of the leaves, the rock, the grit, but I could swallow finally without hurt. That was the first time I knew how to listen without ears, and then I started moving to it, the chords in my body tuning to the chords in the ground. The salving song didn't come always and never at my bidding, but it came often enough to douse all doubt.

Sull, I see your broken face, the acorns on your chair. I remember your hand on Brownboy's back, I feel your breath on my bite. If I could call it for you. If I could stand right alongside you, hearfeel it, and pass it through your skin. If I could tell you what to listen for, if I could name the part that hums.

And how much can life take from you? Sull, your livelihood, lovers, beauty, reputation, dignity. Me, my son, husband, breasts, innocence, righteousness, security. And I am not an ignorant woman. The whole world, I know, is losing, too. Rivers drying, mountains toppling, cities drowning under storms, and not many miles from here, in woods like these, they are even shattering the underground.

But still the land sings. And not just a singing, but louder, stronger, I tell you, every month it gets easier to hear. Because—listen—when everything is losing, everything is lightening, the distance between us thins and sheds. This is what loss gives. In these delicate, sharp, and beautiful, these brilliant unraveling days.

THOSE FIRST YEARS after Sull left, the last years before Brownboy's death, his old body forgot how to shed. Wore into summer a dense, ashy wool a currycomb couldn't begin to unsnag. That was not long after I got married, I was carrying Jesse, and I felt so sorry for Brownboy one evening I took scissors to the mats. But they were closer to the skin than I knew, and when the blood pooled out, grief speared me from my womb to my mouth. Wheeling away, I heard myself sob, even though Brownboy never flinched. Looked at me curious for four or five seconds. Then dropped his head back to graze.

Usually I was home with Rick by dark, but that night I stayed with the old people on Grandmother's porch. Late June, the lightning bugs at their lushest, blowing down out of trees, up out of grass. And at one spot in Brownboy's field, not sailing, or darting, or blinking. But a floating block of them, stuck lit and lurching in the same direction, like a distant house rolling away with its many windows alight.

"Poor ole Brownboy," said an aunt, shaking her head. "Lightning bugs getting trapped in his hair."

The picture has stayed with me, the kind of memory that opens wider with age. A plodding earthbound constellation. A dying body broke out in stars.

FIRST NIGHT OF fall brought a week of rain. You went into the woods daily anyway. Came back soaked through your poncho, then for fifteen, twenty, minutes disappeared into the shower's hot stream. At the beginning, the waste of water would have irked me. Now I was glad I could give you anything.

The evening you told me you had only five more days, we were at the table eating potato soup. The day's strain had runneled your face more rugged, leached your skin more pale. While you cleared the table, I stepped out on the stoop, stood before those staggered hills in the dusk. C'mon, now, I whispered to them. I reached towards them. Waited, but they didn't reach back.

I'd climbed the same three ridges for nearly two months for an answer to a question I didn't have words to ask. By then, I was slipping into it often and easy, I was moving and swallowing earth. But the pulse carried also a hunger, a pull, a gap. I knew always there was some place I hadn't gotten yet.

Then one afternoon, even that knowing dissolved, I was body only, and I let that lead. I ended up on the far side of the last ridge. I listened hard for what I should ask, but it told me only to close my eyes. Time left, place stayed. The hillspeak sank back in the ground.

And they came, Sull, no God we've ever heard of. They came in the song's still center and they blew. Tenderness in gusts that doubled me down, swaddled in a giving from a thousandfold directions, an offering that expected not a thing in return. I sat there lavished, laved, for as long as I could keep my mind at bay. But even now, I hold the memory. I don't have to have faith. I know.

Two days before you were to leave, you caught me by surprise. Late morning, and you at the kitchen door, mud to your calves, wet hair in your face. You wrenched off your boots, grabbed a dish towel, and when you tilted your head to rub it, you gave me a bashful smile. And right there, I saw it. The live coal of you.

I smiled myself, then turned away. Partly to give you privacy, but part because I wasn't sure. I wanted to be for a while with the probably. That sab I took for me.

ME AND MY DADDY LISTEN TO BOB MARLEY

IN THE GOOD Granma smells Mish stands—nighttime powder and church perfume—his fingers tumbling the man in his pocket. His daddy peels the foil from the tiny package he has taken from Gran's dressing table drawer. Daddy, hand tremoring, fishes in the package's dropper of water, snares the lens on a finger and daubs it at his eye as Mish watches. It's not out of curiosity for the contacts—those he has seen his whole life, whenever Daddy can get them, Mish is used to that, looking on from the low single bed at Daddy's house, bedtime, get-up time, Daddy picking plastic in and out of his eyes. Mish watches for the funniness of Daddy at the same dressing table where Granma combs her hair and puts on her makeup, for the strangeness in Gran's mirror of Daddy's raggedy-brimmed Stihl cap, his penny-colored beard. With the effort to keep his eye open, Daddy's top lip is raised, and in the mirror, Mish can see the two big front teeth browning from the middle out. Then the lens pops in, and as though having the thing in his eye grants him the gift of seeing behind, Daddy speaks.

"I told you, wait for me downstairs."

Daddy's right eye streams, and the man somersaults in Mish's pocket.

"Well." Daddy is whispering. "Be very, very quiet. We can't wake Pappy up."

Mish feels around him his coat.

Daddy presses the other contact at the other eye, his hand quivering, the lens falling onto the tabletop, and he quiet-cusses. They are very tearable, very expensive. The contact goes in, and Daddy is stepping away from the mirror, blinking hard, then he turns back, sweeps the little packages into the pockets of his coat, and as he passes Mish, he hisses, "You wait right here, Mish. You hear me? I'll be right back."

Mish follows Daddy. Daddy doesn't hear the rustle-roar of his coat, just like he didn't hear it when Mish walked into Gran's room to watch. Arms held away from his body, his feet in slow motion, Daddy wobbles down the hallway like a cartoon wolf, Mish swishing behind, them passing the bathroom, the closet, to the open door of Pappy's room, where Mish stops. The smells of this room are the inside-out of the Gran room smells—unflushed toilet smells, dead thing in the ditch smells, smells of crusted laundry—and Mish does not go in, he never does.

A floorboard shrieks. Daddy's splayed elbow hooks Pappy's hat rack, the rack bobs, but Daddy teeters on, balancing on the toes of his boots until he can reach into the clutter on Pappy's high chest of drawers. From the door, Mish can see only the standing-up things on the dresser. He knows there is a picture of old-timey people, of Uncle David as a grown-up, another of Daddy as a little boy, looking exactly like a Mish with blond hair. Daddy is unfolding Pappy's hip-worn wallet, and Mish flicks his eyes to the caterpillar shape under the rusty knit blanket on the bed, Pappy's head on its end. The spooky pink of Pappy's shut eyelids without his glasses over them. Mish looks back to Daddy, one hand replacing the wallet, the other tucking bills into his jeans pocket, then back to Pappy. Mish sucks a quick breath. Pappy's blue eyes are open. They hold Mish's there.

Then Daddy is hurrying through the door, scooping up Mish as he does, and they are down the stairs and into the kitchen, where Daddy sets Mish on his feet. "Shhhh." He grabs a block of cheese from the refrigerator, a package of lunchmeat, reaches across to the breadbox and snags one of Gran's mini-doughnuts for Mish—Mish crams it in his mouth right there—and Daddy swings Mish up again, Daddy grunting, staggering back a step, the enormous coat, the cheese and lunchmeat, Mish's lengthening legs, then he finds his footing and they slam out the back door.

It is late afternoon, the land winter hard and unsnowed, the air hard also, Christmas three weeks past. Gran's car is gone, her at Wal-Mart in Renfield a long drive away, exchanging one of Daddy's Christmas presents. Daddy is strapping Mish into his car seat in the old car of Pappy's that Daddy has been driving since he had his wreck in Pappy's newer one—Mish was at Mommy's during that—then they are tearing out of Gran's driveway, gravel splattering, and the Cavalier leaps onto the highway.

Daddy leans into the gas. They swallow Route 30, fast, faster, spewing it spent behind, and as Gran's house vanishes and the woods close in, them alone except for the cars passing in the other lane, Mish feels the man who lives in Daddy ease down. The Cavalier insides are sealed, invisible to the other cars, just *whush* and gone, and by the time they swing onto the county back road that goes to Daddy's house, Daddy has loosened enough to scrabble in the mess on the front seat floor. "Listen, Mish," he calls over his shoulder. "Tater made me this for Christmas." He thrusts a cassette into the deck and begins to sing, a high, chokey string. It is not Bob. Mish reaches into his coat pockets and pulls out the Silver Surfer in one hand, a red Power Ranger in the other.

He'd waited until lunch on the couch at Mommy's in his new coat, a Dallas Cowboys coat given him for Christmas by Gran, the coat reaching almost to his knees on one end and almost to his ears on the other, *Now I got it a couple sizes too big so you can grow into it*, a Ninja Turtle shell, Ranger armor, the Dallas Cowboys coat *is* football pads. The Dallas Cowboys are his daddy's favorite team, and the noise of its nylon, the "I'm here!" crash, the blue star on its back with a white border around it, and sometimes Mish can feel the star there behind him, lit up and hot. Him on the couch and Mommy on the phone, her face bearing down as she made the fourth call to Daddy, then fifth. She sucked a breath and blew it out. "Take off that coat, Mish. You're gonna burn up."

Carlin sat cross-legged in front of the TV, thumbing the iPod his own daddy got him for Christmas, while Kenzie, whose daddy got her nothing, perched at the kitchen bar where Mommy'd put her because Kenzie couldn't keep her hands to herself. Kenzie pitched at Mish pizza coupons folded tight and hard when Mommy couldn't see—"You look like you're a hole with your head sticking out!"—but Mish heard her voice only at a distance, didn't hear her words at all. He was watching Carlin. "Wet me wissen," Mish said it again, low, conspiratorial, his tone simultaneously pleading and leaden with respect. "Wet *me* wissen, Cawwin," because Carlin, thirteen, sometimes gave up a kindness if it cost him nothing (Kenzie, nine, a deerfly, poison ivy, never gave anything at all). But Carlin, bent in concentration, his mouth slightly open, two juicy scabs under his lip, the thumb scrolling, pretended not to hear even though the buds weren't in his ears. "Pwease, Cawwin, wet me wissen," Mish tried again.

"Wet we wissen. Wet we wissen," Kenzie simpered, and Mommy yelled, "Lay off, Kenzie! Mish, Steve's pulling in." Kenzie threw a refrigerator magnet at Mish. "Just three hours late. I guess that's not bad, a busy man like he is. Mish, let's get that coat zipped up—"

Now they are looping down Bonehaul Ridge, the last hill before the last curve before Daddy's house. Daddy's singing trickles to a hush. He brakes, and as they creep up on the curve, Mish slips his men back into his pockets. The car comes to a stop, the man who lives in Daddy back on his feet, finger to his lips, and Mish watches, too. Late afternoon, just this side of dark, Mish holds his breath. But the road in front of Daddy's house is vacant. No taillights of waiting cars. No figure slumped on the crumbly steps. They lurch forward, turn into the dirt tracks by the side porch, and pull around back, where they park right up against the chimney. The yard brown waves of high winter weeds, dogless doghouse coughing bright garbage. Mish strokes with his thumb the Power Ranger's chest.

Their breaths steam around them while Daddy quivers the key in the side door padlock. Mish encases himself deeper in the coat, higher in it, his hands in his pockets to his forearms, his shoulders hackled to his ears. The man in Daddy is full raised now, Mish can see him, behind Daddy's bones. The man is flat and black, out of heavy construction paper snipped, a shape only, and only recently has Mish learned, from a Marvel Comics coloring book, the man's name: Quickshiver. The lock unslots, and Mish trails Daddy through the dim, stale kitchen, into the window-blanketed front room, dark as a groundhog burrow, and Mish, coat whispering, feels right away with his feet for the men he left on the floor last Sunday. Daddy squats to prime the kerosene heater, a stubborn cast-off of Gran and Pappy's, and all around Mish, as ever-present and familiar as the house's sour smell, presses the house's black burring, a static not ear-heard in the way Quickshiver is not eye-seen. Mish finds a man, then two, with his toes, and then he stands still, careful not to smash. With the men safe, he can let down a little, take his hands from the coat. He can feel Bob Marley behind him on the wall, tracing warm the rim of the star on his coat. The heater finally flares, Daddy scrambles upright, and in the pink-orange glow, Mish does his quick accounting: the Blue Power Ranger, Spiderman, the Hulk, Dash Incredible, Luke Skywalker, and a swarm of tiny knights. Mish's shoulders ease.

Then he turns around, and out of the dark, Bob soars. Bob a beam through the static, radiant and still, and although the heater lights only Bob's chest, chin, and mouth, Mish sees the rest clear. Bob has made his face the colors he likes, red, yellow, and green, something Mish'd like to do, something even Jesus cannot, and under the toboggan hat-thing, Mish knows, three little birds nest in Bob's blacksnake hair. Bob does not worry, you see it in his smile, smoke curling it like Santa Claus's in Gran's *Night Before Christmas* book, only Bob is real. When Mish turns away, he feels the heat again on his back, and he starts to kneel to his men, to reach, when a hand closes over his shoulder.

"C'mon, buddy. Let's eat."

Mish sits cross-legged on the kitchen table with a bowl between his legs, gulping Froot Loops as fast as he can. Daddy is watching the window, dipping into a mustard jar some pickle loaf slices he's rolled into tubes, a Budweiser humming in his other hand. Quickshiver crouches. Between bites, Daddy rubs his eyes, pulls now and again on their lids. Mish blinks. Daddy has opened the oven door for heat. They eat in the red U of its element and in a disk of light from a small, goose-necked desk lamp. The room is off the road, but from the side window where Daddy sits, you can see a car's headlights glint off the aluminum NO HUNTING sign tacked to the fence before the car pulls up by the house. Mish hits the bottom of his bowl and slides off the table.

"Keep that overhead off," Daddy says. He watches the window.

Mish stands in the dark doorway. From the floor, the men pull, invisible. To see them at all, he'll have to sit very near the hot cylinder of heater, but right after he thinks that, it doesn't matter anymore. Kneeling, he draws the Silver Surfer and the Power Ranger from his pockets and sets them among the others in their scattered circle. The air over the men is static-less, Mish can feel, and glassy. The black burring pushed up and away. For the first time since this morning, he wriggles out of his coat and lets it drop behind him. Bob has his back. He picks up the Hulk.

The calm almost instantly comes, like a vein from the Hulk into Mish's palm, then up his arm to his heart. The other men begin pulling, showing Mish, and Mish knows what to do. He divides them into the sides they ask for, setting them up for their fight, and as he does, the glassy dome settles, Mish barely notices it with his mind, but the rest of him knows. The dome cupping over, embracing, and inside, only Mish and the men. And soon, Mish hears the murmur, the quiet telling, it comes from his mouth and at the same time from outside of him—

"Mish! C'mere!"

Mish stops.

"Mish!" An amplified hiss. "C'mere!"

Mish leans back. He looks at his men. Then, pulling on his coat, he climbs to his feet and rustles to the kitchen.

Daddy's face is squashed against the window glass. "Look out here." Daddy reaches behind him and snaps off the lamp. Mish rests his chin on the sill and circles his face with his hands like Daddy is doing.

"Look hard. Let your eyes adjust."

Mish stretches big his eyes.

"Do you see something? There by the sycamore?"

Mish strains.

"Somebody moving?"

"I jush see a buncha weedj."

"You're sure?"

Mish looks a little longer, for the sake of Quickshiver. "Nuh-uh. Nuttin dere, Daddy."

Daddy angles his hands around his face, desperate to confirm it. When Mish turns back to his men, Daddy gives up and follows to his own front room spot, the straight chair with the stained pillow drawn up to a crack between blanket-drape and window-frame. He lights his nerve medicine. Mish strips off his coat and studies his men. Half of them sleep in the roofless Lincoln Log house, the other half in the Hot Wheels garage. It is Spiderman wants to be picked up first. Mish does.

Again, the immediate grounding, the vein from man to heart. Whoever Mish holds in his hand, he enters, the man pulling, a speaking way under words, Mish simultaneously following the man and directing him. The men strap on their weapons, pump their muscles, toss back their heads—the Hulk, Luke, Spidey, Knight—Mish both Mish and men and more, the dome settling good now, the block of the black burr. The further he sinks, the calmer he deeps, the good real weight of the men's real world, anchor weight, ballast weight, so different from the daddy weight. Mish speaking not only the men's parts, but the story in between, and always, every word of the murmur understood. Now the men are shouting challenges to each other, girding for the fight, Mish and the men completely endomed, Bob unworrying overhead like a tricolor moon. The first man dies, the second one, the first man resurrects, the dome holding away—

"Mish! Do you have to pee?"

Mish's mouth crackles, two knights crashing.

"Mish, I said, do you have to pee?"

Mish blows out a breath and sits back on his thighs. While one hand has been moving the men, the other has been holding his crotch. "Uh-uh," he mutters, almost to himself.

"Yeah, you do. Do you want me to come up with you?"

He's let go of his pants and picked up Spiderman, trying to follow him back.

"Mish, do you want me to come?" The voice sharpens. "I'm not cleaning up another mess, I'll tell you that."

"Nooo," Mish groans.

"Well, watch that hole. Hear me?"

Up the dark, narrow steps, Mish climbs. The hole in the bathroom floor finally opened all the way through a month ago. The hole's right in front of the toilet, so to pee, you have to straddle it, which Daddy can do, or you have to sidle around and pee from the side, which Mish has to do. Many a time, in daylight, Mish has squatted over the hole and peered down to the stove. Its black coils, its scaley, unwashed pans, the streaked dishtowels borrowed from Gran. Once he dropped a man through to see what would happen, one of the faceless olive army men—he wouldn't have done it to most of the others. When it hit the stovetop, Daddy jumped and cussed. Sometimes, looking through, Mish imagines the what-if of falling himself and frying on a burner. Sometimes, in the night, the bathroom lit, the downstairs dark, like now, Mish sees the hole as not dropping into Daddy's kitchen at all. Mish sees it leading right out of the house to someplace else.

THE DAY AFTER Christmas Mish stood on the footstool in the bathroom off Gran's kitchen, his men battling in the sink. Through the dome arched over them, the shut bathroom door, Mish heard Gran and Uncle David walk into the kitchen and their chairs scrape. Then the grown-up talk, of no more import than the toilet running, as Rescue Hatchet dove off the faucet to save Dash from Darth—when, suddenly, Mish heard his real name. He stopped.

It was Uncle David, of course, who said it. Uncle David, who only came twice a year, *at most*, twice a year, *if that*. And now he was saying it again, in a string of words Mish couldn't reverse and unscramble.

"Steve is thirty-eight years old, Mom. Thirty-eight years old. And has never held a job longer than, what? Three months?"

"Well, he looks better than he has in years. And just happier than he's ever been—"

"Looks better than he has in years with his two front teeth rotted out."

Through Mish, a coldness was unrolling. Starting in his chest, uncurling even into his arms and his legs.

"You know what I mean. Good color in his face. And not all skinny like he has been."

Mish hunched back over the sink, his mouth moving. Rescue Hatchet hacked at Spiderman now.

". . . don't understand why nothing's come of what happened last summer."

"Well, I'll tell you, David, the court system in this county, it's unbelievable how busy they are. At the magistrate's, I heard they're backed up for six months . . ."

Mish made his murmur louder.

"Did you and Dad really press those charges? Or did you just say you did?"

"He's doing better than he has in so, so long. Why, he walked in here yesterday morning with a wrapped present in his hand—"

"Mom, did you press those charges?" Uncle David asked.

Mish threw open the bathroom door and leapt into the kitchen. "Boo!" He landed with a smack on both feet. Uncle David's and Gran's faces snapped towards him like they were fixed on the same pivot. "Ba-ha-ha-ha-ha-ha!" Mish bellowed his best villain laugh. After a couple seconds, Uncle David laughed, too.

"C'mere, Matthew. C'mon. Give me a hug. I'm leaving this afternoon."

"Don't pay any attention to Uncle David," Daddy tells him every time. "He thinks he's better than us."

Mish grinned, shook his head, and ran.

DOWNSTAIRS, THE PHONE rings. Mish freezes. The insides of his ears stand up like a dog's. He lowers himself closer to the floor hole, head tilted. Hears only a wordless rumble spiked here and there by a snicker. He tiptoes to the top of the stairs, but he can tell nothing from there, either. He waits.

"Hey, Mish," Daddy calls. "Get down here get your coat on. We gotta take a quick ride."

Mish's chest clenches. He backs up a few steps and leans into the dark wall, the plaster cold against his cheek.

"It's not a big deal. You can sleep while we're there. And Tater should be around."

Mish breathes deep and blows it loud enough for Daddy to hear, his lips flapping like a horse's.

"C'mon, Mish, it's not a big deal. I'm not gonna stay long."

"Can I sleep in da car?"

"No, it's too cold for you to sleep in the car."

"Daaa-deee."

"Listen, it'll be a nice ride. We'll listen to Bob. And afterwards, we'll stop at Burger King to get you that new toy."

"Wha new toy?"

"I can't remember, I saw it on TV at Gran's. Some kind of man. Now come on down."

"I din see it on teebee at Mommysh."

"Well, I saw it. Get your coat on."

Mish stops on each step, brings his feet together, sighs. When he shuffles into the front room, he sees that Daddy has already swapped the threadbare Stihl cap for the newer one with the Nike swoosh. He's pulling on the canvas coat he got when the Salvation Army came in for the flood victims over in Maddox last year. His usual coat, the one with the tape over the holes to hold in the stuffing, lies on the floor, worryingly close to the men. When Daddy tugs Mish to him, Mish droops, his arms limp, head sagging, and while Daddy threads him into the Dallas Cowboys sleeves, Mish wrinkles his nose against the reek of spilled kerosene in Daddy's coat. Then Daddy is dueling with the zipper, hands buzzing, the cussing a steady grit, but over his shoulder, Mish notices Bob, heater-lit on the wall. Daddy glares at his own hands, stiffens and shakes them. Tries the zipper again. Mish watches Bob, tall and easy on his wall, the smoke from his smile, Mish knows—happiness. Bob can make the feeling seen. The star on Mish's back starts to heat, then to ray, and finally the anticipation of Bob in the car overrides what waits at the end. "Your zipper's broke," Daddy says. Mish stoops quick, snatches the two nearest men, and stuffs one in each pocket.

They hurtle past the NO HUNTING sign. They hairpin back up Bonehaul Ridge. With each yard of asphalt collapsing behind, Quickshiver inside Daddy lies a little more down, the safety of being between place and place, Mish knows this without knowing whose knowing it is. They chute through trees, the house static receding, then burst out into a star-gray field, closer, closer, closer drawing to Bob, and when Mish pulls out the men and sees they are Luke Skywalker and Dash Incredible, he smiles. The Cavalier cuts loose on the first of the road's few straights, and Mish can't help but bounce in his seat; this is where Daddy always asks. And then Daddy does, he calls over his shoulder, Quickshiver nothing but a black puddle at his bottom, "What do you want to listen to, Mish?"

And Mish says, "Bob!"

And Daddy says, "Me, too!"

And Daddy steers with his thigh while he respools the cassette on his pinky, the men warming up in acrobatic leaps, until, finally, Daddy jabs the tape in the deck. And instantly, they are swallowed—Mish, men, Daddy—in the belly of Bob.

Rhythm of reggae, happy heartbeat and a half, Mish reeling it into the cave of his ribs, his pulse recalibrated, the soothe, the joy. The throb patterning, echoing, the loops of the curves, the hills' nods and lifts, Mish swaying, the men flying, the car, Mish knows, if seen from outside, red green and yellow glow, colors of Bob. The Cavalier dances the bends, the banks, and Daddy stringy sings, *This is my message to you-ou-ou.* And Mish's happiness rides on a pillar of memory, sedimented, three years old. Last week, last month, yes, but down, back, further than that, to when Mish stayed at Daddy's half the week, further back still to when Daddy lived at Mommy's house. So much in those layers dark, dangly, shivery, loud, but all that vanishes in the happiness of Bob. The Bob memory constant, soaking up through the sediment and richening each level—memory, memory, memory—whenever Mish was fussy or inconsolable or too tired to sleep, Daddy strapping him in the car, punching the cassette, and they ride in the cradle car to Rockabye Bob.

And three weeks ago, on Christmas night, Carlin stretched out on the bottom bunk with his iPod in his ears, his eyes as blank as if he lay in his coffin, Mish standing behind him, Mish straining with marvel, straining with want, all that glorybig music held in a wafer no thicker than ten Pokémon cards. "Wet me wissen," Mish outright begged, too desperate even to calculate, manipulate. "Wet me wissen," while Carlin paid him no more mind than he did the fluffs of crud under the bed. "Pweeeese, Caw-win, wet me wissen." Mish peering now directly into his face, poking him gently on the shoulder. Until Carlin, his eyes still dead, reached out, planted a hand on Mish's chest, and pushed. Once.

Mish staggered backwards, the tears geysering behind his face. He grabbed the nearest object, a Transformers sticker book, and swung at Carlin. As he did, he yelled, "Me and *my* daddy wissen to Bob Maw-wee." And the tears weren't anymore.

Daddy turns the volume halfway down. "Now, Mish."

"Yeah?"

"Don't say anything to anybody about us taking this ride, okay?"

"Okay."

"It'll just be between you and me."

"Okay."

"Don't say anything to Mommy. Or Gran. Even if they ask."

"Yeah."

Daddy cranks the music back up, even louder than before. It is the Bob beat that propels Mish's blood through his veins. Bob is heart. The car tremors, Mish feels the speaker thrumming against his legs, his hips—beat; beat; beat, beat-beat—and he settles back in his seat, the men catching their breaths in his lap, *everything's gonna be*, music carrying rhythm carry, the car a rocker. Lullaby Bob.

The loss of motion wakes him. He flexes his fingers. One man is still there. One he has dropped. Daddy's unstrapping him—Mish tucks the man in his pocket—lifting him out, and Mish buries his face for a second in Daddy's jacket against the cold, which has shocked him full awake, immediate and blunt. The cold has blacked the night darker, crisped the stars whiter, but over Daddy's shoulder, Mish can see clouds like a dirty blanket pulling over distant sky. They are parked just off the hardtop in the mouth of a dirt road leading into a broad field, and Daddy sets him on his feet on the hood of the car. Mish can feel its heat through his tennis shoes. "See the house, Mish?"

Mish looks past the winter grass, bowed and brittle-humped in the three-quarter moon. The house is the only thing rising off the flat of the field until the mountains start again. Mish nods.

"Can you see cars around it?"

Mish nods. Quickshiver is taut on his toes, his hands splayed, head cocked. Mish pulls his coat sleeve against his side, a muted crackle. Daddy is standing on the ground right next to Mish on the hood, one arm around his waist, and Mish thinks of the apples. "Can you start this for me, buddy?" Mish, bearing down with his small front teeth, breaking the peel and gnawing around in the white to give Daddy a good opening.

Daddy takes a finger and stretches the corner of his eye, his lip lifting. "Do you see Tater's truck?"

Mish squints. "Yeah." Tater's truck is easy. A big white Ford extended cab. "Okay, good." Daddy pulls the corner of his eye again. "Now this is important. This is important, Mish. Look at all of them."

Mish is looking.

"Do you see a blue Toyota Four-Runner?"

Mish wiggles out of the arm around his waist and lifts onto his toes. A heaviness has come into him. One that makes him bigger and tireder. He knew his cars before he knew his colors, that's what Daddy always says, and Mish squints again, drawing on the stingy moon, to untangle the snarl of vehicles around the house. He can't tell blue in the dark, but the shape of a Four-Runner he can.

"Nuh-uh," he says.

"You're sure?"

Mish nods sharp, twice. "Only Toyoda's a Tacoma."

Daddy slaps the star on his back. "Okay. Good. Good job, Mish."

They roll through the field, the house swelling in the windshield. Bob is gone. Daddy drives to the right to straddle the road ruts, the wash of grass against metal, the car cold now because Daddy left the door open while they were looking for the Four-Runner. As the house grows larger, clearer, the heaviness drains out of Mish, leaving something worse. When it's summer, Daddy lets him sleep in the car seat, he leaves the door open for air, and sometimes Mish doesn't even wake up. But in the winter, he has to go inside. The car pitches into a deep hole, and Mish is thrown forward, and he thinks to reach behind him, to the star, but the car seat straps bind him. Then Daddy's carrying him, crunching through frozen mud to planks across cinderblocks that climb to the front door, and when the planks wobble, Daddy stumbles to the side, Mish scissors his legs around Daddy's waist, Daddy finds his balance, and the door opens.

The party explodes in Mish's face. Laughter without fun, heat without warmth, smoke without smile, every party he's ever entered, and the grown-up bodies packed upright and reeling, an October cornfield, rattle and wind. "Hey, Steve!" somebody yells, then somebody else calls it, too, and Daddy grins and yells back. The top half of Tater swims out of the crowd, him brandishing a quart-sized Sheetz cup. "Mish! How you doing?" He strips Mish from Daddy and squashes him to his soft chest, Tater in a T-shirt odored of cigarettes and mildew, and the cup's straw pokes Mish's head and whatever is in it splashes a little on Mish. "Ricky's got it," Tater says, and Daddy says, "Where's he at?" and Tater says, "He'll be here." Past Tater, Mish sees a silver

Christmas tree on a table, listing to one side, drooped with brassy, teardrop ornaments, each exactly the same.

He is set on his feet into the cornfield of legs. No, not corn. Brush, thicket, thorn, briar, the legs pressing, posting, buckling, shifting, and Mish clings to Daddy's jeans pocket to avoid being swept down. "Who's this?" The lady stoops to Mish, and her face reminds Mish of the file Daddy uses to sharpen the chainsaw.

"This is my son, Mish."

"Mish?" This is what they always say.

"That's what I call him. He's named after me, my initials smashed together."

"Oh, isn't he handsome?" They always say that, too, unless they say "cute."

"Yeah, looks just like me when I was little."

"What did Santa Claus bring you, Mish?"

"He can't talk very good. I'm the only one who understands him." Daddy ruffles Mish's hair. Mish ducks. "You got someplace he can sleep?"

Then Daddy is steering him by his shoulders through more legs. There's not even room enough for Daddy to pick him back up. Mish stumbles around mud-splattered work boots, plasticky high heels, tennis shoes with mismatched shoestrings, Christmas gift clogs. He watches the feet, his head lowered, to save him from belts and butts, zippers and belly fat. Hands reach down to pet him—"Ahhh, cute!"—Mish fighting the urge to bite Daddy's fingers, until they're in a skinny hall, passing a vibrating washing machine, and finally entering a back room where Daddy swings Mish onto a coat-heaped bed. He pulls Mish out of the Dallas Cowboys coat and wraps the coat around him like a blanket. Then he sheds his own coat and spreads that over Mish, too.

"Will he fall off?" the file lady asks.

"Nah, nah. He's three years old."

Daddy leans in as if to kiss Mish good night. Mish snakes an arm out of the coats, snatches Daddy's Nike cap, and flings it as hard as he can. One of Daddy's hands flies to his head, the other tomahawks out to intercept the cap. It misses. And there is Daddy's head, naked. The smashed wads of his balding hair like damp caterpillars crawling his scalp, the patchy bare places in between. The file lady giggles at Mish, and Daddy sweeps his cap off the floor, jams it on his head, and shoots Mish a scarlet look. Mish shoots the look right back.

"Sleep tight, cutie." The file lady's voice.

The door shuts, ugly music damps by a third. Mish slings Daddy's reeking coat off himself. He rolls out of the Dallas Cowboys one. Then, his brow hard, his teeth steeled, him holding tight to the Cowboys coat, he windmills his arms and his legs to make a clearing for himself. Furious snow-angel, the foreign coats rolling and bunching away, some of them tumbling onto the floor. Mish's breath comes hard and coarse, and he picks up Daddy's coat and heaves it over the bed edge, too. Then he seizes the Cowboys coat in both hands and clashes it together, nylon on nylon, drowning the horrible music, the coat louder, louder, the coat hollering, screaming. And then Mish stops. His breath comes more quietly. He turns on his side and hugs the coat towards him. He opens his eyes and there's the label where Granma inked his name. M-I-S-H. Matthew Steven Halliday, Junior.

It wasn't long after he began Head Start the fall before that Kenzie started the game. "Let's play school!" She'd grab Mish and push him onto the couch. "I'm the speech therapist! You're the kid!" Her hands pinning his shoulders, one knee on his thigh, Mish squirming, while Kenzie swooped in and out of his face. "Repeat!" in-swoop, "After!" out-swoop, "Me!" in. Then she would hover, inches from his nose, her breath odored of cold, boiled potatoes. "Ma!" she'd bleat. Then, her tongue tipping out and sucking back, thick. "Thew! Ma-Thew!" Mish wiggling, grunting, shoving her away. "Ma! Thew!" Twisting his head to the side, clamping tight his eyes. "Thew! Thew! Repeat!"

Mish reaches into his Dallas Cowboys pocket and touches the man there. It is Dash Incredible. Luke he dropped in the car. He holds Dash quietly in the pocket. He doesn't bring him out into the room.

Suddenly, Mish is being arranged in the car seat again. He recognizes this from deep in a hole of sleep, and after the recognition, he sinks back, but then a knowing pricks him. He blinks, half-opens his eyes, closes them, reopens. And begins clambering up to awake. As he does, he reaches for the man in his pocket. But the man is not there. Daddy is blundering the seat straps, his hands revved to their highest, bumblebees, propellers, the buckles clacking, missing. His face so close to Mish's that Mish can feel the heat off it, smell the salt of sweat. Then Mish feels that it's not just the man who's not there, the pocket isn't there, either, and then Mish understands: the Dallas Cowboys coat is not there.

"Wheresh? Wheresh?"

He is swaddled in Daddy's stinky jacket again. He sees that Daddy's flannel is gone too, him in only his long-john shirt, the yellowed armpits ripped, the sleeves pushed up, and Mish hears himself say, "Wheresh my Dawash Cowboysh coat?"

Daddy is slamming Mish's door and reeling around the front of the Cavalier, one hand scratching vicious the back of his neck, then he drops in the driver's seat. Mish shakes his way out of Daddy's coat and throws his head around, sweeps his arms, hunting the dark car insides for his own coat, and he asks again, panic sparking his voice, "Wheresh my Dawash Cowboysh coat?"

Daddy taps a close-parked car, then another, cusses, pulls forward, tries again. Now he's gaping over his shoulder so he can see behind him better, showing his face to Mish, but Daddy doesn't look at him. "Calm down, Mish. I had to loan it to Ricky for a few days. Then you'll get it right back."

"Wicky? Who Wicky?"

Daddy escapes the mess of cars and throws it into Drive. "Ricky needed it for a few days. Then you'll get it back." They are bouncing down the dirt road, and Mish twists in his seat, the house, little, littler, littler behind them, and then, Mish remembers. Dash is in the coat pocket.

"Go ba ge i! Go ba ge i!"

He is shrieking, his words unraveled to how he talked a year ago, two years ago, Mish hears it but cannot help it. The dirt road levels and they plunge even faster, and Mish smacks the seat beside him, searching for the fallen Luke Skywalker, but hits only Dorito crumbs. Then Mish feels the pressing in his chest. The cave begins to creak. The black to leak. Mish grabs hard, pushes back, and when he shouts next, it is a command, no whine in it. "Take me back to Mommysh!"

At the hard top, Daddy jets left without braking.

"Take me back to Mommysh!"

"Mish," Daddy says, "are you a baby or a man?"

"Take me!"

"I can't, Mish." One front tire drifts onto the shoulder, snags on the pavement lip, the ripping sound of asphalt against rubber, and Daddy jerks it back up, the car swerving into the left lane, then sailing back right. "This is how the judge did it. I've told you a thousand times." He talks the after-party talk, each word deliberate, an egg laid. "It's not my decision. You're with me from Saturday morning to Sunday evening. We have to do what the judge says."

"I doan care wha da judge saysh!"

"Well, I do. It's the law." Now Daddy does look at Mish, his I'm-a-grown-up-and-you're-not look. He turns back to the windshield, his forefinger massaging the corner of his eye. "C'mon, Mish." Now he's lightened his tone, a phony breeze in it. "We'll go in to Burger King tomorrow and get you that man."

Mish's lips are sucked tight in his mouth. His fists are clenched, his arms, too, his stomach, all of him seizing against it, pushing back. But the cave—gradually, excruciatingly—opens. Mish's chest slow-cleaving, the stones cracking, the walls unsealing, until, like always, the first part can't help but spill out. The first part not even plain pain, but the warm wave of pity, and not even for himself, pity for the coat and for Dash, left behind. But once the pity's free, nothing can stop what it's blocked. The grief batter-rams Mish's chest and leaps torrenting out.

The G.I. Joe left at Ponderosa, the Superman shoes outgrown, Kingy run away and the monstrous stench from the ditch, Mommy breaking up with Aaron who liked to play Spiderman, Daddy gone a long time away so the doctors could help him. Daddy gone a long time away. The loss is a tidal wave and Mish strains against it, shoulder to boulder, leaning, gasping, his fingertips shredding from the rough of the rock. *Crybaby. Stop that right now* (*no woman, no cry. No woman, no cry*). Until, finally, Mish feels it. The breach swings back. The cave, heavily, slowly, closing its walls. The rift shrinking from yawn, to gap, to slit to, finally, nothing at all. Mish breathes. As his heart shuts, all that black loss is anviled, smelted. Into a tower of flame-colored mad. And the right words come.

"I'm gonna tell," Mish says. His voice is even. Only he can feel the buzz underneath.

Daddy hesitates. It's less than a second, but Mish hears it.

"You're gonna tell what?"

"Dat you sto dat money fom Pappy." On "you stole," Mish feels a spurt of fear, exhilarating. Not of Daddy, but himself.

Daddy watches the road. Mish watches Daddy. "Pappy owed me that money, Mish. For that wood I cut. I just didn't want to interrupt his nap."

"Dat you sto Gransh contacsh." The cave is sealed completely now, and Mish feels himself growing bigger, even without the coat.

Daddy is quiet. Then, "I'm not going to argue with you, Mish."

"Dat you sto my Dawash Cowboysh coat."

Daddy whips his head around, and the bare anger in his face pumps Mish even bigger. Mish almost smiles, and Daddy sputters, in the tone of the wrongly accused that works so well on Gran. "Mish, I did not steal the coat. I loaned it to Ricky. I'll get it back when I get paid at the end of the week."

"You doan eben hab a job!"

Daddy is watching the road again, each hand clamped on its side of the wheel, his shoulders squared. The model of the safe driver. Trees along the road scroll up gray then disappear. When Daddy speaks this time, his voice is flat again.

"This is between you and me, Mish. It's between men. Babies tell Mommy and Granma." Daddy glances over his shoulder. "You keep our secret . . . I'll get you an iPod." He nods. "Yeah, how about that, buddy? Like Carlin's."

Mish sits motionless in his car seat. It has begun to snow, the flakes driving against the windshield haphazard, bewildered. Then Mish feels, there in the front seat, Quickshiver inside Daddy ease down. Quickshiver drops his shoulders, unkinks his neck, loosens his knees, and lies down. And with each step Quickshiver unwinds, Mish flares a notch higher. Breath to Mish's ember, gas to his blaze. Now both Quickshiver and Daddy think it is over, Mish bought off by a lie, and the cave again bulges, Mish squeezing with all his power back. Daddy is ejecting the Bob tape, jabbing in his new one, and right when he is lifting his finger to PLAY, Mish says, "I'm gonna tell Uncle Dabid."

Daddy's hand freezes, finger extended. For one cold moment, everything hangs in air.

Then Daddy is slamming on the brakes, Mish shot through with gratification and fear, a *hah!* and *uh-oh*, all at once, the car yanked onto the shoulder. With a thud-crunch Daddy throws the gear into Park and twists all the way around, his knee against the back of the front seat, in his eyes a full white circle around each iris, Mish sees them clear. Daddy squeezes the front seat back.

"Mish, listen." He speaks from between the rotted teeth, the others gritted. "You listen." He moistens his lips. "Even if you tell Uncle David, let's say you sit right down and tell him." Daddy's eyes grip Mish's. "Do you think he'd understand anything you said?"

Daddy's eyes hold Mish's. The dry *screek* of the windshield wipers on too fast, the snow too thin. Behind Daddy, the snow spins, scattershot, eddying, like it's not even down it's falling, not even sky it comes from. Finally Daddy turns. Inside Mish, a hundred things scutter away into dark. Daddy drives.

DADDY CARRIES MISH, wound in the canvas coat, through the black kitchen and into the blacker front room, tripping over Mish's men. He totes him up the stairs. He sets Mish down in the cold bedroom, switches on the bedside lamp, and clatters over a stack of CDs. Mish lets the coat spill off him and onto the floor, then, like every Saturday night, he follows Daddy to the bathroom. Both of them wary around the floor hole, Mish pees first, as he always does, Daddy waiting, then Mish waits for Daddy. Back in the bedroom, Daddy shakes out the old Gran covers on the unmade bed, tugs off Mish's shoes, and scoots him under. Daddy drops his cap on the floor and strips off his jeans, his heel catching in the folds and almost bringing him down. Then he crawls under and pulls Mish to him.

"I love you, Mish," he mumbles. He kisses Mish, hard, on his forehead. He reaches over and snaps off the lamp.

Mish lies still, not touching Daddy. He tries to turn himself into a stick on the very edge of the bed. But it is cold in the bedroom, the bed a twin, the blankets thin, Daddy warm. Mish draws a little closer, still careful not to touch him.

"Shit," Daddy says.

He flops over, clicks the lamp, and swings his bare legs over the side of the bed. Rummaging in the junk on the bedside stand, he comes up with a grubby contact case. He pinches the contacts from his eyes and slides them into the case. Then he worms back under the covers and after a single blast of outbreath, begins to snore. The lamp blares on.

Mish squeezes his eyes shut. The light bleeds through. He opens them. The lamp's plastic body is shaped like a lamb. It was Daddy and Uncle David's when they were little boys. Mish watches it. Then he widens his gaze to the photos curling on their tacks on the wall. Various Mishes from baby on up. Daddy snores louder.

Mish slips out of bed. He pads into the hall, the floor numbing his feet. He stops at the top of the steps, where the bedroom lamp throws light before the staircase diminishes into dark. "Ma," he whispers. Then he concentrates, his brow hard. "Yew."

Mish sighs. He licks the roof of his mouth. "Ma," he says again, full-voiced. Then he lifts his tongue, positions it between his teeth like Kenzie does, and sucks it back. "Foo," it says.

Mish drops down one step. He tries again. "Ma. Foo." One more step, and he tries it quick, all run together, a little spit flying, "Ma-foo."

He blows out his breath, knocks his head gently against the wall, and descends another step. And this time he doesn't even try. He just opens his mouth. *Matthew.*

He stops. Not quite believing, he tries again. *Matthew.* Although his ear still doubts, his mind hears it clear. *Matthew*, he practices in his head. *Matthew. Matthew*, once for each cold stair, until he steps into the room where all his men wait.

ACKNOWLEDGEMENTS

MY DEEP GRATITUDE to the friends and editors who helped me with these stories: Lia Purpura, Jane Vandenburgh, Stephen Corey, Patty Boyd, Philip Terman, Carol Tiebout, Laura Long, Ellen Cooper, Jackson Connor, Tracy Oberg-Connor, Sam Pancake, Nancy Morgan, Elea Carey, Suzanne Berne, Melissa Delbridge, Anna Schachner, R.T. Smith, Mary Rockcastle, Christina Thompson, and Jennifer Drew. A special thank you to Jack Shoemaker for his ongoing faith in my work. And to Caitlin Sullivan, first reader always, greatest thanks of all, for everything.